I0768110

Echoes
of Remnant
Light

ECHOES OF REMNANT LIGHT

Book One of The Celestial Tide

Jessica Hope

For Mom

Echoes
of Remnant
Light

CHAPTER 1

The captain was a stickler for punctuality, and she was late. Something had gone wrong, as usual.

Kyzum contemplated the descending sun as it haloed the shore's tree line. It wasn't time for the contingency plan. Yet.

"Should we try to contact them?" Ara, his crewmate, asked.

The surf broke against the rocks of the natural jetty to which their skyship was moored. A gust of wind gathered the sea's spray and cast it across the deck. Ara's short blonde hair whipped about her round, youthful face and mature blue eyes. Kyzum shivered and tightened his cloak, the shaved line across his left scalp cringing at the cold.

"We can't risk giving away their position. This cursed season they call spring up here is probably just slowing them down."

Ara fought a smile. Beneath a long jerkin, she wore a green tunic and trousers tucked into boots, but Kyzum had seen her wear the same thing in the desert. He was not amused.

"You Northerners are crazy," he declared.

Ara didn't agree or disagree, but her wistful expression said much. If they sailed northeast, they would reach Tesinoc in northern Setsea, ancestral city of the galahi and where snow had the audacity to fall below the mountain slopes. If they sailed northwest, they would pass her homeland, Ulydra, and passing was all they would ever do because Ulydra resided beyond the Talons. Snow was an annual aggravation there as well. The sun could be oppressive in the southern grasslands and desert, but no one could say it wasn't warm.

"There!" Ara pointed to a toned figure bursting out of the thicket. A satchel hung from the captain's shoulder, and her wavy locks trailed behind her as she rushed down the rocky beach.

Two men darted out of the trees and blocked her path. A thunderclap echoed in the twilight, and a flash of star kaza hit one in the chest, sprawling his charred corpse upon the sand. Nahzida emerged a second later, her rifle raised for a second shot. Ameara was faster, and her Ryvekian sword cut down the second pursuer in a spray of crimson.

More armed men and women gushed onto the beach, flanking Ameara and Nahzida. Nahzida spun, her kaftan swishing about her slim legs, the hood of her heavy cloak (because she was sensible like Kyzum) falling off her head of close-cropped dark hair. She aimed her rifle, and nothing happened.

A bang from Ameara's pistol resounded across the shore as the man charging Nahzida dropped to the ground, a fatal wound burning with sun kaza. Ameara couldn't bring her pistol to bear for another shot, so she blocked her attacker with her sword. Ameara's quick aid gave Nahzida the seconds she needed to stow her rifle and draw her bow, and she rained arrows on their pursuers as she and Ameara withdrew down the jetty.

The assembly of assailants moved to charge and overwhelm Kyzum's captain and crewmate, but screams suddenly rang out among them as a blur of spotted fur leapt out of the foliage. The band scattered as the leopard slashed and crippled their comrades. The ones who were fortunate enough to avoid attention did what any sane person would do and elected to aid their associates who faced the non-shapeshifters.

Ameara and Nahzida were retreating down the jetty toward the skyship, but a young man and his elder, both with long braided hair, scampered along the slick rocks to get behind them. Ameara and

Nahzida couldn't remove their attention from their pursuers, and even though the leopard distracted the larger group for now, the setting sun boded well for them.

"Permission to go help?" Ara said.

"Do you have enough star kaza to rift everyone onto the ship?" Kyzum asked.

Ara flexed her left wrist. The ametrine and the garnet set in the cylinder seals on her bracelet brightened with stimulated star and sun kaza; the aquamarine was dull.

"I have enough."

"Then permission granted."

Ara called upon the star kaza in her ametrine seal. The air in front of her shimmered, but before the rift could form, the skyship shuddered. A glow began emanating from the helm. Ara rushed to the panel of levers and cylinder seals.

Ameara and Nahzida had reached the bow of the ship, but the rock scramblers hadn't broken their necks on the slick stones and were advancing to cut down Ameara and Nahzida from behind. Obakwe, in leopard form, was still preventing those on the beach from accessing the jetty, but she would have to retreat very soon. The sky was darkening by the second.

The skyship shuddered again. "What is she doing?" Kyzum shouted up to Ara.

"She's trying to rift," Ara said from the quarterdeck.

"What? Rift where? Ameara is literally right next to her."

"Something has her spooked. She won't stop."

"Make her stop."

"I'm trying!"

Nahzida swapped her bow for her short staff and faced the oncoming attackers alone; the narrow jetty creating a bottleneck was the only reason she hadn't been overrun. Ameara confronted the two with braided hair.

Kyzum groaned and tested the knives up his sleeves. Always the messy way with Ameara. He hurried up the stairs to the quarterdeck.

The skyship lurched as Ara slammed her hand onto the anchor seal and grabbed the negative rift seal to prevent it from rotating.

Kyzum said, "Since you're occupied, I'm going to free up Obakwe, but I need to reach her without going through the skirmish that's causing the ship to go crazier."

Keeping one hand on the negative rift seal, Ara flicked her other wrist, re-stimulating the kaza in her bracelet's cylinder seals, and studied the shore. The air parted before her with a gleaming crackle and whirled into an undulating vortex. The rift lapped at Kyzum's cloak.

"Duck when you get there," Ara said.

"Just don't hit me," Kyzum replied. "And make sure the ship is here when I get back."

"Yes, sir."

Kyzum jogged into the ominous vortex, huffed frigid air, and stumbled onto the beach mere feet from leopard-Obakwe. He barely ducked in time as a viscous fireball followed him out of the rift. Men and women scattered as it seared the evening's bite and crashed into a nearby tree, setting it alight. Kyzum jumped to his feet and threw a knife at the first man to recover. Taking advantage of the reprieve, Obakwe bounded toward the jetty. Kyzum sprinted after her but without illusions of catching her.

Obakwe slowed for Kyzum to close the distance, and then she plowed into the cluster of assailants precariously positioned on the narrow causeway. Kyzum followed in her wake, slashing the ones too impolite to make way. They reached Nahzida and formed a defensive line. Their recovering foes began regrouping for another advance. The elder braided warrior was down with a nasty kazashot wound on his leg, and he was wise and stayed there. The other one, not so wise. He attacked Ameara with abandon.

A bolt of lightning struck the jetty, flinging earth and grit. Ara straddled a star cannon. The gems on her seal bracelet were a beacon against the graying horizon. Their would-be adversaries paused and considered the mastless ship.

Ameara's lone attacker didn't blink. Neither did Ameara. She turned with her opponent's charge, elbowed him in the nose, and knocked his feet from under him. Ameara pressed her sword's tip to her fallen foe's neck.

"Stay down," she commanded. "All of you, back off. We're leaving. Attempt to stop us, and you die."

Ameara nodded to Kyzum and the rest of her crew. They slowly backed around Ameara toward their skyship. Kyzum kept his knives at the ready, and Nahzida nocked an arrow on her bow. Obakwe growled at the man Ameara held at bay, as he seemed to be debating whether or not to test his luck. Ameara removed her blade from her opponent's neck. The young man regained his feet and then helped his companion to his own.

"Captain," the elder warrior called. "I don't know what led you to the Vekrym, choice, necessity, or sentence, but no path is permanent. You can choose another."

"Vekrym are always willing to hear offers of contract regardless of the source," Ameara said, "provided we aren't already bound by another."

"Are you sure, Eclipse?" he dared to say.

Whispers of "Eclipse," "Dazmir," and "lost arts" sprouted from the braided elder's associates.

"Vekrym honor their tenets, and their word." Ameara sheathed her Ryvekian sword and turned to join her crew.

The braided youth charged, the elder shouting, "No!" Ameara spun, drawing her pistol, and fired. The youth crumpled to the rocks, sun kaza crackling around his wound. Nahzida was a heartbeat behind drawing her bow. The braided elder became her new target. He stopped midstride, wincing and favoring his injured leg.

Ameara held her pistol steady, primed to fire again. The remaining men and women outnumbered them (everyone always did), but against Ameara's unyielding stance, they were all *dead* men and women.

The old warrior's eyes blazed for his apprentice, but he recognized when a rock would not be moved. He raised his hands, and his comrades reluctantly lowered their weapons.

"Don't follow," Ameara said.

Kyzum and the crew began boarding their skyship. Ameara waited a few heartbeats, then holstered her pistol and pointedly turned her back on their pursuers. The elder limped to the youth's side, but Kyzum knew it was too late. Ameara didn't make idle threats.

They finished boarding as Ara hurried over and did a quick wound count, which totaled a few scrapes and bruises.

"Get us in the air," Ameara ordered. Ara rushed back to the helm.

A groan came from across the deck. The leopard's paws became hands and feet, and its spots receded into dark skin that bore not even a hint of red. Obakwe breathed deep and pushed herself upright with the aid of the gunwale. Her scarlet wrap and the leather straps securing her knobkerries to her back showed no signs of a scuffle.

"Obakwe," Ameara called, "are you going to be sick?"

"Not yet, Captain," Obakwe replied hoarsely.

Ameara turned her attention to Nahzida, who had her rifle open and was turning the cylinder-seal drum with a frown.

"Nahzida, you told me the realignment fixed it," Ameara said.

"I thought it did," Nahzida said.

"Next time be sure, as I might not be there to save your life. Remain here and stand watch until we're at a safe altitude."

A vibration traversed the deck. A familiar glint surrounded the skyship, and a whiff of frigid air tickled Kyzum's nose. His clothes drifted from his body but settled a moment later as the skyship began to rise. Rivulets poured from the hull, and wood creaked as the Dazmir transitioned from the waters below to the currents above, where they would be nothing more than a strange silhouette obscuring the stars and sliver of moon.

As the landscape became dark and darker shadows, Kyzum entered the captain's quarters. Utilitarian at first glance, the worn but clean rug and the trinkets hanging in a corner hinted at the first impression's falsity. Blank and faulty cylinder seals of bone, stone, and wood were kept in a drawer near Ameara's bunk. Various weapons were concealed behind loose boards even Kyzum was ignorant of. The two trunks engraved with Ryvekian knots were aged but polished. The large window behind the desk seemed a painting come to life as the stars traversed the panes.

Ameara stood near the secluded strongbox and was examining the contents of the satchel: a thick roll of loose papers bound with a wax seal. Ameara's olive skin was a shade lighter than Kyzum's own bronze cast, and while the ocean hues of her tunic, vest, and sash were less of an eyesore than other Setseans' attire, he still had to blink away a sting on occasion. The tails of her fuchsia headband cascaded down her dark locks and over her shoulder. Her refined features were thoughtful.

"Retrieval jobs aren't usually so climactic," Kyzum said.

"Usually, no," Ameara said, "but whatever is brewing between these new rebels and the Ora isn't our concern." Satisfied their cargo was intact, she returned the bound papers to the satchel and placed it inside the strongbox. The key disappeared about her person.

"What went wrong?" Kyzum asked.

"Someone spotted us. I tried to distract the fighters while Obakwe and Nahzida picked them off from behind, but they outflanked us."

"I deduced that from all the running," Kyzum said. When Ameara's contemplative expression remained, he added, "Is there a more interesting part to that story, or did Ara break your ship?" Ameara would have felt the Dazmir trying to rift, either exactly or on a general level depending on where her attention was focused. If the skyship was severely damaged though, they wouldn't be in the air, and Ameara wouldn't have wasted time filling him in on the mission's hiccups.

"The two I fought on the jetty. I think they were galahi," Ameara said.

"Why do you think that?" Kyzum asked.

"They fought like Ara, and their hair was braided."

"That is more interesting. It could explain why you were spotted, or you're just getting sloppy." Kyzum raised a challenging brow and conspicuously eyed the strongbox containing their new cargo.

"I asked our patron the appropriate questions. If I had had misgivings, I would've refused the contract," Ameara said.

"First, Whisper's your patron. He doesn't like me—"

"For understandable reasons," Ameara interjected.

"—Secondly, he obviously didn't answer with equal appropriateness."

"The Ora and Yevyrans have both been violating the treaty for years, but officially, it still stands. Telling me we would be retrieving information from rebels was as much as Whisper could say, or he didn't know the Yevyrans were involved, which we have far from confirmed. I was merely speculating."

"Speculating keeps us alive. We could be getting pulled into a conflict and not even know it," Kyzum warned.

"Putting your nose where it doesn't belong is the reason you live on Syra," Ameara reminded him.

"I also stopped a coup," Kyzum said.

"And you go to bed alone."

"Better alone in bed than alone in a grave."

"We don't look at our patrons' cargo," Ameara said firmly.

"Who said anything about looking?" Kyzum asked. "Surely you're not that curious."

"You appear to be. Remember the oaths we both took upon joining the Vekrym. Now see to the crew. Report to me in the heart. I have to check what Ara tinkered with and figure out how long it will take to fix."

Kyzum refrained from noting the untended slash on Ameara's arm (Ara would see to it as they worked), and with a respectful, "Captain," he departed as ordered. Ameara was focused on repairing her ship, the satchel added to a pile of lesser correspondence that wasn't worth a second read. Good. Kyzum was naturally curious and did want a peek at the information they had retrieved. The Yevyrans were said to possess knowledge of the lost arts, and while the kaza-gem-seal mechanics didn't interest him, he knew they were valuable. But he liked living, and therefore tried to avoid anything that could potentially shorten his lifespan. He laughed at the irony of being the feared Eclipse's first mate. He couldn't say it wasn't fun.

Ameara…She knew the flexible bounds of their oaths from the fixed ones. She did. She just needed a subtle reminder now and then, for Kyzum worried she might someday cross one. Then the fun would be over, and he would have to abandon her and the crazy Dazmir he called home.

CHAPTER 2

Obakwe, Nahzida, and Ara paused their conversation when Ameara entered the galley, but recognizing she wasn't there to give orders, they resumed as if the interval hadn't existed.

"No thanks," Ara said.

"We might not be in port long enough," Obakwe added.

"Abylay is a beautiful city," Nahzida urged as Ameara helped herself to bulgur and chickpeas simmered in yogurt sauce. The last of the rosewater had been added to the bulgur. Their dates and pomegranates were also gone, and nuts were running low. They would have to resupply in Abylay.

"It has the finest restaurants in all of Setsea," Nahzida continued. "Theaters, shops, parks. I bet we'll even spot a fashari."

Ameara plopped a piece of flatbread next to the bulgur and poured extra yogurt sauce into a small bowl for dipping. She joined her crew at the narrow table as Obakwe warned, "The fashari are not spectacles for you to gawk at."

Nahzida sighed. "I meant no offense. I'm just trying to convince you to come with me." Her brown eyes brightened as Kyzum entered. "Kyzum, help me out. Tell them Abylay is a magnificent city and we should take some time off this ship to enjoy ourselves."

"Abylay is a magnificent city, and we should take some time off this ship to enjoy ourselves," Kyzum repeated. He scooped dinner into a bowl and opened the spices cabinet in search of a bitter or acidic kick that would please his Masatitoran palate.

"You are no help whatsoever," Nahzida said. She refocused on her other shipmates. "Please come ashore with me. Abylay is even better during the Festival of Shattered Swords. There are performances, competitions; the bazaars are filled with goods you can't find any other time of year. I could get us into a private bathhouse," she said enticingly.

"That sounds luxurious," Obakwe said. "For that, I'll come ashore with you."

Nahzida smiled in victory.

"No thanks," Ara said. "You two go ahead."

"I'm not asking you to attend the offering ceremony," Nahzida said. "I know how you feel about it, even though giving your life to the Ora contributes the greatest light to Orvashka."

"You're getting preachy," Kyzum said as he joined them at the table.

"It's the truth."

"Your defense of that so-called truth, and those who exiled you, remains inadequate," Obakwe said.

"Inadequate, yes. Satisfactory, also yes," Kyzum said between bites of bulgur. "A Wanbasban Vekrym makes as much sense as the Setsean Counselors."

Obakwe furrowed her brow, as if Kyzum had stated he could sail on land. "You say strange things," she smiled.

"My exile was a mercy," Nahzida muttered with finality.

"You were defending yourself and others," Obakwe countered serenely. "You've taken more lives since that first."

Kyzum shrugged and dissolved himself of mediation.

"It's not the purview of a citizen to make that judgment," Nahzida said. "A Vessel is another matter."

"Even if the citizen saves lives?"

"Hence their mercy."

"Do you still want to go back?" Ara asked, interrupting the repeated discussion that never yielded results.

"Of course," Nahzida said, but her previous confidence was lacking. "Abylay is my home. If there was a way for me to return permanently, I would. Although, being a Vessel does have its perks."

She looked fondly at her disassembled rifle lying on the other end of the table. The rotating drum filled with cylinder seals and the pressure dial to regulate power output were identical to Ameara's pistol. Ameara theorized that was why it sporadically misbehaved. The seals needed modification for the stock and the longer barrel that provided accuracy from a distance. They had been working on it for over a year, commissioning the parts in different ports to avoid detection. Ameara thought it well worth the wait. The risk of having it…Well, it wasn't the only item that could potentially crash them into the rocks. Vekrym were exempt from some laws and bent others acceptably, but they kept Kyzum's forged documents just in case.

"Perks of the explosive variety," Kyzum said. "Emphasis on 'explosive.'"

"You know I like all kinds of explosive things," Nahzida said with an exaggerated wink. Obakwe laughed at Kyzum's annoyed expression. Ara blushed and stared at her food.

Nahzida chuckled. "When I return to Abylay as a citizen with an exemption for my weapons, kaza and non-kaza ones, you will all visit and see how much you're missing."

"I have no desire to be run out of another city," Kyzum said.

"Then stop putting your eyes and ears where they don't belong."

"You would have to give the Ora something priceless for them to lift your exile *and* provide an exemption," Obakwe pointed out.

"In our line of work, something's bound to come up," Nahzida said. "If the Yevyrans are working with rebels, that would be a violation of the treaty. The Ora could finally rid Idlium of their presence. That's a priceless gift if ever there was one."

Ara hunched in her seat. Nahzida squeezed her shoulder. "I'm not talking about you. You're one of us."

"Who said Yevyrans are working with rebels?" Ameara asked.

"I was musing about the two braided warriors," Obakwe said.

Ameara spoke to her entire crew but eyed Nahzida. "That's a dangerous claim to make without proof."

"I said 'if,'" Nahzida mumbled, quelled for the moment. Ameara would have to rid her of that entire line of thought in private.

Ameara stood, her dinner half-finished. She had lost her appetite.

"Please visit Abylay with us," Nahzida said to Ara. "We'll be back before the ceremony. I promise. It would be good for all of us to leave Syra and enjoy ourselves. You know I'm right."

"I'll think about it," Ara said. She excused herself and left the galley, claiming she had to check Syra's kaza flow. Nahzida let it be; she was already charting another course to persuade Ara ashore. "Ameara, what about you? Will you join us?"

"I'm replenishing our decoy wild gems," she replied. They had to maintain appearances. If it was ever discovered that Syra was not just a Dazmir, but a Dazmir-vahl-kesh, a survivor of the Schism's birth, they would have to fly to the ends of the world to prevent Syra from being taken. The sentient gems were rare, the sane ones even rarer. Their capabilities forgotten, their power remembered. When Ameara first stumbled upon her, Syra had been lost in a fog of insanity and had almost killed her.

"Always business with you," Nahzida sighed.

"I'm posting a watch tonight," Ameara said. "Other Dazmiri will be close to their berths for stars' sway's replenishing, but Syra needs extra eyes in the pass with the cloud cover and her shield incapacitated. Standard rotation. Obakwe, you're not on it. Kyzum will cover for you."

"I trust Kyzum's tongue more than his sword arm," Obakwe said.

"So do I," Kyzum agreed.

"I've shapeshifted during sunset before," Obakwe said. "The effects aren't new to me."

"You were sick for days last time," Ameara said. "I need you able to veer when we reach Abylay."

"And the garnet seal in my rifle is dull," Nahzida added. "Ameara's spinel seal is probably dull too, and the privy disintegration is dimming."

"Are you expecting trouble?" Obakwe asked Ameara, ignoring Nahzida's unintended implication that she was shirking what she believed was the blessing bestowed by her ancestors. Ameara charged Obakwe with keeping their store of sun kaza wild gems replenished, but it was Obakwe's choice to replenish the cylinder seals. She would be pleased to fulfill a direct, humble request, but acknowledging insinuated directions and cavalier demands was admitting incompetence. She was not "a mindless Setsean kaza supply."

"No more than usual," Ameara said, "but you sleep in your bunk, not on the deck."

"Yes, Captain." Fond remembrance passed over Obakwe's face. "I would use that tone with my daughter when she was being stubborn."

"I'm sure she listened like the responsible young woman you raised her to be," Ameara said.

Obakwe's smile was bittersweet. "For the most part."

"Nahzida, you have first watch," Ameara said.

"Understood."

"And make amends with Ara before we reach Abylay."

"She's not a Yevyran, not anymore," Nahzida said defensively.

"She was raised in Yevyran beliefs," Obakwe said.

"She renounced them."

"Many have done the same under threat of execution."

Nahzida leaned back on the bench and looked thoughtfully in the direction Ara had gone.

"Finish up," Ameara said. "I want a watch on deck within the hour."

She left the galley to replies of, "Yes, Captain." The idea of climbing into her own bunk was appealing, as she would take a watch too, but she went aft toward Syra's heart instead. The heavy door was ajar. Ameara pushed it inward a few more inches and slid inside. The alexandrite set within a cylinder seal in the center of the cabin pulsed with a steady light, its luminance swaying between hues of green and purple. The gem's intensity signaled how hard Syra was working, how much kaza was being expended. It gleamed lazily now, content. Smaller secondary seals for roll, pitch, and yaw hung from a series of pulleys connected to the helm. Kaza from the alexandrite—from Syra—linked to their gems and incorporated their functions. Normally, a Dazmir's seals for positive and negative rift would also be in the heart, but Ameara had moved them. A dangerous, potentially fatal undertaking, but she had been desperate.

The upper hatches were lowered. Ara stood on a ladder, her torso disappearing into the space between decks. Ameara walked beneath a hatch and looked into the branches of secondary seals, pulleys, and gears. Syra's star kaza bounded between the pulsing gems via relay seals. Ameara had modified, rerouted, or done away with numerous branches and safeguards to enable her to fly Syra solo. She had been *very* desperate.

The shield seal remained in its standard location, but Ameara had scraped flat part of its depiction and given the helm control of the shield's power output and shape. It had also given Syra control. All of Ameara's modifications had allowed Syra more freedom to interpret her seal's depictions. Vahl-kesh seals were less precise to accommodate the gemstone's sentience, but their simplicity was specific in what a vahl-kesh could and could not do. Ameara's alterations had blurred that specificity. Its lack had led to some close calls. She had been *very, very* desperate.

Ara had joined her crew just a few months ago, but she already had a grasp of Syra's unique functionality. More than a grasp, considering she had prevented Syra from rifting without disabling her. After temporarily jamming the helm's rift controls, Ara had rerouted the relay seals in the heart leading to the secondary negative rift seal, so instead of kaza forming a loop with the positive rift seal and whisking Syra elsewhere, the majority of that kaza flowed to the shield first, syphoning the power Syra needed to rift. It had also overloaded the shield's seal; the light in the dull diamond was a feeble speck.

"You better not be working on the shield this close to the pass," Ameara said.

"I'm just making sure everything is stabilized," Ara said.

"We both know it is." Between the two of them, they had carefully—very carefully—restored the relay route for rifting and isolated the shield seal and its secondaries. None appeared to be leaking kaza, but it had been a big jolt. Being airborne was not the time to check their integrity and reintegrate them. One missed crack, and they would swerve into a mountainside or be blown from the sky.

"Syra feels…off," Ara said.

"She doesn't like flying without her shield," Ameara said. At least, she thought that was the cause. Syra was definitely apprehensive about something, but inquiring as to the source had led to the deeper parts of her consciousness Ameara couldn't translate with their limited connection.

"I wanted to have her fixed before we reached the pass," Ara said forlornly.

"On a normal Dazmir, you would have. We're on rotating watch tonight."

"Yes, Captain. I'll be done soon." Ara lingered within the hatch, but if she was inspecting the heart's mechanism, she had eyes on the top of her head.

"Do you want to remain on this crew?" Ameara said.

Ara crouched on the ladder. "Have I done something wrong?"

"Your instincts today were spot on. With Kyzum, and with Syra. Anyone else would have crippled her or blown us to pieces. You've proven your value to this crew, and I want to keep relying on you. Whether you consider yourself a Yevyran or not, you were raised in those beliefs and trained as a galahi. The skills you learned have kept you and us alive. Stop second-guessing yourself."

"I don't question my abilities," Ara said.

"Faith and fighting aren't mutually exclusive," Ameara said.

Ara averted her gaze and tapped the ladder where she held it for comfort, not balance. "I used to think I had faith to move mountains. Then when it mattered, my faith was found wanting. Everything I was so sure was true, everything I'd been taught, everything I grew up believing, became nothing more than knowledge. My faith had no belief to stand on. I don't know if I actually believe, or if I just repeat things because they're all I know."

"You left Ulydra two years ago," Ameara said. "You're a Vekrym. You know more now."

Ara regarded Syra's heart. The alexandrite pulsed in a steady rhythm, the play of light across Ara's fair skin reminiscent of a rowshatar-estra. "It's like I'm hanging on to driftwood to stay afloat. There's a dinghy a few strokes away, but to reach it, I would have to let go of the driftwood, and I just…can't."

Ameara shrugged. "As long as the driftwood keeps you in fighting form."

Ara nodded noncommittally.

Ameara hesitated. "When you agreed to join my crew, you said it was where you were supposed to be. If that's true, then everything happened exactly as it should have."

"You don't believe in fate," Ara said.

Ameara didn't. Fate, destiny, someone or something meddling with her life, telling her what to do, where to go, how to live. No thanks.

"You do," Ameara said.

"Yevyra has a plan, but we can choose to follow it or not."

"If Nahzida were here, you would've just started a theological debate. You believe. Now get some rest before your watch. Syra will be fine."

"Yes, Captain." Ara stepped off the ladder, and Ameara left her as she began pushing the hatches shut. The young woman believed crazy things, whether she could admit it or not. Some things she couldn't even explain, but she believed. Or she would believe again, eventually. Maybe. The death penalty accompanying her faith was a great motivator to sail in another direction. If her god did have a plan, if her Creator existed, Ameara preferred the one with Ara alive and caring for Syra.

CHAPTER 3

Harmony Tower's spiral tiers surpassed the hills and dwarfed the surrounding city's crenelated wall. The edifice stood as a testament to the prosperity of Setsea and the attainment all satrapies should strive to achieve. A creation of beauty, peace, and freedom.

Jaleya couldn't stand the sight of it.

The obnoxious bulge gloated from where it had imposed itself onto the land, expecting gratitude for its unsolicited favor as it leached the life from the palm trees and blossoming shrubbery.

Careful, her javati spoke into her mind. *If you glare any harder, you'll reveal your true feelings.*

Isesh, his ivory fur and spectral feathers glistening in the morning sun, joined Jaleya in the bow of the barge taking them to Abylay, their new…abode. Home was a word for a distant village Jaleya hadn't seen in years and could barely remember. A tangible thing reduced to a mere concept. If she ever returned, she wouldn't recognize it.

You want to go there less than I do, she responded in kind.

We managed at our previous posts, and we'll do the same here, Isesh sent, but as they continued down the Nidren River, the simurgh's feathers quivered, and he tested the deck with his paws, as if he wanted to spring into the air and let the wind carry him elsewhere.

It's bigger than our other posts, Jaleya sent. Abylay's wall loomed higher and higher as the barge neared. Towers draped in hanging gardens stabbed the sky. Haughty domes pretended to be gentle clouds. Kaza flashed within a minaret, and Jaleya wondered what deceptions lay in the messages speeding to their recipients.

Its size is not the only thing that's greater, Isesh sent. *A flippant comment that receives discipline on the plains could get us executed here.*

I can control my tongue, Jaleya replied. *I wouldn't be alive otherwise.*

Keep it under tight rein. In Abylay, the people adhere to Orvashka's Ways and the Ora's rule because they choose to.

It's all lies and hypocrisy.

Isesh thumped her with one of his wings, disheveling her dark braids. *And you've just killed us.*

A bargeman eyed them sideways as Jaleya brushed her braids off her shoulders. Knowing javati could share thoughts didn't stop people from being nervous when they knew it was happening.

The barge stopped for inspection between two watchtowers that served as a checkpoint. The Harmony of Orvashka's Ways, six interlocking circles within a ring of cresting waves, was carved below the towers' highest windows and engraved on the boarding solders' leather armor.

One soldier marched up to Jaleya, careful to keep her between him and the mixture of dog and bird that was Isesh. "Orders, javati."

"Assigned to Abylay," Jaleya replied. "Iza Vor. We were delayed upriver, and I didn't have the resources to send a message informing the custodian."

The soldier scrutinized Isesh, specifically the simurgh's wings. Isesh's jowls quivered, the feathers surrounding his canine face ruffling. The soldier wisely refrained from suggesting Isesh should have left her behind to carry a message. However, he wasn't respectful enough to accept her word without a rowshatar attached to her hip. "Orders, javati."

Jaleya had hoped the mention of Iza Vor would speed things

along, but it was the destination for all javati in Abylay, and would therefore be a valuable exploitation for deserters. She went to the rail where she had stashed the pack containing her meager belongings and rummaged through it for her conscription. To the soldier's credit, he only took a small step backward when her absence left him face to face with Isesh.

Jaleya handed the soldier her orders just as there was a stir on the deck. A boy no older than ten scrambled up from below. His wide eyes searched desperately for aid, but the crew, soldiers, and passengers shied away from him. He bolted for the rail.

A man followed the child a heartbeat later. The deck's occupants tripped over each other to avoid his path, as if the Abyss had taken corporeal form. The man's trousers, tunic, and jerkin were unassuming hues of the desert and hills, but his head was shaved and his red sash belt bore a white Harmony. The simple regalia of the shavinashi. He pursued the boy with measured steps.

The child reached the rail and gripped the smooth wood to launch himself overboard. The shavinash moved inhumanly fast and grabbed the boy's frayed tunic. He hoisted him onto his shoulder like a sack of grain. The child pounded his fists on the shavinash's back and kicked his feet in the air.

"Let me go! Let me go! Help!"

Tears lined his cheeks and gurgled his pleas. His impotent blows and terror-stricken sobs did not exist within the shavinash's indifference. No one inquired about the boy's wellbeing. No one interfered.

Jaleya trembled at the shavinash's presence, but her hatred burned hotter than her fear. She longed to snatch his scimitar and hack off his head, even though she knew she wouldn't reach the hilt before he skewered her.

The shavinash paused at the hatch leading belowdecks, the boy still struggling. His attention settled over Jaleya, death seeping from a cold wasteland. Jaleya silently dared him to attack her, to see how he fared against one who could defend herself.

Jaleya. Jaleya, it's not him, Isesh sent, repeating her conclusion from days previous.

The simurgh's words pulled Jaleya back to herself, and she quickly acted the cowed javati. She held her breath as the ice of the shavinash's gaze pierced her, and suppressed a shudder when warmth returned.

The shavinash and his helpless cargo returned from whence they came. The boy's cries were abruptly silenced. The crew resumed their duties, and the passengers answered the solders' questions as if the interim abduction hadn't happened.

The soldier interviewing Jaleya returned her conscription, said a shaken but relieved, "All in order," and joined his comrades to conclude the inspection.

Someday, children will no longer be taken by the shavinashi, Isesh sent.

Yes, when they've fallen with their masters, Jaleya sent.

The barge lurched as it continued downriver. Jaleya strained her neck looking at Abylay's skyline. Soon it would surround her. No more wind caressing her olive skin. No more hills and valleys to roam. She would be confined in brick and stone festering with poison that no amount of stuccowork or mosaics could cure. Surrounded by people who chose the Ora. People who were daft enough to believe Orvashka's Ways were not the Ora's fabrication. People who stood by and did nothing while loved ones were torn apart. Jaleya longed for the day when a rebellion finally overthrew the Ora and the people realized they had brought all their troubles on themselves. She needed to be part of that rebellion.

She had been too young to stop the shavinashi from taking her sister. Lenruz had been so brave, head held high, not a single tear shed. Jaleya remembered her warmth as they embraced, and the aching void when she let go.

Do you think he's in Abylay? she sent to Isesh.

Her javati's feathers ruffled. *My stance on your vengeance hasn't changed. I will not help you with it.*

You won't let me get killed, so when I find him, you'll help me whether you want to or not.

A chirping growl rumbled in Isesh's throat. *Yours is a hatchling's pursuit.*

Isesh padded forward, putting physical distance between them if not mental. Jaleya's stance on her mission hadn't changed over the years either. It had only grown stronger as she became more desperate to fulfill it. Sometimes it was hard sharing minds when they could only agree to disagree.

The raised portcullis spanning the river came upon them faster than Jaleya preferred. The thick bars bore no bolts or grooves, a single metal piece. Made with a rowshatar's aid, it was a creation of the time before the Schism. Jaleya was fascinated despite herself as they passed through the massive wall.

Harmony Tower and its citadel, Iza Vor, dominated the east side of Abylay. Domes designating government, guild, or other official buildings abruptly ended where the Nidren cut through the city. Tiered bridges spanned the water, but glazed bricks and elegant arches abruptly succumbed to coarse blocks and rugged supports. A remnant meeting the aftermath of the Schism's unintended creation. A reminder of what had been lost.

A row of modest but important-looking brick buildings lined the river on its west side, but immediately beyond the tidy waterfront, decrepit structures encroached the narrow alleys, fighting for inches that didn't exist. Flat roofs apologized for having to be built higher instead of wider as they intruded upon Iza Vor's sky.

Jaleya, Isesh sent, his voice hushed with awe.

She followed his gaze upward. Her mouth opened, and her eyes widened. Tethered to a flat tower in Iza Vor, two skyships hovered proud and regal above Abylay. A glimmer faint enough to be attributed to a trick of light surrounded their wooden hulls. It was said Dazmiri could be mistaken for sailing vessels without masts, but witnessing their graceful lines and command of the sky for the first time, Jaleya didn't see how anyone could make that obvious error. One of the most revered relics of a time long past, the Dazmiri would not go quietly to their rest or let anyone forget they had existed.

It must have been amazing to experience the skies from their decks, Jaleya sent.

Perhaps we'll be blessed to witness the Dazmiri's return, Isesh sent. *At the least, we will see one of these depart for the Schism.*

Yes, the work at the Schism. Whatever they might claim, Jaleya doubted the Ora were trying to permanently close it. They would lose too much of their power, their influence, their control. It begged the question, though: what were they actually doing, apart from putting on a show for the people? Or did the Schism have the Ora—"the only ones harmonized enough with Orvashka to lead Setsea"—utterly and helplessly baffled? That thought usually made her chuckle, but not today.

As the skyships declared a time before the Ora, the barge maneuvered toward a dock in the heart of the Ora's territory. Jaleya was suddenly very aware of the shavinash behind her and a hostile city before her.

CHAPTER 4

The barge docked as harbor workers caught lines and secured the ship. The gangplank was lowered, and the captain met the officials waiting on the waterfront. The crew fell into their routine of unloading cargo. Passengers gathered their belongings. Jaleya hurried toward the gangplank, Isesh in her wake. Stepping foot in Abylay was the last thing she wanted to do, but remaining aboard with the Ora's enforcers for one more second would either make her sick or spur her into rash action.

Murmurs and the sudden halt of activity announced the shavinashi reclaiming the main deck. Jaleya stopped, leaving clear the path for disembarking. She had been too slow. A handful of children—new recruits—shuffled into a line between the shavinash from earlier and his female accomplice. The older children put on brave faces while the younger fought to still their quivering lips. Every one shrank beneath the shavinashi's scrutinizing indifference. The boy who had attempted escape favored his left side, but his punishment was otherwise hidden.

As the shavinashi led the children down the gangplank, they seemed bored. As if ripping children away from their families and delivering them to be butchered in what they called training was a morning chore preventing them from riding their favorite horse.

Half of the "recruits" would be dead within the month. Half of the survivors would fail the final test. The remaining remnant would become killers.

The female shavinash paused after the children had passed. She inspected Jaleya with a wicked eye, whatever dark thought she was entertaining curling her cruel lips. Jaleya realized she'd been glaring at the procession of doomed children. She calmed herself. This was not the place or time, and being killed by this shavinash would deprive her of taking the life of the one she hunted. She averted her gaze.

The shavinash gave an amused, derisive sniff and joined her fellow enforcer on the dock. A sailor exhaled in relief, and the passengers swayed, offering each other supporting hands as the threat of violence lifted.

Isesh brushed against Jaleya's hip and whimpered-chirped.

They descended the gangplank next, as the other passengers were disinclined to approach their proximity lest they be associated with the one who had dared stare down a shavinash, even if the one was a javati. Jaleya and Isesh paused amid the hustle and bustle of the waterfront. Officials marched to and fro with clipboards and an air of self-importance. Arguments over tariffs, manifests, and delays blended into a generic buzzing. Crates, sacks, and baskets were loaded onto carts and wagons. Cargo slammed onto the paved bricks, followed by curses and shouts directed at the careless crew. Children in threadbare tunics hovered near intersections, waiting to offer weary travelers directions or help with their luggage in exchange for a small fee; their gullible targets would inevitably find themselves abandoned in a dangerous backstreet and relieved of their valuables. The wily youngsters ducked beneath carts or into alleys when patrols passed by. Harmony Tower was visible even from there.

I guess we go that way, Jaleya sent.

We could ask for directions, Isesh replied.

If we can't find it, we will.

Before they could proceed, Jaleya heard her name. They turned to find a short-haired man wearing an official-looking tunic and simple braided headband hastening toward them; probably an assistant. The Harmony hanging from his neck bore the infinite knot in the circles' center, indicating he endeavored to perfect the Way of Unity within his life force.

"Are you Jaleya?" he said upon reaching them, but his attention was pulled to Isesh. He gawked at the combination of fur and feathers that reached Jaleya's hip.

"Who are you?" Jaleya asked.

"Oh, forgive me. My name is Er'od. Custodian Saunez sent me to escort you to Iza Vor."

Isesh wagged his tail, the feathers shimmering. Er'od tilted his head as if questioning whether or not Isesh could have understood his words, and then nodded to himself.

This one is new, Isesh sent.

Jaleya agreed. Anyone who administered rowshatari, from advocates to personal servants, interacted with javati on a daily basis and learned very quickly that fashari understood everything people said. Fashari often understood people better than people did.

"That was kind of her," Jaleya said. "We appreciate the escort."

Er'od led them away from the docks and down a wide boulevard. Their pace was barely a horse's walk. People were everywhere, and not just Setseans: short Masatitorans in austere, crisp tunics; fair Ryvekians with robust muscles; and even lithe, dark-skinned Wanbasbans in bright wraps and robes, who were presumably Ways sympathizers or spies in the Setsea-Wanbasba stalemate.

Merchants hawked wares; carters made deliveries; vendors enticed passersby with sizzling kebabs and fresh bread; diners enjoyed nougats and fruit stuffed with yogurt on lavish porches; shoppers perused displays; musicians performed at intersections. Kurresh had its bazaars, theaters, and restaurants, but they were contained to specific wards. Here, the bedlam was everywhere, nonstop. It was suffocating.

Isesh slipped through the crowd and walked by Er'od's side, to his unease. People parted before the simurgh, mercifully clearing a path. They crossed a bridge over a branch of the Nidren River, and while shops, eateries, and taverns remained, the crowds diminished. Structures became taller, and domes curved more of the skyline. Jaleya saw buildings that seemed to serve an official function in plenty. One especially elegant façade with gilded stuccowork and an arch of honeycombed mosaics was probably an intarish sanctuary. A temple dedicated to the Way of Love across the lane served as confirmation.

They crossed another bridge, but went only a few streets before the wall of Iza Vor rose before them, Harmony Tower challenging the sun. The citadel spanned for miles, an entire ward—an entire city!—unto itself. It housed the greatest number of rowshatari and javati in all of Setsea. All living within the shadow of the Ora.

The nearest gate was housed in a honeycombed arch like the intarish sanctuary, but it was far larger. Er'od showed the guards his mark of office, and they were allowed entrance. They crossed a large courtyard lavished with flowers, greenery, and a central fountain; hanging gardens adorned the surrounding arcade. They entered a vaulted foyer, and Er'od led Jaleya and Isesh through a maze of arched corridors with mosaics on the floor and ceiling and tiles bordering the windows. The grandeur lessened as they neared their destination: a hall with doors lining the walls. Columns provided the illusion of partitions for the assistants at the desks. Er'od headed toward one of the empty desks and its corresponding door, which had more space allotted to it than the others.

A waiting sirrush noted their approach and lowered its horned head respectfully; Isesh returned the gesture in kind. Jaleya had seen many exchanges between Isesh and other fashari over the years, and from what she had managed to gather, it was some kind of unspoken hierarchy. Simurghs were somewhere in the middle; Isesh deemed sirrushes his equal. Other fashari were…leaders of a sort. They didn't seem to do any leading or governing, but all fashari gave deference to those specific few. Isesh wasn't forthcoming with details, but his limited answers referenced his ancestors and their request to remain in the earthly realm after the heavenly realm had been lost to humanity. It was one of few topics fashari discussed only with other fashari.

A stocky man with arms of corded muscle and hair straddling his shoulders exited the inner room and collected the sirrush. His frown told Jaleya there was an exasperated rant happening between the javati. The sirrush's feline forepaws and hind bird feet made a pad-click-pad-click sound on the stone as the pair left. Er'od didn't break stride and knocked on the open door as he entered. "The new javati is here, Custodian Saunez."

"Thank you, Er'od," a deep feminine voice replied. "Send them in."

Er'od ushered Jaleya and Isesh inside and then backed out, closing the door behind him. A woman with olive skin stood behind a desk laden with paperwork organized into five different stacks. She wore a green, form-fitting dress beneath a fringed shawl fastened with an elegant belt. A tall bonnet embroidered with the luminaries' cycle, the emblem of the rowshatari, crowned her head. Her high cheekbones and pointed chin emphasized her piercing brown eyes and no-nonsense demeanor, which quelled any thoughts of approaching her with foolish inquiries.

Jaleya opened her mouth to greet her new supervisor.

"You're late," Custodian Saunez said. "You were supposed to be here two days ago."

Not one for formalities, is she? Isesh sent.

"The ship we were traveling on was commandeered by shavinashi," Jaleya said. "I had no opportunity to send word. The captain had no communication seal, and the destinations of our delay were small villages that rely solely on horse messengers, none of which came through during our time there."

Jaleya half-expected Custodian Saunez to say that Isesh should have carried a message; she had heard of other custodians making such ignorant suggestions.

Custodian Saunez said, "Word from the harbormaster seems to corroborate your explanation. I will be checking to confirm. Hopefully you're as honest with your duties here. This is your first time in Abylay?"

Jaleya blinked, the thoughts, *She already heard from the harbormaster? No, she's just trying to intimidate me. Right?* still going through her mind. She quickly answered an affirmative.

"And this is your…fourth solo assignment, if you count the brief stay in that backwater village that needed sun kaza to aid its crops."

It didn't sound like a question, but Jaleya answered with another affirmative.

"You haven't been charged with a rowshatar-estra yet," Custodian Saunez said.

"I have not," Jaleya replied.

"Learn fast, then. I won't have sloppy or careless javati looking after my rowshatari." The barest pause. "You're assigned to one of Abylay's rowshatari-estra. Because rowshatari-estra's communion with Orvashka is via the stars, you will be on duty at all times except for a period of four hours three times a week you must request one day in advance. The time does not accumulate, so use it. Your quarters will be adjacent to your charge's instead of with the other javati. When you need to sleep, additional guards will be provided. If something amiss should occur, however, your duty is still to protect your charge. All other regulations remain the same. When your charge has *full* access to kaza, you may come and go as you please as long as he has the appropriate escort. You will follow all of your charge's orders, but you are there to protect him, not to be his servant; his safety has priority over all else, even your javati. If you have a grievance, dispute, complaint, concern, question, and so forth, come to me, and I will address it appropriately. Questions? No? Good. Come with me."

Jaleya spared a glance at Isesh before hopping to follow, as Custodian Saunez marched with purpose, didn't bother to confirm they were behind her, and was already beyond Er'od's desk.

Jaleya looked left and right as they traversed corridor after corridor. The citadel seemed to be laid out similar to other rowshatari complexes, just much, much larger. She didn't need to know her way to know when they entered the rowshatari's palace. She spotted the typical gardens, private parks, and the extravagant branching hallways that no doubt led to a bathhouse, a teahouse, a temple dedicated to Orvashka's Ways, and a pristine horseback riding and recreation arena. The javati compound would be closer to the administration or training section of the citadel, back the way they had come.

The presence of guards was noticeably heightened in the rowshatari's palace. They were stationed inside and out at regular intervals, and some carried a pistol in addition to their scimitar and spear. Kaza weapons had known prominent use before the Schism, but since kaza was now a limited and expensive resource, those weapons had been reduced to a status symbol, an intimidation tactic, and a fleeting advantage.

Custodian Saunez finally paused outside double doors with engraved date palms, but only long enough to grasp the handle and enter without announcing herself. Jaleya was taken aback but followed after a breath's hesitation. Mosaics depicting a desert oasis spanned the columns supporting the domed sitting room. A board of Twenty Squares lay on a table within reach of the gilded chaises and chairs. Vines bloomed on the lattice bordering the archway to the balcony. A heavy curtain to her right probably led to the rowshatar's bedchamber and a private study.

The rowshatar—her new charge—stood before a full-length mirror and scrutinized the silver miter adorning his head while a female servant braided his long black hair. The sash girdling his silk kaftan sparkled. Gold hoops hung from his ears, which appeared slightly too large for his pointed attributes, and every finger bore a ring set with a precious stone. Dead ones, of course. Only the Ora veered the kaza in wild gems. The remshiri were permitted to do so, but they declined to even touch the volatile seal-less jewels.

The rowshatar brightened as he realized who had entered without permission. "Oh, Custodian Saunez. What do you think? It was delivered today. Ow." He glared at the servant braiding his hair; she must have accidentally pulled it when he moved.

"Apologies, Your Radiance," she said.

The rowshatar shook his head and rolled his eyes.

Custodian Saunez gave a cursory inspection of the shining miter. "It suits you. Coin well spent."

Jaleya risked a glance at Isesh. Was that deadpan in Custodian Saunez's voice? Or was she being serious, and Jaleya was imprinting comments of her own? No one else had reacted.

Her new charge beamed at Custodian Saunez's flattery.

"Your new guardian has arrived," Custodian Saunez said. "Jaleya, this is Rowshatar Teza."

The guards posted around the room straightened like a horse smelling a hidden pear upon its master. Jaleya's ears still rung from what she could have sworn was sarcasm, but she stepped forward to greet Teza appropriately.

"You're too young to be a javati," Teza said. "Custodian Saunez, when you said you were getting me another guardian—ow!" The servant apologized again, her cheeks coloring.

Unaffected by the outburst, Custodian Saunez said, "Jaleya has passed the tests, and she is fully qualified to perform her duties."

Teza's face scrunched in skepticism, but fascination lit his brown eyes as he finally noticed Isesh. He stepped toward the fashari. "A simurgh—OW! Empty sky, woman! How incompetent are you?"

The poor servant blushed a deep crimson and lowered her head.

"Leave us, please. All of you," Custodian Saunez ordered. "I have business with Rowshatar Teza."

"They're not finished," protested Teza.

"By the time they finish, it will be time for training, and they will have to undo their work the moment it's completed. They'll return this evening."

Teza thrust out his jaw and puckered his lips into a pout. The excused servants and guards quickly took their leave, giving the rowshatar a wide berth.

"Not you," Custodian Saunez told one of the fleeing guards. "You will escort Rowshatar Teza and Jaleya to the training grounds, as Jaleya is still becoming acquainted with the citadel. Wait outside for the moment."

The guard looked dejected that he had to remain, but his salute was respectful, and his steps were professional as he went to his post. Custodian Saunez closed the door behind him and went to Teza, who still wore a pout, his arms folded.

"I could skip training," he said. "I've already mastered the exercises, and I can rift circles around everyone else. Well, I could if I was allowed to."

"Training is required for all rowshatari," Custodian Saunez said as she began undoing the fine braids around the new miter.

"Then I should get better training," Teza said.

Custodian Saunez removed the miter from his head and placed it in his hands. She gathered his long hair and secured it with a simple band. Jaleya inwardly gaped but kept her face passive. She didn't know any other custodian who took such liberties with her rowshatari. Custodian Saunez didn't seem to think anything of it.

"When you're ready to veer more powerful seals, Seal Keeper Firnak will advance you," she said.

"But I've already learned everything," Teza whined.

Custodian Saunez raised an eyebrow to an astonishing height. "If the seal keeper has not advanced you, then you haven't. Don't despair," she said gently. "Continue training, and in time, you will veer diamond seals."

Teza sighed, but the prospect of veering a diamond seal had taken the heat from his pout, even though Jaleya had never heard of a rowshatar—a Setsean rowshatar—progressing beyond an ametrine. The remshiri who could veer diamond seals were rare and widely known. If a rowshatar obtained such prowess, all of Setsea would hear about it, from Abylay to the smallest "backwater village."

"Jaleya, this way, please," Custodian Saunez said. Jaleya joined her at the corner nearest the entrance. Behind a pillar and a silk curtain was an archway. It led to a modest living area with simple furniture and two adjoining bedchambers; the one with the generous bed was for her, and the stark, empty one was for Isesh.

"Your quarters," Custodian Saunez said. "I'll have your personal effects delivered as soon as possible."

"I have them," Jaleya said, indicating the small pack on her shoulders.

"Good. Send me a list of what your fashari requires, and I'll write an acquisition form presently. If there's something it requires immediately, you may be able to find it in the javati compound. Speak to Quartermaster Bilka; tell her I sent you. She'll get what she can for you."

Jaleya just nodded. After the morning she'd had, she couldn't do anything else. And it wasn't over. She had to escort her new charge to training, and then whatever he did after that.

Custodian Saunez seemed to hesitate, her dark eyes regarding Jaleya thoughtfully. The moment passed. They both returned to Teza.

"I'm not leaving this room with my hair like this," he said.

Unfazed, Custodian Saunez stuck her head out the door and told one of the sentries to fetch a servant quickly. She turned to Jaleya, but she was also speaking to Teza.

"An attendant will be here shortly. I relayed instructions to do nothing fancy, only what is necessary for training. Do not let the attendant make him late. The guard outside will escort you to the training grounds. I'll arrange some time this evening for you to familiarize yourself with the citadel and get settled. Thank you for your service."

Custodian Saunez left then, leaving Jaleya and Isesh alone with their new charge. Teza had sprawled himself onto a chaise, and he studied Isesh intently. The fascination died, replaced with an unimpressed frown, when he regarded Jaleya.

He folded his arms, the pout returning. "What was your name again?"

CHAPTER 5

Teza's new guardian was an arrogant brat with a perpetual frown. Admittedly, training was as entertaining as watching crops grow without sun kaza, but it was no starry night for him either. Seal Keeper Firnak had given him an ametrine seal to veer lighting, but the embedded gemstone was a sliver with a cloudy cast and rough edges; he might as well have been using an opal like everyone else.

At Seal Keeper Firnak's command of "Release," Teza squeezed the cylinder seal, its depiction pressing into his palm, and gathered the stimulated kaza in the gem with his mind. He formed the lightning with barely a thought and tossed it at the clay pot set on a distant pedestal. The pottery shattered with a clatter. The bolt from the rowshatar-estra beside him hit the sand.

Remshiri, the spikes of their helmets begging to be used as targets, replaced the pots and then returned to their positions around the training ring. Teza couldn't see the cylinder seals they carried in their slotted belts, but he knew their ametrine was perfectly cut; they probably even had diamond seals.

Seal Keeper Firnak repeated the release command, and Teza flicked another pot into rubble. Remshiri replaced the targets, again, and Teza destroyed pottery, again. "Release," clatter, "Release," clatter. On and on it went until they were finally presented with a row of three pots each. "Release," clatter, clatter, clatter. "Release," clatter, clatter, clatter. The other rowshatari-estra only achieved a clatter, clatter.

The remshiri collected the lightning seals from the rowshatari-estra and returned them to Seal Keeper Firnak. Teza was glad to be rid of it. The kaza in gemstones behaved the same as the stars', but it felt…foreign, numb. It lacked Orvashka's life.

A remshir handed Teza a cylinder seal depicting a person on both sides of a circle below an eye. A rifting seal. The opal set into one end barely lived up to its name. His capabilities exceeded this stone. Giving it to him was an insult.

Seal Keeper Firnak spoke the familiar instructions, and at his command, Teza applied pressure to the seal and veered the opal's stimulated kaza. The air before him parted and formed a swirling, crackling vortex. Its gentle but insistent pull tugged at the hem of his kaftan as he stepped through. A flash of cold and gleaming air later, he emerged on the opposite side of the training ring. The other rowshatari-estra followed, utilizing their own rifts. Once they had all crossed safely, they rifted back to where they had started, then back across the ring, and back and forth and back and forth they went.

On the last rift, Teza eyed the top of the wall surrounding the training grounds. He fingered the seal in his hand, analyzing its kaza. It might be enough…

At Seal Keeper Firnak's command, Teza did not veer a rift to the other side of the training ring. He focused on the top of the wall, reaching, and parted the air—

Bang! Kaza burst from the opal as it ruptured; Teza felt the seal crack. The guardians lounging about the training grounds jumped to their feet and drew their weapons. Seal Keeper Firnak raised his arms. "It's all right. Just a broken seal."

A remshir appeared at Teza's side and took the now-useless seal. "Are you hurt, Your Radiance?"

"No." Diverting that puff of kaza had been the most exciting thing to happen all week.

The remshir remained by Teza's side as he crossed the training ring and rejoined the other rowshatari-estra. Teza's new guardian watched, but she didn't come to see if he was all right. During training, rowshatari were under the remshiri's protection, but that hadn't stopped previous guardians. They all would have been at his side faster than the remshir after that burst. Well, almost all of them.

Training concluded as normal, and the rowshatari-estra trickled away, their guardians trailing after them. The remshiri were returning the cylinder seals to Seal Keeper Firnak when Teza approached him. "A word, Seal Keeper."

"Of course, Your Radiance," Seal Keeper Firnak said. "May I conclude collecting and accounting of the seals first?"

Nodding permission, Teza waited in the arcade's shade. A few minutes later, Seal Keeper Firnak joined him, the seals' ornate box tucked under his arm.

"How may I be of service?"

"I broke the seal," Teza said. "That means I've gone beyond opals. I want to practice with ametrine, and good-quality ametrine, not the insult you gave me for lightning."

"No insult was meant, Your Radiance. Seals are carefully selected for training. You are slightly stronger than the others; that's why the ametrine was provided for the first exercise. As for the opal…it should have withstood any common error and easily rifted you across the ring. I can't explain its failure, and I take responsibility for the mishap. You have always followed my directions, Rowshatar Teza. I know it wasn't your doing."

Teza blushed in shame, and Seal Keeper Firnak added, "You were following directions, weren't you?"

"Well…mostly…" Teza mumbled.

"I see." Seal Keeper Firnak's frown accentuated the wrinkles around his eyes. "Using seals outside the purview of their gemstone or depiction is dangerous. If that seal had been set with ametrine, you could've hurt yourself. You could've hurt your fellow rowshatari-estra, the remshiri, me."

"I don't want to hurt anyone," Teza said quickly.

Seal Keeper Firnak's wizened features softened. "I know. Which is why my report will state the seal was broken accidentally under no extraordinary circumstances."

"But that would be lying."

"It's not a lie. You didn't intend to break it, and you were training. There's no need to involve your custodian as long as this doesn't happen again."

"It won't," Teza said, disheartened. He didn't want to hurt anyone. He didn't want to disobey Seal Keeper Firnak, who was always supportive. But this current training was so boring. He was never hungry afterward. He had learned everything he could, yet the more powerful gems remained beyond his reach. Maybe he was romanticizing the stars' kaza, remembering incorrectly, as he anticipated the day his strength would progress. He could only access the stars' kaza the two nights surrounding stars' sway, three nights if he was lucky. He had been lucky a lot these past few months.

"Have you thought about my proposal?" Teza asked, not ready to give up yet.

"Rowshatari have individual lessons only when they are new to veering," Seal Keeper Firnak said. "The risk of hurting themselves or others is too great to place them in a group setting. Now that you have mastery, it's better for you to train among your peers, as you will learn from them as they will from you."

Teza wanted to say the only "peers" he might learn from were the Rifters, but Seal Keeper Firnak had forbidden him from speaking of their meetings, or even mentioning that name, in public. And Teza wasn't sure if "learning" was the right word. The Rifters' theories sounded like children's stories with a side of crazy, almost worthy of the radical Yevyrans. They didn't refute Orvashka's Ways, though, and they happily answered his questions. Even if said answers came with a heavy dose of delusion, he appreciated their efforts.

Seal Keeper Firnak maintained the dignity of their stations, as he also did in private, but he lowered his voice and assumed a warm, encouraging tone. "You were a pleasure to have as a student. Continue training, and you will reach the goals you seek. Just be patient." The seal keeper bowed at the waist. "Excuse me, Your Radiance. I have duties to attend to."

He sounded like Saunez. Be patient. Teza was tired of being patient. He glared at the sun shining proudly in the blue sky. He wished it would drown in the Boundless Sea and drag the moon down with it. He wasn't romanticizing or remembering the stars' kaza incorrectly. He wasn't. But if that were true, he would be able to veer an ametrine seal, at least. Seal Keeper Firnak said he wasn't strong enough; Saunez said to trust Seal Keeper Firnak, to not put himself at risk. The people depended on him. Needed him. Be patient.

They didn't know what it was like. They thought they did, but they didn't. They had no idea. A rowshatar-estra's life was waiting patiently for the stars, and disappointment when their light was eclipsed all too quickly. In-between, one was…useless. Inept.

Teza squared his shoulders. He wasn't inept or useless. All of Setsea depended on him. He was a rowshatar-estra.

He left the training grounds and headed for the bathhouse. He had barely turned the corner before his grumpy guardian caught up. He chuckled; grumpy guardian.

The bathhouse was a taste of Paradise, but his guardian refused to enjoy it. The staff making him wait for his favorite pool room and giving him wet towels had been deplorable, but an incident that could be rectified with an education session shouldn't spoil the honor of attending him. Basking in the steam that lathered his body eased his mind, and laying on the warm stone as beautiful girls massaged his muscles with scented soaps and oils soothed away his troubles, for now.

The harsh sun now high overhead, Teza persuaded his guardian to play a round of Twenty Squares in the park, but she refused a rematch after her victory. He always gave the guards and servants who lost to him a rematch, even though they never won that round either. It was only fair.

As they walked down a cleared street toward the theater later that evening—soldiers posted at each intersection for him, the rowshatar—his guardian's scowl deepened. He hadn't thought that was possible, especially being surrounded by such beauty. Iza Vor offered anything he wanted, but the rare occasions when he ventured into Abylay left him awestruck. Mantles of glazed bricks danced across buildings and archways. Porticos stood noble and proud, majestic carvings adorning the capitals. The stone temples devoted to Orvashka's Ways shone like precious gems, their domes glistening in the fading sunlight. Flowers bloomed around the shrines. There was so much to explore, to see, to experience. Teza wished his responsibilities allowed for more time outside Iza Vor. His guardian glared like the city had offended her.

While Teza would be content wandering Abylay for the rest of his life, that evening his attention was drawn to his grumpy guardian's simurgh. Ik-Ish-Itch? I-something had flown to the rooftops and remained there since leaving Iza Vor.

"Tell him to come down," Teza said.

"Our duty is to protect you," his guardian replied. What was her name? Jy…Jel…Keeping track of people's names was so bothersome. There was no reason to learn them since their owners lingered as long as a lightning flash, but he hated referring to others as "servant," "guard," and "you."

"Isesh is keeping a perimeter," his guardian continued. "Outside of Iza Vor, someone might try to harm you or snatch you."

"This isn't the West Ward, and that was an order," Teza said.

"Isesh isn't a pet to command as you please. I'm sure your previous guardians told you the same thing about their javati."

"Simurghs are fascinating, and I want a closer look." Isesh truly was magnificent, fur and feathers blending seamlessly, nobility harboring a brutal predator. Guardians were so fussy about their fashari.

"Gardok let me study Ninlu," Teza said.

"He was your previous guardian?" the frowning girl said.

Teza clamped his mouth shut. He shouldn't mention Gardok. He became so lost the only way to save the remaining light in his life force had been to return him to Orvashka. Teza still heard his manic screams in the shadows of a full moon.

"Isesh stays where he is," his guardian said. "Besides, you wouldn't want him getting too close. His dark life force might infect you."

"I thought your javash kept that in check. That can happen?" No one had ever told him!

His guardian paused midstride, and her eyes narrowed. "No." She continued toward the theater just ahead.

"Then why say it?" Teza said.

"It was a joke," his guardian replied.

"Well, it wasn't funny. Don't sigh at me! I'm your rowshatar."

"Yes, Rowshatar Teza." She didn't sound like she was mocking him, but he felt that she was. One more outburst like that and he would report her to Saunez. He was a rowshatar and deserved respect, especially from his guardian. If not for her hovering like the noon sun, no one could tell he was a rowshatar right now, but he still was one. A few days ago, nobody would have dared question that.

The grand doors to the amphitheater were spread wide. Soldiers stood outside and within. An escort surrounded him and…Jav?… his guardian, and one of the theater staff led them up a flight of marble stairs. Isesh crept about the delegation in a circular pattern; their escort eyed him warily, and the staff flinched as he passed. At the end of a carpeted hallway, two soldiers took post outside the box reserved for Teza. To his disappointment, the simurgh didn't follow him and his guardian to their seats. Teza lounged closest to the rail; flowers of precious stones glided along its tiled length. His guardian drew the curtains and assumed a watchful stance.

"You *can* sit down," Teza said.

"I can see fine from here," she replied.

Teza let her be stubborn. It was her loss.

He waved at a rowshatar-korza occupying a box across the way. She turned to better face the stage. The veins of viscous fire were fading from her skin as the sun gave way to the moon. A serpopard poked its feline head through the curtains of the rowshatar-korza's box. It glanced at Teza with its serpentine eyes, waited the awkward amount of time that indicated a silent exchange was taking place between javati, and then withdrew. The box to either side of the rowshatar-korza was empty, as was the one above. Empty boxes surrounded Teza, too.

Guild leaders, officials, and merchants in formal attire occupied the majority of the theater. They reclined in soft velvet chairs and partook of wine, fruit, and cheese. Belts, broaches, and jewels sparkled in the kaza sconces' light; a rowshatar-korza had replenished the gemstones in the sconces' seals for the play's run. In the highest balcony, citizens squeezed onto rugged benches. Based on the drab colors of their shabby clothing, they were from the West Ward. Unable to afford tickets, a lottery provided them the opportunity to attend the play. It was good to see the Ora helping the less fortunate. No matter how much they gave though, ingratitude continually spurred uprisings. Rebels killed people and basked in their chaos. Children were orphaned.

Teza shook away the dark thoughts as the kaza sconces dimmed. Blue silk billowed across the stage as it trailed behind performers in white. Another performer rose from within the folds and narrated humanity's emergence from Orvashka, the Boundless Sea, and how the rowshatari leadership imparted the Ways of Orvashka, which will strengthen the cosmic sea's light and obliterate the darkness, birthing forth Paradise.

"Alas," the narrator said, "a poison festered in Setsea."

He withdrew as the oscillating silk parted and revealed a backdrop of the once-great city Parvasahalis. Dazmiri hovered beside a stone tower whose name had been lost to history. Gems the size of Teza's torso gleamed from the domed pinnacle. An emerald sea of hills and valleys unfurled from the tiered city, and snow crowned the mountains.

Men and women danced onto the stage, their skin painted white, blue, and red in representation of the rowshatari. They sang of the coming of the Yevyrans and their Creator's tyranny, and how the Ora arose from the rowshatari and delivered the people from the Yevyrans' oppression, bringing freedom to all Setsea. Sadly, the Yevyrans wouldn't relinquish their power, and they created the Schism in retribution.

A second backdrop unrolled. Beneath an angry sky, a crater decimated the land where the magnificent tower once stood. Fallen turrets, broken arches, and sundered parapets drowned in the dust. Rubble and cracked cylinder seals littered the depression. Shards of shattered gems died in the brown hills.

Blue silk descended upon the stage in lifeless clumps. Men and women plodded across it. Exaggerating movements of grief and despair, they wiped the paint from their skin with black cloth.

"But all was not lost," the narrator said. Following the procession of corrupted rowshatari, two men and two women emerged from behind the decimated city. They still bore the white, blue, and red paint. The Schism hadn't tainted the Ora's connection to Orvashka as it had all other rowshatari's. The Ora were still attuned to the Boundless Sea.

The Yevyrans had destroyed Parvasahalis. Their Schism had corrupted the rowshatari and robbed gemstones of their ability to naturally replenish kaza. But for all their efforts, they had failed. The blue silk swelled around the Ora performers and exalted them with a triumphant sphere of whirling fabric.

"With the Ora's guidance," the narrator concluded, "the Ways of Orvashka will continue untarnished. The Schism will be closed, and the rowshatari will again take their rightful place as rulers. All of Idlium will embrace Orvashka's Ways, and Paradise will follow. All is not lost."

Teza applauded as kazalight filled the theater. The players traversed the stage, waving and blowing kisses in appreciation of their audience. Bows were directed at him and the other rowshatari.

Teza had seen numerous versions of this play, but it was always best in Abylay's theater. Iza Vor's was nice, but it was smaller, and the travelling performers relied more on the audience's imagination due to their limited resources and Iza Vor's safety necessities. The paint in this adaptation was new. Usually the actors were wrapped in dyed linen or had tassels sewn onto their clothing. He didn't like the latter; it gave the impression rowshatari leaked kaza, which was preposterous. The former was better, but it reminded him of funeral shrouds.

A pair of soldiers entered the box to escort Teza and his guardian out of the amphitheater. Remarkably, his guardian lacked her scowl. The blank expression was not an improvement; at least the scowl made her look alive. That emptiness must be her version of a smile. Teza shouldn't have been surprised that it was more hostile than her frown.

The soldiers returned them to the street, which was still cordoned off. The audience was flowing out of two different exits. Amid the happy chatter about the play and the Ways, a tone of dissent reached Teza's ears. An angry utterance just loud and near enough for him to hear every other phrase.

"...Ora are the same as other rowshatari...if we want things to be better, it's up to us...Ora won't save Setsea...help ourselves..."

Teza stopped and scanned the line of departing commoners, but he couldn't identify the rebellious speaker. Before he could order a search, surprised and frightened cries erupted from the dirty crowd as soldiers pushed their way through. A woman wearing a headscarf against the night's chill attempted to flee, but she was entangled in the crowd; hands caught the hem of her grungy tunic to prevent her escape. The soldiers seized her arms, and when she struggled, they punched her in the gut and across her cheek. Docile now, the soldiers dragged her away. Silence for a moment, and then someone in the officials' line huffed, and movement resumed. The West Ward audience shuffled faster and hunched their shoulders as they passed beneath the soldiers' scrutinizing gazes.

With a nod, Teza headed back to Iza Vor. His guardian had to correct his direction, but only because the kaza lanterns cast such large shadows. He did know where he was going. Mostly…

"How did you know who spoke?" his guardian asked.

"I didn't," Teza replied. "I was going to have the soldiers find out, but a good citizen must have discovered the rebel and reported her, as good citizens do."

"You were really going to have the soldiers question everyone?"

"Of course! Rebellious thoughts hurt all of us."

"I thought everyone was welcome in Abylay."

"Everyone is, but sometimes a few need to be re-educated. Antiquated and vile ideologies pull us backward into darkness and deprive Orvashka of light." A shadow moved in Teza's peripheral vision, but it was only the simurgh. "Why do you need this explained? Are you neglecting one of the Ways?"

"All the Ways are equal and revered. This is my first time in Abylay; I'm still getting acquainted with the city's protocols."

Teza moaned. It was bad enough being stuck with a guardian who tried to glare everything to death, but an incompetent one, too? Saunez had said she was qualified. Qualified until she found him a new one? "Where are you from?" Teza asked.

"A village west of Kurresh," his guardian said.

Yes, definitely qualified only as a placeholder guardian. Nothing was west of Kurresh except empty plains and reeking livestock. "That explains it. Small villages are uneducated. You'll learn a lot here."

Isesh came alongside Teza's guardian, whose scowl had puffed her precise cheeks. The simurgh nudged her hip with his shoulder.

"We should return to Iza Vor," she said.

"Yes, it's cold out here," Teza agreed.

"Indeed," his guardian said through gritted teeth. She must be getting cold too but didn't want her lips to do anything except hang upside down.

Teza resumed his stroll, and changed direction after hearing, "That's the wrong way." His guardian sounded as exasperated as Saunez had when she discovered he associated with Rifters. His guardian must hate the cold. He really should try to remember her name.

CHAPTER 6

Jaleya's new charge was an oblivious, spoiled child. He fussed over his appearance like a Masatitoran princess, and then he threw lightning and opened rifts with complete disregard for the accompanying responsibility. At least she'd been able to take a moment and catch her breath during his training.

"You must be Rowshatar Teza's new guardian." A Setsean man approached where she observed from the edge of the yard. Wrinkles played around his kind eyes and mouth, and his wiry frame told of a life spent fighting or of manual labor; those were the only choices for a javati.

"Word travels fast," Jaleya replied.

The seal keeper, a burly man with flecks of gray in his beard and bound hair, inspected the trainees as the remshiri distributed the cylinder seals. He took position behind the rowshatari, the remshiri flanked the ring, and training began, the term "training" being relative. The Ora kept the rowshatari on a useful but manageable plateau, where their strength could be checked by the remshiri. It wouldn't do for the rowshatari to realize how powerful they were.

Lightning zapped across the ring and shattered pots resting on pedestals, filling the grounds with the smell of burnt clay. The other rowshatari-estra concentrated and aimed meticulously, but Teza flicked star kaza without thought and made no effort to conceal his disinterest.

The man who had joined Jaleya said, "The javati have been guarding Rowshatar Teza on rotating shifts. They'll be glad you're here."

"Because being responsible for two rowshatari is difficult, or because he is a difficult charge?" Jaleya asked. She suspected—highly suspected—the latter.

"I believe it's a combination," the man said.

The seal keeper ceased the lightning drills and ordered the distribution of rift seals. Vortexes whirled open in front of the rowshatari and then spiraled closed as the trainees emerged from their rift's other end across the sand. Teza popped them into existence with the same enthusiasm he had expressed while tossing around lightning.

"Which one is your charge?" Jaleya asked, nodding at the rowshatari-estra tearing holes in the air.

"My charge is caravans and structures," he replied. "I'm relieved today before I set out tomorrow morning. A short journey, and when I return, I'm assigned to a crew reinforcing a pre-Schism bridge. Natural decay has finally degraded it, and since that art has been lost to the rowshatari, in we go."

"Do you like guarding the caravans?" Jaleya asked. She had hoped for that commission because it would allow her to roam, even if it was roaming the same place over and over again, and she wouldn't have to be at someone's beck and call every hour of every day. Isesh could maneuver cities, though, and his combination of dog and bird made him a potent deterrent and deadly foe. Perfect for protecting rowshatari. This man's javati was probably ill suited (more ill suited) for narrow streets and constricting buildings. She was curious which fashari had chosen him, but asking would degrade the fashari to a prized pet.

"I enjoy the traveling," the man said. "Lizuna prefers the open road as well, even with the risk of bandits. Your javati doesn't seem to mind the city." He indicated Isesh, who lounged in the shade of a tower. The man bowed his head in respect. Isesh accepted it in kind.

"Have you been stationed in Abylay long?" Jaleya asked.

"Going on five years."

That was a long post for a javati, even one that didn't guard rowshatari.

"How may I best serve my charge here?" Jaleya said. Translation: what were the pitfalls of Abylay, as each city had its own unwritten rules, some of which could be bent or even broken while simply nudging others would bestow a quick death.

"Orvashka's Ways are all you need to succeed," he replied with a significant undertone. Jaleya had already assumed the Ora's rule was enforced without leniency here, but she appreciated his friendly confirmation.

The javati lowered his voice. "Since the incident with his previous guardian, your charge has been developing a reputation for being… spirited." Not a good word in Ora territory.

"Incident?" Jaleya said discreetly.

"He was a traitor," the javati whispered.

Bang!

Jaleya dropped into a defensive stance and hefted her newly supplied spear. Isesh jumped up, his feathered neck tall, wings unfurled for flight. The javati beside Jaleya had his hand on his scimitar, and all around the training grounds, other javati bared weapons and searched for danger.

"It's all right. Just a broken seal," the seal keeper announced, his arms raised to calm the alarm. A remshir darted over to Teza, who hadn't rifted with the other rowshatari-estra.

Jaleya's new acquaintance asked, "Aren't you going to see if he's all right?"

"He looks fine to me," Jaleya said. The remshir escorted her pouting charge to the line. Training began to conclude as if nothing had happened. "I think hearing about that incident would be beneficial, so I can avoid those snares and better perform my duties."

The javati gave her a knowing smile. "We all need to guard against deceit. When I return, we can share our stories over a meal in the mess hall."

"I would enjoy that. Thank you for your council…"

"Yongir."

"Thank you for your council, Yongir. I'm Jaleya, and that's Isesh, but you probably already knew that."

"You'll do well here." With a friendly wink, Yongir departed the training grounds.

I think I just met an ally, Jaleya sent to Isesh as the remshiri collected the seals and returned them to their keeper.

He seemed genuine, Isesh replied. *Time will tell.*

Do you think what he said is true? Jaleya asked. *Teza's previous guardian was a traitor?*

I'm sure there's truth in it, but that doesn't mean it's true. You should know that by now.

The rowshatari and javati filed out of the training yard. A frustrated Teza was speaking to the seal keeper; the remshiri waited for him a short distance away. Surprisingly, the keeper seemed to be consoling Teza rather than exalting his prowess. Another oddity about this rowshatar. The first was his…relationship with his custodian, then the supposed traitorous javati, and now what appeared to be an association that went beyond the cold professionalism that was the keeper-rowshatar obligation. Jaleya found herself wondering if Teza wasn't the spoiled, pampered rowshatar she assumed he was. That hope became suspect when he tried to slip away from the training grounds without her, and was dashed by the chaos of the afternoon.

Teza terrorized the bathhouse staff because a rowshatar-mara had overstayed his time in Teza's favorite pool room. The rowshatar-mara bid Teza defer to his schedule since the moon bestowed the more valuable kaza, and Teza responded like a horse that didn't know it was at the bottom of the pecking order. Jaleya had to intervene lest the rowshatar-mara give Teza a bruise to match the amethyst in his ring. The rowshatar-mara's guardian was nowhere to be found.

Then there was the towel incident. The staff had brought his towels as requested, but they had sat unused in a room filled with *steam*. Being a little damp was to be expected. She would have thought the luminaries had fallen from the sky for all the fuss he made.

After watching two servants and a guard let Teza win at Twenty Squares, Jaleya agreed to play one round to put him in his place. It backfired spectacularly when he knocked the board off the table following his defeat. A moment's satisfaction hadn't been worth the tantrum. Thankfully, she was given a brief reprieve after that to speak to Quartermaster Bilka.

Jaleya smelled the javati compound before she reached it. Musty ungulates, dry reptiles, moist fins, polished feathers. It was the closest thing to a home that she knew. Javati indulged in the mess hall, exercised and sparred in the rings, and played cards, dice, and Twenty Squares in the shade. The majority would be guardians to rowshatari-korza, who only required a standard guard detail while the sun dominated the sky and yielded its kaza. The others would be on temporary assignments, allocated to construction or caravan escort, or enjoying their few hours of deserved freedom.

Bilka turned out to be a plump woman who wore a headband embroidered with the Harmony. Her light-brown hair stopped halfway between her chin and shoulders, the chin being the longest permitted length for commonplace citizens. She tallied a shipment of feed on her clipboard with mellow strokes. A heady haze drifted through the curtained alcove behind her. She didn't acknowledge Jaleya when she approached. Jaleya waited an appropriate amount of time, then cleared her throat.

"What do you want?" Bilka said.

"My name is Jaleya."

"Good for you."

"…Custodian Saunez sent me."

Bilka beamed at Jaleya, the feed sacks forgotten. Her pupils were wider than normal. "Custodian Saunez! I like her. She gets stuff done. Any friend of hers is a friend of mine. What do you need?"

Jaleya handed her the requisition form of Isesh's requests. Bilka assured her with smiles and mini bows that she would find everything the simurgh desired, as Jaleya needed all the help she could get to overcome the darkness in her fashari, who were the closest thing Setsea had to empaths now since those deceitful, treacherous people went extinct after the Schism; and it was a shame the magnificent, unique creatures' purpose was also to deceive, and did Jaleya know if fashari were the strange apparitions sometimes glimpsed within rifts?

"I have heard those theories," Jaleya said to placate the woman. Fashari had existed since the dawn of time, but it wasn't until the Schism War that they began dwelling among people and forming javash, which gave the fashari a voice through their javati and people enhanced senses and physicality. Despite javash though, the mystical attributes bestowed upon the hybrid creatures from the past's rare encounters had endured. The Ryvekians believed they were guides for individuals in their gods' favor. They were, and always had been, hunted in Masatitora for being chaos creatures. The Ora taught they were incarnations of the darkness remaining in Orvashka, and only javash could conquer it; any excuse to force Orvashka's Ways on those who were disinclined to them would do. Jaleya couldn't say they were the descendants of guardian spirits from the heavenly realm, as that was Yevyran doctrine and therefore forbidden.

Jaleya excused herself from Bilka before she could be caught in another ramble about empaths, fashari, and rifts. She collected Isesh from where he was getting acquainted with a pegasus, a young kongamato perched atop a tarasque, and a mishipeshu, who was a long way from the Wild Ice. It took a moment to touch Isesh's mind; their javash was always fainter when he communicated with other fashari.

They returned to their charge's quarters just in time to escort him through the barricaded streets to the theater's twisted tale. The thick curtains failed to muffle the lies boring into her burning ears no matter how far she backed into their folds. The Creator was benevolent, and the Yevyrans hadn't been tyrannical rulers. They were common people from the breadth of Setsea's valleys to the heights of its mountains. Yevyrans had held official positions, but that was inevitable when the majority of the country followed the Creator. The Ora had deluded the populace with flowering language and empty promises, and values considered morally wrong were suddenly denied freedoms. The Ora had attempted to eradicate the galahi and empaths—the Ora's fiercest opponents—in Parvasahalis, and those who resisted the Ora had defended themselves. The resulting clash inadvertently created the Schism.

Jaleya had once believed the Ways' doctrine. It had been integrated into every facet of guardian training. She had quoted the tenets as willingly as her peers. But when her sister, Lenruz, risked revealing the Creator's truths, Jaleya recognized them for what they were. The theater's enthralled audience revered the fallacious narrative and hissed at the Yevyrans. Hissed at her and her sister.

Then Jaleya watched the soldiers arrest the poor woman for speaking against the Ora. Teza praised the informer and denounced Setsea's countryside as uneducated while quoting the Ways' benevolence. If Isesh hadn't been there, her words would have caused Teza to report her too, or she would have given him a bloody nose and enjoyed a moment of satisfaction before becoming a fugitive.

And then upon returning to Iza Vor, she was informed that the rowshatar-mara from the bathhouse had filed a complaint against her. She had to write a detailed report so the custodians could determine if her conduct had been appropriate.

"Insane" was the only word that could describe Abylay. It was guardian training on a grand scale.

When she finally retired for the night, she lay in the large bed exhausted yet wide awake. She felt she might suffocate in the fluffy blankets. The growing moon peered through the window's lattice. Sun kaza illuminated the domes and towers of Iza Vor. Its light was cold. It lacked the passion of a flaming torch.

Jaleya untangled herself from the infinite blankets and wrapped a cloak around her shoulders. She crept into Isesh's room and whispered his name. He opened one eye from where he lay curled in an unfinished nest comprised of palm branches, hay, his own feathers, and a shredded wool blanket; the quartermasters weren't pleased when Isesh did that, but they were never surprised.

Jaleya's javati lifted his wing. She sheltered beneath his spectral feathers, snuggling against his ivory fur. *If I had somewhere to call home, I would be missing it right now,* she sent.

Don't despair, Isesh replied. *There is always hope.*

A sad smile touched Jaleya's lips. He always said that, even though nothing improved, nothing changed except the cities and their charges. The Ora still ruled. Lenruz's murderer still walked free. Their only constant was each other.

Tell me about the mountains again, where you were born, Jaleya sent.

Her javati spoke of snow-crowned peaks, green forests swaying like the tide, and spring's first bloom after a white winter. Jaleya fell asleep hoping such a place still existed.

CHAPTER 7

The wild sapphire set in Ezray's necklace returned to equilibrium as she opened her eyes. The kaza she had infused it with was already waning. Gemstones were such an inferior way to access Orvashka's light, and a temptation to stray from the Ways that only the most steadfast resisted. Ezray would not lose her way. Her communion with Orvashka was pure. Her search was important. Imperative. Yet she feared the answers she sought in the future's threads were too elusive for any light but the full moon's to reveal.

A gentle knock sounded on her door.

"Come," Ezray said.

A servant entered and prostrated herself before Ezray.

"You may rise," Ezray said kindly.

The servant went to the basin near the tall windows and washed her hands. She opened the ornate wardrobe and presented selections for the day. Ezray would have normally taken more time to consider, but her mind was focused elsewhere. She chose a blue, full-length tunic with embroidery down the center. Her servant placed a felt tiara encircled with dangling ornaments on Ezray's head and attached an emerald-green shawl that swathed Ezray's body. Ezray adjusted the necklace with the infused sapphire herself, but she let the servant arrange her bracelets, as their gems were dead. After assisting Ezray with her slippers, the servant remained kneeling, eyes down, waiting.

"You've done well," Ezray said. "You may go."

Trying to contain her joy from the compliment, the servant bowed her head and left. Ezray knew it was difficult stumbling through life without a connection to Orvashka, but her servants tried to live as if they had one. Rewards should be given when deserved. Serving Ezray and her fellow Ora was as close to Orvashka as they could get this side of Paradise.

Ezray refrained from perfume but did paint her eyes and lips. She was an Ora. Anyone who looked at her would see strength and confidence. The Ora would close the Schism. Orvashka's Ways would propagate peace throughout Idlium, and Paradise would follow.

Then she could finally rest.

But that day was not today. Her task—the Ora's task—remained unfulfilled. As the many years passed and their numbers dwindled, their purpose seemed beyond even them at times. They couldn't fail, and yet, they were.

Ezray had time to spare before the day's agenda, so she exited her quarters and detoured across an upper courtyard. Sun kaza had encouraged the hanging gardens to bloom early. The Harmony fountain bubbled languidly in the morning sun; it was livelier beneath the moon's cooling light.

Ezray left Harmony Tower behind and strode to the rowshatari-mara repository. Guards standing post outside the arched door lowered their gazes as she entered but otherwise remained vigilant. It was sad and unfortunate that they were a necessary precaution.

The repository's antechamber resembled a school with two rows of desks and a large counter. A woman in a simple belted tunic was collecting papers from the desks. Her short hair peeked from beneath an assistant's bonnet; a stray strand tickled her nose. She looked up as Ezray entered, and almost dropped the documents she carried. She attempted to prostrate herself in the narrow aisle and rescue the collection simultaneously, failing both.

"Where is Custodian Fazrin?" Ezray asked.

"She left a few moments ago, Your Radiance," the assistant replied.

"I wish to speak with her. Bring her here."

The woman straightened and headed toward the arched door. She turned around halfway there, placed the pile of papers on a shelf behind the counter, and then departed. Ezray waited patiently for a few minutes, but when they still hadn't returned, she went through the door on her right.

Beds lined the walls bordered with constellation stuccos. Sunlight peered through the latticed windows. The hall smelled of sweat, ink, and sheets of the paper and fabric variety. The beds were empty now, as the moon had deferred to the sun. Servants swept, sopped up ink spills, and changed the bedding. They paused to prostrate themselves, then continued their work in silence. Ezray walked down the wide aisle and stopped at a door secured with a cylinder seal. A quick tap with the moon kaza in her sapphire had the lock springing open. The room beyond had no windows, but the lanterns flickered to life when she pressed the pressure pad beside the doorway, activating the enclosed cylinder seal. The kazalight was faint. Some of the lanterns had failed to ignite.

Rows of tomes chained to metal shelves spread out before her. The seal locks glowed with a steady blue light. Unlike star and sun kaza, moon kaza required a guiding mind to regulate its power output. That was problematic in complex mechanisms, but it was also why moon kaza made the sturdiest locks. Apart from destroying the gem or its cylinder seal, a moon lock wouldn't cease its function until its kaza was depleted or another source of moon kaza subdued it, and seal locks could be very specific about which negating source they accepted.

It was said the Frozen Wanderers of the Wild Ice utilized moon kaza like Setsea once utilized star kaza and Masatitora and Wanbasba sun kaza, but expeditions in the early years of the Ora's reign had proven unfruitful. One day, Orvashka's Ways would reach even that far, for the Frozen Wanderers' benefit, but the dead land offered nothing except bitter cold and biting winds.

Ezray perused the archive for the most recent volume, which would contain empty pages waiting to be filled. She found it as the door opened and Custodian Fazrin entered. She somehow managed to prostrate herself while in motion. The curve of her bonnet bobbed up and down, and her dark hair brushed her shoulders.

"You honor us with your presence, Your Radiance," she said. "How may we be of service?"

"Have any of the rowshatari-mara been having visions of the spring festival?" Ezray asked.

"We did our standard questings during the full moon. There were threads of skirmishes and rebellion, but those always increase around festivals; nothing warranted recording or investigating. There was an oddity a few nights ago. One of the rowshatari felt something disturbing, but he couldn't articulate it very well, and he didn't know what it meant. He described it as a fork in a road, and both paths were unmaintained, or precarious, or winding. We recorded it. Would that be of interest to you?"

"Show me," Ezray said.

Fazrin opened the wooden cabinet that stored recordings until they were copied, compiled, and archived. After flipping through a stack, she handed Ezray a sheet containing only a few sentences. It read exactly as Fazrin had described, like a commonplace dream. Ezray knew better. Questing into Orvashka unearthed a plethora of futures that would never come to pass or changed in a blink. Too many choices, too many variables. People were predictable, but until they committed to a choice and pursued it, they were decidedly *unpredictable*, birthing a mass of possibilities. The test of a true rowshatar-mara was being able to distinguish between the outcomes that might happen and the ones that were passing fancies.

"Has anyone else had a similar vision?" Ezray asked.

"Not that I'm aware of, but I haven't been through last night's recordings," Fazrin replied. "My assistant is working on that now. I'll inform you if we find a parallel."

"Have tonight's rowshatari-mara focus solely on the Festival of Shattered Swords," Ezray ordered. "If remshiri are available, have them quest today."

"Yes, Your Radiance." Fazrin paused. "Do you have a suggestion of specifics to quest for? A festival of that size will make paths difficult to locate."

The broader a questing, the more numerous the outcomes. If a rowshatar-mara could find one person, or a small group, involved with what he or she sought to see, the outcomes lessened, and a stable future began to form. Individuals. Individuals shaped the future. Even after hundreds of years as a rowshatar-mara and with all her knowledge, it still baffled her. One person, and the choices he or she made, could send the world reeling. That was why it was imperative people made the *right* choices.

Ezray doubted Fazrin's charges would locate any paths, but threads were a possibility. Threads were all she needed.

"A broad questing will suffice for now," she said. "Watch for consistent variables. They will lead you to firmer threads, which in turn will lead you to stable paths."

"It will be done," Fazrin said. "If I may be so bold, Your Radiance…" She glanced at the cylinder seal set with moonstone, the weakest of the moon gems, hanging around her neck. The key to the archive and its precious tomes, it wouldn't have been powerful enough to overcome the archive's lock if its depictions hadn't allowed it. "…A questing of this nature would benefit from a remshir proficient with aquamarine."

"You have my permission to use tanzanite seals," Ezray said.

Fazrin's eyes bulged. "Thank you, Your Radiance." She hesitated. "Your Radiance, is there cause for concern?"

Ezray gave her a gentle smile. "I didn't say you could use sapphire seals. Sifting through this broad questing with accuracy requires tanzanite's adaptability."

Fazrin bowed her head in relief.

"If you find anything, report it to me immediately." Ezray indicated the vision she held in her hand. "Has this been copied? Good. I will study it myself."

Fazrin couldn't hide her apprehension.

"Do not fear," Ezray said. "Nothing is amiss as of now. It is my duty, and yours, to ensure it remains that way."

"I know you'll succeed, of course," Fazrin said quickly. "I didn't mean to question, please forgive me. It's the nature of the questing that has me worried. I would be ashamed to fail you."

"I have as much faith in you as I do in the rowshatari and remshiri," Ezray said.

Fazrin beamed.

Ezray left the rowshatari-mara repository and returned to Harmony Tower. She had a few minutes to spare, but studying the vision would require more than that. She walked slowly as she made her way to the parlor designated for this week's council. She pondered the possibilities of her vision, wondering if the anomaly tucked safely within her tunic was related, and if it was, what that could mean.

She was the first to arrive. The waiting shavinash entered ahead of her and checked behind the silk curtains and among the arches for potential threats. A servant carrying a tray of tea arrived; a rowshatar-korza and his guardian provided an escort. The eagle forelegs of the guardian's gryphon made a clicking sound on the marble floor that grated Ezray's ears. Hoofed fashari had already been banned from the tower. She wondered if it was time to expand that or if her irritation was due to her vision's lingering anxiety. Or maybe it was due to the rowshatar. He looked a rowshatar-korza with veins of fire adorning his red skin, but the sun would reclaim its flame upon setting, exposing the rowshatar for the corrupted pretender he was.

Keeping his distance from the gryphon, the servant placed the tray in the center of the round table. The rowshatar-korza checked the contents for poison and indicated the tea was safe. The servant poured a small cup and sipped. The gryphon drank the other half. Suffering no ill effects, they departed, the shavinash a deadly shadow behind them.

Ezray had the parlor to herself for only a moment before Ahkruz arrived with his new pet shavinash in tow. Ahkruz's preference for loose trousers, patterned tunics, and vests was more akin to the North than the South, a greedy merchant than an Ora. A felt miter rested on his head, and an embroidered ribbon wound within his white braided hair cascading down his back. While Ezray favored garments that complemented her sky-blue complexion, Ahkruz relished the jarring clash between his skin's iridescence and his attire.

Ahkruz dismissed the shavinash, who left without a sound, and the temperature rose a few degrees. The shavinashi were an unfortunate necessity, brave men and women who performed the lamentable deeds required to maintain harmony. They gave Ezray chills. She wasn't afraid of them; for all their training and their enhanced abilities via the zar'sheni's bloodshaping, they were no match for an Ora. But being in their presence was like having death as an uninvited dinner guest. Unless that was one's preference.

"You have extra light in your step," Ezray said.

"You have extra gloom in yours," Ahkruz replied. He picked up the steaming pot and poured himself a cup of tea. "The moon dominates the night sky. Kaza won't be denied you for weeks. You should be less anxious about stars' sway as the years pass, not more." He offered to pour her tea as well, but Ezray drew on the kaza in her necklace's wild sapphire, lifted the pot with her mind, and poured her own.

"You should be more careful with whom you share your bed," she said.

Ahkruz chuckled fondly.

"Any intarish would gladly accept your proposal," Ezray continued. "A coinless whore would accept without payment."

"The poor creatures," Ahkruz said, shaking his head. "We really should work harder to bring them into the Intarish Guild."

"There are plenty of women to make love with who don't know how to kill you ten different ways with a spoon."

"Some find lethal spoons attractive."

"Stop sleeping with shavinashi! They are one moon phase away from becoming a satrapy unto themselves, and we don't want them forming the idea that disposing of a careless Ora would further that ambition."

"Courting death makes you appreciate life." Ahkruz sipped his tea, his rings set with wild diamonds and alexandrites clinking against the Masatitoran porcelain. "But my pleasures with Sentinel aren't what's bothering you."

"You know that's not her real name," Ezray said, deflecting.

"Shavinashi have no names. What did you see?"

Ezray sighed. "I'm not sure…"

She didn't have time to elaborate, for the arched doors opened again, admitting Morhim and Nissa. Nissa's hair was a fierce red, and natural whorls travelled the length of her right side from eye to toe. The eddies flared in the sunlight as if made of real fire. Morhim's communion with Orvashka was subtler. His skin and hair bore a variable ruby cast devoid of molten veins. He dressed as one befitting his station in a full-length tunic and a fringed shawl. His long hair had been frizzed, and it buoyed his gilded tiara. From Nissa's silver miter hung a veil that swayed with the locks brushing her hips. The neckline and cuffs of her form-fitting dress swam with lavish baubles.

They all took their seats at the round table after the two rowshatari-korza poured themselves tea. They sipped solemnly, commemorating the Ora who began the great peace and those who had rejoined Orvashka. Ezray remembered when the Ora filled every seat in vaulted halls and domed assembly chambers. Now they fit in a modest parlor with space to spare, emptiness enclosing them. They were all that remained.

They began their council as usual with the status of Setsea and its satrapies. The satraps managed their provinces to the best of their abilities, but temptations to sway from Orvashka's Ways and pursue their own desires, agendas, and power were ever present. When the satraps corrected themselves, the Ora rewarded them. Sometimes, they needed a nudge. Other times, guidance required a firm hand.

"We need to take an active role in the North," Ahkruz said.

"The last time we did that, we had a full-scale rebellion on our hands," Nissa said. "Satrap Lavoryn hasn't been at her post long, but she knows it is vital Orvashka's Ways be followed. Slowly incorporating them into the people's lives will give them time to adapt, and before they realize it, they will abide by them wholeheartedly. Show the people they can't survive without the Ways, that life without them is chaos and misery, and when the Ways save them, they will become their most ardent supporters."

"The North will be more fanatical than the shavinashi at this rate," Ahkruz commented.

"The satraps will never achieve peace," Ezray said, "but by keeping Setsea in relative rest, we are free to pursue a permanent solution. We need harmony to remain when we are gone."

Morhim spoke up. "If Satrap Lavoryn fails as her predecessors have, she will be replaced. Time will tell if we need to take a more active role."

"Which we will do together," Nissa added.

Ahkruz chuckled at the insinuation and waved a conceding hand. They all bore the weight of their duty differently, but Ahkruz was the most anxious to act, his patience wearing thin. His earlier comment about pleasuring the shavinash to feel alive struck a worrying chord.

"How are the empath tests progressing?" Morhim asked.

"We've had no breakthroughs, but we're confident it will work," Nissa said. "We just have to find the right combination of kaza and the right bloodshaping. The theory is sound."

"In other words, the same as last week, as last month, and all the months before: nowhere," Ahkruz said.

Ezray mentally drifted away from the conversation as it traversed the usual paths. Nissa shared their theory while Ahkruz and Morhim chimed in with speculations they had previously suggested, and the discussion inevitably returned to the foundations from which their theory sprouted: they needed sun, moon, and star kaza in some combination and a way to infuse it into a person. Currently, the combination was wrong, or the transferal bloodshaping was incompatible, or the problem lay with their subjects, which they all hoped wasn't the case. That would put them back at the beginning.

Ahkruz and Morhim's exploit to close the Schism was proceeding better. The rift tests were conclusive and suggested their plan would succeed. But collapsing the Schism required Nissa and Ezray to produce the missing ingredient. *All* power in the Schism had to be cancelled out.

Then there were the Dazmiri. The useless Dazmiri, as they were not Dazmiri-vahl-kesh. Ahkruz and Morhim had been far less successful in that venture.

The vahl-keshi had wreaked havoc across Idlium as the Schism dragged them into insanity. Destroying them had been the only counter to their manic destruction. When the surviving Dazmiri-vahl-kesh retreated inward to a deep slumber, the mountains and valleys had finally exhaled. Now the Ora had to wake a dormant leviathan—an insane leviathan—and coax it back to lucidity, for the Schism shattered the Dazmiri-vahl-kesh's lifeless cousins and couldn't be overcome by those inanimate vessels. Determining which Dazmiri were and were not vahl-kesh was the least of their complications. The one Dazmir-vahl-kesh their agents at the skyship graveyard had managed to awaken had exploded in a mad panic, destroying itself and the warehouse and killing the crystal cultivators. Attempts were being made to create new Dazmiri-vahl-kesh using various methods, mostly bloodshaping, as no gems had gained sentience since the empaths' extinction, but their efforts had yet to bear fruit.

Morhim brought up the point, as he always did, that Ezray and Nissa's work might be unnecessary if the zar'sheni managed to unearth a vahl-kesh bloodshaping. That would be potential proof that bloodshaping could serve as an empath substitute to close the Schism. Perhaps even be a template for a self-sustaining bloodshaping, which was required to fulfill their duty. Nissa bluntly said there was no substitute, and the conversation went in circles as they debated. Ezray made single-syllable responses in support of Nissa, while Ahkruz acknowledged the merit of both and supported pursuit of any valid options.

The relentless obstacles grated on all of them, but until the path to lasting harmony was established, it wasn't time to rid Idlium of the Schism. Its loss would sew division, hatred, and violence. Chaos would ensue. Kaza was secure in the Ora's hands, and they distributed the valuable resource where it was needed. The people could not be trusted with it.

"Are you all right?" Nissa asked. "You've been very quiet."

Ezray stirred as she realized the question had been directed at her. Across the table, Ahkruz spread his hands in invitation.

"I had a vision," Ezray informed them. "It's occupying my thoughts."

"What was it?" Morhim asked.

Ezray titled her head, tried to articulate with words what no vocabulary could adequately express. "I stood in a scorched crater. Blood rained from the sky, but then reversed and fell upward. The earth turned to ash and was blown into oblivion, only to reform at the last instant into a blooming garden."

She paused. Her fellow Ora frowned in contemplation, but they didn't voice interpretations. Kaza visions were not only what one saw, but also the feelings they evoked, the instincts that arose. The *knowing* when one had no proof. Ezray knew far too little.

"I can't see around it," she concluded.

"It gives me the chills," Nissa said.

"No. I can't *see* around it. Everything between the Festival of Shattered Swords and my vision is…hazy, shapeless."

"You're not thinking of refraining from the offering?" Ahkruz accused.

"Of course not. But my inability to see around the festival means the future is hinging upon it. Something is stirring. Important choices are about to be made."

"Do you know who is going to make these important choices?" Morhim asked.

"If I did, I wouldn't be sitting here."

"We must be vigilant and assist Ezray in locating the source of her vision," Nissa said.

Nods of agreement.

"Forward Orvashka's Ways," the Ora intoned, "to Paradise eternal."

CHAPTER 8

Ameara lay on her bunk and stared at the deck above her head. Syra's creaking beams usually lulled her to sleep, but tonight they were a tick in her ear. Flying without the shield wasn't foreign water; the occasions were rare, but they had done it before. Maybe Syra's strange unease wasn't related to her temporary vulnerability. Perhaps the Dazmir-vahl-kesh was absorbing Ameara's misgivings about their cargo and reflecting it back to her. A vicious circle.

Ameara sighed and rolled over. She couldn't deny she was curious about the circumstances surrounding their contract, but they seemed ripe for dragging her and her crew into a conflict that had nothing to do with them. She wasn't *that* curious. Kyzum didn't need to remind her of the Vekrym's neutrality.

This anxiety wasn't hers.

Ameara pressed her hand against the bulkhead. The familiar grain had witnessed wonders only spoken of in whispered awe and decaying tomes, but it culminated in knots of horror and despair. Awakening from such a place hadn't been easy. Syra touched Ameara's mind, sending disquiet, urgency. Hastening her to her heart. Something else accompanied the sending, but Ameara couldn't discern what it was. Without javash, the depths of Syra's awareness were incomprehensible, but their communication had come a long way since the beginning.

Ameara climbed out of her bunk and put on her boots and weapons belt. The star and the moon kaza seals glowed beneath the hood of her pistol; the sun seal was dull.

She left the captain's cabin and followed her ship's vague directions to the lower deck. She halted at the bottom of the stairs. Something wasn't right. Ameara scanned the shadows, listening for irregular creaks. She reached out to Syra and advanced aft, avoiding the squeaky planks even as she lengthened her stride. Something was wrong. Something was very wrong.

Syra yelled alarm as Ameara plunged into the heart, pistol in one hand and sword in the other. A tall broad-shouldered figure stood beside the heart seal; a headscarf concealed his features. The intruder's hand paused a hairsbreadth from the pulsing alexandrite while his other hovered near the kaza stream connecting the roll seal to Syra's heart.

As the words "don't move" formed on Ameara's lips, the intruder thrust his hand into the channel, and kaza burst from the disrupted connection. Syra listed sharply port, oscillating from stern to bow. Shielding her eyes, Ameara flicked the dial on the side of her pistol to concentrate the blast and not exacerbate the star kaza jolting around the cabin, aimed at the intruder's chest, and fired. The man staggered, but he remained on his feet. Ignoring the part of her mind telling her that was impossible—that he should be dead—she increased her pistol's power output and fired again. The shot knocked him into the hull, and he collapsed to the deck. Ameara shifted her balance automatically as Syra leveled herself.

Running footsteps behind her. Ameara spun, pistol raised. Her crew stopped short, Obakwe's knobkerries poised for a charge, Ara's double-edged sword held defensively while her seal bracelet glowed red. Kyzum covered them with a crossbow. Ameara lowered her weapons, and her crew followed suit. The red light from Ara's bracelet faded.

Boots pounding on wood announced Nahzida's arrival. An arrow was nocked on her bow, but she lowered it as she perceived her crewmates' relaxing stances.

"Why is the skyship trying to be an acrobat?" Kyzum said.

Ameara cleared the doorway and nodded at the prone intruder. "That's why."

Her crew filed into the heart. Obakwe examined the shrouded man while Ara, carefully avoiding the stray sparks of kaza, inspected the seals for damage.

"I searched Syra when we left Masatitora," Nahzida said. "No one else was aboard."

"We're all having the same hallucination, then?" Kyzum said.

"Captain," Obakwe said gravely. She had removed the intruder's headscarf, and his pate had no hair to speak of. Foreboding trickled down Ameara's spine. Obakwe presented his bared forearm, where his vambrace and sleeve had concealed Old Setsean script branded around his upper wrist. Then she pulled low the collar of his tunic. A shard of obsidian was embedded in his chest, and even though she couldn't see it, Ameara knew the dark stone contained a bloodshaping seal. The etch of a shavinash. Cracks fractured outward from a jagged cavity in its center.

"Empty sky," Nahzida said. "Ameara, what did you do?"

Ara's seal bracelet glowed red. Obakwe's features were grim. Kyzum was quiet. Never a good sign. The hum of Syra's heart pounded in Ameara's ears, amplifying the frantic beat of her own.

"Nahzida, Obakwe, take him to the brig and secure him," she ordered. "Ara—"

"You're going to hold a shavinash prisoner?" Nahzida blurted, and while no one else voiced opposition, Kyzum's furrowed brow, Obakwe's wide stance, and Ara's terrified expression indicated they were of the same mind.

Ameara kept her face blank. "Yes." The one word carried the weight of her authority and reminded them why Eclipse was rightfully feared.

Nahzida rushed to obey, and she and Obakwe carried the unconscious shavinash out of the heart.

"Ara," Ameara said, "make sure he didn't tamper with anything, and then you and Obakwe search Syra from bow to stern, deck by deck. Confirm no one else is aboard."

"Why didn't Syra warn you about him?" the young woman asked.

"Shavinashi instill fear," Ameara said, then hardened her tone as if speaking to Syra, "but that is no reason to yield to it. One of many things we will be discussing."

Ara accepted the explanation with a thoughtful nod, but Ameara was far from satisfied. She doubted another stowaway lurked in the hold, as Syra wasn't sending alarm and shavinashi usually worked alone; sabotaging a Dazmir didn't scream "group effort." Syra's disquiet had only leveled off, though, not disappeared. Assurance failed to soothe the Dazmir-vahl-kesh's state of mind, and seeking the cause of the omission returned the unintelligible sensation given in her cabin. Syra wouldn't elaborate, and she withdrew when Ameara pressed. An enigma for another time.

"Kyzum, with me."

Ameara recounted the confrontation in the heart as they ascended to the main deck and crossed to the captain's quarters. Her friend and first mate was very quiet. The click of the closing door finally prompted him to speak. "Did you annoy Whisper?"

"He was as cordial as always during our meeting," Ameara replied.

"Subtly threatening with his crooked smile but assuring you he likes your arrangement with his good manners?"

Ameara gave his wit a brief frown. It was the reason Whisper didn't care for Kyzum and wouldn't hesitate to kill Kyzum if he ever approached him without Ameara. Their arrangement was strictly between Eclipse and Whisper.

Ameara thought back to said meeting, running it through her mind. Had she missed something? She shook her head. "He gave no indication he was displeased with us."

"Trying to blow up our ship is a good indication," Kyzum said.

"At least he's not trying to steal her," Ameara said.

If Syra's secret had been discovered, the goal would be capture, not destruction, and that *would* require a joint effort. They had been lucky the shavinash hadn't sent them hurling into a cliff. They had been lucky the pass's crest was behind them.

"Another cadre maneuvering to overthrow Whisper in the shashvin hierarchy?" Kyzum offered.

"Very possible," Ameara said, "but what would our deaths accomplish? We're just Vekrym. Whisper could recruit another Dazmir captain."

"Whisper didn't recruit you. You went to him," Kyzum reminded her. "His fellow shashvini may be warming to his unorthodox methods. The one who removes Eclipse would have a substantial advantage in a very limited pool."

Ameara conceded the point with a nod. Ora agents, guilds, and others of status secretly hired Vekrym to keep Orvashka's Ways clean, but shavinashi were the hands-on type. Whisper didn't need her skills. Openly dealing with her was a declaration of the shavinashi's strength and their independence from the Ora. A bold move. Yet, the Ora hadn't reined in their assassins. The shavinashi were becoming a power unto themselves.

"What if Whisper discovered the origin of our newest crew member?" Kyzum said. "That could be enough to convince him to kill us, guilt by association."

That was one of the first theories Ameara had considered, and dismissed. "Ara was allowed to live as an example of the Ora's benevolence. But the cargo we retrieved was on its way to rebels. It could be used to frame us and claim breach of contract. Why wait until we're in the pass, though, to make the attempt?"

"That is odd," Kyzum said. "Even an amateur would know you need the debris for evidence in the frame job. Unless the goal is simply to dispose of us for an inadvertent offense."

"We're being used, or we've lost favor with Whisper," Ameara agreed. They both breathed deep.

Ameara steeled herself. "Either way, our course doesn't change. This shavinash has failed his shashvin. He failed his mission. I'll take him before Whisper, demand to know why he's lost faith in me, and insist on a chance to regain it."

"You're going to bring Whisper the shavinash he potentially ordered to kill us back to him and demand to continue working for him," Kyzum said, deadpan. "That is a terrible plan."

"We need to know who wants us dead," Ameara said, "and the safer way to do that is being an arrogant fool Whisper gets to chasten. Parading a subdued shavinash from a rival cadre in front of him would make him look weak and incompetent."

"I never thought I'd be hoping to be caught in a shavinashi power play," Kyzum said. "At least you didn't aim higher. Then we'd be in real trouble."

A living shavinash presented possibilities, albeit fragile and dangerous ones. A dead shavinash dealt one fate. Ameara hadn't thought her pistol was powerful enough to damage a shavinash's etch. Rowshatari and remshiri had bombarded etchs and not left a scratch. Beheading a shavinash was easier than overcoming the pure, dense obsidian that encompassed the bloodshaping seal, easier being a relative term. Or so she had believed.

Syra's hull creaked, buffeted by the night's wind. Wary, the Dazmir-vahl-kesh reached out to Ameara. Ameara kept her out. She couldn't soothe Syra when her own fears were tightening her chest.

"If Whisper is behind this, and he won't be persuaded, I'll buy the rest of you time to make yourselves scarce."

Kyzum's hazel eyes hardened, a glimpse of the resolve that had gotten him exiled. "Ameara…"

"It's decided."

Kyzum bit back what Ameara knew to be a stream of arguments originating from their suddenly uncertain future. "It's a terrible plan."

Ameara waved away his concern. "We've lived through terrible plans before."

"That doesn't mean you should keep implementing them."

The door burst open, and Ara rushed in. "He's waking up."

A hush enveloped the captain's quarters.

Ameara spoke into the silence, defying its constricting dread. "Let's not keep him waiting."

CHAPTER 9

The bazaar was awash with awnings, tents, booths, and carts. Trinkets clinked, jewelry glistened, rugs swayed, and pottery gleamed. Sizzling meats, simmering curries, and fresh bread intermingled with nougats, fruit, and pastries. Jaleya should have been shouldering her way through a bustling, buzzing crowd, intense bartering intermittently interrupting the chatter.

She could have run laps around the cleared bazaar.

Only those whose hair fell past their shoulders could enter with the rowshatari present, but they had servants for such things. Indeed, the servants who had been removed waited impatiently down side streets for the soldiers to let them return.

Jaleya plodded along behind Teza, who stopped at every stall to admire the pattern of this or that rug, try on cuffs and earrings only to declare them too modest for a rowshatar, and appraise every shawl. The latest item to capture his interest was a glass bowl with embossed whales swimming its circumference. Tints and shades of blue refracted the late-morning light, as though the glass had captured a wave.

"That came all the way from the Wild Ice," the merchant said proudly.

"Uh-huh," Teza said as he moved his head back and forth, back and forth, following the play of light.

Jaleya almost lifted her headscarf to conceal her aggravation, but the breeze from the canals running through Abylay was refreshing. Having distance from Iza Vor was refreshing, even though it never let anyone forget its presence.

Patience, Isesh sent. He watched the bazaar from a wall's triangular crenellations. His jowls opened wide in a relaxed yawn. The perch he occupied probably belonged to a guild; they were near that ward. Jaleya could see the crest of a dome and a minaret beyond her javati.

I hate bazaar days, Jaleya sent. *They never buy anything, or they clean out the merchants without paying.*

Rowshatari don't have to pay, Isesh replied calmly.

'Gratitude' for the rowshatari's 'service' doesn't extend to an entire livelihood.

I doubt our charge will leave a merchant coinless, especially one who can afford a space in this bazaar. He didn't bring servants to carry acquisitions or arrange transport.

He better not ask me to do either of those things.

He seems content to just look.

He could look faster.

You have somewhere you need to be? Isesh sent dryly.

He could come to the bazaar with everyone else, Jaleya replied. *Isn't protecting him why we're here? He doesn't need special treatment.*

You know why the Ora provide it.

Bored with the intricate bowl, Teza straightened and jumped over to the next booth like a foal let out to pasture. Jaleya offered the merchant a polite smile before following.

A rug with a hexagon pattern trimmed with gold had caught Teza's attention. He glanced over his shoulder as Jaleya approached and rolled his eyes. "Stop hovering like a vulture. You're ruining bazaar day."

"As you wish, Your Radiance." Jaleya was glad to put space between them. She took position within an awning's shade.

Other rowshatari and their guardians wandered the bazaar. The javati were relaxed and inspected merchandise for themselves. The rowshatari paid them no mind. They were unsolicited accessories. The rowshatari-korza, their skin crackling with the sun's light, had no javati, only an escort detail. Soldiers guarded the streets to the bazaar and stood post on the roofs with vantages of the stalls and surrounding city; they gave a wide berth to the fashari who had claimed the high ground. If a threat arose, it would have to get past the soldiers and perched fashari before even reaching the bazaar. Jaleya might as well not be there.

Teza lost interest in the rug and bounded from booth to booth much quicker now, stealing what he thought were inconspicuous glances into the surrounding streets and to where she stood watch. A heated exchange broke out between a flustered servant and a soldier. Teza ducked down that lane and bypassed the distracted soldier, who gave a shout as the rowshatar disappeared into the line of impatient retainers.

Jaleya sighed, unsurprised. With a sweep of his wings, Isesh crossed the bazaar to an opposite roof.

"He's testing you," Yongir said from a tent where he was evaluating a set of Masatitoran porcelain. Jaleya still couldn't tell which fashari was his javati. A qilin lingered nearby, but it wasn't being territorial or familiar.

"They always do," Jaleya said. *Especially this one,* she thought but knew better than to say in public. "Welcome back," she told the other javati; she hadn't realized he had returned to Abylay until that moment.

Jaleya hurried after Teza, waving away the frantic soldier who had inadvertently let him pass.

You have eyes on him? she sent to Isesh, who paralleled the streets from above.

Just follow the parting crowd, Isesh sent.

Citizens naturally yielded roadways to rowshatari, but once

awe replaced timidity, they closed in, wanting to touch Orvashka's Harmonized or even just the hem of their shawls. Jaleya reached the back of one such bottleneck, and she spotted Teza's tiara turn down a side street. She utilized an arch and an oriel window to reach the rooftops, and she and Isesh seamlessly intersected.

Without the hindrance of the crowds, they easily trailed Teza through hanging gardens, around domes, and from terrace to terrace. Whenever their makeshift path dead-ended, Isesh carried them over the gap. If they had been west of the river, they would have been able to walk across the flat rooftops unimpeded. The streets were narrow there, people living on top of each other. Here, the wide boulevards created a meandering warren.

I think he's lost, Isesh sent after a quarter hour of following their charge around in circles.

Agreed, Jaleya sent.

We could announce ourselves and help him, Isesh suggested.

He told me to stop ruining his day. He'll realize we're here eventually, and he'll order us to take him back to Iza Vor. If he doesn't, we'll return him by force. Either way, we'll be back before he's missed.

You're enjoying this, Isesh scolded.

He's the one that ran off. It's not my fault he doesn't know the way around his own city.

Teza looked left and right at an intersection, and chose at random. It led to a street on the Nidren. A long line of people extended from a two-story building with glazed bricks and a small portico.

Do you think he's asking for directions? Isesh sent.

Let's get closer, Jaleya replied. Something felt off.

As they closed the distance, Jaleya couldn't tell if the uneasy feeling in her stomach was indicative of danger to Teza or due to what was taking place below. The bread line stretched from the distribution center all the way across the nearest bridge spanning the Nidren, and stragglers were coming up behind. She saw them in every city and town. Faces changed, but the people didn't. There were the servants of the guild and government officials who hadn't bothered to remove their headdress or mark of office. There were the men, women, and children with dirty faces and no shoes, their soiled tunics patched, frayed, and hanging off their starved shoulders. There were the ones whose clothing was well kept if simple, but the wearers' features were haggard, having labored diligently only to have the Ora steal their earnings and leave them without enough to feed themselves, forcing them to make the choice of continuing to work themselves to the bone or join the ones who had nothing but what the Ora "graciously" gave them. Those that lived on the crossroads were always the least in number, and that number was shrinking even with a thriving black market. Without majority control of the Schism, all of Setsea would already be divided into the West Ward and the Ways' enforcers.

It made Jaleya's blood boil.

She reminded herself that these people—these Illuminated —followed the Ways willingly. They championed the mire that was suffocating them.

Keeping out of sight of the civilians and officials but close enough to track Teza, Jaleya and Isesh alighted on the building adjacent to the distribution center. Chin high, Teza marched up to one of the center's guards and ordered he take him back to Iza Vor. Jaleya and Isesh shared an unsurprised look.

Mournful cries erupted from the bread line. The official who seemed to be in charge upturned an empty crate, stepped upon it, and spoke over the crowd. "I'm sorry, but we are out of bread for the day and are closed. Other distribution centers may be able to accommodate you. We will be resupplied tomorrow morning, and you are encouraged to come back then. Thank you." She stepped down and disappeared into the building, leaving the assistants and guards to deal with the hungry populace.

The families stuffed into the long line stared grief-stricken, hopeless, at the empty crates. Then resignation took over, for what could they do? Not a single tear was shed. The line began to disperse.

Some headed home in despair; some sought a spot where patrols might not find them to spend the night and wait for the morning shipment; a few began to wander to other distribution centers, even though they would also be empty.

"Citizens!" The disbanding crowd stopped. Teza stood on the crate the official had vacated. His chest puffed with importance, his gold cuffs and necklace gleaming in the sunlight, he proclaimed, "Do not despair."

Jaleya hid her face in her hand and groaned.

"The bread ran out today, but it will return tomorrow. All deserve food on their table. That's why the distribution centers exist: to ensure all have food on their table. Orvashka's Ways give everyone a bountiful life, and with the Ora leading us in them, harmony will continue to reign and spread."

"I'm standing here because of their harmony," a man in the crowd shouted. Jaleya and the guards straightened, alert. A pregnant silence settled. Teza hesitated, then continued.

"Yes, the Ora ensure we all have a life of dignity that strengthens Orvashka's light and will bring about—"

A rock grazed Teza's shoulder; he jumped in surprise and toppled to the ground. The thrower shouted, "They're thieves and liars!"

The guards tore into the stunned crowd, converging on the dissenter. A woman begged for mercy, but a sharp slap silenced her cries. The guards dragged the stone thrower, who wore simple but sufficient clothing, to the portico's steps. The woman with a swelling cheek and another man followed. The official emerged on the second-floor terrace. She glanced at the assistant brushing dirt off Teza, the guards binding the stone thrower, and his friends on their knees pleading for leniency. The official waved the guards to carry on. The woman burst into tears as the prisoner was dragged away. The remaining guards established a human barricade between the bread line and the distribution center. The crowd hurried to be anywhere else. The man comforting the woman urged her to leave, and it was only with continual appeals that she acquiesced. In her parting expression, Jaleya recognized the anger that comes from grief. Anger that leads to rash action.

Jaleya dropped to the street and strode over to her charge; Isesh kept a watchful distance.

"I'll take it from here," she told the guard Teza was haranguing into escorting him back to Iza Vor.

"You!" Teza said. "What are you doing here? I ordered you to stop hovering."

"Guardian," the guard greeted.

"Hovering is my job," Jaleya said. "We're going back to Iza Vor. Now."

Teza stuck out his chin, crossed his arms, and puckered his lips. "I don't take orders from you. I'm perfectly capable of returning to Iza Vor myself. Now be gone."

Jaleya itched to slap the smugness off his face. A man was going to be executed for expressing justified outrage, and Teza didn't care, just like he hadn't cared at the theater. Did he even know? Informing him the shelter he lived in was a cage was how javati got executed, but the bars were staring him in the face. Why couldn't he see them?

"As you wish, Your Radiance," Jaleya said far too sweetly. The guard was shrinking away from the arguing rowshatar and javati, but he froze beneath Jaleya's sudden attention. "You'll see he returns safely?"

"Yes, guardian."

Jaleya turned on her heel and collected Isesh. He flew them back to the rooftops, and they paralleled Teza and his escort as they made their way to Iza Vor. Jaleya's hands still itched to whack Teza upside the head.

Is it just me, or are the rowshatari getting more pompous with every passing day? she sent.

They're reared to believe they are Setsea's rightful rulers denied their reign because of the Schism's corruption, Isesh replied. *You expect them to behave otherwise? This one does seem more mischievous than others, but I thought that would please you.*

Not when it ends like it did today, Jaleya sent softly.

If a rebellion ascends to challenge the Ora, something you advocate for and bluster about daily, that man will be but the first of many casualties.

You want the Ora to fall, too.

I want freedom to return, even with its dangers. I hope it can be achieved without bloodshed, but you humans shout so loud and speak so many words, no one can hear when something is actually said.

Jaleya grimaced. A skyship crashing into Harmony Tower wouldn't even make the Ora *consider* relinquishing their power.

Jaleya, Isesh sent urgently.

She looked below. Teza and the guard were strolling up a quiet side street. The guard had taken the route that exposed Teza to the least amount of people; Jaleya would have done the same. A fleeting figure paralleled them on an adjacent street, slinking from doorway to doorway. Two others maneuvered to intersect.

Jaleya sent Isesh to flank the pair gaining from behind, and Jaleya ran ahead, seeking the ambush point. At a junction with no street-facing windows, she slowed, crouched, and peered over the edge of the roof. A man and a woman pressed themselves against a wall, ready to surprise Teza and his escort. Jaleya eyed possible routes, searching for the best angle to confront the ambushers.

Isesh sprang into her mind. *The guard is injured. Teza is heading toward you.*

What?

The two behind us. I let them see me, but instead of retreating, they attacked. I scared them off, but our charge fled, too.

Jaleya sighed in exasperation. *Make sure they don't double back. I'll handle things over here.*

Responsibly, please.

Jaleya shut him out to let him know what she thought of his comment.

Keeping low, she backtracked until she spotted Teza barreling toward the waiting trap. His tiara bounced side to side, the fringe on his shawl horizontal. The fleeting figure matched his pace but kept to the parallel street. Three against one really was unfair.

Jaleya dropped to the paved bricks and crossed to the parallel street. Keeping her steps light but quick, she gained on Teza's shadow. The man turned down a lane to initiate the snatching, but Jaleya rushed him from behind, driving him to the ground. He rolled onto his back, but his exclamation was cut short by Jaleya's fist. He blinked, dazed but still conscious. Jaleya punched him again. The man went limp.

Jaleya frowned at the would-be snatcher. His clothing was poor cloth but well fitted. The dust on his face was equivalent to an honest morning's work. The folds of his tunic didn't suggest any concealed weapons. He had nothing to shelter his head from the sun or conceal his features. Snatcher, bandit—threat—this man was not.

Jaleya hurried to the street where the other ambushers waited. She peered around the corner as they leapt from hiding and tackled Teza to the ground. They forced him onto his stomach, and the man sat on him and seized his arms while the woman forced a gag into his mouth. She flinched each time Teza struggled, afraid to get her fingers bitten. The man urged her to hurry, his grip slipping as Teza twisted beneath him.

Jaleya readied her short spear and wandered a few steps.

The woman bound Teza's hands with twine and slipped a dirty sack over his head. The sack further muffled Teza's screams.

Jaleya ambled a few more steps; it was a shame a whistled tune would draw attention. The snatchers could see her if they looked aside, but they were invested in their task.

The man and woman hoisted Teza to his feet; Teza still shrieked against the gag. Jaleya supposed the time was ripe. She stepped hard and cleared her throat. The would-be snatchers finally noticed her, but before they could react, she was upon them. She knocked the man into a brick wall and slapped the spear shaft across the woman's torso, sending her sprawling. Teza stumbled over his own feet and toppled sideways.

Jaleya stood over Teza, the ambushers on each side of her. She recognized them. The weeping woman from the bread line and the man who consoled her.

Jaleya lowered her spear. "You should go. Now."

The man began backing away, wisely following her good advice. The woman hesitated, desperately eyeing Teza at Jaleya's feet. Her one chance for the condemned man to return to her.

"It won't work," Jaleya said. "You'll all die. You, him, and everyone you involve."

"At least we'll die together, standing," the woman said. Tears lined her cheeks, her eyes sunken, lost, hopeless.

"Live, and take a stand when the ground will hold," Jaleya said, the words echoing from the past.

The woman tore her gaze from Teza and affixed it to Jaleya. Jaleya recognized the battle raging inside her. If she attacked, Jaleya would skewer her, but it would all be over. No more pain. No more grief. If she heeded Jaleya's words, she had no promise of anything besides toil, misery, and a slow descent into poverty. She might never see justice for the one she lost.

"Ravorna," her companion called from the shelter of the cross street.

A final tear dripped from Ravorna's eyes. She rose slowly. Paused. She joined her friend, and together they fled. She might never see justice for the one she lost. That thought was a great motivator.

Jaleya helped Teza upright and drew her knife to free him. Teza whimpered and flinched.

She rammed the hilt into his nose, and he crumpled back to the paved bricks.

Jaleya, Isesh scolded as he and the guard approached. The guard carried his helmet, and he leaned on Isesh's shoulder for support. That was why her javati had taken so long to arrive.

Jaleya cut the twine binding Teza's wrists and dragged him to his feet. He fumbled with the sack, so she removed that, too. Teza blinked in the sunlight. Blood trailed down his chin. Jaleya rid him of the gag, and his moaning reached full volume. He touched his tender nose and yelped in pain.

"You broke my nose. You broke my nose!"

"It's not broken," Jaleya said.

"Yes, it is."

"You weren't hit that hard."

"Yes, I was! It's broken. Empty sky!"

Jaleya ignored her charge's complaints and went to Isesh and the guard. "We'll take it from here. Can you reach a physician or your barracks on your own?"

"I'll manage," the guard said quickly, removing his hand from Isesh. His balance was questionable, but he probably wanted to be as far from a bickering javati and rowshatar as possible. He left with a hurried salute, anxious Jaleya would change her mind and require further assistance.

"It won't stop," Teza wailed. Rivulets of blood lined his chin and dripped onto his disheveled purple shawl, which had acquired a layer of dust.

Jaleya retrieved the discarded gag and pressed it into his hand. "Use this, and keep your head back."

"This? That's disgusting."

"Keep your head back," Jaleya repeated, pushing his forehead skyward.

"I can't walk like this. I'll trip. I'm riding your pet the rest of the way."

Isesh rumbled-pealed a warning. Teza flinched, blood splattering. Jaleya pushed his head back again.

"He's not a pet. You're not riding him."

"*You* ride him."

"I'm his javati. If you attempted it, he would burst into the air and drop you from hundreds of feet, and you would have far more to complain about than a bump on the nose. We're returning to Iza Vor. If you don't keep up, you will be left behind, and whoever else wants to snatch you will see no resistance from me."

Her patience at its end, Teza withered before her. His chin drooped toward his chest, and he hastily stuck it skyward.

You should've done that at the beginning, Isesh smirked.

Shut up, Jaleya sent.

She took the lead down the lane. Teza stumbled every few steps as he continued to stem the blood flow from his nose, but he didn't fall behind. Isesh brought up the rear, ever watchful, but he and Jaleya knew the snatchers wouldn't return. It had been an impulsive plan birthed from desperation and wouldn't have been attempted outside the cloud of grief.

Teza whined the entire way, but he did so in mumbles and whispers, like a child testing the boundaries of his parents' ire. Jaleya treated him like the spoiled child he was and ignored him. She wished she *had* broken his nose.

CHAPTER 10

"She's horrible, the worst. I want her and her pet removed, replaced, banned from Abylay! Ow." Teza winced as the rowshatar-korza's fingers roamed too close to his healing nose. On the threshold between discomfort and pain, the sun kaza prickled his nostrils inside and out like thousands of needles.

Saunez stood at the foot of the infirmary bed Teza sat upon. She pretended to listen, but her crossed arms divulged her disinterest. Being deprived of kaza except for one week a month, if he was lucky, didn't make him a lesser rowshatar. The greatest inventions of Setsea had been constructed with star kaza. It wasn't his fault the knowledge had been lost and the once-magnificent creations were shattered remnants. He was a rowshatar-estra and deserved respect.

"I order you to get me a new guardian," he said.

One eyebrow almost disappeared under Saunez's embroidered bonnet. Never a good omen. How did she raise a single eyebrow so high? How did it say so much with just an arch? It was uncanny. He had never been able to do it, even when they were children. His eyebrows were attached to each other. Teza cleverly took cover in the rowshatar-korza's healing. She gave him a you're-in-trouble look.

The prickling in his nose ceased, and the rowshatar-korza's hands stopped glowing. Saunez's eyebrow returned to its natural plane.

"Return tomorrow and the morning after for your follow-up healing," the rowshatar-korza said.

"You hear that?" Teza said to Saunez. "Because my guardian *broke* my nose, I have to come back to the infirmary *twice*."

"It was bruised, not broken," the rowshatar-korza said. "The first follow-up is standard procedure to verify the healing has taken and to reinforce it if it hasn't. The second is because you're a rowshatar, and as you should know, different kaza sources don't get along." She turned to Saunez. "Tomorrow morning, and the morning after. If the healing begins to deteriorate, have him return immediately, or it may collapse. Ask for Paruna."

"Thank you, Rowshatar Paruna," Saunez said.

"I'm not Paruna." The rowshatar-korza who was not Paruna pranced away like a goat glad to be out of its pen. At least, what he assumed a goat would be like. He had never seen one up close except for when it steamed on his dinner plate.

Amused—*amused!*—Saunez watched her disappear through an arch that led to rowshatari suites, private exam rooms, and supply closets.

"When will my new guardian be ready?" Teza asked.

Saunez's smirk died. "Jaleya is not being reassigned."

"What? She *broke. My. Nose.* She assaulted me—a rowshatar. She disobeys my orders, has her pet chirp at me, talks back—"

"What were you doing outside the bazaar?" Saunez said.

Teza's teeth clicked as he clamped his mouth shut. "Um…I…It's good to see the people we serve. Right?" He was proud of himself for coming up with that answer so quickly.

Saunez's eyebrow summited a mountain. She knew he was lying. She always knew when he was lying. He waited for the reprimand, his shoulders clenching.

"Guardians protect you; they protect all rowshatari," Saunez said. "That is their solemn duty. They are not your friends. It is regretful that your previous guardian was a traitor—"

"He wasn't—"

The eyebrow defied gravity, and the words died on his lips. The madness that followed the loss of a guardian's fashari had descended upon Gardok quickly. He had raved he was being framed, that he was innocent, as he flinched and cowered at hallucinations. He had blathered up to the moment the ceremonial dagger plunged into his chest. Teza didn't like to think about that day.

"It's regretful," Saunez repeated, "but all rowshatari must have a guardian. There are those who seek to destroy Orvashka's harmony and bring chaos to Setsea. Eliminating our rowshatari would greatly aid their misguided efforts.

"You will stop evading your guardian, and you will put all ideas of roaming, wandering, exploring, and so forth, aside. You might not like her, but as long as she stops the knife meant for you, your dislike is inconsequential. Is that understood?"

His head lowered, Teza nodded.

"I said: Is that understood?"

"Yes, Custodian Saunez."

"Good. An escort will return you to your quarters. Your guardian will be along after I've heard her report."

Saunez left his bedside with the commanding air of a custodian, having given him none of the comfort he had hoped to receive. He knew the infirmary was a public place, but he had almost been snatched. He could still taste the sweat on the foul gag and feel the dirty sack cutting off his air. No matter how he twisted his wrists, the twine held. No matter how much he thrashed, he couldn't get free. No matter how loud he screamed, no help came. He was doomed to be a ransom for antiquated, thankless, uneducated rebels who had no intention of upholding their end of any bargain. He would be tortured to death and his body dumped in the desert to be picked apart by vultures.

Gardok would have saved him. But he was gone now. Returned to Orvashka so any remaining light in his life force would be spared corruption and would be able to foster Paradise, as he had refused to recant his dark ways even before the madness overcame him.

Maybe Gardok wouldn't have saved him after all. Only the irredeemable were returned to Orvashka.

Teza sighed. He didn't want another guardian. He had thought if he could reach Seal Keeper Firnak's house just outside Iza Vor —surprise him, surprise Saunez—everyone would see his competence. A guardian wouldn't have to trail him everywhere and wouldn't betray him and Orvashka, as javati were wont to do. His actions had only proved how helpless and incapable he was without one.

But he was still a rowshatar-estra. Providing star kaza to Abylay and Setsea was a vital duty, and the citizens recognized that with gratitude. They loved him, respected him. He was important and valued. He veered the stars' kaza. He was Rowshatar-estra Teza!

His thoughts echoed in his mind like words echoed in the infirmary. No one paid him any mind. Without the stars' iridescence adorning his olive skin, he could be any high official. Without kaza coursing through his veins, he too had to remind himself of who he was.

* * *

Jaleya followed Custodian Saunez down the corridor. Her supervisor's back was straight and her shoulders were tall, her steps decisive but not hasty. Jaleya expected a stern lecture after the attempted snatching, but seeing Teza knocked from the stars was worth a little reprimand.

They entered Custodian Saunez's office. "Your fashari stays outside."

Jaleya was about to protest, but Isesh accommodated the absurd command and sat beside Er'od's desk; Er'od shuffled his chair a few inches. Jaleya moved to the center of the enclosed room, her hands clasped before her like a good, obedient javati. Custodian Saunez's lips were a thin line, her dark eyes hard.

"Do you understand the nature of your duty?"

Jaleya blinked. The protocol was for her to report on the incident. "Yes," she answered.

"Remind me," Custodian Saunez said.

"I am to protect the rowshatar in my charge and obey his orders. I have done so."

"Like stars at noon you have," Custodian Saunez retorted. "You deliberately endangered his life."

"He ordered me to give him space. I never ceased my watch, and I intervened when it became necessary."

"You should have intervened sooner. He could've been killed."

It took Jaleya longer than she wanted to respond. Custodians weren't distressed when one of their rowshatari suffered a scrape. Anxious about the implications for their position, yes, but not genuinely concerned about the rowshatar, which Custodian Saunez seemed to be. This was Abylay, though. If their rowshatari were hurt or perished, the Ora couldn't force their rule on Setsea and their claimed territories. Custodians would be more high-strung as a result.

Jaleya said, "Considering the contradictory parameters of my duty, I performed as best I could. There was no danger until we left the bread line, and when the threat arose, I acted accordingly."

"The safety of your charge supersedes everything else, including orders given by your charge," Custodian Saunez said, her eyes blazing. "You protect him, even if that means protecting him from himself. All guardians know that."

Jaleya bowed her head in the manner other custodians accepted as deferential.

Custodian Saunez curved her lips. "You think you're clever walking the line between willful but willing guardian and outright defiance. That line is far thinner than you think, and testing its boundaries is the action of a child. If you want to turn traitor, commit to it, and do it soon; I'll need time to arrange another guardian for Rowshatar Teza before the Festival of Shattered Swords. Otherwise, don't let him get another scratch. You walked the line well this time, but attempt it again, and I will give you to the shavinashi or execute you and serve your fashari as the main dish at the Ora's table. It depends how generous I'm feeling."

"Yes, Custodian Saunez," Jaleya said automatically, then added because she had threatened Isesh, "It's just a bloody nose."

Saunez raised one delicate eyebrow. She pulled a cord hanging in the corner behind her desk. The summoned soldiers entered and stood at attention. "Custodian Saunez."

Jaleya looked between the guards and the custodian, her stomach fluttering. She was serious. Custodian Saunez would drag her away right now, dispose of her and Isesh, and replace them without blinking. They were nothing to her.

"It won't happen again," Jaleya said, a hint of true submission tingeing her voice.

"Never mind," Custodian Saunez told the guards. They saluted and left.

The custodian said, "I look forward to reading about Rowshatar Teza's bloody nose in your full report. That will be all."

Custodian Saunez sat behind her desk and turned her attention to paperwork, dismissing Jaleya from her office and her thoughts. Jaleya wanted to slap the smugness off Custodian Saunez's face. She retreated instead. Jaleya had dodged an arrow, but she hadn't even known the archer was there.

CHAPTER 11

Saunez looked up from the document as the door closed behind Jaleya. She leaned back in her chair and pushed aside the missive she had been reading but not comprehending in her current state of mind. When word of Teza's attempted snatching had reached her, it had been all she could do to not abandon Iza Vor and return him to the citadel herself. Then to discover he'd been injured…Exaggeration was as natural as breathing to Teza, but Saunez had no trouble believing Jaleya was responsible for his "bloody nose." Reading the half-truths woven into the arrogant child's report would be interesting. She was a green guardian if ever there was one, still enveloped in the invincibility of youth, but she had learned to mince words. Her control needed work; Saunez had noted several instances when Jaleya's carefully framed sentences were awkward on her tongue and contrary to her thoughts. At least she had brought Teza home. She seemed honorable in that regard, and that was what mattered. Teza was safe. And Saunez was late.

She left her office and paused by Er'od. "Now I am going to speak with Quartermaster Bilka. Let's hope another crisis doesn't arise before I reach the door."

"I'll tell the crisis it has to wait," Er'od replied.

Saunez traversed the corridors to the javati compound; she

scrunched her nose against the pungent odor of livestock. Quartermaster Bilka informed her there was nothing she could do about the outstanding acquisition requests, as she was waiting on a delayed shipment. The merchant had been caught delivering faster than regulation, so the entire stock had been deferred until the others regained the lost ground. Saunez listened with half an ear. It wasn't the first time this had happened, and it wouldn't be the last. Iza Vor paid in the shadows to have its shipments prioritized, and some merchants were more discreet than others. Saunez told Bilka she expected the orders to be filled the moment the shipment arrived. After much reassurance from Bilka, Saunez slipped her more "incense" and left the reeking javati compound behind.

She turned a corner to take the long way back to her office. She strolled through a garden of pomegranate trees and roses before entering an arcaded hallway utilized by staff. A main corridor in the citadel's early days, it had been reduced to an inconspicuous shortcut as Iza Vor expanded.

Saunez paused when she felt eyes on her, but she saw no one. She looked up into the arches' shadows. A reptilian head crowned with a horn regarded her with glossy orbs, its lithe, scaled body curved into the corner where it perched precariously on feline paws and bird talons. It flicked its forked tongue without an accompanying hiss. No one was near who shouldn't be.

Saunez continued past the sirrush and entered an obsolete parlor filled with splintered crates and excess furniture. The lack of alarm on her three co-conspirators' faces told her Hossa had alerted Enlu of her arrival.

"You're late," O'rin said. A slim woman with a pinched nose and brown hair that tested the bounds of decency, she was an official in the Dyers' Guild. Opportunities to slip away were few, but her incessant reminders made one think they were sane vahl-keshi.

"Apologies," Saunez said to all of them. "Rowshatar Teza's new guardian is proving to be troublesome."

"You have no one to blame but yourself," Enlu said, his ample muscles flexing as he crossed his arms. He wore his long hair partially bound, and his glower intensified his pronounced cheekbones.

"I regret Gardok's death, but it was necessary," Saunez said. "The trail couldn't lead back to me—to us. It was the only way to protect what we're doing."

"You were protecting Teza," Enlu argued.

"Yes, I was. Loyal to the Ora he may be, but he is still a rowshatar-estra, and to keep the Dazmiri in the sky, we need rowshatari-estra."

"Enough," Firnan said, his firm tone cutting between Enlu and Saunez. Flour sprinkled the sleeves of his brown tunic similar to the gray speckling his short dark hair. Wrinkles encircled his unyielding eyes even as his shoulders carried a minor hunch. He was without his apron, which meant his delivery cart was hidden nearby. Time was short.

"What's done is done," Firnan said. "Our plan remains hidden. We've all had to make hard decisions, and we will have to make more until Setsea is free from the Ora's tyranny."

Saunez bowed her head in apology. Enlu's nod was much smaller.

"Do we have any new information on the spy?" Firnan asked the room.

"It has to be someone in Iza Vor," Enlu said.

"That's like saying it has to be someone in Abylay," O'rin remarked. "Obviously the spy is within the custodians' circle, or Saunez wouldn't have been able to frame Gardok so indisputably. I'm glad you're on our side."

Saunez brushed aside the painful compliment. "The spy does appear to be knowledgeable about the custodians and their responsibilities."

"I asked for *new* information," Firnan said.

They all shook their heads in the negative.

"Very well. We'll continue with our increased precautions until we can determine who the informant is. Apart from that, is everything for the festival proceeding according to plan? O'rin, will the cylinder seals be ready?"

"Imlay will have them by week's end," O'rin said. "She wasn't able to procure as many as she hoped, but she's confident there will be enough to take the armory and deter the remshiri."

"Our targets?" Firnan said, looking to Saunez.

"I'll receive the replenishing assignments the week of stars' sway, and I'll pass them along through channels," she replied. "The assignments have been the same the last few months, and I haven't heard any indication that this is changing. Four guards, and possibly a guardian, will be escorting each rowshatar-estra, in addition to the ones posted near the skyships. The Dazmiri will be useless to us until they're replenished, so the ship teams must wait until the rowshatari-estra finish."

"That gives us a very short window to gain control of the skyships, especially since we have to confront the Ora before the bloodshaping ritual renews their life," Enlu said.

"It's our best chance," Saunez said.

"Even if the ritual completes before we arrive, the plan doesn't change," Firnan said. "The Ora aren't going to shoot down the solution to closing the Schism."

"Unless they don't need the skyships and their work at the Schism is all for show," O'rin added.

Silence followed the voicing of the fear in all their minds. Compelling the Ora to the negotiating table hinged upon the Dazmiri's significance.

"Then the Ora will have revealed themselves to be liars, and the people will lose faith," Firnan said. It wasn't an encouraging alternative. Even O'rin didn't say how easily the people's faith would be restored.

"What if they call our bluff?" Enlu said. "By stealing the skyships, we're admitting to knowing their importance. What if the Ora don't agree to terms because they know we won't destroy the skyships?"

"Who says we're bluffing?" Saunez replied.

A heavy silence.

O'rin exhaled. "I'm *very* glad you're on our side."

"Damaging the skyships is a last resort," Firnan said. "If it does become necessary…They're magnificent creations, but they are not vahl-keshi. New ones can be built. We all knew this wasn't going to be easy. Do not let the risks deter you so close to the end. Think of the future about to begin." He paused, as if reminding himself of that very future. "How are the ship teams?"

"As nervous as children mounting their first horse," Enlu said.

"Informing them they may have to destroy a Dazmir will help with that," O'rin said drily.

"The intelligence coming from the North will bolster them," Saunez said.

Firnan rubbed his bearded chin. "Will they be able to fly the skyships without that intelligence?"

Saunez shared a concerned glance with the other two.

"There's a problem," Firnan confirmed. "Ora spies caught wind of lost arts changing hands. The good news is they don't suspect our involvement; we can thank our northern brothers and sisters' unruly reputation for that. The bad news is the shavinashi were tasked with interception."

The temperature in the room dropped. They fiddled with the hems of their tunics and shawls and glanced side to side as if a shavinash would materialize from the dusty shadows. O'rin began flicking her fingers, a nervous tick she needed to learn to control.

"The meeting is taking place in Masatitora," O'rin said, her voice unsteady. "If shavinashi are discovered carrying out clandestine orders, the treaty between our countries would be broken. That's why we chose that location."

"They would risk it if it was sufficiently important," Saunez said.

"Yes, they would," agreed Firnan. "However, I don't believe they consider this of treaty-shattering significance. Eclipse's Dazmir, *Skyheart*, was spotted in Abylay a few days ago."

"Empty sky," Enlu spat.

O'rin looked between them. "What's the problem? We're fortunate the shavinashi aren't sending one of their own. We can fight Vessels. They're just mercenaries."

"Eclipse is not a common Vessel," Saunez said. "She killed the first crew she served with, yet the Vessels still admitted her to their ranks. And that was after she fought as a Schism gladiator and stole a Dazmir, which no one managed to take from her, and now no one dares try. She's the only Vessel who works for the shavinashi, and if her ship was seen after they were told to intercept our information without implicating themselves, you can be sure they hired Eclipse to do it."

"I thought the stories about her were…stories," O'rin said.

"Most are, I'm sure," Firnan said, "but she does have a Dazmir."

"Can we send a message to warn our contacts?" Enlu said.

"The risk is too great with Ora spies aware of the meeting," Firnan said. "They'll be anticipating communications, and the trail can't lead back to us. We have good people up north. They'll be expecting trouble, and they'll hear about the threat through their own channels."

"What if Eclipse does intercept the intelligence?" O'rin said.

Firnan replied, "That close to stars' sway, everything running on star kaza will be low on power, including her skyship. She'll be forced to use the Tethmet Strait to conserve kaza. That will be our chance to get it back. But it will be our only chance. So I ask again: will the ship teams be able to fly without the additional information?"

Enlu wore a sober expression. "They'll fly or die trying."

O'rin looked sick, her fingers ticking incessantly. Unease stirred in Saunez's stomach. Their entire plan depended on controlling the Dazmiri. It was the only leverage they had. She and others had been passing along the bits and pieces of lost arts documentation they had managed to scavenge from archives, libraries, and records, but they were still working off of a lot of assumptions.

As their meeting concluded, they agreed to push forward. Too many pieces were already in place, and they might not have another opportunity for a long while, especially with an unidentified informant among the custodians.

O'rin and Enlu left first, filing out a few minutes apart. Saunez hung back and caught Firnan's knowing eye.

"You could use the communication seal. You could warn them."

"Its kaza is too low," Firnan said. "I'd rather hear Eclipse stole the information and have enough kaza to coordinate a retrieval than warn them and have the outcome be the same but have no kaza to confirm if the information will reach us or not."

Saunez bit back a frustrated but concurring sigh. "What if Eclipse has kaza reserves and doesn't take the strait? What if we have to force her ship out of the sky?"

Firnan scratched his beard as he pondered. "I do have something. I was saving it for an emergency, but it might work."

"If we don't have those instructions, reinforcements could arrive before the ship teams are able to get the Dazmiri airborne, and our plan fails," Saunez warned. "I'd say this qualifies as an emergency."

"We'll wait to hear from our people," Firnan said. "Eclipse may fail."

"You don't fail the shavinashi."

"We're waiting," Firnan said firmly. "I'll keep you apprised."

He cracked the door, looked both ways, and proceeded into the arcaded corridor. Saunez lingered for a few moments, counting the seconds to let him gain distance; reminding herself to purchase cinnamon dates for Er'od as explanation for her long absence; trying to ease her growing disquiet. Their comrades up north were good people. They understood the severity of what they were attempting. If the shavinashi had sent any other Vessel, Saunez would have given their people a fighting chance. But this was Eclipse. All the stories about her couldn't be true, but stories had their roots in truth, and reputations—names—were earned.

You don't fail the shavinashi. Not if you want to live.

CHAPTER 12

Obakwe and Nahzida dragged the shavinash to the brig and secured him to the bars. Lacking manacles, they tied the knots extra tight. Nahzida guarded the brig while Obakwe and Ara searched Syra for more stowaways. Despite being out of reach of the unarmed and bound shavinash, Nahzida held her short staff with a white-knuckled fist. When Ameara and Kyzum arrived, Kyzum positioned himself opposite Nahzida. Ameara alone approached the prisoner.

The shavinash stared at the hull. None of them were worth his attention. The shadows cast by the lantern's light slashed across the shavinash's strong jaw and stern cheekbones. He seemed part of those shadows. He was a shadow. His dark clothing and sandy skin were the illusion.

Ameara interrupted his view of the hull, and he finally acknowledged her. Eyes as blue as the ocean but colder than its black depths commanded her submission. Ameara's sword and pistol were a reassuring weight.

Would they be any help against this predator?

The shavinash spoke. "Release me." His voice was deep and smooth, and oh so cold.

Ameara met his gaze. Shavinashi were all the same. Never show them weakness. But never deem oneself superior.

"What cadre are you with?" She didn't bother to ask if he knew who she was. Shavinashi always knew whom they dealt with and the significance of their targets. "What or who was your mission?"

"You presume to ask me questions?" the shavinash said.

"I'm not presuming. What cadre are you with?"

The corner of his lips twitched in what was probably a condescending smile. "Release me. I'll overlook your egregious actions."

"Like your shashvin will overlook your failure?"

That gave him pause. Maybe. Or he was calculating the most efficient way to discard his restraints and strike her dead with his bare hands.

"We're bound for Abylay, as you no doubt know," Ameara said. "There, we're going to have a long talk with my shashvin patron. He'll be very intrigued seeing us arrive together. Unless you want to tell me which shashvin ordered you here. Then this misunderstanding can be cleared up right now. Your choice."

"The choice is yours, Captain, and it will lead to the death of you and your crew. You will spare them if our encounter is forgotten by all, myself included. Now release me."

Nahzida drew a sharp breath. Ameara defeated her fear with anger. How dare he threaten her crew!

"The conversation in Abylay bodes better for me," she said. "If you change your mind, I'd be willing to consider alternatives."

She locked the brig and ushered Kyzum and Nahzida to the stairs' shadow, very conscious, as she always was, that she had turned her back to a shavinash.

"He is never to be left alone," she ordered in a whisper. "He is not to be approached or engaged under any circumstances. It's three days to Abylay. His etch will sustain him for that time, so no food or water. I am the only one who speaks to him."

Obakwe and Ara joined them as Kyzum and Nahzida gave affirmative nods and a round of, "Yes, Captain."

"There's no one else aboard," Obakwe reported, just as Ameara had theorized, and desperately hoped.

"We'll guard our guest in shifts," Ameara said. "Nahzida, you have first watch. Do not approach the bars for any reason. Ara, search his belongings. Look for anything that could indicate who ordered him here or who his target is. I'll watch the main deck. Kyzum, relieve me in an hour. Obakwe, try to get some rest. I still need you able to veer in Abylay."

Another round of, "Yes, Captain," and they dispersed to their assignments. Ameara climbed to the main deck, resisting the impulse to take the stairs three at a time; her crew was watching her every gesture. She breathed deep of the chilly night air, and attributed her limbs' tremble to the wind's bite.

"His offer was strange," Kyzum said, coming up behind her.

"His offer?" Ameara said. "The implied 'let me go, don't tell anyone what happened, and your crew will be spared'? The one where he didn't specify how long or in what way we would be spared? That's standard shavinash."

"It's strange that he proposed such an offer," Kyzum clarified. "When shavinashi want to ensure someone's silence, they're a one-method-fits-all kind of group, and we are his mission. Shavinashi don't give quarter once they've been loosed."

"That is strange," Ameara said, contemplating the angle she hadn't seen. "There must be more moving parts in this shashvin power play than we think. Or he and Whisper are toying with us. It doesn't change our situation."

"That would be too easy," Kyzum agreed, "but it is something to bear in mind if he summons you."

"Unless his offer has a heading for us to escape this mess alive, our guest can make as many as he wants. I'll accept none."

"We could cut his head off and throw his corpse into the sea, unless you could convince Obakwe to burn it to ash," Kyzum suggested halfheartedly.

"And when we return to Abylay and the shavinash doesn't, we'll be just as dead as if he'd killed us now. He isn't to be harmed."

"But we could run together then before we're slaughtered. I like that scenario better than you confronting Whisper alone."

Ameara didn't point out that confronting Whisper was the one scenario that could possibly spare their lives. Kyzum knew that. He was dreading it as much as she was.

Syra pressed against her mind, but the sending wasn't focused enough for Ameara to understand. Her own doubts and fears were mixing with her ship's, making for a tangled mess of incomprehensible knots.

"Ameara?" Kyzum said, seeing her confused squint.

"It's Syra. She's trying to tell me something, but I'm not sure what."

"Probably 'get the assassin off me.'"

Ameara allowed herself a smile. "Go get some rest, Kyzum."

"No one is getting any sleep tonight."

"At least try."

Kyzum released a dramatic sigh. "I'll pretend for half an hour."

Ameara took position at the helm. The wind nipped at her long locks, the brisk air filling her lungs. Stars shone bright beside the sliver of moon. Syra swayed beneath her, a heightened tremor to each gentle list. Pale shadows glinted in the kaza propelling them through the sky.

It would have been a beautiful night if not for the shavinash in her brig.

The brig Syra was urging her to return to.

Ameara closed her mind to her ship, but that allowed her own dark thoughts to surface. She had worried since the beginning that her arrangement with Whisper would be too much for her to keep up with, that it would eventually overtake her; she hadn't expected it to last this long. Maybe that day had finally come.

She hadn't meant to take others with her.

*　　*　　*

Kyzum relieved Ameara at the end of what felt like a very long watch. Too restless to sleep, Ameara went to check on Ara's progress, and frowned when she discovered Obakwe was guarding the shavinash.

After a silent exchange, she let her be. Kyzum was right: no one would be able to sleep tonight. They were all waiting for the shavinash's escape attempt. If he drew on his etch's bloodshaping, he could probably loosen the knots or dislocate his thumb to free himself. Why hadn't he? Surely he had a means of defeating the brig's lock hidden about him somewhere, even though they hadn't found one. Obakwe reported he hadn't made a sound since the start of her watch, and Nahzida had told Obakwe the same. The suspense was paralyzing Ameara's crew. Perhaps he was waiting until they were completely incapacitated.

Ameara left Obakwe and returned to the galley. Ara had the shavinash's belongings spread out on the table; Nahzida circled with interest. Twine, needle and thread, flint and steel, and dried meat and nuts lay in an ordered pile beside an empty belt pouch. Vials filled with liquids of various viscosities were divided into two rows based on Ara deeming them poison or antidote.

"Anything?" Ameara asked.

"Nothing," Ara replied. "This could belong to any shavinash."

Nahzida picked up the dual scimitars from among the collection of blades; they had found three concealed knives on the shavinash's person. The scimitars Nahzida eyed with admiration were more austere than most shavinashi's. Their preferred weapon was their only distinguishing trait.

"Shavinashi do know fine steel," Nahzida said. "Even his belt knife is quality craftsmanship. If any of these are vahl-keshi, I'm laying claim to them now."

"I don't think they are," Ara said. "There are no gemstones, and vahl-keshi don't like bloodshaping. They wouldn't communicate with a shavinash."

"Shavinashi risk corrupting their own life force to purify Orvashka's light! Bloodshaping is their deserved shield, as Orvashka's last appeal sadly requires implementation—"

"Why would a vahl-kesh dislike bloodshaping?" Ameara interrupted. She wasn't fond of the practice, especially how it was utilized in Setsea, but proving or disproving its purpose and origin was not her interest, or her responsibility. Ara seemed to be implying vahl-keshi had a special aversion to the zar'sheni's power.

"Captain…" Nahzida said with lowered voice and emphasizing eyes, "she's yapping Yevyran nonsense."

"Syra has been tense since the shavinash, and his etch, came aboard," Ameara said.

"We've all been tense since you shot the shavinash."

Ameara turned to the young galahi. "Ara?"

Ara shifted her feet and chewed her lip. She spoke to the table covered with the shavinash's belongings. "Bloodshaping was adopted and developed as a replacement for empath power, but it's a regressive imitation, a warped reflection at best. Vahl-keshi know its power is counter to their own."

Nahzida rolled her eyes and said to Ameara, "What has Syra impressed about bloodshaping?"

"Nothing specific, but if you think you can interpret her better than me, you're welcome to *try*."

"I didn't mean—" Nahzida's zeal withered. "I simply wanted confirmation from the source."

"We don't have much confirmation at all right now, which is why we're exploring any route that may provide some."

Nahzida nodded. She sheathed one of the scimitars, and paused. She bared a few inches of the blade, her fingers questing around the scabbard's ornamented throat. "What have we here?" She pulled a leather cord from within a hidden compartment.

"Be careful," Ameara cautioned.

Nahzida reached the cord's end, and hanging from it was a transparent crystal the length of Ameara's little finger. It caught the lantern's light, but its crude faces failed to reflect it onto the hull. Ara leaned closer, intrigued.

"That's an odd thing for a shavinash to carry."

"Gratitude for an independent cleansing?" Nahzida suggested.

"He could be killed for that," Ameara said. Ara's frown told Ameara the young woman also had thoughts on the subject, but she didn't voice them.

"Only if he was distorting Orvashka's Ways. Not even shavinashi can be a law until themselves." Nahzida squinted at the crystal, and chuckled. "If it was an independent cleansing, it was in a backwater village. This crystal's flawed. It's worthless." She tilted the stone to reveal a jagged crack at its center. The lantern's light was funneled to that inner fracture, where it became trapped. It glowed like a star in a thin fog.

Ameara's heart skipped a beat. The hull she stood in suddenly wasn't Syra's. It was another ship, another time. A ribcage of creaking timber. A rainstorm momentarily brightened by the inner light of a single flawed crystal. Her hand swatting it aside, the radiance lost beneath the missing boards. Desperately digging through the mud to save it.

"Captain?" Ara said. Nahzida stared at her with a furrowed brow. How many times had they addressed her?

Ameara took the stone from Nahzida and ran her finger along its facets. Its interior might be flawed, but the outside was smooth, if crude. A common, worthless stone. How many of those had a fracture exactly where she remembered that also glowed with an inner star? Hundreds. Thousands. Her memory was unreliable. She had been a child when she watched the crystal leave.

Trailing behind a shavinash. In the hands of a boy with eyes as blue as the sea.

"Care to share with the rest of us?" Nahzida said.

Ameara shook herself. She tossed the crystal onto the table. "Look through his things again. Inform me if you find anything significant."

"Whatever just happened seemed significant," Nahzida said.

"Look again."

Nahzida frowned at being kept in the dark. Ara studied Ameara out of the corner of her eye. Ameara left them to their work. She paused out of sight. Took a breath. She eyed the stairs to the lower deck, where the brig contained a shavinash. A blue-eyed shavinash who carried a flawed crystal.

Syra shuddered against her mind.

CHAPTER 13

Ezray's eyelids drooped as she studied the recorded visions. By themselves, they were meaningless fragments, but together, they began to form an image. An image of what was the question. Details were changing too quickly. All she knew for certain was that a metaphorical storm was building around the approaching festival, a storm that would determine the course of the future. An Ora refraining from the offering could shift the future thus, as only three would then remain. Only three to secure harmony for all of Idlium. Ezray didn't think any of her fellow Ora were going to refrain. She certainly wasn't.

She had quested for large-scale rebellions, but the threads were too numerous and too fleeting, and none pierced the thick haze beyond the spring festival. Intelligence from eyes and ears reported nothing besides the average grumblings of ungrateful citizens with antiquated ideas. Nothing arrests and education couldn't solve.

No, her vision indicated something…unique. Something she had not yet experienced in her very long life.

Ezray had procured ancient tomes from the dark archive for research and possible corroborative visions, but she had yet to find anything of use. The few pre-Schism books that had survived the giant rift's creation and the war that followed were filled with absurdities and backward ideologies. No wonder the Yevyrans and their supporters had lost. Any knowledge from the time of their influence should be destroyed, but it had been preserved as a warning and a reminder to not return to those beliefs. Ezray supposed it was a sound argument, as long as the information remained available only to a select few who understood its dangers and wouldn't sway from Orvashka's Ways.

A servant entered her quarters. "I'm sorry to disturb you, Your Radiance, but—"

"Good afternoon, Ezray," Nissa said, brushing past the servant. "You've been so sequestered lately I came to see how you're faring. You may leave," she added to the servant. He hastily obeyed, but his bow wasn't quite low enough.

"Ahkruz's insinuation that I'm going to refrain from the offering is groundless," Ezray assured her.

"Of course it is," Nissa said. "Ahkruz spoke what he fears for himself. You have noticed the increase in his nightly activities?"

Ezray nodded, relieved she wasn't the only one concerned. "Morhim has spoken to him?" The rowshatar-korza was a crackling fire on a cold winter night. Never let that fire escape the hearth, though.

"Morhim and I have both conveyed our distress, and we will continue to counsel Ahkruz until an intarish replaces the shavinash," Nissa said.

Ezray was taken aback. Nissa had more patience with Ahkruz than Ezray did, but that patience was an active volcano, and when exhausted, woe to those in her path. Nissa's disquiet regarding Ahkruz's lover had clearly originated before Ezray's.

"We are all that remain to secure peace for Idlium," Nissa continued, "but our responsibility is also to each other." She paused significantly. "You haven't been supervising the zar'sheni or the remshiri working on our experiment, much less touched it yourself, and when you're not delving the future's threads, you're pouring over dusty books and ancient scrolls." She sniffed at the mottled stack from the dark archive.

"My vision is imperative," Ezray said.

"I didn't say it wasn't. However, your mind can shatter just like lesser rowshatari-mara's. Ahkruz incorrectly predicted your refraining from the offering, but you're well on your way to proving that outcome."

Ezray regarded the books, scrolls, and loose papers piled haphazardly on the desk and chaises. Wild gems drained to dullness rested on the low table before her. When was the last time she had slept?

Her point made, Nissa asked, "Have you made any progress?"

"No," Ezray replied. "I see a shooting star in some variations now, but its significance and meaning are veiled. Another thread among countless others that refuses to coalesce." She stood and went to the wine pitcher. She filled two glasses and offered one to Nissa. "My vision's future is certain, but its form has not yet taken root."

Accepting the wine, Nissa said, "Have you been able to see past the festival?"

Ezray sipped the chilled sweet liquid. It refreshed her tired limbs and aching back, which she hadn't been aware of until now. "No. Whenever I quest beyond it, I see only fog. Something is stirring, Nissa, but I don't know what. It might be too fragile, or there might be too many moving pieces, or I might be looking in the wrong place…I don't know, and it's…aggravating."

Nissa grinned into her glass. "I can tell. Have the rowshatari or remshiri been any help?" She took a seat in a gilded chair and set aside the ledger she'd been carrying. Ezray reclined on the chaise opposite.

"Some of their questings contain similar threads, but beyond the festival, they fray into nothingness. The fog I see is the key; I know it. I just have to find who is causing it."

"Do the rowshatari and remshiri see this fog?" Nissa asked.

"They can't quest deep enough to see it, but I'll not give them more kaza or information."

"I wouldn't suggest such a thing," Nissa said, appalled. "Providing them tanzanite seals was barely appropriate as it is."

Ezray nodded agreement and took another sip of wine. "I feel like I did when I quested for the first time," she admitted. "Everything is uncertain."

"It must be strange to remember a time so long ago," Nissa mused.

"'Remember' is an incorrect term. It's like looking at a portrait, and you can vaguely recall that you were there, but details are far and few."

"A dream you can't recall," Nissa said softly. "Who knew living could make one feel so weary?"

Silence settled between them, a moment of empathy only the Ora could comprehend.

Nissa set her wine aside. "You are not questing for the first time. You have more experience, knowledge, and strength than all the lesser rowshatari-mara and remshiri combined. You will see beyond this, for without you—without us—there is no future."

She retrieved the ledger and offered it to Ezray. "It may be nothing, but it is unusual. According to my eyes and ears, a rowshatar-estra was seen at a bread line less than an hour before he was almost snatched. The same rowshatar-estra recently acquired a new guardian, as his previous one was a traitor and returned to Orvashka. Apart from being at the bread line, the report contains no undue actions by the rowshatar-estra, but if you read between the lines, an image begins to form. An alarming one, if true. However, neither an advocate nor the custodian has brought the incident before the Advocate Council for review. My eyes and ears may be seeing something that doesn't exist, as that is their trade. Determining future threats is yours."

Ezray skimmed the report. A traitorous rowshatar-estra trying to abandon his duty by way of a snatching? Interesting, but fanciful.

The post-Schism rowshatari had their quirks, acclimating a new guardian was never without friction, and javati were brewers of chaos at heart. It probably wasn't connected to her vision...

Ezray straightened, noticing the date on the report. Her vision had first revealed itself around the time the rowshatar-estra's new guardian arrived in Abylay. This might be worth looking into after all.

"You do well, considering your limited resources," Ezray said with a shrewd grin.

The identical one on Nissa's lips bore an avid undercurrent. "Since rowshatari and javati are difficult to quest, my limited resources are at your disposal."

Ezray considered the report in her hands. "What did you have in mind?"

CHAPTER 14

Jaleya spotted Yongir in the mess hall. He was laughing with a group of javati gathered at one of the long tables. Archways opened the pavilion to the courtyard. The javati compound's mustiness mingled with baking bread and simmering stew. It would cause most to lose their appetite. Jaleya breathed deep as she made her way to Yongir's table.

A few patrons waited near the counter for dinner or drinks. Others played Twenty Squares or cards. Jaleya avoided the latter, as the fashari created their own game within the game. The cockatrice perched on one of the men's shoulders could be helping or attempting to sabotage him for its own gain. Dice were the safer option when fashari were around.

As Jaleya approached Yongir and the other javati, Yongir hushed the woman speaking to him and proclaimed, "The javati of the hour!" He raised his mug, and others at the table did likewise. "To Jaleya, and her courage to do what we've all imagined." The javati indulged in their drinks, hiding their grins.

"What did I do?" Jaleya asked as the javati made room for her on the bench. All but two of Yongir's party chose to find other company. Apparently, her courage was also infamous.

"The tale of your exploits in the city has spread far," Yongir answered.

"It was un unfortunate incident," Jaleya said tactfully.

"Especially for your charge's nose," the woman sitting across from Yongir chuckled. Her full lips men would find appealing were tempered by an arrogant brow. Jaleya was fairly positive her name was Fusi; they had only met in passing. Gevruz, the man Fusi leaned against, concealed his amusement by scratching his wide nose. Yongir hollered a loud belly laugh.

Jaleya tried to not let the praise unbalance her. She'd been expecting a thorough questioning from an advocate, but no one had summoned her. Since a few days had passed, her report must have been a satisfactory explanation. Which didn't make sense. Custodian Saunez suspected her of evading the truth. She couldn't prove it, but suspicion was enough to decree guilt, or make one confess it. Teza had been unsupervised in Abylay's streets and almost snatched. That in itself should have had her reporting to an advocate or the Advocate Council. Jaleya was prepared for it. She had rehearsed her responses and memorized her report so the appropriate amount of natural inconsistencies would exist without being suspect. And…nothing.

Custodians could have more influence and autonomy in Abylay than in other cities. Setsea's capital had more important things to worry about than a rowshatar stubbing his toe, like spreading Orvashka's Ways across the country and into others, whether they wanted it or not. Advocates couldn't be bothered with every incident. But considering rowshatari were crucial to the survival of Abylay's way of life…Something was amiss. Isesh, who lounged outside in the twilight, had cautioned her about seeing something that wasn't there, but he hadn't denied the situation's peculiarity.

"It sets a bad precedent," Jaleya said.

"True, true," Yongir relented. "We will treasure it discreetly and entertain it in our minds only."

Fusi said, "You did well holding back your…instincts as long as you did. I'm surprised it didn't happen sooner. One day with him was enough for me."

"He was your charge?" Jaleya asked.

"Only on a rotating basis." Fusi shifted in Gevruz's arms so she could meet his eyes. "Other javati did not have the pleasure."

"It felt like I did, hearing you complain about the assignment," Gevruz said.

"I thought the other javati on the rotation were exaggerating. They weren't."

"Give him some sympathy. He's probably very mistrustful of javati right now."

"It's been over a month. The Ora remind everyone of our 'tendency to rebel' every opportunity they can. It shouldn't have been a surprise when it actually happened."

"The traitor had overstayed his assignment, too," Yongir added. "Whether it was clerical error, custodian error, or initiative on his part, in hindsight it seems indicative of nefarious activity."

"His custodian had nothing to do with it," Gevruz said. "If all custodians were like Custodian Saunez, life for the javati would be easier. You're fortunate in that regard," he told Jaleya.

She stared. "I'm fortunate to have Saunez as my custodian?"

Fusi laughed at Jaleya's incredulous expression. "Oh, she's a horrible person, but she does her job well and lets us do ours without hovering over your shoulder like the noon sun, unlike my custodian who has soldiers chase me down if one thing I say doesn't match my reports."

"Or custodians who thinks they have more power than they actually do," added Gevruz.

Fusi nodded and downed the rest of her beer. "I'm turning in. I have an overzealous rowshatar-mara to keep track of tomorrow."

"You enjoy it when she mutters about her visions," Gevruz said, rising with Fusi.

"Knowing what futures the Ora might pursue is valuable information. But having to acquire that information from inane mumbling is enough to drive me insane."

"You like being the source of gossip too much to stop listening,"

Gevruz said as they turned away. Fusi's response was lost in an outcry from the card table. The javati of the cockatrice pointed a threatening finger at the reptile-chicken hybrid, who was perched on a sirrush's head, its co-conspirator. The cockatrice puffed its chest proudly.

"The life of a javati," Yongir reflected.

No one approached to take the vacant space on the bench, so Jaleya turned her focus to the reason she had sought out Yongir. "The traitor you spoke of, my charge's former guardian. Was my charge just as…unruly with him?" A rowshatar without an inflated ego was like Isesh not shedding; a wonderful thought, but a fantasy. However, there were degrees of shedding.

"Your charge was always a handful," Yongir said, "but while the traitor was assigned to him, he seemed somewhat tempered. He's making up for it now, eh?"

"At least it's not all because he doesn't like me," Jaleya said lightheartedly, but her mind wandered to her situation's peculiarity. Adding Teza's traitorous guardian made it even odder that the incident in the city hadn't received more scrutiny. Orvashka's Ways did not wipe clean one's association with a traitor, even though they claimed otherwise.

"How did Rowshatar Teza discover him?" Jaleya asked.

"Why so curious?" Yongir said. "It doesn't matter how traitors are exposed, only that they are. A traitor is a traitor." He recited the idiom like a model Setsean, but his eyes were downcast. He swallowed a generous portion from his mug.

"Of course," Jaleya said, treading carefully. "But if there's anything I can do to soothe my charge's distrust of javati, I would know of it. And…it makes me sad when javati fall prey to their fashari's corruption and reject what the Ora have given us." She could have choked on those words. "I muse on how I could have prevented it."

Yongir considered for a moment as he ate his bulgur and

flatbread. When he spoke without suspicion, Jaleya could have sagged in relief.

"Gardok was an upstanding citizen and master of his fashari. His one failing was his impressionability. Tales of my caravan journeys fascinated him, and he often wondered what life would be like if we didn't serve the rowshatari. Perhaps he…*mused* farther than he should have."

"We should both be careful with our musings, then," Jaleya said.

Yongir gave her a fond, conspiratorial smile as he lifted his mug to his lips. He hid it well, but Jaleya recognized the light in his eyes when he spoke of traveling across Setsea and the parroting undertone when he recited the Ways' dogma.

Yongir regarded Jaleya over the rim of his mug and covertly glanced around the mess hall. Satisfied no one was listening, he slid his earthen plate toward Jaleya. Only a few bites of bulgur and a strip of flatbread remained.

"Details are expectedly sparse, but we do know the traitor's fashari was killed when he resisted arrest." Yongir spoke in a quiet voice, his lips hardly moving between sips from his mug. Jaleya began eating the remains of food on Yongir's plate as slowly as possible. She knew he would stop speaking the second the plate was empty, and there were barely two mouthfuls.

"The madness took him almost immediately," Yongir continued, "but its quick arrival proved to be a mercy, as his questioning was cut short."

Only one fate awaited traitors: death by means of sacrifice to Orvashka. The lucky ones were taken to Harmony Tower and killed immediately. The unlucky ones were put on display and executed in front of a cheering crowd. The poor souls given to the shavinashi for questioning died the moment they were condemned; it was just a matter of time before their bodies stopped clinging to life.

"In-between jumping and hollering at 'voices,' he professed his innocence until he was returned to Orvashka," Yongir said. "It was almost certainly a result of the madness, but if not, did he reach that conclusion on his own or was he encouraged?"

Jaleya began ripping apart the flatbread and chewed pieces no larger than her fingertips until her teeth ground together.

"Overstaying his assignment alone wouldn't mark him as a traitor, but expressing his reveries to someone with power? The resulting change, though subtle, would be noticed by a close, attentive person, and that person would quickly deal with the dissent once its origin was ascertained."

Jaleya skimmed her fingers for more flatbread, but even the crumbs were gone. Yongir reclaimed the empty plate, and hesitated.

"I like to pretend there was a reason for the traitor's foolishness; perhaps others who were just as fanciful, and he couldn't help but be caught up in it. However, fancies are rarely as grand or as satisfying in reality, and silent musings that comfort will betray you once spoken."

Yongir collected the empty dinnerware and stood. "Welcome to Abylay."

Jaleya remained at the table for a moment, pondering Yongir's theory: Gardok rebelled against the Ora and began opening Teza's eyes to his gilded prison, hence the agreeable behavior, but Custodian Saunez discovered what was happening and exposed him. She might have kept Gardok in Abylay past his assignment's end so she could confirm her suspicions. Horrible woman. Typical Illuminated. What part had Teza played? The way Yongir described it, Teza had been…innocent. That couldn't be right.

Jaleya passed beneath the arches to the courtyard. The lifeless kaza lanterns and the setting sun cast long shadows over the compound. Jaleya located the one belonging to her javati as javash directed her steps. Isesh lay in the corner of an upper walkway, his paws hanging over the edge. His feathered neck was erect, his canine ears alert. Instead of the stairwell's long way around, Jaleya utilized the arcade to ascend to the walkway. She settled beside her javati and swung her legs over the wall.

The Schism opens, Isesh sent.

They couldn't see the giant rift that absorbed the world's kaza, but if she concentrated, Jaleya could feel it. A buzzing in her blood, a heaviness to the north. The Schism revealed itself this night, spewing forth the only new crystals able to be cut into gems the rowshatari could infuse and replenish, as the Schism had robbed all other precious stones of their natural ability to replenish, vahl-keshi being the only exception. Jaleya had never seen the Schism, but she knew what a rift looked like, and she had heard enough descriptions of the colossal vortex to imagine its might.

She thought it odd that she was aware of it at such a distance, when she focused, and the rowshatari were not. She credited it to javash, as fashari were mindful of its opening. All around her and Isesh, silhouettes sat, perched, curled, hung, and lay among Iza Vor's domes and towers, curious sculptures in the twilight. They all faced north, toward the Sojourn Mountains.

It's early this month, Jaleya sent. When she had asked Isesh why the fashari observed the Schism's opening in mournful vigil, he had replied, *It reminds us of our oath to watch, guide, and protect.* Isesh didn't keep secrets from her. There were instances when he explicitly told her he wouldn't discuss something, mostly when the topic involved the fashari, but he never evaded her. Jaleya didn't want to sew distrust into their javash, even if it was just for cards.

It remains within its cycle, Isesh sent.

The Schism's opening couldn't be predicted with absolute accuracy, but one could determine the week. There would be no Schism games otherwise.

As the sky darkened, Jaleya told Isesh about her conversation with Yongir. *What if he's right? What if Gardok didn't rebel on his own? The resistance could be here.*

She could be one step closer to fulfilling her revenge and purging Setsea of the Ora. Finally. Now she just had to find the resistance.

It is a possibility, Isesh sent. *Abylay would provide an uprising with abundant and much-needed resources. However, Abylay also houses the most ardent Illuminated, as Gardok discovered the hard way, provided Yongir's speculation is accurate, which we have far from confirmed.*

Maybe that's their con! Jaleya sent, the pieces clicking into place in her mind. *Teza pretends to be a faithful but naïve Illuminated to lure resistance members into complacency, and then Saunez reports them.*

Exposing those who question Orvashka's Ways is a vocation of all Setsean citizens, Isesh sent, *and Teza's behavior, regrettably, contains the consistency of authenticity.*

Jaleya's shoulders drooped, her proudly deciphered conspiracy snapping apart. Admittedly, the pieces had been forced to fit.

You're right, Jaleya sent. *That's giving Teza way too much credit.*

What was his role, then? What advantage did Saunez gain by downplaying Teza's disobedience and attempted snatching? If custodians allowed their rowshatari to become disloyal, they would be lucky if they only ended up west of the Nidren. If Jaleya hadn't been contemplating Illuminated, it would seem like Custodian Saunez was protecting Teza, shielding him from scrutiny, from attention that could turn him into the living dead. Maybe Saunez's profit had something to do with her and Teza's odd relationship. Were they a...couple? Even if that had been permitted, Jaleya couldn't make that thought fully form. It felt so, so wrong.

We need to find out what they're up to, she sent.

Your desire to soothe your injured pride could place us in a precarious position, Isesh sent.

This isn't about me, Jaleya replied more defensively than she intended. *We could already be in a precarious position. Something is going on, and if we don't find out what, we won't know if we're in danger or not.*

That is a valid point, but have we been in Abylay long enough to make that judgment?

It felt like they had been there forever. It had only been a little over a week.

Saunez is up to something, Jaleya insisted. She wasn't going to be a pawn in whatever web the custodian was weaving. That woman knew her opponent's moves three in advance and had a counter to every one, but she wasn't the only one who could read between the lines. It would be good for her to be knocked down a few pegs; Teza, too. Jaleya would beat them both at their own game.

They lingered a few minutes more, and then made their way to Teza's quarters. Jaleya's free time was over. When they arrived at the lavish double doors, the two guards standing post crossed their spears.

"Apologies, guardian," one said. "Rowshatar Teza is receiving an intarish, and they are not to be disturbed."

"I don't want to disturb them," Jaleya assured him. "But my quarters are in there too, and I need to sleep. Look at it this way: I'm back on duty, which means you have less to worry about. You'll have even more to not worry about if we're within."

The guards considered, exchanging glances and raised brows.

"Or I can bypass the guards on the balcony and enter that way," Jaleya said. Isesh flexed his wings.

Realizing they wouldn't be able to stop her—wouldn't be able to stop Isesh—the guards allowed her entrance. Teza and the intarish were thankfully not in the sitting room. Getting any rest with them making love on the chaise would be a lost cause. Teza seemed like a loud one, and so the intarish would be louder.

Jaleya paused in the middle of the room, looked to the drawn curtain concealing Teza's bedchamber.

Jaleya? Isesh sent from the archway to their quarters.

Does it seem too quiet to you? Jaleya replied. Javash enhanced her senses, but Isesh's were still superior.

Isesh scrunched his hybrid features into a very human expression. *I'd rather not speculate on our charge's sexual activity.*

Jaleya blanched at the thought. That was the last thing she wanted crossing her mind! But it *was* too quiet. She crept to the curtain, her boots silent on the stone. She tilted her ear to the thick silk. No creaking wood, no moans of ecstasy, not even voices. Teza wouldn't spend his limited time with an intarish simply enjoying her company. An intarish didn't come for that. A quick check confirmed the guards on the balcony weren't alarmed, and the guards at the door hadn't been either. Jaleya heard a creak and a shuffle of movement within, like a person changing position. Someone was in there.

Don't disturb them, Isesh sent, venturing closer. *An intarish wouldn't risk the destruction of her sanctuary and the death of her sisters and brothers for the elimination of a single rowshatar. She would receive greater profit from reporting the conspirator to the Counselors.* Isesh sniffed the curtain's border. *There's no death in that room.*

Jaleya hesitated.

Jaleya—

Something isn't right, Isesh.

—I sense kaza.

What?

Stars sway was weeks away. Teza couldn't access kaza, and he was forbidden seals unless supervised by a keeper. The keepers never let the cylinder seals entrusted to them out of their sight and were prohibited from distributing them without orders. Intarishi acquired seals through contacts, favors, and bribes, but they would be foolish to bring one into Iza Vor, as they were not officially permitted to possess them.

I sense kaza, Isesh repeated, his feathers bristling. *It's very faint, but it's there.*

You're sure it's not from the lanterns? Jaleya could smell Isesh's wet fur hours after the top layer dried, but javash hadn't granted her the simurgh's ability to distinguish subtle kaza sources.

Isesh huffed at her suggestion.

All right, then, Jaleya sent.

She drew her scimitar, tore back the curtain, and rushed inside, Isesh covering her flank. The intarish lay on the gilded four-poster bed. Her dark, unbound tresses cascaded over her refined shoulders to the curve of her hips. Her magenta and green dress glorified the female form and teased pleasures no mere commoner would ever know.

In her delicate hands she held a book.

Jaleya blinked, straightened, reassessing the situation. Teza was nowhere to be seen. Isesh reported he wasn't in the inner rooms either.

"Where's Rowshatar Teza?" Jaleya asked the woman.

The intarish regarded her and Isesh with painted eyes of disdain. She seemed insulted they had so rudely interrupted her reading.

Jaleya sheathed her scimitar. "You're not going to tell me anything, are you?"

The woman curved the corner of her lips, somehow making even that small gesture sensual and alluring. Intarishi held their patrons in the strictest confidence. But in this case, who was the real patron? Teza couldn't use the privy without permission. He wouldn't have been able to get his hands on a rift seal without aid.

"Give my regards to Custodian Saunez," Jaleya said.

The woman's shrewd smile didn't falter. Jaleya left her to her book.

"Don't forget your place, guardian," the intarish said, her eyes focused on the leather-bound tome. Even her voice was sultry sexuality; she made "guardian" sound like "peasant." Jaleya drew the curtain.

Do you think we should tell the guards? she sent.

I think we do not know enough to safely make that decision, Isesh replied. *All is calm here. Perhaps Gardok was condemned not because he was resistance, but because he discovered and openly spoke of condoned illicitness. Teza could be more astute than we believe and might have devised this disappearance with the intarish.*

That's unlikely, Jaleya sent.

But not out of the realm of possibility, Isesh countered.

Jaleya considered their next move. The situation did appear to be one of intentional ignorance on the guards' part. Maintaining the façade the intarish was helping perpetrate would be easy with collaborators always posted outside when she was present. That could be arranged, but as far as Jaleya knew, custodians had no say in the guards' rotation, and every accomplice was a potential report to the Counselors. Not intentional ignorance, then; the regular kind. The guards assumed Teza and the intarish were climaxing in his bedchamber. As if on cue, moans of pleasure began emanating from behind the curtain, wood rocking to the intarish's rhythm.

Let's take a walk, Jaleya sent. *I told you they were up to something.*

She didn't believe for a second that Saunez was uninvolved, especially since custodians managed intarish proposals. The unknown in this subterfuge was the rift seal that had let Teza off the lead rope. Where had he acquired it? The intarish? A foolish risk for little reward. Custodian Saunez? Most likely, but she would be arrested if found in possession of a seal. An unidentified third party?

The guards wore superior grins as Jaleya and Isesh exited Teza's quarters. Let them think what they may. It was the perfect cover.

Where would he go? Jaleya pondered as they walked down the corridor. Isesh tried picking up Teza's scent, but the trails were stale.

He can't rift beyond Iza Vor's shield, so he has to be somewhere in the citadel, Isesh sent.

Unless he decided to take another stroll into Abylay, Jaleya sent.

He would've been stopped at the gate. Iza Vor's soldiers know rowshatari don't always bear the appearance of one.

They paused at an intersection. Through a window, Jaleya could see the dome of Iza Vor's library. The other direction led to the training grounds. Teza wanted to advance his veering skills. Maybe he knew a secluded spot to do just that. His rift seal couldn't be very powerful since Isesh hadn't sensed its kaza until he had been right next to Teza's bedchamber, but it was all they had to go on.

As they traversed the corridors, Isesh sniffed the air and stone every so often, trying to catch their charge's freshest scent. By the time they reached the training grounds, Jaleya was certain they wouldn't find Teza there. Isesh would have located a trace. They searched anyway; it didn't take long. The training rings were empty except for a group of sparring javati.

Let's try the library, Jaleya sent.

Why do you think he would be there? Isesh asked. Teza could visit any time he wanted. They had accompanied him more than once as he spent hours pouring over approved tomes.

Jaleya couldn't explain it, but the library's dome caressed her mind like a fair breeze.

Call it a hunch, she sent.

The library was mostly empty when they arrived; it would be closed within the hour. The lingering patrons studied books in cubicles or asked the scholars to reserve their selections for tomorrow. A remshir was speaking to the scholar at the entrance counter, allowing Jaleya and Isesh to slip past without being bothered. The library was open to anyone within Iza Vor, but finding what one sought in the rows of unlabeled shelves that spanned three stories would take days. The fastest way to get a book in one's hands was to employ the help of the scholars, as they had every aisle, row, and shelf memorized. One would have the requested materials in minutes. The scholars would also know exactly what one was researching, which was the point.

Fortunately, Jaleya and Isesh weren't looking for bound paper. Isesh started sniffing the moment they lost sight of the entrance counter, and he caught a whiff of Teza's preferred perfume: mint and lemon with a hint of saffron. It was faint, but it was fresh. What was Teza doing here?

Jaleya followed Isesh deeper into the library. They paused when they reached a narrow archway in a secluded corner. After confirming no one was around to question them, they went through to a short hallway crammed with shelves piled high with dusty tomes and scrolls.

A single sun kaza lantern hung from a hook on the plain brick walls. There were no windows. Situated between two sections of the library, the nook was probably an overflow space or where less-requested books were housed.

They rounded a rickety shelf, and found thick bars blocking their path. A cylinder seal secured the gate's latch.

He's in there? Jaleya sent.

Yes. Isesh sounded surprised. Jaleya was annoyed.

She marched to the seal lock and threw back the hood. She examined the potently glowing deep-blue gem and the depictions to no avail. The intricacies of cylinder seals were not her forte. The seal was keeping the gate locked, and without its key, it would remain locked. Shattering the gem—a sapphire!—was out of the question. The kaza blast would take the whole archway with it, bars, bricks, and her and Isesh.

Jaleya, Isesh cautioned.

Jaleya stepped back, glaring at the cylinder seal. *Why do they need a sapphire seal in a library?* she sent.

To contain information the Ora deem unsuitable for the people, Isesh replied. *Sometimes the best hiding place is in plain sight.*

What kind of information do you think is in there? Jaleya sent.

The kind that is less sky-shattering than you hope. It's here instead of Harmony Tower, and it must not be shielded since Teza rifted inside; his scent originates within. What I wonder is why there's no guard.

You just said they're hiding whatever is back there in plain sight, Jaleya sent.

They could easily explain a soldier's presence: the seal requires safeguarding and is in use because the books beyond the gate are old and must be handled with the utmost care, therefore special requests are required to view them.

Jaleya hated when her javati was so reasonable.

We should leave, Isesh sent.

What about Teza?

Unless you have a rift seal, and you've learned to use it, we're not getting in there. The longer we remain, the more likely our presence will be detected. Despite the pretense, I doubt the scholars would be pleased to discover us here. Custodian Saunez would be especially displeased.

Saunez's name rang like a challenge in Jaleya's mind. Teza was in a forbidden area of the library, having rifted with a cylinder seal of pathetic power that had been provided by persons unknown. What game were they playing?

Jaleya eyed the sapphire glowing in its seal. *We don't need to rift,* she sent. *We just need obsidian.*

CHAPTER 15

Jaleya could have invented a legitimate reason for requesting obsidian, but she didn't want to submit the mountain of paperwork and endure the interviews just to be denied, which she would be despite javati technically being able to borrow small quantities of obsidian if it helped protect the rowshatari. Then there was the paper trail to consider. It was better if that didn't exist.

Jaleya hadn't established contacts in Abylay, so she asked Yongir if he knew where she might acquire the kaza-negating stone. Even though she liked and trusted Yongir, she withheld as much information as possible. This was still Abylay. With a knowing eye, Yongir didn't ask questions and told her he could arrange a meeting. She nearly choked on the price. Fortunately, Yongir's contact was willing to barter. Teza's extravagance was going to be beneficial for once. He wouldn't notice the perfume bottles were emptier than they should be; the wine that was too watered would be blamed on the merchants; and subtle—maybe not so subtle in Teza's case—comments would deliver delicacies right into Jaleya's hands. Adding her weekly stipend, Jaleya could come up with the payment. Barely.

Are you sure you want to proceed down this path? Isesh asked later that day as Teza feasted on rosewater bulgur, roasted quail, bread served with cheese and jam, pickled vegetables, and a yogurt and pomegranate salad. Servants waited in the corner of the private dining room. Jaleya stood at attention behind Teza's chair while Isesh kept watch by the oriel window.

Teza and Saunez are up to something, Jaleya sent.

That may be, Isesh sent, *but schemes and plots abound from Abylay to the smallest village. Don't let your juvenile motivations propel us into a situation where you cannot bear the consequences.*

Jaleya replied gently but firmly. *Don't let your fear of Lizuna's condition propel you into a hole. I won't allow it to happen.*

They had finally met Yongir's javati: a pegasus with a gleaming black coat. Her mind was muddled and hazy. She had forgotten too much of herself. Isesh grieved for the lost fashari.

Lizuna's condition can occur naturally, although rarely, Isesh sent. *Most often it results from ignorance or abuse of javash.*

You think Yongir did that to her intentionally? Jaleya sent, aghast.

I've made no conclusions. Yongir's affection for Lizuna appears legitimate, but he has no obligation to divulge the intimacies of their javash. We can't dismiss intentionality as a possibility.

Yongir wouldn't do that.

Do we know him well enough to make that judgment?

Teza slurped the glaze off a quail leg and tossed the bone aside. Isesh gave the discarded scraps a mere glance.

He's helping us get the obsidian, Jaleya reminded her javati.

Yes, but why? Isesh sent.

He wants to know the truth about Gardok, and Saunez and Teza are the only lead.

Since Yongir was frequently away from Iza Vor, any investigating on his part would draw suspicion. He hadn't asked Jaleya to fill that gap, but they were both hungry for answers. Javati stuck together.

A qilin told me a storm is stirring, Isesh sent.

Does it involve us? Jaleya asked.

He couldn't say either way, so as to not influence the future. However, revealing its approach suggests that it may, or if we aren't careful, we may find ourselves caught up in a whirlwind we are not prepared for.

The qilin's warning made Jaleya hesitate. She could leave Saunez and Teza to their game; she wouldn't be ensnared. She could pretend to be the dutiful, oblivious guardian they expected her to be. But what if not acting landed her and Isesh in the future the qilin sensed? What if Gardok had found the spark that could obliterate the Ora? They all needed to pay.

Teza stood and ordered the servants to clear away the remaining food. He wandered into the corridor as he munched on jam-covered flatbread.

No one noticed when a wine bottle vanished.

A few days later, that wine and other forms of payment changed hands, and Jaleya left a dark alley with a cutting of obsidian that could overcome the library's sapphire seal. She kept a sharp eye out for spies, but the shadows remained still. Isesh's concerns, however outlandish, should never be dismissed out of hand, even when they proved unfounded.

*   *   *

Teza's next engagement with an intarish coincided with Jaleya's free time. Not a coincidence. Saunez and Teza were definitely hiding something.

Jaleya and Isesh returned to the library midway through Teza's supposed lovemaking. They took the long way around and avoided any place rowshatari lingered so they wouldn't sense the obsidian's void. Evading the scholars' attention, they crept into the overflow room. No guard stood post this time either, although one had been present when Jaleya had scouted for opportunities to bypass the sapphire.

He's in there, right? Jaleya asked.

Isesh confirmed their charge's scent was fresh beyond the locked gate. Jaleya withdrew the obsidian and approached the cylinder seal. The sapphire set within began to flicker, its light pulsing erratically. She brought the obsidian beside the seal, and the sapphire went dim with a futile sputter. Jaleya pocketed the dark stone and released the lock. The gate swung inward on well-oiled hinges.

Jaleya and Isesh entered the forbidden space, closing the gate behind them but not locking it. They needed to circumvent the seal, not dull it. The sapphire was already flickering back to life.

Isesh sniffed the stale tomes and aged wood as they traversed the shelves crammed with brittle, flaking scrolls and spines peeling from their binding, their titles faded. The poor lighting and plain walls were reminiscent of a storage closet, but the lack of cobwebs indicated the state of decay was due to age, not neglect. Their passing left no footprints on the uneven brick floor.

Seeing no guards, and Isesh smelling none, they crossed the narrow aisle and followed the far wall until it gave way to nooks with cracked, desiccated tables. Teza occupied the furthest one. A kaza lantern illuminated the old tomes before him as he scribbled on wrinkled paper.

"You're supposed to be pleasuring the intarish in your bed-chamber," Jaleya said.

Teza jumped in his seat, and the wobbly chair toppled sideways, taking him with it. Jaleya contained her laughter to a smirk. If Teza had had access to kaza, he would have sensed the obsidian's void long before they reached his nook.

"What are you doing here?" Teza said.

"I'm perusing the library in my free time," Jaleya said.

"How did you get in here?"

"Special requests. How did you get in here?"

Teza's hand leapt to an inner pocket of his kaftan. "I have p-permission to be here," he stammered. "I order you t-to leave."

Jaleya seized Teza's arm, twisted it around his back, and relieved him of his rift seal. She held it before her, careful to conceal the ametrine the obsidian was cancelling out; the less Teza questioned her presence in this forbidden archive, the better.

"If you had permission to be here, you would've used the door," Jaleya said.

Teza paled, his dark eyes darting about in panic. Jaleya subtly passed the obsidian to Isesh, who wandered away from the nook. The dark stone would dull the ametrine, trapping Teza in the archive and paving the way for lots of dangerous questions.

"What are you doing in here?" Jaleya asked.

Surprisingly, Teza kept his mouth shut.

Jaleya snatched the paper he'd been inscribing.

"Don't—! Be careful," Teza said.

Jaleya skimmed the writing on one side, then turned it over and found more writing on the back. It was all related to the history of the rowshatari, specifically their accomplishments and abilities. She pulled one of the open books closer. Beyond the fact that it was text, she couldn't make heads or tails of it. Certain symbols looked familiar, but nothing she could comprehend.

"You're translating," she said.

Teza paled even more, a breathing corpse.

Trusting a hunch, Jaleya took a stab in the dark. "You're translating Old Setsean."

"I don't speak it," Teza said much too quickly. "Only the Ora are harmonized sufficiently with Orvashka to speak it."

A loophole, Isesh commented as he returned.

One he probably didn't come up with himself, Jaleya replied. *He looks like a guilty child when he lies.*

"I b-barely understand it," Teza continued. "Just the basics. The idea of a sentence, not w-word for word."

Honesty is a virtue, Isesh sent.

So is staying alive, Jaleya sent.

She took another glance at the translation in her hands. "I think the basics serve you well."

Teza's shoulders slumped. "Please don't tell Saunez."

Saunez? Not Custodian Saunez? The lack of her title prickled Jaleya's ears, but Teza believing Saunez was unaware of his clandestine rifts to a forbidden archive sent her mind racing. A third party *was* involved, and was probably the source of the rift seal.

"Do you hear me scolding you?" Jaleya said.

Teza hesitated. "No?"

Jaleya offered the translation. Teza accepted it carefully, as if it was a viper.

"You know Old Setsean," Jaleya said, surprised despite herself. "Who taught you?"

His features miserable, Teza said, "No one. Modern Setsean is descended from its old form, and with the records here and the offering ceremonies, I…filled in the gaps."

Jaleya regarded the open books. "*Why* are you translating?"

He mumbled something indiscernible, even to her ears. Isesh's peaked in interest.

"Speak up," Jaleya ordered.

"Rowshatari," Teza said.

Jaleya kept her confusion from her face. He *was* a rowshatar. He also seemed to think that explanation was enough, as he didn't continue. Jaleya let the uncomfortable silence build, wishing she could raise her eyebrow to uncharted heights like Saunez.

"What they could do," Teza blurted. "What they built. The Dazmiri, the skimmers, kaza weapons—even though weapons are hateful—the rift lanes in Parvasahalis, the oases in the desert. They could cross mountains in a blink, move stone with just their minds, create structures we can't comprehend. Rowshatari-estra could *fly*! When the Ora close the Schism, all those things will be possible again. We could make those wonders, revive them, see them new in our present, not as remnants of the past. They're not just stories. They did do it. It is possible."

"You're trying to find *how* they did it," Jaleya said.

Teza's passion waned as the size of his undertaking reared its ugly head. "Trying, and having little success." He gazed hungrily at the shelves filled with brittle scrolls and old tomes.

Teza could be manipulating her, concealing an ulterior motive. But he really was horrible at deception. The excitement that brightened his eyes had been…innocent. Sincere.

"We won't keep you, then," Jaleya said. "What a rowshatar does with an intarish is between them, and rowshatari have no interest in what their guardians do during their free time."

Teza stared at her in confusion, so she raised her brow meaningfully. Comprehension finally dawned.

"Oh! Yes, I am with the intarish, and you were not in the old archive, not that I would know that because I was with the intarish."

Amazed at his denseness, Jaleya placed the rift seal on the dilapidated table. The ametrine still glowed. Good. She turned to leave.

"You're really not going to tell Saunez?" Teza said, his voice caught between confusion and hope.

"She won't hear about this from me," Jaleya said.

"But…guardians are supposed to report their rowshatar's misconduct."

"I don't recall any misconduct while I was on duty. I can't speak for your actions when you're in the care of others." A slim argument worthy of Saunez.

Jaleya lingered a moment more to confirm Teza understood their silent agreement. Any mention from either of them that the other had been in this forbidden archive would expose both of them. Teza's benefactors would learn of her presence due to his inability to mix words, but when she remained silent, they would feign ignorance. Another problematic guardian so soon after Gardok would invite unwelcome scrutiny.

When Jaleya was as confident as she could be, she left her charge to his translations. She retrieved the obsidian from where Isesh had stashed it, went through the gate, and locked it. The sapphire's glow returned as the dark stone left its proximity.

I fear Teza is being used, Isesh sent.

The lost arts are the bait, and while he pursues them, his benefactors hope he'll stumble upon what they seek, Jaleya agreed. Whatever they were after, it had to be important to risk smuggling a cylinder seal, hiring an intarish for cover, keeping the library guard away, and letting a rowshatar study forbidden information. Rediscovering lost arts for the sake of rediscovering them seemed to be Teza's only goal.

Where do you think the rift seal came from? Jaleya sent. *Saunez wouldn't directly involve herself with something that could lead back to her so easily.*

We know one other person who is a constant in our charge's life, Isesh sent.

Jaleya searched her brain for whom Isesh referred to as they left the library behind.

Seal Keeper Firnak? she sent.

Seal Keeper Firnak, Isesh confirmed. *No one would question his presence in Iza Vor.*

What's in it for him? Jaleya sent.

I've heard rumors that Seal Keeper Firnak is a Rifter. Perhaps he seeks verification of the secrets he believes are contained within rift passages.

And if you really can see the Schism circling the word within the passages, as the Rifters believe, Jaleya sent, *that could potentially aid the Ora and give Seal Keeper Firnak a lot of commendations. What a mess.*

You have no one to blame but yourself for stepping in it, Isesh sent.

They arrived at Teza's quarters just as Teza and the intarish emerged from his bedchamber. Teza avoided eye contact like the guilty, but the intarish bid him goodnight with a leisurely kiss. She glided past Jaleya and Isesh as if they didn't exist.

Teza scurried back to his bedchamber and drew the curtain. Isesh wandered to their accommodations, ready to retire. He paused when he noticed Jaleya wasn't following.

I'll be right back, Jaleya sent.

Be careful, Isesh cautioned.

Jaleya navigated the corridors on an intercept course and caught up with the intarish as the woman turned down an arcade that bordered a garden. Jaleya carefully peered around the corner.

The intarish maintained her elegant stroll, but at one of the flowerpots resting beneath the arches, her hand brushed to the side and dropped something within it. The motion was so subtle it would have been imperceptible to someone who wasn't watching for it.

Jaleya froze in indecision. Follow the intarish, or see who came for what she had deposited in the urn?

The intarish turned down another corridor and was lost to sight. Jaleya hesitated a second more, glancing at the flowerpot where she assumed the rift seal now lay, and then hurried after the intarish. She trailed her to a secluded courtyard lit with kaza lanterns. The dead light cast deep shadows beneath the arcade. From those shadows a figure emerged. The intarish paused, and soft words were exchanged. Jaleya couldn't discern what was said (Isesh would have been able to), but their composed postures and polite tones signified someone reporting to a superior, or the real patron.

A small pouch—the payment—passed between them, and after a moment of friendly banter, the intarish continued on her way toward the nearest gate. Jaleya couldn't pierce the shadows' depths to identity the other person, but based on height, build, and tone of voice, the intarish was working for a woman. Jaleya had a deep suspicion she knew which woman. The intarish's patron finally turned, and a ray of lantern light illuminated Saunez's proud profile.

Suspicion confirmed, Jaleya hurried back to the flowerpot. She arrived just in time to witness Seal Keeper Firnak disappear into the garden. Another suspicion confirmed.

The seal keeper must have enticed the intarish to carry the rift seal to and from the drop point. The intarish, seeing the profit in it for herself, had reported the seal keeper's treacherous proposal to Saunez, not Iza Vor's guards. Since Saunez was the one who hired the intarish, their dealings could be said to fall under patron-intarish confidentiality. Seal Keeper Firnak was manipulating Teza only because Saunez allowed it. What was Saunez after in the forbidden archive? Or was the scheme just a way to ensure her unruly rowshatar remained under her control?

Her unruly, ignorant, oblivious rowshatar who would rather study old books than make love with an intarish. The rowshatar who lit with joy and passion at the wonders the world had forgotten.

Jaleya shook her head. What a mess indeed.

CHAPTER 16

Kyzum slowly took the stairs to the main deck. Two feet on each board. Backward a few times. He emerged beneath a cloud-covered sky with a slit of moon. He pulled his cloak tighter. They were descending, but the air still had bite. Kyzum cursed whatever god had thought cold was a good idea.

Ameara didn't seem affected by it. She wore a cloak, but it flapped freely in the wind. She apparently had no interest in securing it, and why would she? Ameara had been born with the sea in her blood, and the winds renewed the waters she had claimed as her own. She sat on the helm in front of the wheel, which made minute independent adjustments. Kyzum's friend and captain wasn't navigating, but she stared ahead as if she was, deep in thought.

"I heard you found something interesting in the shavinash's possessions," he said.

"It has no bearing on our shashvin problem," Ameara said. "It's insignificant."

"Anything that makes my captain freeze is not insignificant."

"I don't freeze."

"Flinched."

"I don't flinch."

"Surprised. Everyone gets surprised."

Ameara breathed an ill-tempered sigh. "Who told you?"

"It was a collective effort."

Ameara gave him one of her I'm-acting-angry-but-no-one-is-really-in-trouble glares.

"Want to share?" Kyzum said.

Ameara ran her hand along the wooden wheel, which shifted toward her palm. A breath later, it readjusted. A silent communication between Ameara and her ship. In their many fights and frantic flights, they piloted as well as any javati, but it was in the mundane, quiet moments, the simple yet intimate gestures, that Ameara and her ship truly seemed as one, even though they weren't.

"When I was a child, before I ran away," Ameara said, "I would visit the Ryvekian merchants when they were in port not only because of their goods but because some of them were willing to teach me the sword; they thought it a cruel joke that I couldn't defend myself.

"A boy from town would accompany me. My mother disapproved of our sparring. She told me to respect my future position as an intarish, to be dignified and honorable, associate with the right people, not roll around in the muck and smash people's faces like an uncivilized brute."

"The more I hear about her, the more wonderful she sounds," Kyzum said sarcastically. Ameara had divulged tidbits of her childhood before, but she had failed to mention her friend in her previous telling.

"After my mother struck the deal with the magistrate, he encouraged his son to confirm I was an acceptable payment for elevating my mother's whore house to an intarish sanctuary."

Kyzum's ears tingled. The son was new information.

"The magistrate's son and his lackeys started harassing me, and one day it became violent. My friend witnessed it and came to my defense. One of the lackeys was killed. A shavinash took my friend the next day."

"There was nothing you could've done," Kyzum said gently, "not against a shavinash, not against a plot you were ignorant of."

"There was much I could have done," Ameara said. Her hard eyes and dark tone revealed there was more to the story, but if Kyzum pushed, she would lash out, and the significance of the flawed crystal would remain a mystery.

"That's why we keep picking up strays," Kyzum said. "It all makes sense now. You're trying to atone for not helping your friend."

Ameara glared at him; she hated when he referred to the crew as strays. "You were a stray, too."

"No, I was a stowaway."

"'Stowaway' means your presence was unknown. I saw you jump aboard. You're lucky I didn't throw you over the side and let the vengeful prince have you."

"I'm too charming to throw overboard."

"Your charm has never worked on me."

"Then why didn't you throw me over the side?"

"I was debating between that or cutting off your head, but then we had to run for our lives. I was less decisive back then."

"One thing you have never been, Ameara, is indecisive. That's why you needed my charm. Without me, people thought you were mean and scary."

A smile tugged Ameara's lips. "You have been useful."

The changing wind gathered Ameara's wavy locks and headband and blew them across her face. A meandering gleam lengthened below. The Tethmet Strait.

"How does the crystal fit in?" Kyzum asked.

"It was all I had to give him before the shavinash took him away," Ameara said. "An apology. I thought he was pursuing my future services, but there was no ulterior motive. He was…honest. Kind. My one true friend. And I let a shavinash take him."

Again the itch that Ameara wasn't telling the whole story.

Kyzum said, "You think our shavinash friend is your friend…? This is the part where you tell me his name."

Ameara hesitated, looking to the lengthening water below. "Dorian."

"You think our shavinash friend is your friend Dorian?"

"There are thousands of worthless crystals and gems in Idlium," Ameara said. "Hundreds of shavinashi. I haven't thought about that day in a long time. It surprised me," she concluded grudgingly.

True words, but empty nonetheless. Kyzum had softened Ameara's harder edges and honed her eyes and ears, but Ameara's mother had ingrained the foundations. Being an intarish was more than elegant appearance and pleasures of the flesh. Setting people aflame with a single look and implying everything while promising nothing required precision, skill, and wisdom of when to employ said skill. Despite Ameara having tried to purge her mother's influence, the foundations had remained, and Ameara had eventually conceded their value. Kyzum would have preferred Ameara *not* use those foundations to barter a deal with a shashvin, but what was done was done. She couldn't fool Kyzum, though. At least, not often. Only when she really wanted to. And he could still see through it. Probably.

Kyzum spoke gently. "Whoever this shavinash was before being coerced into their murderer guild, he is not that person now."

"I know that," Ameara said. "Dorian is long dead. He wasn't a killer. He danced circles around me more often than not when we sparred, but not a killer."

"Are you sure he didn't let you win due to emerging manhood?" Kyzum said.

Ameara scowled and hopped off her perch. "I'm going to check in with the crew. Mind the helm while we descend."

"You know I'm a horrible pilot," Kyzum said.

"You won't have to fly. Syra likes the company. And we have to keep up appearances."

"Aye, aye, Captain."

Kyzum leaned on the wheel as Ameara left the quarterdeck. She definitely wasn't telling him the whole story. Misjudging a friend who was taken by a shavinash was sure to affect a young girl, but not to the extent that said girl grew up to accumulate strays and let them live on her debatably stolen skyship. Letting a friend take the blame for someone's death…Ameara said her childhood friend had been honest, kind; probably the quiet type who knew the value of listening. Not a killer. And yet, a boy had ended up dead.

The wheel jerked, and Kyzum stumbled. He frowned at the wheel, which was course correcting. "That was uncalled for." Kyzum leaned against the helm instead. "Is this all right?"

The skyship didn't respond, of course. She could understand him, if she was listening, but she never touched his or the crew's minds. It did seem, at times, she knew what he was feeling, though, and translating emotions to thoughts was easier than people believed.

CHAPTER 17

Syra swayed to the strait's gentle rhythm as Ameara approached the brig. Ara was on watch. The young woman had cleared the shield seal and returned it to Syra's kaza flow; it would take time for Syra to replenish and reintegrate the restored seal, but a measure of protection was better than none. The Dazmir-vahl-kesh was no less anxious. Her sendings continually turned to the brig, as did Ameara's thoughts. The dual focus had become vexing, and Ameara had decided to confront the source of their disquiet. She would not run from a shavinash. The shame of her past would not rule her.

The shavinash's eyes were closed, as if he was meditating. Whatever his game was, he thought he had it all in hand. He might be right. He hadn't attempted to escape when they passed a portion of the strait where swimming to shore would have been possible if he drew on his etch. Surely the bloodshaping had recovered from Syra's kaza blast and the jolt from Ameara's pistol. Assuming the etch wasn't strong enough to free him would be their last mistake. What was he waiting for?

Ameara planted herself in front of him, arms relaxed at her sides but near her weapons. "Let's talk."

"I've disclosed what you must do," he said.

"I've never been good at taking orders. Tell me what your mission is or which cadre you belong to, and I'll reconsider your proposal."

"Forget our encounter and tell them nothing, or you will all die." It wasn't a threat. It was a fact.

"Because it won't turn out well for you if I reveal your failure," Ameara countered. "No other captain can claim she captured a shavinash."

"None living," the assassin said.

"Threatening to kill me and my crew when you haven't made a single escape attempt indicates you're not in a hurry to do so. You have unfinished business. I may be inclined to alter the narrative of our encounter if I had an adequate reason."

"You'll all live," the shavinash said.

"We'll all live after I hand you over."

"You won't."

"Such confidence. Indulge me. Why would your shashvin be more displeased with us than with you?"

"Why do you court annihilation?" the shavinash said. "The more you know, the more you'll have to forget."

"My memory isn't very sharp," Ameara said.

"I doubt that."

Ameara studied the bound but far from helpless assassin. A shavinash would gladly kill someone who knew too much, or was suspected of knowing too much. This shavinash's obsession with feigning ignorance implied her crew was walking the knife's edge of such a situation, but as Kyzum had noted, bargaining with victims was out of character for the trained murderers. Ameara's guard tightened. The water she treaded really was as deep as she feared, probably deeper. It didn't deter her from her intercept course with Whisper. She hadn't come to the brig looking for alternatives.

She hesitated, and then crouched to meet the shavinash's eyes. Blue eyes as cold and dead as the Wild Ice.

"You're right," Ameara said. "My memory is exceptional." She lifted her hand and dangled the flawed crystal from her finger. "This is an odd trinket for a shavinash to carry, much less conceal. It can't hold kaza. The most desperate merchant wouldn't try to sell it.

We weren't introduced until you tried to blow up my ship, but I swear I've seen it before. A long time ago. Where did you get it?"

She watched him for a reaction, a hint. *Anything.* He might as well have been a ship's figurehead.

"Forget, or die," he said.

Ameara could have punched him. But that would reveal he was getting to her. No amount of force would make him speak, and even though he assumed docility, he wouldn't accept the abuse.

"Does the name Dorian Dagrin mean anything to you?" she asked calmly.

Was that a flicker of recognition, or a trick of the light? Or was it the growing impression twisting her stomach that this wasn't their first encounter?

Syra pressed against her mind, but Ameara shut her out. She was close. She could feel it. That name fit him like a seal's gem.

"What about Ameara Osana?" she asked.

Something did stir in his eyes that time, but the ice claimed it before it could draw breath.

"Eclipse isn't your given name," the shavinash said.

Syra pressed against her mind again, urgent now. Ameara sent back that she was being careful and Syra didn't need to worry.

"Do either of those names mean anything to you?" she said.

"Should they?" the shavinash replied.

Yes, she thought they should.

Syra screamed as Nahzida's replenished rifle broke the night's silence. A muffled warning of, "Skimmers!" reached the brig, and running footsteps sounded on the deck above. A boom echoed, and Syra jerked from a heavy impact. Ameara toppled; Ara quickstepped to keep her footing.

"That was kaza," the young woman said.

Another bang rocked the ship, and a wave of Syra's fear rolled over Ameara.

"The shield won't hold if we're hit with more blasts like that," Ara said. "The ship's kaza is low."

Thumps sounded against the hull. They were being boarded.

"Stay here and make sure he doesn't escape," Ameara ordered.

"Captain, I think I'll be more use on the main deck."

Ameara lowered her voice. "If he gets loose, you have the best chance of stopping him. Do not let him escape."

The gems in Ara's seal bracelet brightened. "Yes, Captain."

Ameara hastened to the main deck, and ducked as a scimitar attempted to remove her head. She cut down her assailant and joined the fray. Nahzida, who had been on watch, provided cover from the quarterdeck, her rifle thundering and sparking with each shot. Kyzum dashed along the starboard gunwale severing the ropes attached to the hooks embedded in the wood. Obakwe engaged the intruders whose climbing was faster than Kyzum's cutting.

Another blast hit the skyship, and the failing shield shimmered. More grappling hooks bit into the port gunwale. Obakwe rushed to intercept their owners, leaving Ameara and Kyzum to deal with the starboard skimmer's remaining crew. Ameara parried two consecutive blows from an intruder, twisted, and slashed his belly. Nahzida's rifle split the night, and a woman rushing Ameara toppled to the deck with a spray of blood. Ameara thrust her sword into Kyzum's opponent's neck, and he toppled forward. Kyzum backpedaled and raised his long knives defensively. He lowered them upon recognizing Ameara.

"Three skimmers," he said. "Highly manned. Their hearts weren't powered; probably used sails to sneak up on us. One is hiding behind the stern and killing our shield."

Kyzum didn't ask, but Ameara heard his question: why hadn't Syra noticed their approach? The skimmers could have been eliminated before they became a threat; they were too close now to employ Syra's cannons.

Syra had noticed. Ameara had allowed the shavinash to distract her. She wouldn't let her crew pay for her lapse.

Ameara glanced beyond Syra's stern. A skimmer's silhouette, similar to a large skiff, was outlined by the stars' blaze and the crackling halo ringing the barrel of its cannon. If the skimmer was flying colors, Ameara couldn't see them. These were pirates or rebels; Vekrym had no reservations about attacking other Vekrym, but they would give a warning as a professional courtesy. They were heavily armed for rebels—a cannon in the hand of rebels?—but if galahi were allied with them, this rebellion might have more bite than its predecessors. Whoever they were, they were after something. One didn't bring a cannon to a fight unless one intended to use it. Replenishing its seal was not cheap.

Across the deck, Obakwe faltered as more interlopers climbed over the gunwale.

"Go help Obakwe," Ameara ordered, and Kyzum left her side. He and Obakwe were outnumbered, but with Nahzida overhead, they would manage. However, Nahzida's rifle, Obakwe's fighting prowess, and Kyzum's aptitude for always being where he was most needed in a scuffle meant nothing if the cannon defeated Syra's shield and blasted through the hull. Then they would be dead in the water and outnumbered. They had to take out that cannon.

Ameara extended her consciousness to Syra, a lifeline to help the Dazmir-vahl-kesh focus and overcome her fear, a familiar presence to spur her into action. Ameara was sorry she hadn't listened in the brig; Syra had performed beautifully. Ameara had a plan to expel the intruders, but she couldn't do it alone. She needed Syra's help.

Syra began to emerge from the recesses of her consciousness, but Ameara was forced to take a mental step back as she noticed three trespassers attempting to break into her quarters. Whisper's cargo was in there. Rebels after all?

Ameara abandoned the gunwale and crept behind the would-be thieves. She slit the throat of one before they realized she was there. Ameara knocked the second into the quarterdeck's stairs and ran him through as he faltered. The third intruder managed a few good parries before she slashed him across the thigh and chest.

Syra's scream reverberated through Ameara's mind as another

jolt shook the deck. The shield shimmered as it deflected the blast, and then peeled back with a whoosh. The shield was down. The next shot would tear through the hull.

Ameara sprinted starboard, calling to Syra. She knew the shield was gone, knew Syra was vulnerable. But Syra needed to listen to her right now. Ameara reached the gunwale and, without pause, leapt off the ship. Her momentum carried her upward for a moment, and then she began to fall. She called to Syra. *Listen! Now! Right now!*

A hairsbreadth from the water, Ameara felt the familiar pulling sensation and smelled crisp air.

She plopped onto wood to startled exclamations. She jumped to her feet and fired her pistol at the man who charged her. The lost art's thunder made the rest of the crew pause, and she took advantage of their hesitation. Pistol in one hand and sword in the other, she shot and stabbed her way to the cannon in the bow. The gunner's motions quickened as she neared; he was aiming for Syra's middle deck, where the heart was—where Syra was. Judging by the light leaking from the ill-fitting hood, the cannon's seal wasn't charged for a full blast, but it would still breach Syra's hull. Ameara dispatched the last crewmember as the gunner reached for the firing lever. Ameara pulled her pistol's trigger, and the concentrated kaza slammed the doomed gunner into the cannon. The skimmer was hers.

The gunner slid backward, and pulled the firing lever with his last breath.

A sphere of sun kaza soared toward Syra, toward Ameara's crew. Toward Ameara's home.

Clashing kaza lit the strait as Syra's weak shield dispersed the projectile. *Good girl,* Ameara thought, praising both Syra and Ara.

The momentary radiance revealed a fourth skimmer moored to Syra's stern. Where had that one come from? A series of grappling hooks and ropes created a makeshift ladder from the skimmer to the quarterdeck. Her crew had been flanked.

Anger eclipsed Ameara's relief. Did these people really think they could attack her crew and her ship and get away with it? Had they forgotten who she was? She would remind them.

Ameara threw back the cannon's hood and located its heart. The cylinder seal's gemstone pulsed slowly; it only retained one more shot. Or two small ones. Ameara aimed the cannon at the skimmer harassing Syra's stern, lowered the power output, and fired. The skimmer snapped in half, and the current eagerly devoured it. Ameara offered the depths the skimmer on the starboard side, too. Exclamations carried over the water. The intruders were realizing the tide had turned.

The cannon's heart fluttered feebly. Not enough kaza for her purpose. Ameara could fix that. She removed the sun-kaza seal from her pistol. That left her with just the dim star and dull moon ones, but so be it. The invaders would fall to her sword instead. A quick modification to the heart's mechanism, and the pistol seal was incompatibly inserted into its kaza flow.

Ameara swiveled the cannon toward the skimmer's stern and pulled the firing lever. The cannon heaved, choked, and began to vibrate. Angry red light burst from its heart. Ameara dove off the skimmer. The cold water engulfed her as the cannon exploded in a barrage of wood and metal.

*　　*　　*

Kyzum ducked as another man tried to kill him. Obakwe intercepted the man's blade on the backswing, and a tricky blow shattered his windpipe. Kyzum inwardly flinched because there was no time to physically flinch. Obakwe was quickly re-engaged, and Kyzum defended himself against a man who seemed much too eager for his blood considering they had never met. That was why Kyzum preferred words over swords, spears, staves, kaza-insert-dangerous-projectile-spewing-weapon-here, and anything else that administered an undignified end. It was so messy. Blood always left trails.

Kyzum slashed his attacker on the thigh, making him stumble, and he kicked him where no man should ever be kicked, dropping him to the deck and hopefully removing him from the fight. The next violence enthusiast instantly replaced him, but his attacks were tempered. None of the intruders were as eager as they had been upon initial engagement.

Kyzum could see their thoughts as expectations vied with reality. How could they be losing? They outnumbered the skyship's crew. Kyzum answered in his head because no one was doing him the favor of asking out loud: This was Eclipse's ship, and one did not attack Eclipse's ship lightly. Ever. And Nahzida's new contraption was proving more advantageous than her bow. He prayed it wouldn't explode.

Except…he hadn't heard the telling thunder from the quarterdeck after that quick succession a moment ago.

An impact rocked the ship, and the shield failed. Not good.

Nahzida dropped from the quarterdeck, a swift figure on her heels. Nahzida raised her rifle like a club and smashed it against the head of her pursuer. Another foe breached the main deck from above, but she didn't claim two steps before Kyzum's throwing knife stopped her heart. Nahzida exchanged her dull rifle for her short staff as the reinforcements who had forced her from her perch poured onto the main deck. They spread out in a crescent, trapping Kyzum and his crewmates between them and the gunwale. Very, very not good.

Two interlopers resumed the work of their fallen comrades at the captain's quarters; others broke off to the lower decks. They were searching for something. The only cargo this ship carried was the intelligence they had appropriated from the rebels. Were these rebels? With a cannon?

A man stepped forward from the barrier of foes. "Drop your weapons," he commanded.

Kyzum and his crewmates shared a glance, the women's gazes deferential. It was his call; Ameara had disappeared. The last time

Kyzum had seen her was when she had killed the men trying to raid her quarters. She was probably off doing something dangerous, foolish, and very Ameara-like. Leaving him with this responsibility. Capture or death? In his experience, trusting Ameara to be Ameara was the best option. With no shield, facing fresh fighters, and the cannon threatening to blow the possessed ship sky-high, Kyzum could live with surrendering now and escaping or being rescued later. He would *live*. They all would. These aggressors—these rebels? —only seemed interested in retrieving what had been taken from them; they had made no effort to commandeer the valuable skyship.

A figure emerged from below. Ara finally arriving as reinforcement? No. The silhouette was too tall, its shoulders too broad. A ray of light from the sliver of moon reflected off a bald pate. The shavinash. He crossed the deck without a sound, a shadow among shadows. Death incarnate.

Ara was dead, then. They would join her momentarily.

There was no surrendering now. Better to die at the hands of these rebels than at the hands of the shavinash. Or worse, become the shavinash's prisoners. The heightened alertness of Nahzida and Obakwe told Kyzum they had noticed the looming end. Kyzum didn't need to consult them to know they were all of one mind. They gathered back to back and dropped into defensive stances.

"Very well," the spokesman said regretfully. The rebels raised their weapons. Two dropped dead. The shavinash was upon them. Kyzum, Obakwe, and Nahzida rushed the startled intruders as they regrouped to counter the shavinash cutting them down like barley.

The cannon's bang broke through the clash of steel, and Kyzum knew the skyship was dead. But the blast met a flickering dome of light and was dispersed. Ara must have rigged the shield, again, before…

The cannon fired again, rocking the skyship, but it didn't feel like the shot had made contact. The cannon fired a third time, and a waterspout splashed over the starboard gunwale, depositing fractured boards onto the deck. The remains of the intruders' skimmer.

Kyzum smiled. Ameara. Gods bless that crazy woman.

Realizing their greatest advantage had been turned against them, the rebels hesitated. Then an explosion shook the strait. Ameara, again. That one better have been on purpose.

"We'll give you one chance to surrender," Kyzum said into the sudden silence.

He felt a flicker of cold air, and a whoosh spat Ameara onto the deck. She fired a flash of kaza into the sky and then aimed her pistol at the largest cluster of trespassers.

"Get off my ship."

Ameara dripped from head to toe and stood brazenly alone as the night's diamond current glistened behind her. A wrathful sea goddess to make the most powerful shahs tremble.

"I destroyed your cannon. I will destroy you, too. Leave, or die."

The rebels fingered their weapons, their boots scraping against the deck's grain. Oddly, the shavinash was primed to strike but hadn't moved since Ameara interrupted the skirmish.

Ameara turned her pistol to the side and fired. The men outside her quarters died in a spasm of charred flesh.

The rebels hastened to the port gunwale and leapt overboard. Kyzum heard their last skimmer hum to life, the steady purr rapidly lost within the waves as the failed aggressors accepted Ameara's goodwill. Within a few moments, the only trespassers who remained were the dead ones; Kyzum wasn't looking forward to cleaning up the mess.

Ameara whipped her pistol around and aimed it at the shavinash's heart. Nahzida and Obakwe held their weapons ready, but they dared not approach. They had all witnessed the speed with which he moved, how efficiently he cut down the rebels. Why wasn't he attacking?

The shavinash dropped the sword he carried. It was Ara's. Ameara must have recognized it, but she didn't blow the shavinash's head off. Was Ameara's pistol out of kaza? Was she bluffing? The standoff would end the second she lowered her arm, and seal all their fates.

The shavinash and Ameara locked gazes. Something beyond Kyzum passed between them. He could have cut the air with a knife.

The shavinash shuddered, clenched his fists. He swayed, righted himself, and collapsed to the deck with the thump of the genuinely unconscious.

CHAPTER 18

They waited, but the shavinash didn't stir. Ameara directed Nahzida and Obakwe to approach very carefully. Obakwe prodded him with one of her knobkerries. He didn't react.

"Is he dead?" Nahzida asked.

"He's alive," Obakwe said.

Ameara gripped her sword's hilt, tempted to correct that. She forced herself to not look at Ara's sword lying on the deck. If she killed the shavinash, none of them would survive. She had to protect the ones she still could.

"Nahzida, find Ara and secure the lower decks," Ameara ordered. "Obakwe, Kyzum, take him back to the brig."

Ameara went to the helm and eased Syra back on course. She reached out with calming thoughts. The threat had gone. Her shield would be properly fixed. It was only two days until stars' sway. She knew Syra was stressed and tired, but Syra wouldn't let them down. The Dazmir-vahl-kesh's consciousness brightened, and her fear diminished beneath Ameara's soothing touch.

After a quarter hour without incident or indication that they were being followed, Ameara left the helm, but she kept her connection to Syra forefront in her mind. She slowly descended to the lowest deck, preparing herself for what she would see.

Her crew had congregated around the brig. Ara was with them. Alive. The vise constricting Ameara's chest released, and she inwardly breathed a sigh of relief.

"Four dead. No one else is aboard," Nahzida reported.

"We're very happy Ara is not dead," Kyzum added.

"What happened?" Ameara asked Ara.

She replied softly, as if speaking pained her. The shavinash must have injured her jaw. "I left my post to restore the shield. He must have drawn on the etch to escape. I saw him come up from below, but he moved so fast I barely finished the shield before he attacked."

"She was out cold," Obakwe said. "Like he is now."

"He won't remain that way," Ameara said. "Ara, I need you at the helm if you're up for it. Nahzida, keep watch. Obakwe, find an explanation for his collapse. Carefully."

Her crew separated to perform their tasks. Ameara tapped Nahzida's arm and nodded toward Ara. Nahzida nodded in return: she would make sure Ara was all right and able to stand post, and if not, make her rest until Obakwe could heal her.

As Obakwe examined the shavinash, Ameara eyed the bonds he had loosed. They bore fresh blood. His thumb was bent at an odd angle, dislocated. Obakwe had secured his torso in addition to his hands and ankles this time, for all the good it would do. Escaping had cost him, but not enough to deter a second attempt.

Kyzum steered Ameara a short distance from the brig, and Ameara spoke her thoughts.

"Why didn't he kill Ara? Why didn't he kill any of you? Why remain aboard only to surrender?"

"Please don't make me say 'I don't know,'" Kyzum said. "I've been saying that too much lately."

"Haven't we all," Ameara said.

"Captain," a nervous Obakwe called.

They hurried over. Ameara crouched beside Obakwe, who had pulled low the shavinash's tunic. She indicated the etch embedded in his chest. Dark-crimson sludge writhed within the chipped obsidian and sprouted outward in jagged lines, creepers burrowing into the shavinash's body. They already consumed his torso.

"What in the gods' names is that?" Kyzum said.

"Get Ara down here," Ameara said.

Obakwe returned a moment later, Ara in tow; a nasty bruise was surfacing on her jaw. Ara walked resolutely to the shavinash and knelt before him. If one fell out of the rigging, the best response was to climb right back up.

Ara cautiously studied the angry veins permeating the shavinash's torso.

"It's the bloodshaping," she said.

"We assumed as much," Kyzum said.

"What is it doing?" Ameara asked. "I'm far from an expert on etches, but that doesn't look normal."

The shavinash's eyes popped open, his head sprang up, and he gasped a deep breath. Ara lurched back, her sun seal flaring. Obakwe brandished a knobkerrie, and a knife appeared in Kyzum's hand. Ameara started but drew no weapon.

"Outside, all of you," she ordered. Obakwe hesitated a fraction of a second before obeying, Ara following. Kyzum whispered a warning, "Captain."

"*All* of you," Ameara repeated, her eyes fixed on the wakening shavinash. Kyzum resisted a moment more, then complied with the minimum required submission for a first mate.

The shavinash blinked as if clearing his head. He tested his new restraints, undoubtedly ascertaining the easiest way to circumvent them.

"It's called an escape attempt because you're supposed to flee your current predicament," Ameara said. "The concept seems to be lost on you."

The shavinash's lips twitched. "Unfinished business."

Why hadn't he finished that business during the skirmish?

What was his mission if not to dispose of Ameara and her crew? What was the ulterior motive she couldn't see?

"So you killed the pirates just to pass the time?" Ameara said.

"Securing the Dazmir," the shavinash replied.

Sinister forewarning, or diversion? He could be the inside man for an ambush deployed to steal Syra, but then why try to destroy her? His actions didn't make sense.

Or was she dismissing the answer because it was too simple?

The shavinash spoke. "Tell your patron I attempted to secure your cargo, but when you discovered me, I retreated. It's the only way your crew will live."

Ameara scoffed. "That's a different story than the one you told before. I still like my plan better."

"Pretending we never crossed paths is no longer an option."

"I never considered it one."

Another twitch, this time touching his eyes. "They won't exchange clemency for my delivery. They'll kill you. The situation has changed."

"Because we were attacked? Or because of what that thing in your chest is doing to you?"

"Yes."

That was oddly and unexpectedly forthcoming. Ameara crouched before him, studying him, looking for his objective, the deception in his words.

"If I were to do as you propose, to alter our narrative, what becomes of you?" Ameara said.

"We immediately part ways and forget all our interactions apart from our fabrication," the shavinash said.

"And we're back to your first offer, where I just trust that you won't return and kill us."

The shavinash's jaw clenched. "Assets shouldn't be lightly thrown aside."

He could be proposing an accord. She doesn't tell Whisper about his failed mission, and he doesn't tell his shashvin she shot and imprisoned him. Except his mission involved her, her crew, or Syra, or a combination thereof, and he was compelled to complete it. Confronting Whisper was their only chance to recall him. Surely he didn't think her dense enough to disregard his shashvin. She was missing something.

The shavinash gasped a breath, breaking her thought trail. His harsh features contorted. Ameara studied him anew. The facial twitches, the uneven breathing. Sweat beaded on his brow.

He wasn't patronizing her. He was in pain.

Ameara's eyes were drawn to the fractured obsidian in his chest. "Your etch is killing you."

His sharp inhale and unsteady exhale were answer enough.

"Will you even reach Abylay?" Ameara said.

"One way or another," the shavinash said.

That was what she was missing. If she told Whisper she had seen a shavinash and he never reappeared, the cause of his death would point to Ameara and her crew. Even if his brethren never found his body, her ship was the last place he'd been seen. The shavinash was trying to trick her into telling his fellow assassins she had killed him.

Ameara stood and left the brig.

"Tell him you saw me," the shavinash said. "It's the only way you'll live."

Ameara ignored him and ascended to the upper deck, where she found Kyzum and an uncomfortable Ara hovering near the landing.

"Tell me about the etch," Ameara said to Ara.

Surprised Ameara hadn't called out their eavesdropping, Ara said, "To make an etch, you need a…sacrifice. The victim's life force is connected to the shavinash by the bloodshaping seal. The obsidian protects the seal and the shavinash from kaza. The bloodshaping sustains the life force and allows the shavinash to access it, and to replenish itself, the bloodshaping draws strength from the shavinash. A symbiotic relationship." She paused, continued gently. "Syra's kaza must have weakened the obsidian, so when you shot him, you damaged the seal, too. The bloodshaping is losing power and trying to replenish itself, but since the seal is damaged, it's unchecked."

"Is it a danger to us?" Ameara asked.

"It shouldn't be. It's still connected to the shavinash. Otherwise, it wouldn't be able to…feed off him. When he dies, its power will dissipate, just like a kaza seal, or if he'd been decapitated. But to be safe, I wouldn't touch it."

"I second that," Kyzum said.

"How long does he have?" Ameara asked.

Ara glanced down the stairs. "It must have been killing him since it was damaged…Drawing on it seems to have accelerated its hunger." She paused, hesitated. "If it doesn't slow down…he'll probably be dead before we reach Abylay."

"Can we stop it?" Ameara said.

Ara shook her head in thought. "Bloodshaping is vulnerable to kaza, but this bloodshaping is connected to him. I don't know how to separate the two, and unless we can break that connection, anything we do to destroy the etch would likely kill him, or the etch would unintentionally kill him while defending him."

"Of course it would," Kyzum said.

Dragging a defeated shavinash to Whisper and demanding to know what had caused his displeasure was one thing; Ameara was clearly an asset. Dragging a shavinash's body to Whisper was another. Asset or not, he would kill her and her crew to remind them of their place. Ameara was going to have to rethink her plan.

"Thank you, Ara," Ameara said. "Well done with the shield."

Ara blushed as she left Ameara and Kyzum alone.

"Don't teach Ara your bad habits," Ameara said.

"Listening is a habit more people should practice," Kyzum said.

"Eavesdropping is not."

"Depends on the situation."

"What's your impression of ours?"

"Your shavinash friend is trying to get us killed."

"You're slipping if you needed to spy to determine that."

"Confirmation is never a bad thing."

"Do you have anything to add besides redundant confirmation?"

"You won't like it."

"I don't like anything about this situation."

Kyzum's features hardened, and his back subtly straightened. The Masatitoran spymaster who had simultaneously earned his gods' esteem and his exile.

"Tell Whisper nothing. The shavinash is already dead. We should end it now and dispose of his corpse. His brethren *will* kill us if they think we killed one of them, but they only *might* kill us if he just disappears. His death would be attributed to a rival or a scheme before pathetic Vekrym." He paused. "I'll do it."

"You're assuming Whisper isn't behind this," Ameara said.

"Assuming otherwise means we're as dead as that shavinash." Kyzum pursed his lips. "Whisper likes you. The rival shashvin will believe his assassin's demise was due to Whisper's intervention, and Whisper will commend your quiet removal of the threat as long as neither of you ever speak of it. Probably."

Ameara considered her first mate's plan. It hinged on a lot of speculations proving correct, but Kyzum thrived on speculations, and it was all they had to work with. The shavinash was dying. Ameara had to change course. Toward the shoals to avoid the squall. A lesser risk among a slew of perilous routes.

Syra's consciousness heightened, and the anxious impression of the brig skimmed across Ameara's mind.

"It's the best option we have," Kyzum said.

"Probably," Ameara said.

Kyzum waited for her authorization, but when she didn't give it, he realized she was contemplating deeper—and perhaps imagined —currents they had not yet explored.

"What are you thinking?" he asked.

Dangerous thoughts. Maybe Ameara couldn't decipher the shavinash's mission because there was no mission. At least, not from his shashvin. He showed no interest in disposing of Ameara or her crew. He wanted her to pretend his presence on Syra had been fleeting or nonexistent. Was he operating outside the shavinashi's doctrine?

Being associated with a rogue shavinash would be equivalent to killing one, but it was a possible, if implausible, interpretation of his actions and the lies he claimed would save her crew. Would Whisper spare them to cover up a defector among the Ways' most zealous disciples? Killing her for killing a shavinash was understandable. Killing her for being implicated in a shavinash's death, also understandable. Killing her when she returned successful from a contract…Some would question the reason. Not openly, but whispers would circulate. One of those whispers might carry a truth the shavinashi must silence.

Or the dying shavinash was just trying to get her killed. It didn't explain what he'd been attempting to do in Syra's heart. Ameara hated sailing blind.

"Ameara?" Kyzum said.

"You need to look at our cargo," Ameara said.

"We don't look," her first mate said firmly.

"*We* are not. *You* are."

"Nope. Next plan."

"Something is happening that is beyond us. If we know what our cargo contains, we may be able to determine if a shashvin could use it to undermine Whisper, which in turn will determine what I report to Whisper.

"There's no going back after we kill him. We have some time. Let's use it."

Kyzum frowned, caught between his instinct to not get involved and his desire to keep living. He sighed in acquiescence.

"No one is to know what you're doing," Ameara said. "You are the only one who sees it."

"Yes, Captain. What are you going to do?"

Ameara squared her shoulders. "I'm going to have another talk with our uninvited guest. Maybe the pain will loosen his tongue."

CHAPTER 19

The bloodshaping leeching the life from the shavinash made him even more reticent. He only spoke to repeat his commands concerning Ameara's course. Ameara eventually conceded he wasn't going to deviate from his reiterations, even with his deteriorating condition. The bloodshaping continued to burrow into his body, spreading up his shoulders and reaching for his neck. Bursts of pain made him gasp and groan despite his efforts to remain silent. Ameara kept her crew on guard shifts, but she removed herself from the rotation. The more the shavinash succumbed to the damaged etch, the more… human he seemed. Her judgment was already impaired. No need to make it worse.

Their last full day at sea passed without incident; the rebels must have thrown everything they had into their attack. Unfortunately, the lack of interruptions didn't help Kyzum with their cargo. The intelligence was in Old Setsean, and encoded.

"How long will it take to translate?" Ameara asked.

Kyzum blew a breath. "The cipher is absurdly simple, so I'm assuming the intended recipients don't know Old Setsean and a key was made for interpretation. Unfortunately for us, the rebels were smart and didn't include the key with the documents. I'm very good, so I will get some of this to make sense, but I'm on a very tight deadline, and my Old Setsean leaves much to be desired."

Kyzum sequestered himself in his cabin and attacked their cargo as only Kyzum could, but they both doubted he would be able to translate enough to aid them. Abylay would crown the shoreline tomorrow afternoon. The shavinash had to be a distant memory long before that.

The idle time did allow Ameara to get the shield fully operational. Ara could have done it, as Obakwe had healed her injuries at dawn, but Ameara needed time alone to think. Well, almost alone. Syra was a constant presence in Ameara's mind, nudging her ever so slightly to achieve perfect kaza flow. The sendings seemed Ameara's own thoughts as she reconnected the shield's secondary cylinder seals to Syra's heart. A gleeful spurt of star kaza signaled her success.

Ameara wished knowing what to tell Whisper could be just as simple. Every instinct she had developed as a Schism gladiator and a captain told her to omit the shavinash from her report. Any narrative that had her recognizing a shavinash could lead back to his death at her hand. The bloodshaping was doing its grisly work all too well, but if the shavinash still drew breath with morning's first light, she would have to finish the process. Kyzum's reasoning was sound. Whisper did like her; she shuddered.

Yet something vied with her instincts and her first mate's infallible reasoning. Something that would not let her dismiss the shavinash dying in the brig. A feeling his lies dwelled only in the unspoken.

*   *   *

Evening came far too fast for Ameara. The smell of onions, thyme, and vinegar wafted from the galley. Kyzum was on meal duty; Ameara had forced him to take a break from the translation. Dinner was probably lentils and chickpeas with pickled vegetables. They might have some bread left. Simple, as meals usually were. The one time Nahzida had made lemon tarts was still wistfully remembered.

Ameara should eat, but she had no appetite. She didn't want to sit with her crew and be reminded of what the impending dawn would bring. She would face it. She refused to run. She just wanted to pretend for a little longer that there was another way out of the storm.

Ameara left her quarters and descended to the lower deck. Obakwe and Ara sat silently in the galley. It would be a somber meal. Even Kyzum couldn't save it. Ameara continued down. The lone lantern flickered as Syra swayed to the waves' rhythm. Dark shadows cloaked the hull. Nahzida acknowledged her with a subdued, "Captain."

"Any change?" Ameara asked.

"He's not dead yet. The bloodshaping is still spreading. I've seen it moving. I thought it was a trick of the light at first." She shivered.

"I'll take over," Ameara said. "Go get some food."

"Are you sure?" Nahzida asked meaningfully.

"Go."

Nahzida offered Ameara her rifle, but she declined. She would better defend herself with the pistol and sword she was familiar with. Although, there didn't seem much left to defend from.

Ameara took the lantern from its hook and entered the brig. She set the light down near the gate and leaned against the bars. The shavinash's head was tilted back, a drowning man about to be consumed by the waves. His breath was shallow and ragged. Sweat beaded his brow and soaked his tunic. The bloodshaping's thorns coiled his neck. Nahzida was right: it *was* moving beneath his skin, writhing like an enraged viper.

The shavinash's sunken eyes opened. The dark circles beneath them seemed as bruises on his ashen complexion.

"My crew tell me you're refusing poppy powder," Ameara said. "We're not trying to poison you. Your etch is already doing that."

"Tell your patron I attempted to secure your cargo," the shavinash said, "but when you discovered me—" He groaned, his jaw clenching as another wave of pain broke upon him. He gasped as it subsided. "Tell him—"

"Stop. Just stop. You don't have breath to waste on pointless words."

"It's the only way you'll survive," he said. Insisted. "The only way your crew will survive."

"Why does it matter what happens to us? You're dead either way."

"Assets shouldn't be wasted."

Ameara hesitated, then steeled herself and ventured closer. Close enough for him to plunge a dagger into her gut. Close enough to touch. She caught his bloodshot eyes with her dark ones, and held them, searching. Searching for what her heart was telling her.

"Why did you aid my crew?" she asked. "And don't tell me it was to secure my ship. I know you're not here for her."

"Presuming you've anticipated the shavinashi will end you," the assassin said. "Tell your patron I attempted to—" The bloodshaping clenched its fist again, and he gritted his teeth.

Ameara shook her head. If only the bloodshaping had exhausted his faculties. Even now he would not be deterred. She paused. Shavinashi discipline, or something else?

"When I was a child," Ameara said, "I knew this boy who was as honorable as they come. His father wasn't Setsean and didn't worship Orvashka's Ways, though, so the village never let him forget his mother's corruption or his selfishness for evaluating his father's 'antiquated ideas.' But that didn't stop him from intervening when some older boys tried to have fun with a whore's daughter. He was outnumbered, but he stood his ground anyway. He was beaten and bloodied. But this gave the whore's daughter an opportunity, and she crushed one of the boy's skulls with a rock. Then she blamed his death on her defender. He went along with it, didn't deny it. Accepted the blame. A shavinash took him the next day. Honor, bravery, valor—whatever you want to call it—it's all foolishness. No one will thank you for it, and you will end up dead."

"Says the captain keeping a shavinash prisoner to save her crew," the assassin said.

Ameara remained unfazed. She hadn't said she wasn't a fool. As Kyzum often reminded her, her crew was composed of strays. But they were *her* strays.

"A shavinash who hastened his death to aid intended victims," Ameara countered, even though she now doubted that had been his mission.

The shavinash's intense regard emerged from the depths of his tortured frame and settled upon her. Syra's attention sidled closer.

Another jolt of pain seized the shavinash. "Poppy powder won't help," he said as it passed. "The etch would consume it."

Ameara lowered her gaze, feeling…pity. He was a shavinash —child abductor, enforcer, murderer. And dying in agony. If he hadn't been a shavinash, he would be thrashing and screaming his throat raw.

Ameara retrieved the flask she had brought with her and offered it to the shavinash. He eyed it warily.

"It's only water," she said. "Promise."

He hesitated, then, surprisingly, nodded. Ameara gently poured the water into his mouth. It dripped from his cracked lips.

"You don't remember, do you?" Ameara said.

The shavinash didn't respond, but neither did he recite his repeated command.

Did he remember and was refusing to admit it, or was she seeing recognition in his blue eyes when none existed? Did it matter at this point? He was dead either way.

The shavinash stiffened as the bloodshaping burrowed deeper, but it didn't subside as before. An anguished cry escaped his lips, and he strained against his bonds. Syra roiled in Ameara's mind. She wanted the bloodshaping gone.

The shavinash finally collapsed against the bars, his eyelids drooping. The black veins had crested his chiseled jaw, a vice slowly suffocating him.

Ameara drew her belt knife. Hesitated. She cut the ropes binding his torso. The shavinash slumped, and his breath came easier. A mistake…probably. But his death throes were not a feint or a trap; the bloodshaping brazenly gorged itself, and was progressing faster as the night wore on. She could probably loose all his bonds, and he wouldn't move even if Kyzum's gods ordained it. She stayed her hand. It would only take one swift blow to shatter her windpipe.

Ameara left the brig and returned the lantern to its hook. She settled beneath the wavering candlelight, her back against Syra's sturdy hull. A witness to the end of the shavinash's life.

"What happened to the girl?" he murmured.

An anomalous question for a shavinash. For anyone in his position.

Ameara regarded him across the short distance that spanned leagues. What happened to the whore's daughter? Betrayal, grief, despair.

"She ran away to the stars."

"Not…foolish…"

A heavy silence swallowed the deck. The shavinash had finally succumbed to the etch.

Ameara wasn't certain if his last words had been about the girl who ran away or the boy who defended her.

CHAPTER 20

"Aren't you forgetting something?"

Jaleya proffered the sealed letter as Saunez passed the column behind which Jaleya waited. The custodian's composure never faltered as she extricated herself from the congregation departing the Way of Law temple. Jaleya's ears still burned from the sermon, which conveyed like an official address rather than a teaching of a revered higher being; no matter the conviction of its duped constituents, the Ora's lifeless collective morality could not provide what it inevitably suppressed. Arriving early had been necessary to intercept the information meant for Saunez, but then Jaleya had dared not leave lest she attract the attention of the Counselors lurking behind the altar. They scrutinized the congregation and the ministers alike.

"This isn't your free time," Saunez said. "While devotion to Orvashka's Ways is essential, shirking your duty to fulfill that devotion is not acceptable. I'll decide what disciplinary action is appropriate when I return to Iza Vor. The quicker your abandoned post is reoccupied, the more lenient I will be inclined."

Jaleya didn't flinch. She'd been weighing the outcome of this confrontation for days, weighing her suspicions against her surveillance. Saunez was exceedingly careful and covered her tracks well —very well, but Jaleya had noted the long detours to deliver or retrieve reports, the "coincidental" encounters, simple errands that took longer than they should, and a clandestine meeting in an old wing of Iza Vor; Jaleya hadn't been close enough to identify Saunez's accomplices due to a sirrush keeping watch, but a small conference had definitely taken place. Saunez had not been pleased afterward.

Jaleya hadn't been certain of her conclusion when she left Isesh with Teza and ventured into this temple, but now, standing before Saunez as the custodian tried to intimidate her, facing Saunez's commanding, confident demeanor, she was. It was subtle, but Saunez was *too* confident, wielding her authority *too* forcefully. Too eager for Jaleya to leave.

Jaleya had set out to expose Saunez's scheme so she and Isesh wouldn't be caught up in it, but what she had found was the chance she'd been yearning for. She didn't want Saunez to be the one to give it to her, but if one rejected a fashari, another might never appear.

"While you're pondering disciplinary action," Jaleya said, "make sure you choose an appropriate one for Teza using a smuggled seal to rift into the restricted archive in Iza Vor's library."

Saunez raised a curious but unsurprised eyebrow. "That is distressing information. Thank you for bringing it to my attention. I'll look into it when I return, after we've discussed your misconduct." Dismissal rang clear in her tone, but Jaleya pressed forward.

"You won't look into it, and you won't have anyone else look into it because that would reveal you know Seal Keeper Firnak has been bribing the guard away from the archive and smuggling a rift seal to Teza via your intarish informant, and you've let it continue to benefit your own interests."

"That is a very serious accusation," Saunez said, her composure unwavering. "Have you reported me? Thought not, otherwise I'd be before a Counselor. If this is an attempt at extortion, it will not end the way you hope."

"I'm not trying to blackmail you, and we both know threatening me is an empty gesture."

"Is that so?" Saunez said.

"Yes. Teza has been attracting a lot of attention lately. More scrutiny could easily shift from routine rowshatar management to questionable private matters, such as a custodian attending a secret meeting in a servant corridor and retrieving letters hidden under cushions." Jaleya twiddled the message in her hand. "Those actions could be interpreted for what they truly are, and that would be dangerous without *allies* watching your back."

The corner of Saunez's mouth curved in a condescending grin. It wasn't the reaction Jaleya had been expecting.

"Whatever you think you know, you don't," Saunez said. "Return to Rowshatar Teza, and we will both pretend this conversation never happened."

Saunez walked past, head high. Jaleya grabbed her arm. "I can help."

Saunez pinched Jaleya's elbow and calmly but painfully drove Jaleya beyond the columns to a Law shrine. A featureless Ora clutched the haloed sealed scroll as its rays descended upon the contour of citizens basking in its enlightenment. Saunez pretended to read the inscribed Way of Law tenets as she glanced around the temple for prying eyes and ears. The ministers sifted through the devotions for the ones worthy of addition to the altar tome. The remaining parishioners meditated or huddled near the ministers hoping their deeds had progressed Orvashka's light. The Counselors had left with the congregation.

Saunez's pointed nose flared in vexation. "You help by looking after Teza."

"You're resistance and a custodian," Jaleya protested, glad to finally drop the pretense. "Of the two of us, I'm the one who has more time on my hands."

Saunez strolled to the second plaque of tenets. "Without an accompanying rowshatar, you and your fashari are noted wherever you go," she hissed. "Even if you weren't, even if you were in the perfect position to provide aid, I wouldn't let you. You're arrogant, impulsive, and you have a chip on your shoulder as large as the Nidren.

You will keep your head down and be an obedient guardian. If you bring unwanted attention, it will be easy to shift all of it to you."

"Is that what happened to Gardok?" Jaleya said.

Guilt flashed across Saunez's stern features. Mastering it, she said, "That's all I will say on this matter. We should both return before we're missed."

"How would Teza react if he knew you were resistance?" Jaleya said, circling Saunez to the next plaque; instead of tenets, this one spewed the virtues of the Ways.

"He would respond as any good citizen would, which is why he is not involved," Saunez said, reclaiming her forefront position.

Jaleya pursed her lips. "He is involved. He just doesn't know it."

"He has legitimate deniability, his status, and his ignorance. And it will *remain* that way."

Jaleya edged sideways, but not because of the lethal threat behind Saunez's dark eyes. Jaleya had been trying to determine the nature of Teza and Saunez's relationship since she arrived in Iza Vor. An odd romance was what first came to mind, but lovers fit as well as a square peg in a round hole. She had dismissed them as siblings because family members were prohibited from supervising each other. Distant cousins…an exception might be made. But witnessing the protective flame in Saunez's eyes, hearing the fatal warning in her voice…

"Teza is your brother…" Jaleya said.

Saunez blinked. "Of course he's not. What gave you an absurd idea like that?"

"My older sister would have done anything to protect me, too."

Saunez hesitated. Triumph soared within Jaleya. She had finally bested her!

"Return to Iza Vor," Saunez ordered. "Someone will realize you've gone."

She bowed her head to the shrine, touched her heart and forehead with crossed palms, and strode away with the smugness of the Ways' most devout. Jaleya's triumph deflated. She had caught

Saunez red-handed. She had enough information to blackmail Saunez into doing her bidding, to condemn Saunez and Teza as rebels; Counselors didn't require proof. And Saunez just walked away?

"You're not worried I'll report you out of an arrogant impulse?" Jaleya said.

Saunez paused and looked over her shoulder. "You won't. It would prove I'm right about you."

Jaleya fumed. Saunez had no right to deny her. Jaleya could help! She wanted to help. *Needed* to help. Playing wet nurse to spoiled, entitled rowshatari was getting her no closer to the shavinash she sought or to destroying the Ora. Her training was wasted on the rowshatari. She was being wasted. Being correct that Saunez was plotting something, even if it wasn't what she had initially assumed, was small consolation.

Jaleya's temper did not improve as she snuck back to Iza Vor, and it soured further when she realized the letter was gone.

CHAPTER 21

Saunez marched down the arched hallway leading to Advocate Badaad's office. Her stomach felt like it had been pecked by the sparrows chirping in the garden. She'd been aware of Jaleya's spying and had outmaneuvered her when the occasion dictated, but she hadn't known the girl had followed her to the resistance meeting; she must have kept a great distance to not alert Hossa. Jaleya was sharp; Saunez would give her that. Dangerously inexperienced —calling attention to her in a crowded temple of all places!—but sharp. Inferring her relation to Teza had thrown Saunez off balance. She always thought if anyone discovered their secret it would be due to Teza's error.

Jaleya wouldn't expose their relation. The simmering rage in the girl's eyes when she spoke of her sister concealed great heartache. But Jaleya was an unknown factor in the impending confrontation, and Orvashka knew Saunez didn't need something else keeping her awake at night. Firnan had received word that Eclipse and her crew had stolen the skyship intelligence. His retrieval plan was sound, but Saunez feared the skyship teams would be going in blind.

You don't fail the shavinashi.

She reached Advocate Badaad's office, knocked, and entered when bidden. Badaad sat behind his desk signing and sealing documents, his back to the latticed window. His beard was neatly trimmed, and his tall bonnet ornamented with a gold rowshatari emblem bound dark hair that rested between his shoulder blades when loose.

Records, reports, and manifests occupied one wall. Chaises and chairs encircled a low table laden with a pot of tea and half-empty cups; steam still wafted from the pot's spout. The last time Saunez had been in this office, she'd been minimizing Teza's attempted snatching by emphasizing the freshness of his guardian pairing and his budding reputation for being eccentric, even for a rowshatar. She needed to rein in her brother before said reputation developed further. Being singled out even slightly was dangerous for both of them. Despite what she told Teza, she would have to get Jaleya reassigned. Those two were a volatile combination.

A matter for after stars' sway.

Badaad looked up from his paperwork and smiled fondly. "Custodian Saunez, punctual as always."

"Advocate Badaad," she greeted.

"I have your rowshatari's replenishing assignments," Badaad said. He withdrew a scroll from a stack on his desk and offered it to her, but when she took it, he held tight. "You're managing quite a roster, a quarter more than other custodians."

"If I couldn't handle it, I would inform you," Saunez said. In a mock conspiratorial tone she added, "Besides, we both know I'm worth three custodians."

Badaad held her gaze for a moment, then released the scroll and chuckled. "True. Very true, even though I will be obligated to deny it should anyone ask. If only others were as reliable as you."

Saunez glanced meaningfully at the cooling tea. "Trouble, sir?"

Badaad leaned forward and lowered his voice. "Ora Ezray visited the rowshatari-mara repository, as is her custom, but she asked them to focus their questings on the Festival of Shattered Swords. She even requested remshiri and authorized the use of tanzanite seals. The rumors surrounding her instructions have made the guild leaders...nervous."

"It does sound serious," Saunez said in the tone of the interested audience even though her stomach had just flip-flopped.

"That's what I thought, too," Badaad said, "but patrols haven't been increased, a curfew hasn't been implemented; festival preparations are proceeding as planned; there haven't been any raids or arrests, and, thankfully, the shavinashi have stayed in their hole. If trouble was coming, something would be stirring."

"The future is said to be always changing," Saunez said. "Perhaps what Ora Ezray roused the repository for has been dismissed as a possibility. If the Ora thought a threat was imminent, they would prepare and respond."

"Exactly, but try telling the guilds that."

Saunez smiled sympathetically, but her mind raced frantically. The future did change until it became the present, and even if a predicted future came to pass, it might not happen as expected. A small-scale questing was difficult to sift. A large-scale one involving the festival, or a rebellion…The precious gemstones would be discarded with the dross.

But if the rowshatari-mara searched long enough, if they quested deep enough, they could find the individuals around which future events turned. Intervening then could render those axes insignificant and drastically alter the future, or it could bring about the very future they sought to prevent. That was why Saunez and the other ranking resistance members always bore a chip of obsidian. Too small to be noticed by rowshatari, it wouldn't stop kaza, but it made them "slippery" in questings. Despite that and their other precautions, the Ora had turned their attention to the festival. Exactly where the resistance needed it to not be.

Saunez opened the scroll to hide her troubled thoughts, but she found no refuge as she skimmed the roster.

"If you ever need a respite, I can assign some of your rowshatari to other custodians," Badaad said.

"That won't be necessary," Saunez said, her gaze transfixed on Teza's name and his assigned replenishing.

"You've proven yourself a valuable asset, Custodian Saunez, but two lamentable incidents in two months doesn't reflect well on either of us," Badaad said. "I like being able to rely on you. A temporary leave, just a few days, would revive your life force and reaffirm your devotion to Orvashka."

Saunez looked up. Badaad's posture was formally erect, his hands clasped before him on the desk.

Saunez said, "The incident in Abylay resulted due to a guardian better suited for the countryside, but since the outcome proved favorable, disciplinary action wasn't necessary. We would have had a very different conversation if harm had come to the rowshatar-estra. As for the traitor, if there had been any indication of what he truly was, apart from the willful streak all javati possess, I would've reported him immediately. I did err in transferring other guardians despite the traitor being at the head of the rotation, but that also aroused my suspicions: a guardian and rowshatar are rarely so amiable near a term's completion. My devotion the deplorable traitor sought to exploit proved his undoing. My devotion does not waver."

Badaad considered for a moment that lasted an eternity. A knot tightened between Saunez's shoulders.

Badaad leaned back in his chair. "If you had followed protocol, the traitor wouldn't have been apprehended so promptly, or worse, he might have swindled someone into his obscene beliefs."

The tension in Saunez's shoulders abated. She wouldn't be delivered to the desert, as Teza had been. Badaad wouldn't have been lenient if he knew the truth of her error.

Keeping Gardok in Abylay had been intentional, but not to frame him. Teza had never had a friend before. Unfortunately, Gardok had been in the best position to become the scapegoat. Saunez had done what was necessary to protect the resistance. To make new laws—better laws—fair laws. To make Setsea better for everyone. The justifications stung. Orvashka wane that spy! Who was it?

Realizing she had been silent for too long, Saunez said, "I know your concern stems from care, and I appreciate it. Perhaps when stars' sway has passed I'll take a few days to recuperate from the festival's replenishings."

"Your rowshatari will be well taken care of during your absence," Badaad said.

"Thank you, sir."

Saunez withdrew as if her pulse wasn't throbbing against her neck. The Ora were questing the Festival of Shattered Swords. Badaad, and possibly the Advocate Council, was questioning her loyalty. She had to alert Firnan and the others straightaway.

Teza's name on the scroll in her hand—his assignment for stars' sway—burned into her palm. Could she get him out of it? Assign another rowshatar at the last minute? Make an excuse? Alter the document? There must be something she could do.

As she scrambled for options, no matter how desperate, she relaxed her fist lest she crush the roster handing her brother a death sentence and someone ask her why her eyes were blurred with tears.

CHAPTER 22

Saunez paused outside her brother's quarters. Took a breath. Reminded herself of her responsibilities, of the people counting on her. Composed, she entered. Teza lay on a chaise outside, his legs over the backrest, his gaze heavenward. Saunez joined him on the balcony and frowned when she discovered he was alone.

"Where's your guardian?"

Teza raised his hand, and sparks jumped between his fingers.

Saunez's frown deepened. The moon was a bright slash in the sky, but her brother could already command the stars' kaza. She doubted he could do more than what he had demonstrated, but other rowshatari-estra couldn't even accomplish that.

"Stars' sway is two days from now. Star kaza is far from fully accessible. She should be here," Saunez said.

"My guardian isn't required to be present when I can veer kaza," Teza said. "Be glad I can reach the stars. Otherwise, you would've walked in on a corpse and a bloody mess of feathers."

The corpse would've been yours, Saunez thought.

"I don't know where you found her," Teza continued, "but take her back. Get me someone else."

Saunez patiently clasped her hands in front of her. "I'll make a bargain with you. If you can singe the top of my bonnet from where you're lying, I'll request a new guardian."

Teza eyed the few feet that separated them. White light illuminated his hands and highlighted his chiseled cheekbones as sparks tingled his fingertips. His brow furrowed in concentration, and a strand grew between his fingers, writhing and flashing.

The lightning sputtered out with a pitiful crackle.

"When the stars hold sway, your guardian can go where she pleases," Saunez said. "You will tolerate her presence until then and not dismiss her on a technicality. Is that clear?"

Teza crossed his arms and pouted. "Yes, Custodian Saunez."

Saunez patted his legs, and he lifted them off the backrest and dropped his sandaled feet to the stone. She sat beside him and spoke quietly, even though the interior guards that should have been present in Jaleya's absence were not. Countryside guardian indeed.

"I know the days since Gardok turned traitor have been difficult for you, but that is no excuse to put yourself in danger. Enduring the inconvenience of a guardian is a small price to pay for what you've always wanted."

"I wanted to throw sun kaza," Teza grumbled. He summoned the stars' power again and bounced a single bolt from finger to finger.

"Stars at noon you did," Saunez said. "The rowshatari-estra fascinated you the most."

"And what a disappointment they are." The bolt hopping between his fingers increased its cadence, leaving an afterimage in her vision.

"All kaza types have their strengths and weaknesses," she said, "but all are important. It's an honor to veer any of them…"

The lightning amid Teza's fingers was a sizzling blur.

Saunez whacked the back of his hand, startling him and stopping his display.

"And should be treated as such. Which means no wasting it on childish games." Saunez flexed her fingers, relieving the shock she had received.

"Kaza doesn't run out," Teza said, "so while I can veer, I'll do as I please."

"Kaza is infinite, but your body is not," Saunez retorted. "Or have you forgotten how hungry you were after last stars' sway? You will not waste your strength on foolish amusement when its entirety is needed to safeguard Abylay and its people."

"I only lost a few pounds," Teza shrugged. "That's normal. The communication seals need a lot of kaza." He veered more lightning and fashioned a net between his palms.

"You won't be replenishing Iza Vor's minarets," Saunez said.

Another shrug, this one tinged with irritation. "Replenishing cylinder seals is the same no matter what they're hooked into."

Saunez hesitated, and reminded herself once more of her responsibilities. She softened her tone. "You've been assigned to the skyships."

The rustling web dancing among his palms sputtered, and a stray bolt singed the stone wall. The stars' kaza cut out, plunging the balcony into a deeper night.

"W-what?" Teza said. "I always replenish the minarets. I d-don't replenish the Dazmiri."

Saunez was grateful the sudden shadows obscured his expression, for she didn't want to witness his fear as well as hear it.

"You will this time," she said.

Her brother shook his head. "No. I d-don't replenish the Dazmiri. Send someone else. Ch-change it."

"It's not my decision," Saunez said. If it was, she wouldn't be in the mess she currently found herself. The rowshatari replenishing the skyships had always been a potential threat to the resistance's mission, and if a confrontation did occur, the ship teams only had two options. No one could be allowed to escape. If Teza opposed them, the likelihood he would end up dead was high, especially if his brat of a guardian shoved herself into the altercation. Considering their mutual hostility, Jaleya probably wouldn't be present since she wasn't required to be, but either way, Saunez hoped her brother would make the wise choice and surrender.

Teza gripped a chunk of his hair and twiddled it through his fingers. He didn't seem to be aware that his skin had acquired an iridescent sheen.

She had let him progress too far. The advocates had noticed.

Saunez cupped Teza's hands in hers. "You will replenish the skyships, and you will live to tell about it."

"Lots of others haven't," Teza said. "They need t-too much."

"The honor has taken lives, yes, but plenty have lived after numerous replenishings."

"And were reeds for weeks afterward."

Saunez couldn't refute that fact. "What happened to others doesn't matter. You can do this; I know it. I'm not looking forward to your boasting, however well deserved. Few can say they stepped aboard a skyship, much less saw the gemstone in its heart, experienced a wonder lost to the Schism."

Teza's iridescent luster seemed to brighten. "It would be amazing to see one up close." He frowned. "Even though it will be the last thing I see."

"It won't," Saunez said firmly. She eased her brother's clenched fist and brought a portion of his long hair before his eyes. Even with stars' sway two days hence, it had already begun to lighten.

"Fat lot of good it's done me," Teza said, but his tone was softer, his shoulders straighter.

"It will help you this time," Saunez said. She tapped his nose with a paling tuft. "As long as you have your full strength for stars' sway."

Teza sighed. "Are you sure you can't get me out of this?"

Saunez should lie to him. It was easy. She'd been doing it for years. But giving him false hope could leave him unprepared for the task ahead, and Teza needed to be prepared. She didn't want him to become another casualty of the Ora's supposed quest to close the Schism. Attempting to reassign him would draw attention, and as Jaleya had perceptively asserted, any attention was bad attention right then. Too much was at stake.

"There's nothing I can do," she said. "I'm sorry." And she was. For so much. For all she would continue to do.

Teza nodded, but his gaze wandered to the sear left by the kaza that had escaped his control.

Saunez squeezed his shoulder. "You'll be master of the Dazmiri, Rowshatar Teza." She stood. "When your guardian returns, inform her a smidgen of kaza is not permission to abandon her duty. Only when you gleam like the stars may she indulge herself."

"Yes, Custodian Saunez," Teza said.

"Goodnight, Teza."

"Goodnight."

Teza returned to his back and plopped his feet upon the chaise, but he didn't summon the stars' kaza. Saunez refrained from scolding him for his mistreatment of the furniture.

For all her responsibility to the resistance, to Abylay, to Setsea, she had a deeper one to her brother. Her actions—or rather, inaction—would be placing him in harm's way, could potentially result in his death. She should do everything in her power to guarantee he wasn't anywhere near the skyships come stars' sway, that he was away from danger. That he was safe. But one person couldn't be weighed more valuable than the greater good. She loved her brother, but he was just one person. One person wasn't more precious than an entire city, an entire country, all of Idlium.

For a moment though, a short moment, he was.

CHAPTER 23

Torches burned in the javati compound, but the ones within the training grounds were extinguished. The stars' tapestry stretched across the sky. An iridescent sheen that gleamed in the pools of surrounding torchlight tinted the rowshatari-estra's skin. The rowshatari-estra delighted in the kaza they could now veer, hopping lightning across their fingers, attempting to hit targets they wouldn't be able to scorch until tomorrow, and blasting the sand in the hope of birthing lightning's unique glass. Javati goaded their rowshatar to outdo the others.

Jaleya paused in the arcade as she noticed a familiar silhouette on the far side of the training grounds. She had tried to rid herself of thoughts involving Teza, but they returned like tenacious horseflies. His sister was using him! Defeating the Ora would be difficult and would require sacrifice, but to so manipulate one's own flesh and blood...Saunez's actions didn't support her protective resolve reminiscent of Lenruz. Teza was just a piece on a board, easily disposed of when his use lapsed.

Jaleya wandered closer to her charge. A small detour to the festival wouldn't hurt. Isesh trailed her curiously.

Guards bordered the training grounds and observed from the upper walkway, but they wouldn't intervene unless the rowshatari-estra began rifting beyond the surrounding wall. Jaleya doubted this lot, or any Setsean rowshatar-estra, could rift that far. The guards' actual purpose was to watch and report. Spies under the guise of protectors. Just like her?

Jaleya leaned against an archway, a torch's natural flame casting her in shadow. Beneath the night diamonds, Teza practiced alone. The iridescence adorning his skin was no mere sheen. While the other rowshatari-estra performed lightning tricks between their palms, Teza cracked holes in the air. The shimmers huffed mountain chill, but then sputtered and collapsed, the rifts failing to form. Teza growled in frustration. He gathered his braided hair and examined the twists that were more white than gray. His posture became intense concentration.

What do you think he'd do if he found out his sister is resistance? Jaleya sent to Isesh.

I hope he would listen to her and see reason, Isesh replied, *but I fear Custodian Saunez's prediction is more accurate.*

Isesh's confirmation eased Jaleya's bothersome, misguided sympathy. Teza was an Illuminated. His sister was using him, yes, but she wouldn't have to use him if he thought for himself and accepted the Creator's truths.

Isesh continued. *The equal sorrow is that he would report her in the belief she would be granted mercy.*

The Ora's idea of mercy is murdering people for the moral code they worship, Jaleya sent.

Clemency is not for rebels, Isesh agreed.

They watched Teza attempt another rift. It almost formed.

He has concealed his relation to Custodian Saunez thus far, her javati commented.

That surprises me more than Saunez being a rebel, Jaleya sent.

Does it? If their relation was discovered, Teza would be removed from his sister's charge, and she would be sent to another city, at least.

He doesn't want to lose the free rein she gives him.

Isesh's disappointment was as clear as day on his bird-dog features. *He doesn't want to be separated from his family.*

He's loyal to the ones who would take his sister from him, Jaleya reminded him.

Not entirely it seems.

Jaleya sighed. *Your incessant optimism is very annoying.*

As is your cynicism.

The air in front of Teza shimmered once more, and finally expanded into a vortex. But Teza wasn't popping anywhere with a rift that size. Perhaps he was considering cutting off a limb to avoid replenishing the Dazmiri. Jaleya would be tempted to do the same in his position.

Dazmiri required an enormous amount of star kaza. After the Schism and the following war, the cost of wild gems or a rowshatar's service to replenish the Dazmiri that had not gained sentience became extraordinary, leading to most skyships being decommissioned. The Masatitoran skimmers had faced similar issues, but unlike star kaza, sun kaza was available every day. Replenishing skimmers could be done gradually. Replenishing Dazmiri was known to be a rowshatar-estra's final assignment.

The rift's rotation slowed, its gleaming border a wave suspended at its crest. Isesh's ears peaked, his feathered neck stiffening. The rift stuttered, spat star kaza, and collapsed with a whoosh. Guards glanced at the disturbance, but seeing all rowshatari unharmed and accounted for, they returned to their superfluous posts.

"That wasn't a normal rift," Jaleya said.

Teza jumped, spinning toward the sound of her voice. He hadn't realized they were there. How oblivious was he?

"What are you doing here?" he said. "I don't need you." Lightning flashed from his hand and struck the dirt. Jaleya privately admitted it was impressive compared to the game the others were playing.

"Don't need me, or don't want me?" Jaleya said as she stepped beneath the stars. Isesh alighted on the archway's peak, a deterrent to prying eyes and ears.

"Go away," Teza said.

"Why so eager for me to leave? Are you doing something you're not supposed to, like rifting into a forbidden archive?"

Teza looked anywhere except at her, a child caught eating nougats before dinner. He recovered quickly, but like he was reminding himself how to lie with a straight face. Jaleya suspected if she had asked about Saunez being his sister no recovery would have been necessary. Saunez would accept nothing less than perfection. Fortunately for Jaleya, Teza's discipline was lie specific.

"I don't like you or your pet," Teza said. Isesh chirp-growled from above. Teza continued with the minimum amount of obligatory civility. "I want to enjoy the time when you're not hovering over my shoulder."

"By experimenting with frozen rifts," Jaleya said.

"They're not—" Teza clamped his mouth shut and folded his arms. "Go away."

Jaleya almost did. She also wanted to enjoy the time when she wasn't forced to hover over him. The Festival of Shattered Swords was in full swing. She'd been looking forward to a dinner of peppers and squash stuffed with fried fish and mint chutney, followed by a tournament (she wouldn't be able to find a performance that didn't spout Ways nonsense). She wanted to surprise Isesh with a new brush, too; she hoped she could afford the kind he favored.

The vacant space before Teza made her hesitate. The last time she had caught him being secretive, he had been in the forbidden archive researching lost arts. With the stars frolicking overhead, he could test that research to his heart's content. As long as he was alone. Jaleya considered the distant but watchful guards. As long as Teza *thought* he was alone.

The lost arts must be very important to Teza for him to knowingly exploit loopholes that circumvented his devotion. His rebellious streak had Jaleya interested despite herself. Was it a crack she could employ to finally make him see the error of his Ways?

"It looked frozen to me," Jaleya said. She had foundational

knowledge of the rowshatari's abilities and how to neutralize them, but she was far from an expert. Guardians couldn't have too much knowledge.

"Of course it looks that way to you," Teza said. "You're from the countryside."

Meaning she was less educated. "Not indoctrinated" was the accurate term.

Keeping her sarcasm to a minimum, Jaleya said, "Then enlighten me."

"You wouldn't understand," Teza said.

"I'm sure you can dumb it down for my simple intellect."

"Then it wouldn't make sense."

Jaleya gritted her teeth. "I'll go away if you tell me. If not, I'll hover all night." She went to a closed water barrel and seated herself upon it.

Sparks haloed Teza's whitening crown. "The rift wasn't frozen," he grumbled with an eye roll. "There was a time bubble in front of it."

"You can veer time bubbles?" Jaleya said. She thought the Ora didn't let their rowshatari-estra become that strong. Teza's replenishing assignment suddenly adopted a nefarious purpose.

"Only small ones," Teza said. "I've been trying to expand one into the rift, but whenever the bubble touches it..." He spread his fingers and hands in an imitation of an explosion.

"Why are you trying to do that?" Jaleya asked.

Teza sighed. "See, I told you you wouldn't understand." But as he began to explain, a light that had nothing to do with kaza brightened his eyes.

"Rifts seem like doorways, but they're actually a hallway that's been compressed. The journey through the passage goes by in a blink, but for that blink, you are *in* the Boundless Sea—*in* Orvashka. If you could slow down that moment, you may be able to alter the passage and move the exit and leave somewhere else."

"Somewhere else?" Jaleya said. All rifts led somewhere else. That was their purpose.

"To rift, you have to know where you're going or be able to see where you're going if you're unfamiliar with the destination. But Orvashka is everywhere. It sustains and permeates the world. If you could slow down that blink when you're inside it, you could potentially go somewhere you haven't been before because you would be traveling *in* Orvashka instead of through it."

"You could go anywhere," Jaleya said. She and Isesh shared a mutual dread.

"Rowshatari-estra used to be able to do it," Teza said, oblivious to the terrifying scenarios running through Jaleya's mind. His childlike passion rivaled the brightest star. "Rediscovering this lost art would benefit everyone. Harmony would be solidified in the North and could spread beyond Setsea. There would be no more rebellions and no more fighting and no more killing."

The depth to which he believed that was chilling. His experiment could spread the Ora's reign across countries in a war that would ravage Idlium. His intentions were pure, but the Ora were masters at perverting such intentions. Their rise to power was paved with them.

Resisting her desire to fling his fallacies at his iridescent face, Jaleya glanced around the training grounds, at the guards above, at the other rowshatari-estra and the off-duty javati. "Do you experiment here every night you can veer?"

"Yes. This is the only safe place to practice," Teza said condescendingly.

"In full view of everyone here, you experiment with rifts."

"The other rowshatari can't see me, and the guards don't understand what I'm doing."

"Maybe, but the guards report to superiors who do."

Jaleya waited for him to catch up, but he just stared, lost. She sighed. "Whatever you think you're hiding, you're not. The advocates know exactly what you're doing, but they want you to keep doing it, so they're pretending they don't know."

Why assign him to replenish the Dazmiri, then? Different factions could by vying for position, but more likely the danger of Teza's growing strength had finally outweighed the potential gain.

Teza laughed incredulously. "You country folk are so paranoid. That makes no sense. If the advocates want me to pursue this lost art, they would've provided a substitute method instead of denying my request."

"Wait. You requested to experiment with rifts?" Jaleya said.

"Of course. The advocates have to assess the risk associated with any new veering. They were right to deny my request. I could've been hurt, and I wouldn't have been able to fulfill my duty to Abylay's people."

Jaleya stared. He couldn't be that deluded. She was witnessing it, and she still couldn't believe it. Orvashka's Ways were a *sham*. How could he not see that?

"But you're doing exactly what you were denied permission to do," Jaleya said.

"No, I'm not. This way is different."

Jaleya tilted her head. "Did you request permission to use this method?"

Teza paled beneath the stars' iridescence, Jaleya's discovery of his loophole finally dawning on him. Jaleya let him squirm in his own imagination, keeping her posture nonthreatening.

Swallowing, Teza said, "You may report my misconduct in general terms. Custodian Saunez advised me to conserve my strength for stars' sway, and I see now I should have heeded her wise counsel."

He was more worried about Saunez's reaction than the Advocate Council's? Another priority he had backward. Neither would accept his false humility as genuine.

"Do I seem like I'm going to report you?" Jaleya said.

"You always seem like that; you're always angry," Teza said.

Isesh huffed from his perch. He could have been discouraging a buzzing insect, but he wasn't.

Jaleya sighed. "I'm off duty."

Confusion and hope vied for dominance on Teza's face. Jaleya had witnessed the same dilemma in the archive.

"I just want to help," Teza said.

His sincerity caught Jaleya off guard. She studied him in the torchlight that seeped from the surrounding arcade. Misplaced loyalties aside, she recognized the desire to act—to do something, and the disappointment of being unable to.

Her words carried less heat than usual. She wasn't always angry! "You replenish cylinder seals. How is that not helping?" He was helping the wrong side, but she put a lid on that for the moment—a very short moment.

"It's an important duty," Teza said hastily. "I'm glad to serve the Ora and Orvashka's Ways in the position they've given me." He paused, his skin's iridescence muting his blush. "But the rowshatari used to do so much more. I wanted to be one when I was young; I admired them, knew them all by name. Now that I am one, it's... very different."

"You feel...powerless," Jaleya offered.

"I'm not powerless," Teza said much too quickly. "It's just... frustrating, sometimes, that I can't do more."

Frustrating was putting it mildly. Jaleya hated the guardian's oath she'd been forced to assume, but she had hoped it would provide opportunities to rectify Lenruz's murder. Oh, how quickly she had been disillusioned of such fancies. It infuriated Jaleya knowing she was helping sustain the Ora's rule, but if she outright rebelled and fled their tyranny, her chances of achieving her revenge became nil, unless she was lucky and the shavinash cadre sent to hunt her down contained the monster she sought. Joining a rebellion would lessen her odds initially, but when it gained ground, sooner or later it would face shavinashi. And now, even that slim possibility had been ripped away from her.

"The Dazmiri have the secret," Teza said with a stamp of his foot. "I don't know how they fly, but it's theoretically similar to manipulating a rift passage. The Dazmiri's seals still work, so it is still possible…" The passion faded from Teza's eyes, and his face fell. "Maybe seeing their depictions tomorrow will help. Have you ever b-been on a Dazmir? It's said to be magnificent."

"No," Jaleya said.

"I suppose I'll find out soon enough." His attempt at a lighthearted smile resulted in a grave twitch.

Jaleya winced, but with pity. He was a tool for everyone to use or exploit, even his own sister. His sister should have been protecting him.

"Maybe Custodian Saunez will approve your request after you've seen a Dazmir's heart seal," Jaleya said.

"The advocates approve veering requests," Teza said.

"So, Custodian Saunez delivers the requests on your behalf and informs you of their denial or approval?"

"Yes." Teza rolled his eyes. "How do you not know that?"

He had missed her point, as anticipated. Jaleya bit back a retort. "Custodian Saunez has a lot of responsibilities."

Teza nodded in agreement. Then he added, "You country folk really need better education."

Jaleya's cheeks burned with fury.

Careful, Jaleya, Isesh sent.

Jaleya cooled her flared temper. "I'll let you enjoy your evening," she said to Teza. She even managed a civil tone.

Isesh descended from his perch and joined her in the lit corridor as she retraced her steps to the intersection that led to Iza Vor's nearest gate.

If Saunez didn't submit his request or altered it to appear harmless, which is more likely, the advocates might not be fully aware of what he's attempting, Isesh sent.

There's no 'if' about it, Jaleya replied. *It's another ploy to obtain lost arts. Being able to travel within rift passages would be a huge advantage to the resistance. Which means Teza's replenishing assignment is just protocol for removing a problematic rowshatar. And Saunez isn't lifting a finger to save him.*

You seem concerned for him, Isesh noted.

His situation is of his own making, Jaleya retorted. *If he didn't believe the Ora's lies, he would see what's really happening. As it stands, he's a danger to the resistance.*

Jaleya looked over her shoulder. Teza had veered another rift, and it fizzled out like the ones preceding it. Teza leaned on his knees in disappointment. He might have more strength than the others, but it wasn't anywhere near what the rowshatari of old had supposedly possessed.

Jaleya's charge straightened, his shoulders tall, and formed another rift. So determined. The best of intentions. He could bring war to all of Idlium. She would definitely be able to say, "I told you so," then.

Would she still want to?

Jaleya might have something stronger than tea with her dinner, which had suddenly lost its appeal.

CHAPTER 24

Jubilant music quickened the evening air as kaza displays flashed in the skyline to accompanying awe. Cheering and clashing steel rang from the tournament field. The Temples of Love beckoned with warm light and incense. Enraptured citizens in their festival best scurried to and fro beneath streamers and banners that wove the Way of Love's sword-breaking tulip across intersections and squares. Harmony and Ways flags crowning towers and domes danced in the breeze skimming the Nidren.

Jaleya huddled in the corner of a teahouse's porch, Isesh lounging beside her. Laughter from taverns and temporary pavilions gushed into the streets. Lottery winners from the West Ward paused every few steps, overwhelmed and enchanted by the trappings of luxury, and indulging as if this night was their last. Their rigorous bathing and borrowed opulent clothing that professed value in truth only served to advertise the Ora's charity. Jaleya's untouched tea no longer steamed.

Food vendors carrying pastries, cheeses, sweets, an assortment of fruit juices, and grilled kebabs passed through the small square adjoining the teahouse. Isesh followed the tidbits with his avian eyes, unless his canine nose detected a particularly appetizing scent deemed worthy of his entire head's attention. Jaleya had settled for a simple dinner of bulgur mixed with figs and almonds. She and Isesh had shared a handful of cinnamon dates for dessert; their price had been almost a whole week's stipend. Isesh's favored brush had been abandoned at the merchant's booth even before the dates. Jaleya had done her best to conceal her disappointment, for the gesture alone pleased Isesh like a warm updraft.

Jaleya's mind continually wandered to her charge—her naïve, childish, oblivious charge. He had made his choice. He chose to be an Illuminated. His experiments were a threat to the resistance. If Saunez could turn that threat into an advantage, all the better. The Ora's rule had to be broken. Jaleya's appetite shouldn't be ruined. She had suppressed the urge to punch Teza again on more than one occasion.

The person Teza should be able to trust above all others was manipulating him.

Jaleya idly rubbed the handle of her teacup, and spotted Yongir amid the complicit revelers. Lizuna trailed him lethargically, her graceful neck bowed low. Noticing Jaleya, Yongir and the pegasus changed course.

"Jaleya," he greeted. "I'm surprised to see you here instead of enjoying the festival's activities."

"I'm enjoying them from a distance," Jaleya said.

Yongir chuckled and indicated the vacant seat across from her. "May I?"

Jaleya nodded. "How is the bridge reinforcement?" she asked.

"Tiring and menial, but it keeps me fit. How is your charge?"

"Still a rowshatar."

Isesh dimmed in Jaleya's mind as he attempted to engage Lizuna. The black pegasus lingered at the rim of the teahouse's kazalight. Isesh had raised his head to exchange the customary fashari greeting when she approached, but Lizuna had merely stared, ears forward, as if trying to recall why Isesh's actions were familiar.

"I heard he'll be replenishing the skyships tomorrow," Yongir said. "Is this true?"

Jaleya nodded in what she thought was a casual manner, but Yongir returned her effort with an understanding grimace. "Be mindful of where you place your sympathy. Do not become emotionally attached to the person who controls your life. It leads to refraining from festivals and brooding in corners while your excellent tea goes cold."

Jaleya flinched beneath his astute observation. Surely she wasn't that transparent. In defiance of his conclusion, and her muddled state of mind, Jaleya calmly sipped her tea. It was colder than she anticipated. Her nose scrunched as she swallowed the flat liquid. Yongir chuckled, and Jaleya shrugged in defeat, her cheeks blushing scarlet.

A server arrived and asked Yongir if he would like to order a beverage. Caught up in amusement over Jaleya's tea drinking, he declined with an overenthusiastic grin. The server departed with a sniff, assuming the mirth was at her expense.

Yongir sobered, and knowingly regarded Jaleya, glancing once at her inedible tea.

"Rowshatar Teza is the first rowshatar-estra I've been assigned," Jaleya said. "With rowshatari-korza and mara, I can walk away as soon as the sun and moon show up. But with Teza, that opportunity only comes once a month. I see everything. Every part of his life. He seems so…alone. And I never thought I would associate that word with a rowshatar."

"Our duty is to protect them," Yongir said gently, "but with that duty comes the inevitability that we see the rowshatari as ordinary people. That's why we're frequently reassigned. The rowshatari don't like being reminded that they are closer to commoners than Orvashka."

Jaleya glanced around the porch. Complaining about one's charge in Iza Vor surrounded by other javati was one thing, but it was another matter entirely to demean rowshatari in public. Counselors had ears everywhere. None of the populace appeared to have heard him, though, or if they had they weren't scrambling to report him.

"What you must remember…" Yongir trailed off as Lizuna wandered into the square. The silence of a javati's exchange settled upon Yongir.

Isesh? Jaleya sent. The simurgh's ears were peaked in interest.

Something is amiss, Isesh replied.

Jaleya scanned the thoroughfares filled with tipsy revelers and scrutinized the shadows for suspicious movement. *What is it?*

I'm not sure. Isesh stood. His gaze trailed Lizuna as she ambled down a side street. The festivalgoers parted like a river around a rock.

"Lizuna!" Yongir called, and sighed when she didn't return.

Isesh regarded Yongir sitting calmly across from Jaleya. *Be cautious. Reveal nothing.*

Isesh trotted off the portico in pursuit of Lizuna, the crowd yielding him a much wider berth than the pegasus.

"He thinks something's wrong, but he's not sure what," Jaleya explained to Yongir's puzzled expression.

The older javati bowed his head as a heavy burden seemed to saddle his shoulders. "Lizuna's…condition distresses other fashari. When she becomes distracted, her attention narrows onto the diversion, and it can be difficult to reach her. She probably wandered after a fruit cart."

Yongir twisted in his seat, caught between wanting to retrieve his javati and remain with Jaleya. He paused, and then resolutely faced forward. He spoke lightheartedly, but his eyes were pained. "I will have to fetch her, unless your javati does so for me. But regarding your charge, Jaleya. What you must remember is that, in the end, they are rowshatari and you are a javati, and our lives are worth less than theirs.

"Gardok also pondered if life could be otherwise, and while hope and sympathy are amicable, admirable even, I would be saddened if you likewise lost sight of what is."

Jaleya hesitated; Isesh had cautioned her before pursuing Lizuna. But his wariness of Yongir stemmed from the pegasus's condition. Yongir was a fellow javati, and he had proven himself by helping her obtain the obsidian to bypass the library's seal lock. He might parrot Orvashka's Ways like a good citizen, but a carefully contained inner fire undermined his words.

"Perhaps Gardok saw as well as you and I, and circumstances simply took advantage of his fancies," Jaleya said.

Yongir's attention peaked like a simurgh's ears. He kept his expression neutral. "Circumstances can be crafty, especially if you're otherwise occupied."

Jaleya chose her words carefully. She had no proof either way of Gardok's status with the resistance, but her inclination was that he had simply been one of Saunez's pawns. Perhaps a pawn the resistance had been aiming to recruit, if anything she had heard about him was true, but one not yet initiated into the alliance. He had been innocent of the charges that led to his execution. A common practice with Orvashka's Ways. Saunez still bore responsibility for the javati's death (horrible woman), but the means had been provided on a gold platter.

"Our charges require the majority of our attention," Jaleya said, "which is why we have custodians as our eyes and ears. They see the changing conditions we do not and act accordingly. But even the most attentive custodian is not always forthcoming, and actions she believes are in the best interest of a javati can actually be detrimental and escalate into misfortune."

Yongir leaned back in his chair and loosed a steadying breath. That should diminish Saunez in the javati's eyes. At least she would somewhat get her due.

"A bitter tragedy," Yongir said, shaking his head. "If only Gardok hadn't denied the accusation. Re-education is not uncommon among javati; he would've survived." Yongir paused, thoughtful. "Unless he wasn't meant to survive, and he was incited to escalation…"

The underpinnings of a question clung to Yongir's musing. Jaleya wasn't sure how he had arrived at that speculation; she hadn't implied any such thing. At least, she didn't think she had.

"I don't know the specifics of his arrest," she said, "but Isesh often tells me that good can come from tragedy. He hasn't convinced me yet, but maybe this time will prove him right."

Yongir pondered her words for a moment, and then sidled closer. "This affair seems to run deeper than we were expecting."

Jaleya hesitated, and Yongir latched onto it like a starving man consuming crumbs.

"Jaleya, what else did you find?"

Isesh's warning rang in Jaleya's mind, but it was also Isesh who claimed hope was a needed remedy Setseans lacked; that it was always present even amid a lightless sky. Yongir could definitely use some hope. His desperation was a dammed river barely contained, the heartache he bore for Lizuna a cracked seal gem refusing to shatter even as seeping kaza eroded its facets. Yongir was a javati.

"I stumbled upon reassurance that we are not alone, and that a fancy can satisfy, even if its reality is different than expected and an attentive custodian is the source of hope and tragedy."

Yongir leaned closer at her mention of the attentive custodian, his fingers trembling with anticipation. His words were a breath among the festival's joviality. "Resistance? Here?"

Jaleya inclined her head no more than a twitch.

The blow struck her cheek and uprooted her from her seat. She crashed against the porch, only her javash with Isesh preventing unconsciousness. More stunned than wounded, Jaleya blinked to clear her double vision. Yongir loomed over her. Gone was the desperation for hope, the genial glint that never strayed far from his lips. The heartache for Lizuna. The acute lines of his face had calloused, his eyes pitiless. His dense muscles clenched in eagerness to harm.

"You traitors are all the same." His voice was a stranger's.

He lifted his booted foot to fully incapacitate her, but a spectral blur slammed into his chest and hurled him into the square. A pealing bark pierced the evening's revelry. Festivalgoers screamed and scattered. Doors and shutters banged shut.

Jaleya stumbled to her feet and staggered into the abandoned square. Isesh guarded Yongir's prone form. Blood leaked from a head wound sustained when Isesh had tackled him, and bite marks encircled his neck. Kaza spectacles thundered and flared the skyline.

Are you hurt? Isesh sent. *Jaleya?*

It took a moment for his sending to pierce her lagging mind. She shook her head. Her jaw ached, but she didn't think it was broken. Speaking would be painful, and her cheek would be purple by tomorrow, but nothing that wouldn't heal.

Calls of alarm echoed up the streets. Inquisitive citizens in the surrounding buildings peered through cracked shutters. They wanted to be the first to report to the approaching guards; the most loyal would have the most information.

Isesh began digging his nose beneath Yongir's torso. *Get him onto my back. We need to delay the guards.*

Is he dead? Jaleya sent. Still in a daze, only Isesh's steadfast, familiar presence was keeping her grounded. Yongir had attacked her. Had called her a traitor. It didn't feel real even as she faltered while heaving him onto Isesh.

No, only unconscious, Isesh sent. *Come. Hurry.*

Jaleya trotted behind her javati as he wound through alleys and side streets but remained parallel to Iza Vor. When he stopped at an unlit dead end, they were on the border of a residential area blocks from the teahouse.

How much did you tell him? Isesh sent as he shed his burden.

Jaleya stared at the javati lying unconscious on the paved bricks. The javati who had welcomed her with a warm chuckle and counseled her through Abylay's pitfalls. It had all been a ruse.

Jaleya!

She tore her gaze from Yongir. A javati. An Illuminated.

How much does he know?

Isesh's question recalled her conversation with Yongir. He had been too eager near the end, too forceful. She should have seen his unusual bluntness as the warning it was. But she hadn't. So many warnings she hadn't seen. And she had told him…

Everything, Jaleya sent. *He knows…everything…*

Dear Creator, what had she done?

Jaleya.

An infinite radiance rippled in the dark pools of Isesh's eyes. His powerful muscles swelled, and his spectral feathers gleamed with celestial light as he seemed to grow larger amid a deep, fierce aura not of the earthly realm.

Be strong now. Weep later.

Latching on to their javash, Jaleya managed a nod.

Isesh trotted to the cross street. On hind legs, he chomped free a streamer spanning the dead end. He dropped the fabric at Jaleya's feet.

Tie him quickly, Isesh instructed. *The longer it takes the guards to find him, the more time we'll have.*

Jaleya gathered the streamer automatically. The embroidered Harmonies seemed to jeer. She pulled the emblems taut.

We should kill him. The words came from her mind, but she felt detached from the cold sending. Detached from her body, as if she had stepped outside of it and someone else was directing its movements. *He's an Illuminated.*

Isesh sidled between her and Yongir. *His death will not change the outcome of this night. The trail leads to Saunez regardless. And I will not allow cold-blooded murder.*

Would he then deny her her revenge when she caught Lenruz's killer? The passing thought wasn't new, just stirred from its slumber.

In truth, it was a relief to loosen her white-knuckled grip on the mocking streamer.

Jaleya strode to Yongir and began binding him, her muscle memory compensating for her besieged mind.

Quickly, Isesh urged. *Lizuna will delay as much as possible, but it won't be for long.*

Lizuna? Jaleya sent.

We are not the first to fall prey to Yongir's deception. Lizuna resists when she can, but her strength is failing, and her spirit wanes. Yongir must have realized Lizuna's intention, hence their precipitate attack.

She attacked you? Jaleya sent.

Reluctantly. I broke her leg.

An injury which would see a horse put down without kaza healing. A pegasus could survive due to support from its wings, but without kaza would endure weeks of suffering. Isesh's sending carried grief, remorse, and acceptance.

So her condition isn't accidental, Jaleya sent. *He did that to her.*

Isesh had recognized the warning. He had seen all the warnings. She hadn't listened.

And you still want me to spare him?

We will find a way to expose him, Isesh sent, *but we don't want to be hunted for murder in addition to being traitors.*

They *would* have to run now. Jaleya had admitted affiliation with the resistance. Lenruz's killer might as well be a ghost.

Jaleya began to tremble with rage, her fingers pausing on the last knot. She breathed deep, quelling the fury warming her cheeks. Harboring it until the time came to unleash it.

How could he do that to his javati? She finished the last knot with an unnecessary jerk, punctuating her disgust. Her sending had been rhetorical incredulity, but as she and Isesh rolled a bound Yongir into the deepest shadows, Isesh replied, *Some humans do not have the wisdom to accept sound guidance, or truth, when they hear it. Most humans,* he amended. *But you can learn it.*

Sorrow tempered an ancient anger in the fashari's avian eyes, but there was no condemnation. It was worse than if he had mauled her with javash unrestrained.

Isesh offered his back. *Come. We must warn Saunez.*

A weight dropped into Jaleya's stomach, jarring her out of her stupor. Warn Saunez. Jaleya subconsciously knew that would be necessary; she had exposed the horrible woman. Of course she would have to be warned. But hearing Isesh pronounce it suddenly made the necessity a very present reality. Jaleya would rather face a pride of lions than Custodian Saunez.

She forced her resisting legs to move and mounted Isesh. The simurgh seemed to diminish as they took to the star-speckled sky, even though he was no smaller than he had been in the alley.

The guards posted at Iza Vor's nearest gate stood at attention, but they barely glanced at Jaleya's guardian pass before admitting her. Iza Vor's grounds were quiet apart from the intermittent private gatherings. Yongir's accusation hadn't reached the citadel. Jaleya and Isesh were ahead of the hunters. For now.

Isesh led Jaleya to the custodian hall; unexpected at the late hour, but not surprising. Only one other desk was occupied by an assistant. Jaleya and Isesh approached Saunez's office, but Er'od barred their way with a raised hand and a polite but stern, "May I help you?"

"I need to speak with Custodian Saunez," Jaleya replied.

"Is she expecting you?"

"No, but this is important."

"I see," Er'od said dismissively. "Why don't you have a seat, and I'll ask her if she will see you."

Jaleya fumed. If a rowshatar had come to her, he or she would have been admitted immediately, no matter the hour. She and Isesh couldn't waste their precious time on bureaucratic nonsense.

Jaleya shoved past Er'od into Saunez's office. Saunez looked up from a document, her custodian seal dripping fresh wax. Er'od apologized and ordered Jaleya to leave while edging aside of Isesh, who crept into the room behind them.

Saunez raised her hand, and Er'od ceased his feeble attempts to remove them. How did she do that?

"It's fine, Er'od," Saunez said, and added for Jaleya, "I'm sure there's a good explanation for the interruption." She didn't speak the word "rude," but Jaleya heard it.

Er'od eyed Jaleya dubiously, but he obeyed his mistress and returned to his desk. Isesh positioned himself next to the closed door, listening and smelling for Iza Vor's eyes and ears. Saunez's civil expression became rigid stone.

Mouth suddenly dry, Jaleya said, "There's a problem."

"Regarding what?" Saunez said in an overly polite tone.

Jaleya swallowed, and then quickly and concisely relayed the events at the teahouse. Saunez's brow furrowed as she spoke, until it rivaled her pursed lips for displeasure. When Jaleya finished, Saunez calmly set aside her custodian seal and the stamped document and placed her clasped hands on the desk, perhaps to stop them from wringing Jaleya's neck. Jaleya had never seen Saunez expend such effort to master herself. It was terrifying.

Saunez's even voice pierced the taut air as no shout ever could. "It never occurred to you that there are Illuminated among the javati?"

A javati Illuminated had never entered Jaleya's mind. Her cheeks burned with shame.

"You might have unwittingly located the spy we've been searching for," Saunez said. "And you might have ruined everything."

The custodian summoned her assistant back into the office. Despite herself, Jaleya was impressed by how quickly Saunez's polite, official demeanor returned.

"Er'od, I'm needed to settle a disagreement between javati. The correspondence I'll leave on my desk must be delivered tonight. After that, you may retire, and we'll reconvene after stars' sway."

"Yes, Custodian Saunez," Er'od replied. "Is everything all right?" He studied Jaleya, committing her description to memory.

"It's nothing serious, but to prevent escalation, I must attend to it immediately. You know how prickly javati are."

Er'od nodded with complete disregard for Jaleya and Isesh's presence and returned to his desk. The pleasantness dropped from

Saunez's expression. Jaleya restrained dozens of questions as Saunez opened a desk drawer and shuffled through the papers within. After selecting ten seemingly at random, she dipped a stylus in the inkwell, addressed them, blew the fresh ink dry, and secured the messages with her custodian seal. Piling them on the center of her desk, she told Jaleya, "Come with me."

They departed the custodian's office with routine professionalism, but the second Er'od lost sight of them, Saunez's pace increased to a purposeful march. Jaleya detected a door opening and closing on the edge of her enhanced hearing.

"Your assistant isn't one of us?" Jaleya whispered, but she wasn't surprised; she had never seen him without the Harmony around his neck.

Saunez replied, "He will consider opening the letters for a few moments, and when he decides their late deliverance and my hasty departure are suspicious enough to warrant doing so, all he will find are festival well-wishes and meeting requests. He'll reseal the letters and deliver them, and by the time anyone is the wiser, we will be gone. However, if he discovers the code in a select few, our window of opportunity will vastly diminish."

She led Jaleya down servant hallways and back staircases, but Jaleya remained oriented enough to realize they were heading to the javati compound. She could already smell fashari musk and sweet straw.

Saunez paused when they arrived, searching, and then approached a man with a bold face and bulging arms. Jaleya had seen him around the compound but never spoken with him. He was assigned to a rowshatar-korza and was javash to a sirrush. The same sirrush that had been covering the secret resistance meeting?

The javati respectfully lowered his head to Saunez. Isesh's presence dimmed.

"Enlu, I have good news," Saunez said. "Jaleya here has spoken with her fashari, and he will be more conscious of where he lounges so your fashari won't feel like he's being driven from his territory."

"Isesh—" Jaleya began, but Saunez drowned her out. "You may

still file a formal grievance, of course, but as long as her fashari behaves as agreed, I don't think it's necessary."

Enlu studied Saunez and Jaleya. It became clear to him, just as it was dawning on Jaleya, that what was being spoken was not what Saunez was there to say.

"Will there be repercussions if this incident isn't recorded?" Enlu asked.

"I've noted it in my daily report, but if Jaleya's fashari doesn't behave as agreed and the dispute escalates, that note might not sufficiently support your side of the grievance."

Enlu pretended to consider. "I will trust the honor of the noble fashari."

"Very well. I'm considering this matter closed."

"Agreed," Enlu said, and after a raised eyebrow from Saunez, Jaleya responded likewise.

As they turned to leave, Saunez brushed past Enlu and pressed a small folded paper into his hand. Jaleya was alarmed at the daring move in the exposed courtyard, even with the night's shadows, but no one was paying them any attention. It was just a custodian performing her duty, and the other javati were pleased to not be the object of her interest.

"What is he going to do?" Jaleya asked quietly.

"Keep people safe from your egregious error," Saunez said. "Where's Teza?"

Jaleya stopped dead. "Teza? He's an Illuminated."

"Where is he?" Saunez repeated sharply.

Jaleya couldn't blame Saunez for being angry with her; she was angry with herself. It was the fear creeping into the older woman's voice that worried her. Contingency and evacuation plans were essential, but leaving behind coded messages? Warning other resistance? This seemed full blown worst-case scenario.

Hollowness gnawed Jaleya's stomach. The repercussions of her inadvertent mistake ran deeper than she realized. She had a feeling something was about to go horribly wrong.

"He was at the training grounds, but that was hours ago," Jaleya said.

"Stupid boy," Saunez growled. She did some quick calculations. "He'll be in his quarters by now."

They arrived a few minutes later, slowing as they approached to not arouse suspicion. The guards admitted them without question, opening the double doors in perfect sync with Saunez's steps.

Teza turned in his seat from where he ate dates, cheese, bread, and pomegranate jam. "Saunez, what are you doing here?" he said. His large ears might as well have been laid flat with guilt.

Saunez went to a bas-relief of palm trees and pressed a combination of frond segments. A hidden panel swung open, and she retrieved a light but full pack and two heavy cloaks from within. She tossed a cloak to Teza, who recoiled as if it contained the plague.

"Put it on," Saunez ordered. "We have an emergency assignment outside Iza Vor."

"What? That's not right. It's the middle of the night. And why are you storing things in my quarters?"

Because no one would suspect a Setsean rowshatar of rejecting Orvashka's Ways. Saunez had planned well. Why was she risking it all to bring Teza along? Their relation meant nothing to her, and he knew nothing of Saunez's rebellion. He was a liability only if he accompanied them.

And yet, here Saunez was consuming their precious seconds trying to persuade her obstinate brother to come willingly. His rift theories must be more important than Jaleya realized. The conclusion rippled in protest.

"This is not a discussion," Saunez said firmly. "I am your custodian, and you've been given an emergency assignment."

"I won't be spoken to like this," Teza said. "I'm a rowshatar."

"A rowshatar who's been illicitly experimenting with rifts, and who now, judging by the food you're gorging, can't rift to save your life, which is what you will have to do if you don't listen to me."

Teza's haughtiness diminished as the gravity of the situation finally began to register. He considered the hidden pack in his quarters, the lack of procedure and escort, and the late hour and abruptness of their departure. "Saunez, what's going on?"

Saunez grabbed the cloak at his feet and thrust it into his hands. "An emergency assignment."

Teza opened his mouth to ask another question, but he cowered in defeat when his sister's eyebrow rose to an incredible height. Jaleya needed to learn how to do that.

Teza grudgingly put the cloak over his shoulders and tied it closed. It was a little big, but that helped conceal his fine clothing and iridescent skin. Saunez had planned very well.

"It smells," Teza complained.

"Come," Saunez said, calmer now that they were moving again.

The guards eyed them askance as they left Teza's quarters, but at their continued silence, Jaleya began to think they had overcome another obstacle.

"Custodian Saunez…?" one of the guards said hesitantly.

Jaleya's instincts screamed for her scimitar. Saunez turned gracefully, the picture of innocence. "Yes?"

"I don't mean to infringe upon your duty, but where are you going?"

"You are infringing, and I am not at liberty to disclose our assignment." She paused, pretended to deliberate out of sympathy, and covertly backtracked to the skeptical guards. "Guild business," she whispered. "A seal is…malfunctioning."

The guards exchanged alarmed glances. "Should we be worried?"

"I believe this is a cautionary measure, but I can't be certain from here."

"Of course, Custodian. Pardon us, Custodian."

"One of the guild's seals is malfunctioning?" Teza said as they resumed their steady pace down the hallway. "I'm not certified to fix that."

"Hush," Saunez replied, and surprisingly, he did.

Saunez took the most direct route to the stables, regardless of a corridor's occupants. She stood in the center of the barn aisle with the posture of one expecting to be waited on. Why weren't her needs being taken care of? The stable boy finally appeared. Saunez commanded two horses to be saddled, but the boy apologetically replied that he hadn't received orders to provide mounts for her. Saunez feigned sympathy while conceding the rowshatar would be late to his assignment and someone was going to be reprimanded. The underhanded threat got the boy moving; he didn't want anyone getting in trouble, and as long as the documentation was on its way, he could ready two horses.

"You'll have to walk," Saunez said to Jaleya, who had expected no less. Appearances had to be maintained, Saunez's plan hadn't accounted for her and Isesh, and Saunez didn't like her.

As they rode out of the stables at a brisk walk, the deep sky flared with light. In the direction of the main communication minaret. Yongir had been found. Their time was up.

"Saunez," Jaleya said.

"I see it," Saunez said, but she maintained the horses' walk.

Why wasn't she going faster? They would be captured if they didn't flee!

The message must reach one with authority to seal Iza Vor, and then that order must be relayed, Isesh sent. *We have a few minutes yet. Be calm.*

Jaleya heeded her javati, but it didn't repel the knife teasing her spine. Anticipation knotted her gut as she awaited the flare that would stab the blade into her flesh.

Iza Vor's gate loomed ominously as they approached. The stars swam in their tranquil pool. The guards halted them, and Saunez presented a very official-looking scroll. The guards inspected it in the lanterns' kazalight. Despite the cool night, sweat dripped down Jaleya's back.

A flash, behind her. She maintained her composure, but she couldn't stop her eyes from darting sideways in panic. She slowly moved her hand near her scimitar's hilt, but a subtle shift from Isesh deferred it back to rest. The guards turned from Saunez, who sat her horse like a Masatitoran princess, and scrutinized Jaleya and Isesh at Teza's side. Her heart threatened to burst from her chest.

The guards waved them through. Jaleya expected a spear to suddenly impale her, but nothing stirred as they crossed the sinister stones. Jaleya felt a dash of pride amid her racing pulse. She and Isesh had just saved Saunez from having to bluff her way out of Iza Vor.

Saunez immediately kicked her horse into a swift trot. Teza bounced in the saddle like a sack of flour, his arms flailing; Jaleya wondered how long it would be before he met the paved bricks. She mounted Isesh and trusted him to keep up with the horses. She watched the skyline for the light that would doom their final escape.

"Isn't the Guild Ward the other way?" Teza asked.

"We aren't going to a guild," Saunez said.

"But you said we were. Where are we going?"

"I'll explain everything when we arrive."

"No, explain it now. You lied to the guards. Ah!" Teza tilted sideways but grabbed the pommel of his saddle and managed to right himself.

"I can't explain now," Saunez said. "Time is pressing."

Jaleya expected Teza to continue arguing, but when he didn't, she thanked the horse he rode for occupying his attention.

A few blocks from Iza Vor, a telltale flare shone behind them. The citadel was being secured. Abylay's gates would be next. Jaleya gripped Isesh's feathers until he whimpered-chirped in discomfort.

Saunez wound through side streets at a breakneck pace, only slowing at corners to prevent a horse from slipping. Fortunately, most standard patrols had been allocated to the festival and its unofficial nightly revelries, so witnesses were scarce. Although, Jaleya wouldn't have been surprised if Saunez had memorized the patrol routes while crafting her evacuation.

They slowed dramatically a half block from Abylay's east gate. Every creak of shutters, every swish of a horse's tail, every rustle of a banner seemed an ambush about to spring.

Saunez handed the gate guards another official-looking scroll. It received similar but longer scrutiny than Iza Vor's, but the guards finally opened the gate and let them pass. The stifling salty air had never smelled so clear.

Thank you, Lizuna, Jaleya thought. She and Isesh shared a mutual sadness.

Abylay soon became twinkling earthen stars on the undulating horizon. Saunez pulled back on the reins. Breath steamed from the horses' nostrils.

"Where are we headed, since we're not actually going to the caravansary?" Jaleya asked.

"We're not going to the caravansary? You told those guards we were," Teza said to Saunez.

"We need to keep moving," Saunez said. "We have a hard ride ahead of us."

"Saunez, what is going on?" Teza demanded. He jerked his horse to a halt, but since he didn't stop pulling the reins, the poor creature started backing up. Saunez turned around to assist, and their party came to a dead stop. Saunez reached over and pulled the hood of Teza's cloak over his head. "Keep your hood up. You're glowing."

Teza shoved it back down, scowling. "I don't glow."

"A glimmer on a dark landscape is a signal fire," Saunez said. "Put your hood up, or you'll expose us."

"Expose us to what?" Teza said, exasperated.

Saunez's shoulders momentarily slumped. "I'll explain everything. I promise," she said gently. "But right now, we need to ride. You're just going to have to trust me."

"But…" Confusion, suspicion, and trust circled Teza's kaza-touched face. He glanced at Jaleya, and his lips twitched at the ridiculousness of said glance. Jaleya sat quietly on Isesh, knowing anything she said would shatter the fragile silence.

Teza sighed and drew the hood of his cloak over his white head. Saunez gently squeezed his shoulder, an oddly intimate gesture for her, but one that evoked pained remembrance for Jaleya.

They continued cantering east on the main road. Beyond the wheat and barley fields cast in the gentle red radiance of their agriculture seals, they walked the horses for a few minutes, and then took up the canter again, and so on and so forth as Abylay receded from sight. Teza almost fell from his horse more than once, so Saunez took command of his reins, and Teza clung to the saddle's pommel. Isesh and Jaleya periodically ascended and scouted for pursuit and bandits. Jaleya caught Teza looking longingly at Isesh, but a rigid stare made him refrain from voicing his demand. Despite the dire situation, the wind's embrace and the hills roaming the wide plains warmed Jaleya's heart, and for a moment, she was free.

Saunez eventually turned them off the main road onto a narrow dirt one. Buttes began intermingling with the hills. As they neared a sharp rise crowned with a crag, Jaleya discerned an estate nestled at its base. Kaza lanterns illuminated the parapets, their light systematically interrupted by guards patrolling the wall. Beyond the manor, silhouettes of outbuildings and simple houses slept beneath the starlight. Considering the proximity to the rocky hills, Jaleya assumed this was a mining estate. The precious stones would be useless for cylinder seals, but they would still boast a substantial price. Why was Saunez taking them there? The guilds were as zealous as the Counselors.

They halted before the dense wooden gate, and the guards on the wall ordered them to identify themselves. The kaza lanterns highlighted the Mining Guild emblem on the keystone.

"I am Custodian Saunez of Abylay, and I have urgent information regarding Batebi and Imlay's interests in Sarvis. Their foundations might not be as solid as they believe."

"How did you come by this information?" one guard said.

"Please, just give them the message. If they don't wish to see us, we'll leave. But they will want to see us."

The guards hesitated, whispered back and forth. "Wait there," one ordered, and then descended the wall. He returned a few minutes later, and they were courteously admitted. Saunez and Teza entered first, Jaleya and Isesh behind. Nervous yet fascinated whispers followed the simurgh's passing.

Blooming tulips bordered a paved stone path, and a long courtyard sheltered fig trees lining its center. An arched door nestled in the low wall on each side; rustling leaves peered over the tiled crenellations on Jaleya's left.

The manor was a three-story building of glazed bricks and stucco reliefs. Their escort directed them to a sitting room and instructed them to wait. Moldings with silver scroll bordered the two entrances, the Mining Guild emblem carved into the lintels. A trio of tapestries displayed the Ora dedicating the first temple to Orvashka's Ways; citizens raised their hands in praise in the foreground. Jaleya turned away in disgust. Saunez seated herself on a plush maroon chaise, the significance of their flight seemingly forgotten. A servant arrived and presented a tray of refreshments. Teza dashed to the tidbits and guzzled the tea, fruit, and yogurt. Isesh licked his jowls as he watched their charge.

Shortly after the servant departed, a shapely woman in a sunstone dress and with dark hair that caressed her upper back entered through the opposite door. A middle-aged man in a long tunic girdled with a sash accompanied her. His salt and pepper hair was of equal length. He ordered the guards to wait outside.

Jaleya hung back as Saunez approached the newcomers. After pleasantries that Jaleya was certain contained a coded verification were exchanged, Saunez said, "I've been compromised. We must alter the plan to obtain the skyships."

Their hosts, who Jaleya assumed were Imlay and Batebi, exchanged alarmed looks.

"How much could potentially be exposed?" Batebi asked.

"If they dig deep enough, they could link me to Firnan," Saunez said, "but that connection will be a dead end by the time they uncover it; I warned Enlu directly. They will most likely discover my interest in lost arts and manipulation of assignments and personnel. I left no trace of my objective, but the more direct means I've had to occasionally employ couldn't be completely erased. Everyone I've interacted with, however remotely, will be suspect. The Counselors may assume command of the custodians and oversee tomorrow's replenishings, or they may utilize subtlety in the hope it will expose defectors. Either way, there will be increased guards and maybe a shavinash cadre."

"Perhaps we should reconsider more than just the skyships," Imlay said gravely. "The attempt to reclaim the intelligence from Eclipse was a failure, and now this."

"Our people were unable to recover the information?" Saunez said, dismayed but not surprised.

"We received word earlier today," Imlay said. "Heavy losses, the cannon destroyed. Only one skimmer survived."

Saunez paused, but not for long. "No," she said firmly. "We may never again have this opportunity. A real opportunity to save Setsea! Others know Iza Vor's layout and protocols as well as I. We can still do this, but we must act quickly. We'll have to use the communication seals, and we'll need a distraction."

Their hosts hesitated. Isesh's ears twitched. Jaleya's pulse throbbed. She hadn't just compromised Saunez. She had potentially compromised the resistance's entire plan.

Please let there be a way, she prayed. *Please.*

"You're rebels," Teza whispered. His voice thundered in the pregnant silence. "You're *rebels!*"

Saunez's fists clenched in exasperation. "I'll explain later," she said over her shoulder.

Teza threw back his hood; yogurt was smeared on his cheek. "No. You'll explain now."

Their hosts flinched. "What have you done?" Batebi said. Red light tinted Imlay's hand. A remshir? Her hair wasn't long enough. An illegal seal obtained through bribes or the black market, then.

Saunez carefully crossed to Teza, a farmhand attempting to wrangle a horse that preferred to remain in the pasture. Her posture was resolute, but her tone was gentle. Regretful?

"Yes, I am resistance. This isn't how I wanted you to find out, but what's done is done. Understand my actions are for Setsea's benefit. You'll see that soon enough. For now, you're just going to have to trust me."

Teza stared at Saunez, aghast. "You're a rebel," he muttered, his voice thick with the sting of betrayal.

"I'm your sister," Saunez said softly, too softly for Imlay and Batebi to hear. "You're my brother. That hasn't changed, and it never will."

Teza's mouth moved, but no words formed. Isesh crept behind him to prevent escape, as rifting was beyond him at the moment. Jaleya eased a sheen of blade from its sheathe. The kazalight illuminating Imlay's hand deepened. Batebi adjusted his stance for a charged tackle, rowshatar or not.

Teza seemed oblivious to everyone except Saunez. She stood uncompromising, but patient instead of forceful. She didn't want to intimidate him into accepting this. If she hadn't been Saunez, Jaleya would have described her as desperately, fearfully hopeful.

Saunez's brother blinked, coming back to himself. The rowshatar haughtiness retreated, and he averted his gaze. Saunez raised her hand to clean the yogurt off his cheek, but Teza cringed. He hastily wiped the smear with the sleeve of his cloak.

"Why did you bring him?" Batebi asked, seeing the immediate threat had passed. "His presence endangers all of us."

"It created doubt," Saunez said. "Rowshatar rebels are rare, but it does happen, however much the Ora otherwise proclaim. Every resource investigating if he is or isn't loyal is one less resource devoted to hunting us."

"He would've served that purpose in Abylay," Imlay pointed out.

Jaleya had thought the same initially, but she had had hours to re-evaluate during their ride. If Teza and Saunez's relation had been discovered during the routine interrogation, the Counselors would wonder what else he was hiding. He might have been given to the shavinashi to ensure he wasn't holding anything back. And he wouldn't hold anything back. Not under the physical and mental torture of the shavinashi. That was the real reason Saunez had smuggled Teza out of Abylay. She couldn't trust that him being a rowshatar-estra would protect him, because it might not have. Perhaps Saunez retained a trace of humanity after all. A trace. Evading Teza's prolonged death sentence had been a coincidence.

"Yes, but not as effectively," Saunez said. She waved a dismissive hand. "It is neither here nor there now. If we're going to salvage the situation, we need to begin immediately."

Their hosts hesitated once more, but then Batebi clenched his jaw, and Imlay's lips thinned. They nodded as one.

"Come with me," Imlay told Saunez. "You can tell me everything that's happened while we contact our allies. As for that distraction we need, I have an idea. Abylay has been reinforcing a failing bridge…"

Imlay's voice faded as she took Saunez elsewhere. Batebi recalled the guards and covertly instructed them to mind Teza before following the two women. Jaleya was left in the sitting room, dismissed, forgotten. She fumed at being relegated to the sidelines, again. She could help fix this. She *needed* to fix this. Instead, she was consigned to play nursemaid to a rowshatar.

Teza stared into the empty space where his sister had been. A tear slid down his iridescent cheek.

Jaleya's anger vanished. She reminded herself that people exactly like Teza made the resistance necessary in the first place, but it failed to buffer her defeat. The Ora on the tapestries reveled in their triumph.

Isesh brushed against Jaleya's hip, his presence a warm light in her mind.

This is all my fault, Jaleya sent.

All the blame does not fall at your feet, Isesh sent. *Yongir and others could've made different choices. While the error was yours, the circumstances were not of your making. Grieve for your mistake, and then stand atop it to reach the higher peak.*

Jaleya sent her javati her gratitude. His optimism was irritating, but at times, it was all she had to cling to.

*　　*　　*

Time passed in a daze. Teza's sister and her conspirators did a lot of anxious waiting, followed by hopeful anticipation as responses arrived via the manor's communication seal; it was probably housed on the uppermost level, as Teza sensed its kaza originating from above. Jaleya abandoned her guardian duty at the first opportunity. She hovered around the insurrectionists, edging closer inch by subtle inch, interjecting comments when discussions lulled. Saunez wasn't pleased with her intrusions, but the others seemed to be warming up to her.

Teza drifted through the manor's main level as the hour progressed. His guardian's pet trailed him like a shadow. Estate guards maintained a respectful distance, as was his due, but they were quick to steer him away from windows and main hallways. Teza wasn't fooled. He was a prisoner. Perhaps a hostage. He didn't think Saunez would use him as such, but before tonight, he had also thought she followed the Ways. She spoke and behaved like she honored every one; like she knew, just as he did, that Orvashka's Ways were right and good for everyone. It couldn't have been a lie, an act. And yet, she consorted with rebels mere feet from him.

Teza wandered onto the veranda and reached for the stars. Their kaza embraced him like a warm blanket. How could Saunez do this? Rebels had orphaned them, and in the coinciding chaos, they had lost each other. Years and years alone, the day they had finally found each other was one of the happiest he could remember. Saunez's insurrection would cause more loss akin to the one they had suffered. She and the rebels would bring war, people would be killed, loved ones torn apart, lines drawn in the sand. Setsea would descend into chaos. And all for nothing. Only the Ways could perfect Orvashka's light and birth Paradise. If not for the ungrateful, antiquated rabble, Setsea would already be harmonized with Orvashka, and other countries would joyfully accept the Ways and the Ora's leadership. Why couldn't she see that?

The rebels must have deceived her, poisoned her mind with pretense and lies. It wasn't Saunez's fault. That is what rebels did. She wasn't truly one of them. She had just lost her way. She could still come home. He would help her.

But he wouldn't be able to help her if she was caught with rebels. Whatever they were planning would be the death of them all. Intending to commit treason blighted one's life force, but not beyond healing. Committing treason obliterated any light one could contribute to Paradise, and the only way to save the remaining uncorrupted source was to return the person to Orvashka. A life wasted.

Teza thought of Gardok then, and it was impossible to remember him without seeing him being returned to Orvashka. Had he been a traitor, or had he just been deceived as Saunez was? Teza didn't want to remember his sister as a squandered life force returned to Orvashka. She had made mistakes. She let herself be misguided. But she could be made to realize her errors. She could be re-educated about the truth of Orvashka's Ways, the necessity of the Ora's leadership. She would again see the only path to Paradise and embrace the Ways with renewed vigor.

The rebels' plan could not be allowed to succeed. It wouldn't just doom Saunez. It would doom all of Setsea.

Teza studied the brick and stone horizon across the garden. The wall concealed the land directly beyond, and the lanterns muddied the rocky hills. He would need a better view to progress. He sensed kaza defenses surrounding the manor, but they were dormant. Either the seals weren't fully replenished, or they were only used in emergencies.

Two rifts. Two rifts and he would be clear of the estate. How many would it take to reach Abylay? Could he even make it? Saunez's deduction that he had stopped experimenting with rifts because his strength was exhausted had been accurate. The food he had eaten since then hadn't fully satisfied his hunger. The sky remained a dark, twinkling canvas, but he felt the stars on the precipice of waning.

His guardian's pet sidled closer, wings flexing, ears forward. The simurgh probably sensed him drawing in kaza. Teza would have to be faster than the chaos creature, or his plan would be over before it began.

Could Teza muster enough strength? Could he make it in time? Could he save his sister and avert a disaster?

Teza focused on the closest section of the constraining wall, and shaped the stars' kaza to his will.

He would find out soon enough.

*   *   *

"What do you mean 'he's gone'?" Saunez said to Jaleya. "You can't find him, or he rifted?"

"He rifted," Jaleya replied. "Isesh is searching for him."

Imlay and Batebi began conferring in hushed tones but kept an eye on the communication orb, which was idle at the moment. The diamond's light was a steady, calm luminescence; Imlay had opted for power and reach for her missives. The tower had been designed as a study or observatory, and the communication orb hung from the ceiling in a nook hidden by a bookshelf. The smaller cylinder seals fastened to the metal casing enclosing the heart seal would pulse when a message was received. Saunez longed to see them gleam. She knew how to maneuver those obstacles.

"Why weren't you watching him?" Saunez said.

Jaleya scoffed. "You're still holding to that farce while we plan the Ora's downfall?"

"Your only part is to mind Teza, which you have failed."

Jaleya crossed her arms. "The stars hold sway. I can do as I please."

Batebi spoke up before Saunez could pointedly, if not outrightly, remind Jaleya that the resistance was facing disaster because she had done just that. "We'll go after him. We can spare some guards."

Saunez set aside her fury at Jaleya, and her fury at herself for underestimating her brother. She had honestly thought he wouldn't be able to rift until stars' sway. She and Seal Keeper Firnak had both underestimated his strength, and his determination.

"You won't catch him," she said. "Neither will the fashari."

"We have fresh horses, and our guards know the area. Rowshatari-estra tire after three, maybe four, rifts," Imlay said. "He hasn't gone far beyond the estate."

"He won't tire," Jaleya said. Her gaze held accusation. Saunez accepted it and added it to the list of her transgressions. Yes, she was responsible for Teza's strength growing beyond his peers', but it had been a calculated risk. The lost art he was trying to realize would be a great advantage to the resistance. She had intended to smuggle him out of Abylay when he had been close to a breakthrough, tell him the truth gradually, slowly. Would his reaction have been any different? For all her planning, for all her claims about Teza's loyalties, she never believed he would abandon her.

"He'll return to Abylay," Batebi said.

"We need to evacuate resistance on the estate, and you two have to disappear," Saunez confirmed.

Jaleya interrupted, again. Her continual intrusions were expected, if tiresome, but her words were not. "You really think he'll go back to Abylay?"

Old heartache surfaced behind her eyes. Saunez had witnessed it before when the girl had deduced her and Teza's relation. Jaleya knew what it was to grieve for family.

"We can't afford to believe otherwise," Saunez said tersely. She faced Batebi and Imlay. "I'm sorry."

"We knew what joining the resistance would entail," Batebi said.

"It's a blessing this day was delayed for so long," Imlay added. "But we're going to evacuate as many as we can, resistance and Illuminated. They won't be shown mercy even if they uphold Orvashka's Ways."

"We might not have time for that," Saunez warned.

"Nevertheless, we will try," Batebi said firmly.

Noting their resolve, Saunez didn't argue. They didn't have time to debate. "Our plans must be finalized quickly. I doubt stars' sway has deterred Ora Ezray's questings. A few hours are all we can hope for."

CHAPTER 25

"Your Radiance," the servant said as he prostrated himself before Ezray. Ezray withdrew from her meditation, but her bright old eyes remained closed. The future undulated like a lake before a storm. Ezray was the rock that must guide the current downriver or divert it into the bank. A single mistake in the delicate process could create a flood.

Iza Vor was abuzz with speculations and whispers regarding the investigation in the custodian offices. Nissa's spy had produced ripe fruit, but the traitorous custodian was nowhere to be found. The recipients of her coded messages had absconded; that assistant would never again see Setsea's great cities. The rowshatar and javati that had drawn Nissa's interest were also missing. Whether the rowshatar was a willing or unwilling participant was yet to be determined. Reports from the gates had the traitors heading east, their most likely destination Isedbi. That was incorrect. A glimpse with her sapphire had revealed that thread's frailty.

The night's insurrection was a step toward her terrible vision, but she now had individuals upon which to focus her efforts. She'd been surprised to learn the custodian's death had the potential to be insignificant or the catalyst that caused calamity. Dread stole her breath when she quested the latter path. It must be avoided at all costs.

"Pardon the interruption," the servant continued. "A rowshatar-estra is demanding to see the Ora. Under normal circumstances, he would be denied, but you ordered—"

"I know what I ordered," Ezray said, but not harshly. Her lips curved. The missing rowshatar had come home. Ezray would find the axes around which the precarious future turned. She would ensure the land bloomed.

"Have him brought to my sitting room."

"Yes, Your Radiance," the servant said, bowing low as he left her quarters.

Gray light filtered through the latticed windows. Even when eclipsed by the stars' obnoxious twinkling or the sun's frenzy, Ezray knew the night orb remained. She could feel its kaza on the edge of her consciousness, unveerable yet ever flowing. She considered tapping the kaza in her sapphire, but dismissed the notion. She would learn nothing new. Even the tangible threads rippled from a precarious origin. Caution was needed to shepherd the present onto the correct path, especially with such chaos surrounding the custodian's death. Push too hard, and the future would career to disaster. She had already ordered a company of soldiers to prepare and stand by. That was sufficient for now. With the moon and the future's depths as her allies, Ezray wouldn't fail. She couldn't.

Ezray rose from her cushion and strolled to the sitting room. The fugitive rowshatar-estra huddled on the edge of a chair and twiddled his tousled braid, unbefitting conduct even for a corrupted rowshatar. His disheveled kaftan was slightly loose on his shoulders, and he had tightened the sash around his waist. At least he bore the iridescence of a true rowshatar-estra beneath the sweat and dust. But the eve of dawn hadn't diminished the façade. Interesting.

Ezray veered a smidgen of kaza from her sapphire. As with all rowshatari and javati, he was indistinct, hazy, slipping from the future's threads before she could pluck them. But proximity honed her finely tuned abilities, and her brief questing revealed the rowshatar was a mess of contending knots. Ezray recognized him.

Not his physical features. His life force. He was an axis. She would have to tread very, very carefully.

Finally noticing her presence, the rowshatar-estra stumbled over his sandaled feet as he rushed to prostrate himself. Ezray hid her disgust. How far the rowshatari had fallen. These were sad times indeed.

"Rise, Your Radiance," she said genially. "Orvashka shines from both of us."

The rowshatar-estra returned to his seat, but now he seemed to be trying to melt into its low back. Ezray sat calmly opposite him.

"I was told you requested to see an Ora, that you wouldn't speak to anyone else."

He nodded, kaza-lightened eyes averted. He adjusted the sash around his waist.

"You must harbor something of great significance if you can only reveal it to us," Ezray prodded.

A nod, then nothing. Was he simply nervous, intimidated? Or was he conflicted? Her brief questing indicated the latter. That was dangerous. Conflicted people were unpredictable.

"Has someone hurt you? Threatened you?" she asked.

"No," the rowshatar-estra said quickly. "No. I have…information."

"All right. What kind of information?"

"My…friend…She g-got involved with m-misguided people, and they're p-planning something bad."

"Rebels?"

"They haven't done anything yet," the rowshatar-estra said. "They're only talking about it, and they're just deceived, and they've lost their way and they can still lighten Orvashka we just have to remind them that Orvashka's Ways—"

"Be calm, Your Radiance," Ezray said, raising her hands. "Please, be calm."

He settled and took a deep breath. Ezray inwardly sighed as he resumed fiddling with his braid.

"Now, these people who deceived your friend are plotting treason but have not yet acted?"

He didn't answer immediately. Considering his words seemed to be a new concept to him. His face scrunched in concentration.

"I don't want anyone to get hurt," he said.

"Of course not," she assured him. "We don't want anyone to be hurt either."

She waited for him to continue, but he just tottered in his chair. In other circumstances, she would have admired this rowshatar-estra for having the spine to demand an audience with an Ora, and then given him to the shavinashi, who would pry from him every secret he knew and drain every last drop of kaza from his unworthy being. A rowshatar, associating with rebels! Orvashka's Ways had given him everything, and he would jeopardize harmony for ungrateful peasants who refused to accept the truth? But the future was frayed ropes pulling in different directions. The slightest contact would snap them all. The smoothest future resulted when this rowshatar-estra cut the opposing ropes himself.

"What is your name?" Ezray said.

"Teza," he answered.

"Rowshatar Teza, I see you care deeply for your friend. Revealing her unfaithfulness took great courage, and it was the right thing to do. She might not be completely lost."

"She's not," he said—insisted. "We can help her, re-educate her. She'll uphold Orvashka's Ways again; she will. She's just confused because of the rebels." He paused, and Ezray suppressed an enjoyable fantasy where she called upon the kaza in her sapphire and choked the answers from him.

"I don't want anybody getting hurt," the rowshatar-estra said. "I can show you where they are so you can stop them, and since you'll stop them before they act on their treason, they don't need to be returned to Orvashka. We'll help them instead."

We? He counted himself among true rowshatari? The audacity!

"The Ora are merciful," Ezray said.

He didn't accept her words as agreement like she expected. This one was new to negotiations and subterfuge, but he had felt their sting before, probably recently.

"If I tell you where they are, they won't be returned to Orvashka? You'll grant mercy and help them see their delusions?" he said slowly and clearly.

"We will be merciful," Ezray said.

"I have your word my friend, and the others, won't be returned to Orvashka?"

The future's frayed ropes pulled tighter, straining, creaking.

"You have the word of all the Ora."

Snap!

CHAPTER 26

The advance guard arrived as dawn's first luster crowned the craggy hills. The soldiers and the remshir searched the outbuildings and houses, but their inhabitants were crowded into the manor's courtyard. The remshir attempted entry, and was answered with kaza and arrows. The advance guard positioned itself around the manor to prevent anyone from leaving and hunkered down in anticipation of the imminent main force.

Batebi had taken charge of the evacuations. A tunnel led from the kitchen to the hills, where the staff, miners, and their families could follow a ravine to the main road and hopefully reach the nearest town. A few wanted to stay and fight, but Batebi forbid it. This was not the ground on which the resistance would make their stand. If they wanted to help, they should use their skills to protect their evacuation group.

Illuminated had endeavored to open the gate when the remshir prodded the manor's defenses, but they were subdued and locked away. Most of the civilians were not fanatical loyalists or resistance but found themselves in the middle regardless. They opted to flee from both sides.

Imlay managed the communications with the resistance. Saunez assisted. She paced back and forth in the tower as oranges and reds overcame the gray sky far too quickly. The sun had barely crested the hills when one of the estate guards entered, his features grim.

"They're here."

Saunez and Imlay exchanged foreboding glances. Three evacuation groups remained in the courtyard. Some of the resistance hadn't responded with confirmations, and others were holding their ground, insisting the festival plan be abandoned or refusing to commit resources to what was now a fool's errand.

Since none of the seals' gems were pulsing with waiting messages, Saunez and Imlay hurried to the wall, where Batebi surveyed the landscape through a spyglass. The approaching host was a black line on the horizon, a dust cloud marking its passage. A scout from the advance guard rode to meet it.

"Empty sky," Batebi swore. "Ora Ezray and Ora Morhim are leading the company."

"The Ora don't directly involve themselves with rebellions, especially one that hasn't even begun," Imlay said thoughtfully.

A spike of despair struck Saunez's chest, but she kept her voice even. "Unless they deem it a threat."

She should have reassigned Jaleya after the attempted snatching or returned her to the countryside where she belonged. The javati's pride might have destroyed Setsea's deliverance.

"Your rowshatar is with them," Batebi said, offering the spyglass to Saunez. She eyed it warily, fearing to confirm what she had predicted, what her heart already knew.

She took the spyglass and lifted the eyepiece. Her brother rode beside the Ora on a chestnut horse, even though he detested the creatures. His ornamented kaftan glinted in the morning light, and he wore elegant trousers beneath it; he hated those, too. His elaborately braided hair and tall metal tiara declared his authority, and the gravity of the march. He was the Ora's second. He agreed with their purpose. He probably wasn't aware of the message he silently proclaimed.

"Can we get everyone out?" Imlay asked.

Batebi considered the advancing force and the remaining evacuation groups waiting in the courtyard; they'd been sending the groups in intervals to avoid detection in the hills and on the road. The Ora's company contained mostly soldiers, but Saunez had spotted a squad bearing the spiked helmets of the remshiri. Whatever Ora Ezray had seen, she wasn't taking any chances.

"We'll need to move faster," Batebi said, "but it's a risk we'll have to take."

Imlay nodded grimly. "The rift seal isn't designed for so many." She paused. "We should delay activating the shield until absolutely necessary. It won't last long."

"Agreed. I'll ask for volunteers among the estate guard. We may need more time."

"Any defense on our part will last shorter than our shield," Imlay said.

"It may also be the few minutes that make every difference."

A silent exchange passed between the husband and wife. Affection and sadness tugged Imlay's lips. Batebi squeezed Imlay's hand, and then left the wall with his escort.

Saunez and Imlay regarded the inevitable onslaught.

"I'll finish with the resistance," Saunez said. "See to your people."

"Our allies might not respond in time," Imlay warned.

"Then I'll send final instructions, and they'll have to fill in the blanks."

Imlay regarded her suspiciously. "Do not wait until the last moment. You know too much now."

"They'll get nothing from me," Saunez said.

Imlay's sniff combined admiration with admonition. "Wait in the sitting room when you're finished. The last of us will use the hidden rift seal to escape."

They parted to attend to their tasks, neither voicing what they were both thinking: if everyone escaped, it would be a miracle. But perhaps the time when such miracles were required was dwindling. The Ora did not involve themselves in fruitless uprisings.

Just let the estate's blood be worth it.

Let the ache in her heart be worth it.

*   *   *

"We've apprehended a group of civilians in the hills," a soldier reported. His rank must have been worthy of addressing the Ora, but Teza didn't know how they distinguished that when everyone's caliber was covered by a helmet or restrained by a cord. He assumed it had something to do with the insignia on the man's sash. The company's scale armor all looked identical.

The high-ranking soldier continued. "They appear to be the miners, staff, and families that live in the estate's community."

The horse Teza had been burdened with bent a leg. Teza shifted to regain his equilibrium. The beasts were a horrible form of transportation. They bounced, they reeked, and they had a mind of their own, unrestrained by javash. He never thought he would agree with one. The host had surrounded the manor a good half hour ago, and yet all it had done since was sit there. No one had approached the gate to deliver the Ora's benevolent pardon. Maybe the commanders were worried the rebels would attack the messengers, resulting in unnecessary death. The shield forming a dome over the manor glinted red in the chilly morning air.

"Have you located the means by which they arrived in the hills?" Ora Morhim asked the soldier. Draped in shades of fire with a gold miter crowning his frizzed mane, he was the sun's kaza made manifest. How the soldier managed to reply without stuttering, Teza didn't know.

"A concealed tunnel heads toward the estate, but its passages are numerous and dark. A child fled into the warren and managed to evade capture as the civilians were secured. The detachment believes the child was wounded, but if he manages to warn the traitors, they could place traps in the tunnel or collapse it."

"Does it merit pursuit?" Ora Morhim asked Ora Ezray.

The wild sapphire in her silver necklace gleaming steadily, Ora Ezray momentarily gazed into Orvashka's undulating depths. "Not anymore," she said.

An explosion convulsed the nearby hills. Teza's horse flinched, and he jerked the reins to prevent the beast from bolting. The other horses shied this way and that, ears peaked, eyes wide, but none fled. Teza sensed kaza, but it was the lifeless kind within gemstones.

"The blunt way, then," Ora Morhim said.

"Cautiously blunt," Ora Ezray replied.

Ora Morhim rode his horse to the front of the gathered company, archers flanking him. The flame of his being intensified as kaza formed between his hands. He hurled the viscous fire at the manor, and the shield shimmered as it absorbed and dispersed the blast.

Ora Ezray spoke to the high-ranking solider. "Captain, proceed with the attack. The custodian and the estate administrators are not to be harmed. They must be questioned before they're returned to Orvashka. You may dispose of any others who won't surrender, but prisoners are preferred."

The captain bowed at the waist and began barking orders. The blood drained from Teza's face as the remshir squad formed a line on either side of Ora Morhim. Lightning and liquid fire pummeled the manor's shield. Archers fired volleys of arrows, the projectiles disintegrating upon contact.

Teza kicked his horse and flapped the reins and managed to maneuver the unsavory mount beside Ora Ezray. "Your Radiance—"

A wave of moon kaza knocked him from his horse, and he hit the dirt hard.

"This rowshatar seeks to usurp Orvashka's Harmonized," Ora Ezray said. "Shackle him with obsidian and keep him out of sight."

Soldiers hauled Teza to his feet, and another approached carrying manacles set with the menacing stone.

"You said you'd be merciful," Teza said frantically as Ora Morhim and the remshiri continued to bombard the manor; the shield began to buckle beneath the onslaught. "You said you wouldn't return them to Orvashka. You gave me your word."

"I did," Ora Ezray said, "and if you were an Illuminated, I would be honor bound to abide by it. Alas, you are a traitor, as is everyone in that estate."

Cold metal clamped around his wrists, but the shackles that inhibited the stars' kaza were warm compared to the pit in his stomach.

"Be grateful," Ora Ezray told him. "You will witness firsthand why Orvashka's Ways are necessary, and your contribution to Orvashka will be greater than your fellow traitors.'"

The manor's shield crackled, and then disintegrated with a rumbling fizzle. Ora Ezray squeezed her horse forward and halted beside Ora Morhim. The sapphire in her necklace flared with the moon's light as she raised her cerulean arms. The manor's gate creaked, dust falling from the hinges. She clenched her fists as if trying to squeeze juice from a pomegranate. Metal groaned; wood splintered. The gate burst outward and fell with a thud that shook the ground. The soldiers and remshiri rushed through the gap, weapons drawn and cylinder seals ablaze.

*　　　*　　　*

This was madness. The civilians the soldiers had captured were dead, or they soon would be. Even if Jaleya managed to free them, they would be apprehended again before they reached the road. The dead child drove her onward. Imlay had tried to save the bleeding boy, but he died in her arms, his strength and her cylinder seal insufficient to heal him.

Isesh had utilized the morning sun to thwart the arrows of the enemy and escape the siege. The Ora no doubt knew of their flight, but one javati wasn't a threat to their forces, and any aid Jaleya and Isesh might muster would never arrive in time to spare the estate.

After a few minutes of being airborne, they landed in the rocky hills north of the tunnel's entrance among shrubbery and sparse trees. They progressed south using the slopes for cover. Voices drifted to their ears. Jaleya and Isesh pressed themselves flat against the ground and peered over a rise. The evacuees knelt in a circle, bound and roped together. Five soldiers equipped with scimitars and bows surrounded the prisoners. The sixth proceeded downhill to waiting horses. He mounted and trotted off toward the estate. Horse messengers. Good. No remshiri had been sent with this detachment.

I'll circle around and flank them, Isesh sent.

Jaleya readied herself while her javati took position. A child evacuee sniffled, and a woman quickly but gently hushed her. A soldier raised a threatening hand, and the woman recoiled in fear. Jaleya anticipated stabbing the Ora's lackey.

The horses shied on their pickets. Isesh was set.

The fashari burst from the rocky underbrush and collided with the nearest soldier. The others turned in surprise, and Jaleya rushed down the slope and struck two from behind. Isesh finished another, and Jaleya claimed the last one. Her javati responded to her satisfaction with sadness.

The evacuees huddled together as Jaleya approached with a drawn knife; children screamed. She cut them free, and the tears of fear became ones of relief. Women embraced Jaleya and wept on her shoulder. The men nodded in gratitude and jealously enfolded their families. Children peered at Isesh from the safety of their parents' arms. Jaleya and Isesh shared mutual gratification.

As eyes dried, the evacuees made to return to the tunnel. Jaleya barred their path.

"You can't go back. The Ora are attacking the estate; there's no safety there. Your best chance is following the ravine to the road and getting as far from here as possible."

They hesitated, but the children trembling amid the bleeding corpses spurred their decision. Jaleya discreetly suggested they take the soldiers' weapons, and was answered with aghast incredulity.

The evacuees began ascending the overgrown switchbacks seemingly to escape Jaleya as much as the Ora's assault. Had she just saved Illuminated?

As the column passed Jaleya, a man near the end gradually lost ground. His surreptitious glances drew his lagging steps aside, toward the idle scimitars. A woman and a young boy abandoned the switchbacks and began searching anxiously. The man considered the pair upon the rise and steeled himself, but then he acknowledged his fellow evacuees who had recoiled at Jaleya's suggestion. He matched his pace to theirs.

Jaleya caught his arm. He was perhaps ten years her senior with short hair; the Mining Guild emblem swaggered on his headband and sash belt. She met his conflicted gaze. She silently offered the knife she had used to free him.

His family watched as he and Jaleya stood as a rock in a river. He grasped the hilt and concealed the blade within his long tunic. He rejoined his wife and son. Her perceptive eyes were equally conflicted, but she was silent and clutched her husband's hand.

Jaleya ventured into the dark tunnel; the brambles and brush obscuring the entrance had been trampled. She sensed kaza in her immediate vicinity. Just beyond the shaft of daylight, she located the dual support beams and knocked on the lintels until a hollow echo answered. She dug her fingers into the nearly imperceptible crease and pulled. A thin panel detached, revealing a small compartment. A cylinder seal as long as her forearm rested within on wooden feet. Jaleya removed the seal's hood, and the nook filled with ruby light.

I found it, Jaleya sent.

Set it quickly, Isesh replied. *We've lingered here too long.*

Set it. Right.

The horizontal seal depicted two parallel gemstones, one with its crown disjointed from its pavilion, and the other whole with rays sprouting from its facets. Right of those was another depiction of a disjointed jewel, but a band of smooth stone separated the pavilion from the rotatable cap bearing the crown.

Three clicks? Jaleya sent.

Three clicks, Isesh confirmed.

Jaleya braced the seal and carefully turned the cap, further separating the disjointed segments. She felt and heard inner gears connecting, once, twice, three times. Jaleya ceased the rotation and prayed the seal wouldn't explode in her face.

She pressed the cap inward, and the smooth stone slid into the cylinder seal, eliminating the gap dividing the depiction and activating the timing mechanism. Jaleya beamed.

The crown on the cap rotated toward its pavilion. Click.

Jaleya bolted. Click. She threw herself out of the tunnel as kaza spewed from its mouth and thundered the surrounding hills. When the dust cleared, fallen rock and shattered wood blocked the passageway. The manor was safe from infiltration. Its breach was still inevitable, yet Jaleya was proud of her actions. All evacuees had reached the hills. The enemy's victory would be in vain.

She was finally fighting back.

Jaleya and Isesh ascended to the sky and crested the hills. The manor's shield was gone. As Isesh circled closer, they witnessed the Ora's host overrun the first barricade erected across the courtyard. The defense, led by Batebi, retreated to the second barrier while Imlay and archers hampered the advancing soldiers with sun kaza and arrows. The stumps of the fig trees felled to aid the crude fortifications smoldered with liquid fire. The Ora sitting on their elegant mounts and surrounded by an honor guard remained outside the wall, abstaining from the battle. For now.

Of one mind, the javati dove toward the manor. Jaleya leapt off Isesh, rolled as she hit the paving stones, and dispatched a soldier caught in the wooden web stretched across the barricade's summit. Isesh barreled into the swelling human tide, lashing with his claws and mauling with his powerful limbs. Estate guards speared the attackers through strategically placed slits in the fortification. Archers defended the summit, and Imlay rained down liquid fire where the defense faltered. Arrows and kaza pummeled a remshir until his shield seal failed and the bolts penetrated his flesh; two other remshiri lay dead before the first barricade. Jaleya slashed, hacked, and thrust the life from her enemies, yet the tide of soldiers did not ebb.

Jaleya found herself next to Batebi amid the clashing steel, twang of bows, and crackling kaza.

"Success?" he asked, his features grim.

"Yes," Jaleya said, even though it no longer felt like one.

Relief softened the lines of Batebi's blood-splattered face.

A shockwave slammed into the barricade. Furniture, foodstuffs, and timber tore apart; defenders and attackers were hurled aside; and the paving stones caved into a furrow. Three remshiri with seals glowing blue stepped back as one. Soldiers surged into the sudden gap. The estate guard captain ordered a retreat to the final barrier, but the flood of soldiers made disengaging impossible.

Liquid fire engulfed the riven barricade and bombarded the channel through which the soldiers charged. Imlay's hands clutching a cylinder seal burned like the sun; sweat matted her hair. The estate guards struck hard and fast, cutting themselves an opening. The blazing wall guarded their hasty withdrawal.

Jaleya and the estate guards scrambled behind the last fortification. It barely surpassed her head and only spanned the manor's entrance; the double doors were ajar. Isesh hurdled to safety with buffering wings. He carried an unconscious Batebi.

"The shockwave," the guard captain said. He guided Batebi off of Isesh and sat him against the doorway's pillar. Imlay rushed to her husband's side. His eyes flickered open, but he squinted and blinked as if a desert haze blighted his vision. His mouth moved, but speaking proved difficult. Imlay drew a small seal from her sash belt. The sun gem pulsed softly as Imlay delved Batebi's wounds. Imlay swallowed, and gently explored the back of his head. Her hand came away dripping crimson.

Love saturated Batebi's bleary gaze as he beheld his wife. Imlay's healing seal dimmed. Restrained grief glistened in her eyes.

Soldiers and remshiri cautiously advanced through the smoldering breach. Two detachments investigated the arched doors on both sides of the courtyard and found them barred from the inside. Remshiri bashed the archways asunder, and soldiers ground the crumbled crenellation tiles as they proceeded into the gardens and the veranda, seeking the manor's rear entrances.

A handful of estate guards remained; none had evacuated. One quiver held arrows. Blood smeared every spearhead and stained Isesh's jowls and ivory coat.

"Our people are safe," Batebi murmured. His lips barely moved.

"I will see you in Paradise," Imlay whispered.

Only Jaleya and Isesh heard the intimate farewell.

Imlay turned to the captain and repeated her husband's words. "Go to the sitting room and use the rift seal. You must hurry to outpace the forces at our back."

The captain hesitated. "What about you?"

Imlay withdrew from her embroidered tunic a ruby the size of a date, and it wasn't fixed to a seal. "I will ensure pursuit from the front is sufficiently delayed."

The captain wanted to protest, but he considered the organizing soldiers, the remshiri switching seals, and Batebi's body resting against the pillar. The captain saluted and gathered the remnant of his men into the manor.

Jaleya stood rooted to the porch, even as the enemy noted the guards' retreat and began advancing, seals kindled and steel bared. Isesh nudged her urgently.

"Come with us," Jaleya begged, powerless to stop what Imlay was about to do. Javash enhanced her speed, but she wasn't faster than thought. "Imlay, please!"

Imlay stared at the Ora's host marching across the decimated courtyard of her home. Her wild gem flared a vengeful red. Jaleya's skin prickled as the air fizzed with kaza.

"Fly, javati."

Jaleya fled, Isesh at her side. She looked over her shoulder as her reluctant steps bore her away from the foyer, and through the fissure of sunlight, she saw Imlay settle beside Batebi and take his hand. The Ora's forces swarmed the abandoned defenses. The wild gem blazed red, yellow, and white.

Isesh tackled Jaleya into a side corridor as an explosion rocked the manor. The ground buckled; walls cracked and crumbled. Unbridled kaza roared, and screams were engulfed.

Silence afraid to exhale.

Jaleya uncurled from Isesh's bodily shield. The whisper of his wings and the creak of her weapons belt seemed to echo into infinity.

They peered into the foyer. One splintered door hung precariously from a lone pillar; the other was buried beneath a mound of stones and bricks. Smoke and dust mingled in the beams of light. The scent of burning flesh twisted Jaleya's stomach. Shattered tiles crunched beneath her boots.

Isesh pressed against her hip. Jaleya laid her hand on his shoulder, the smooth transitions of fur and feathers a familiar, steadying comfort. One second the foyer had been there, and the next…gone. Just like Imlay, and Batebi, and the guards slain upon the barricades.

They had paid for her mistake.

Soft feathers caressed her cheek. Isesh's eyes were fierce from battle but beheld her gently.

Their deaths were not in vain. Come. The final retreat awaits.

The javati took the most direct route to the sitting room harboring the rift seal; it was the same room where Imlay and Batebi had received them in the dead of night. That meeting felt like a lifetime ago, not mere hours. And now they were gone.

Jaleya and Isesh slowed as they approached, and jerked aside as an arrow shot into the corridor. Jaleya pressed her back against the wall and called softly, "It's Jaleya and Isesh. Stand down."

She cautiously looked inside, and two estate guards lowered their crossbows.

"Apologies, javati," one said.

"Batebi and Imlay?" Saunez asked. She stood before the trio of tapestries. Jaleya was pleased to see the middle one had been torn down. The dozen aids and servants who had disposed of incriminating items and helped build the barricades clustered by the discarded propaganda.

The knot in Jaleya's stomach wound tighter. "They…didn't make it."

Saunez nodded grimly and shed her confirmed fear like a cloak. She began tracing the mortar of the exposed bricks, seeking the ones that triggered the hidden alcove's opening mechanism. Jaleya sensed the rift seal behind the wall. The kaza sconces weren't lit, and the residual kaza from the battle and explosion was waning mist.

"The estate guards are on their way," Jaleya said. They should have already been present. Something must have diverted them. The enemy soldiers entering through the kitchen and the veranda? Surely she, or at least Isesh, would have heard their clash.

"Hope they arrive before we rift," Saunez said, locating the first of three bricks; it grated as she pressed it inward. "We can't wait for them. We've already lingered too long."

The servants shifted in distress, and the guards' lips thinned, but no one countered the custodian. Jaleya was surprised they'd waited as long as they had, especially Saunez. The explosion must have been the deciding factor. Had it also delayed the captain? No, his squad had been ahead of Jaleya and Isesh, and the inner corridors hadn't been affected by the blast.

Isesh's ears peaked, and he whipped toward the room's open entrance. He sniffed deep. All Jaleya could smell was charred brick, smoldering kaza, and melting flesh. The rank reached even there.

A whisper of a boot across stone. A lone soldier paused in the doorway. He wore the scaled armor of the Ora's host, but he didn't seem to feel its weight. A frozen wasteland stretched unending in his barren eyes and seeped the warmth from the air. A military metal and cloth headscarf concealed his head, but Jaleya knew it was smooth.

Isesh's hackles rose, and a pealing growl rumbled in his throat. The two guards fired their crossbows. The soldier—the shavinash —*moved*. The arrows struck the corridor, the servants screamed, and Isesh charged.

"Get the door open," Jaleya called to Saunez as she rushed to her javati's aid. The dread all shavinashi evoked threatened to numb her limbs, but Jaleya's vow thwarted his terrible aura. This was why she trained, why she endured the lies and pretended to believe them. This shavinash wasn't the one she sought—too short, shoulders too narrow, and his eyes were too dark. Always too dark. But one less evil would plague Setsea.

The two guards hefted their spears and followed; the shafts trembled in their hands. Dark delight twisted the shavinash's cruel lips as he drew his dual short swords. The frigid wasteland laughed at their audacity to challenge its might.

Faster than Isesh he crossed the room. The slash of his blade that sliced a guard's throat was nothing more than a whoosh of movement in Jaleya's peripheral vision. She managed to block the attack that came for her, and Isesh interrupted the follow-up strike. The shavinash targeted the remaining guard. Blood sprayed as the poor man died before he knew what was happening.

Isesh snapped and swiped at the shavinash, disrupting his trajectory. The fashari's presence receded in Jaleya's mind. Jaleya thrust at the back of the shavinash's knee, but he parried, suddenly facing her seemingly without turning. He drove her backward, and it was all Jaleya could do to defend. But defend she did. The shavinash could be playing with her, as they were wont to do, but her skin tingled just before he moved impossibly fast. The intervening blink when he called upon his etch swayed against her like a deep current.

Jaleya plunged into that current, drowning her rational mind, enveloping herself in instincts she hadn't known she possessed. Isesh continually harried the shavinash, and the javati earned the assassin's attention.

The trained killer dodged Isesh's jaws, spun, and sliced Isesh's flank; the simurgh cried a chirping whimper, his leg buckling. The shavinash drew upon his etch, but Jaleya read the ripples too slow, and he twisted her scimitar from her hands. A bloodshaping-enhanced kick sent her sprawling. Before she could recover, the shavinash was upon her. He seized her braids and slammed her head against the wall, once, twice, three times. Blood gushed down Jaleya's cheek. The room spun, her ears ringing. The shavinash twirled his short swords, the steel embodying the macabre pleasure in his dark eyes. Always too dark. He raised his blades for a fatal blow.

A blur of feathers and fur barreled into the shavinash, and Jaleya heard barking chirps, hybrid and human bodies grappling.

Isesh.

She tried climbing to her feet, but simply lifting her head roiled her stomach and dimmed her vision. She crumpled onto her back and had to breathe deep to defer unconsciousness.

Bricks ground together. A door burst open. Screams and dismay pierced her ears like a spike. She felt the vibrations of rapid footsteps.

Someone grabbed her shoulders and dragged her across the smooth stone. Jaleya's watery limbs provided no leverage for escape, and the futile effort made her stomach empty its contents. Black plumes stifled her sight.

A peal of pain. A presence nestled in her mind trembled.

Jaleya lurched toward the resilient consciousness. "Isesh..." she mumbled. "Isesh!" She struggled to go to the aid of her javati, but her captor would not be deterred.

Jaleya was dragged into stale shadows and dropped beside an earthen pedestal. A white radiance flowed over the hollow's brick walls. A woman inspected its source. Squinting against the stinging brilliance, her head ringing, Jaleya woozily rolled onto her side. Isesh was in trouble. Her javati needed her.

A silhouette eclipsed the daylight beyond the alcove. His short swords bled on the threshold. The shavinash.

The woman before the pedestal cried out in surprise as the shavinash seized her. She thrashed and knocked her head into his, but the shavinash's arms were an unyielding vice, and he dragged her from the alcove.

"Get out!" she yelled. "Get out!" Her voice sounded familiar. Saunez?

Jaleya fought the thickening fog smothering her mind. Coherent thoughts slowly, painfully formed. The estate. The attack. The shavinash. Isesh! The last retreat. They had to get out. Saunez had been trying to get out. But how?

The white radiance finally registered as more than pain, and Jaleya recalled a connection between light and passages. Passages leading…somewhere, anywhere.

Another silhouette darkened the threshold. Jaleya discerned the garb of an Abylayan soldier.

Her javati needed her. He was hurt, possibly dying. She felt his presence, but deeper awareness was currently beyond her. However much she longed to fight her way to Isesh's side, she knew her first punch wouldn't even land.

Jaleya raised her hand, grasped the light, and hoped she wouldn't wake up on the other side of the Sojourn Mountains.

CHAPTER 27

Jaleya carefully surveyed the battle's aftermath from a gnarled second-story window. The estate's few survivors and many wounded had been herded onto skimmers and chained together; she spotted Saunez among them. Bodies were strewn about the courtyard, left to lie where they had fallen. Gore stained the paving stones. The flowers wept crimson tears.

Isesh hunched in an undersized cage loaded on a large skimmer. Dried blood matted his flank, and one wing was bent at a grotesque angle, but his canine ears swiveled, alert. A five-foot perimeter surrounded the cage. Isesh bared his teeth, feathers ruffling, when a foolish soldier ventured into its bounds.

Jaleya couldn't distinguish the shavinash among the Ora's host, but that didn't mean he wasn't there. Did he conceal his identity to hide in plain sight? In this instance, it served no purpose Jaleya could conceptualize. His masters had denounced the estate. Harmonizing Setsea composed his existence.

Jaleya reached out to her javati. *Isesh, I'm back. I see you.*

Isesh didn't physically react, but his relief was palpable. *Your approach was heartening. I feared when you didn't respond.*

Sorry. The nasty bump on my head put me out for a while.

The sun had reached its zenith. She had been unconscious and fumbling her way through the hills for a few hours. Jaleya thanked the Creator Imlay's seal had rifted the entire alcove. Otherwise, she would be in the courtyard with the prisoners.

They've finished clearing the estate, Isesh sent. *They'll be returning to Abylay momentarily. The Ora debated searching for you, but they concluded your death resulting from mine would be satisfactory. They're being very cautious.*

How do I get you out of there? Jaleya sent.

Her javati didn't answer.

Isesh?

You don't. Their numbers are too great.

Jaleya swallowed the dread creeping up her throat. She wouldn't accept that. She couldn't.

The Ora rode forward and addressed the company's commanders. Orders to commence marching formations echoed down the courtyard, soldiers jumping into line, the skimmers humming to life. Ora Ezray eyed the one carrying Saunez as she and Ora Morhim proceeded to the head of the column.

There has to be a way, Jaleya sent, unable to filter her desperation.

Do not reveal yourself, Isesh commanded. *Both of us as prisoners will not present a means of escape, and I don't want to watch you being tortured to death or murdered on an altar.*

The Ora and their honor guard passed through the decimated gateway. Decorated with silks and jewels, the Illuminated Batebi had imprisoned rode on resplendent mounts immediately behind. Configurations of remshiri and soldiers flanked the accelerating skimmers laden with tapestries, coin chests, vessels of gold and silver, and the prisoners.

I'll figure something out, Jaleya sent. *I'll come for you.*

Bittersweetness clothed Isesh's sending. *You would need an army of rowshatari. They're taking us to Harmony Tower. Shavinashi and zar'sheni have been summoned.*

The skimmer bearing Isesh joined the column departing the estate. The urge to jump to the courtyard and fight through the soldiers, the remshiri, even the Ora and a shavinash to free him was an ache in Jaleya's gut. Her feet shuffled, and she grasped the window's splintered lattice.

Isesh's presence blossomed in her consciousness, staying her impulse. Jaleya clung to his bright, ever-present light. Calm, bold, undaunted. He was right. She couldn't defeat these foes. And doing nothing while her javati was hauled away to be executed was a vicious torture.

You can survive the madness, Isesh sent. *It is possible to overcome it.*

An anguished chortle escaped her lips. Altruistic unto the end. And she loved him for it. But false hope ignored imminent reality better prepared for than denied. Jaleya would welcome the madness. It would ease the pain constricting her heart.

That's a children's story, she sent.

Isesh was driven through the gateway, and he began to shrink with the lengthening distance. The rest of the soldiers filed after.

Then you will be the first to prove it true.

Her javati closed his mind, and no matter how much she poked and prodded, pounded and railed at the light that was Isesh, he kept her out.

Jaleya sunk to the floor. Strained, harsh sobs racked her shoulders. She wanted to scream. How many times must she stand by while a loved one was stolen from her? Let the madness come. It had to be better than this.

Fresh smoke tingled her nose. Voices drifted through the mangled window from outside. Jaleya thought everyone had left. She peered into the courtyard. A small squad of soldiers and a Seal Keeper convened in the center. Infant flames licked the gardens. Beyond the wall, the community's wheat fields withered beneath a scorching mantle. The squad was completing the estate's "purification." It was time to leave.

Jaleya froze as another soldier emerged from the manor with one last prisoner. Stripped naked, hair hacked off, Teza staggered into the soldiers' midst. Manacles embedded with obsidian bound his wrists. Bare scalp peeked through his remaining tufts.

Rage boiled Jaleya's blood at the sight of the rowshatar-estra. He had led the Ora to the estate. He had endorsed the ruthless slaughter. He was the reason Isesh had been taken from her—the reason Isesh was going to die, murdered by Teza's deceitful, faithless, tyrannical overlords and their Ways. Jaleya's entire body trembled. Her fingernails bit into her palms as her hands clenched into fists. Isesh was right. None of this was her fault. It was Teza's.

The soldiers taunted the rowshatar with torches, the flames passing within a hairsbreadth of his exposed skin. Teza cowered at his jailors' malicious hands. Jaleya felt no pity. He was reaping what he sowed. Hidden from the resistance after reinforcing the rowshatari's devotion to harmony, he'd been condemned by the very Ways he affirmed. The Ora would decree the events of his death, and their followers would believe it, regardless of what their own eyes had witnessed.

The Seal Keeper let the punishment continue for a moment, and then ordered it halted. The soldiers tossed their torches aside. The Seal Keeper opened a chest at her feet and retrieved a cylinder seal the size of her thigh. Its ruby encompassed three-quarters of the depicted surface, and a band of smooth stone encircled one end. Just like the bomb in the tunnel.

The Seal Keeper carried the explosive into the manor.

Jaleya bolted down the hallway, scanning the intersecting corridors for the outer wall paralleling the veranda. A glimpse of hazy sky, and she swerved toward it. She saw the hoped-for roof extending below an open window, and she jumped through the frame. She rolled as she landed and unfolded into a sprint. Reaching the end of the veranda, she leapt for the manor's distant battlements. Her momentum fell short. She slammed into a crenel and slid backward, her boots unable to find purchase. She grabbed the sides of the adjoining merlons, halting her descent, but her fingers immediately began to slip.

The manor boomed. Brick and stone burst, and the ceiling collapsed. Viscous kaza whooshed through the crumbling structure and latched onto doorways, lattices, and furniture, gnawing the bones even though it hungered for meat. Smoke and dust spewed forth and clouded the sun. Jaleya was knocked from her precarious hold and landed hard among the burning landscaping. Fragments pelted her, and she curled into a ball, hands shielding her head.

The raining rubble ceased. Jaleya scrambled to her feet and crouched through the thickening smoke to the veranda's outlet. She sheltered in the remnant of a courtyard barricade and, through a muffling elbow, coughed air back into her lungs.

The Seal Keeper and her entourage marched clear of their purified ruins, towing Teza by his shackles. Rage greater than the explosion's thundered in Jaleya.

Deceased guards lay sprawled upon the crushed defenses. Spear shafts jutted from their backs. Jaleya yanked the spears free and also salvaged a knife for good measure.

She stalked the squad and their prisoner to the ruptured gateway. She paused and cautiously looked around its pillar. The soldiers were ushering Teza into a small skimmer a stone's throw from the wall. Jaleya climbed onto the fractured battlements. She hefted one of the reclaimed spears and secured the second in her belt. She would only get one shot, and it needed to be fatal.

The soldiers' backs were turned to the desecrated manor. No telling glow emanated from the Seal Keeper's hands. Jaleya leapt into the air once more.

*   *   *

A figure dropped from the sky and crushed the Seal Keeper to the ground, a spear impaling the base of her neck. The female assailant thrust a second spear at the nearest soldier, but his quick evasion caught the head between his Abylayan scales. Exploiting the sudden leverage, she drove him onto his back and stabbed his exposed face with a knife. The remaining two soldiers charged the attacker, and Teza tumbled out of the skimmer as he tried to hide.

Spears collided and scraped across armor, shouts of rage drowned cries of pain, and the inferno seethed. Teza huddled behind the skimmer, wishing he could burrow into the ground. Steel found flesh, and what sounded like water gurgled onto the dirt. Wet, sticky drops splattered the skimmer. Teza told himself it was red ash.

The discord ceased as suddenly as it began. The cleansing blaze rumbled undisturbed.

Teza slowly peered over the skimmer. And beheld harmony's soldiers frozen in a grotesque tableau of violence and agony. He swallowed the bile bubbling up his throat. Jaleya stood in the center of the carnage, spear in hand, face and jerkin awash with crimson. She scanned the surroundings, and lowered her weapon, satisfied the danger had passed.

She stalked toward Teza with death in her eyes.

The hope he had felt upon seeing his guardian was killed as quickly as the soldiers had been. Jaleya wasn't there to save him.

Teza fled, but he only achieved a short distance down the road before Jaleya tackled him from behind. She seized the remaining tufts of his hair, yanked him to his knees, and rained down blows on his face and belly; his lungs ached from the forced expulsion of precious air. Cold steel pressed against his throat as Jaleya jerked his neck taught. Teza grabbed her knife-wielding arm, but she was as strong as the manacles inhibiting the stars' kaza.

"Wait!" he gasped. "P-please!"

"Do you have any idea what you've done?" she snarled.

Teza had been struggling to comprehend that since the soldiers arrested him. "I was trying to do what's right."

"What's right? What's *right*?" The blade pressed harder, and a bead of blood trickled down his neck. "The torturous death your Ways had in store for you was fitting indeed. But your fellow Illuminated will not have that pleasure. Isesh will receive justice by my hand."

"Isesh?" Teza said. It was only then that he noticed the simurgh's absence.

The knife poised to sever his throat trembled. "I won't leave him to be tormented by shavinashi and murdered on a Ways altar. We will fly one last time before we perish, together, as it should be." Her voice was cold, resigned. She…expected death, and yet she would still attempt to free her pet.

"I'm sorry," Teza whispered.

"Not sorry enough."

Teza closed his eyes and waited for his guardian to end his life. Even if the stars had held sway, the obsidian set in the manacles prevented him from reaching their kaza. He was powerless, helpless. Useless. He couldn't stop her.

His neck muscles strained as Jaleya tightened her grip on his mortifying wisps. An involuntary whimper escaped his lips. Jaleya's sharp inhale announced his end. The knife pierced his skin—

Teza looked up, wishing the stars gazed back.

Jaleya screamed and shoved him forward. He hit the ground like a rock and lay sprawled in the middle of the road, his limbs and lungs paralyzed with anticipation.

Jaleya sheathed her knife and returned to the soldiers' corpses. Quaking uncontrollably, Teza lifted his head. Jaleya was rifling through the squad's pockets and belt pouches; Teza's stomach squirmed. She rose from her grisly looting and buckled an appropriated scimitar around her waist. That was why she hadn't killed him. She needed a blade better suited for hacking his body apart.

Jaleya strode toward him. Teza swallowed and stared at the ground; he didn't want to witness his death. His guardian's footsteps came closer, and closer—she was alongside him (something thumped in the dirt)—and…she continued past him.

Teza propped himself onto his elbows. Jaleya didn't stop. He quivered to his knees. She still didn't stop.

"Aren't you g-going to k-kill me?" he said.

A pause in her stride. A heavy silence. Her voice cracked with tears. "He wouldn't want me to."

She resumed her march. Toward Abylay. Toward Iza Vor. Toward the Ora's tower. Where she would endeavor to rescue Isesh regardless of the grim outcome.

"I can get us in," Teza blurted.

Jaleya stopped. Looked over her shoulder. Teza flinched. What in the Ways had possessed him to reclaim her attention? She was leaving!

"Us?" she said menacingly.

Teza staggered to his feet, the incredulity that he was going to live just as overwhelming as his expected death. Words that were articulate in his mind turned to gibberish on his tongue. The bloodied guardian began backtracking like a lioness debating if she was hungry enough to kill the lost sheep.

"Saunez," he sputtered. "Ora Ezray—um, she, uh, she wanted Saunez alive, to return to Orvashka. That's—that's where Saunez is. Harmony T-Tower. Offerings are housed in the tower. I can rift us into Iza Vor, and you can find Isesh with your guardian life force connection. It d-does work that way, right?"

Jaleya halted outside of arm's reach, but well within her scimitar's reach. "Iza Vor is shielded against rifting."

"The shield is dormant when its seals are replenished to guarantee maximum kaza absorption."

"There'll be extra guards to account for the lowered defenses," Jaleya said. "Hence the 'us.'"

Was that why Teza had called after her? Subconsciously, he knew he would need her help? Once inside Iza Vor, he could rift within the citadel's shield, but one misstep, one misrift, and he would be skewered.

"Give me one reason why I should trust you," Jaleya said.

"Um...I'm a rowshatar?"

"A rowshatar who could rift us inside Iza Vor and hand me over in a futile attempt to regain his status."

Teza chortled self-deprecatingly. "Apparently, I've been surrounded by conspiracies for a while now, and I recognized none of them. You think I'm capable of creating my own? The Ora said they would grant Saunez mercy; they'd re-educate her. But they lied. They outright lied, and I believed them, and now Saunez is going to die, and it's my fault. I wouldn't have told them where she was if I'd realized—"

He sighed and reached for his braid that no longer existed. "She's all I have left."

His shoulders bowed with the weight of that admission. He'd been pronounced a traitor. The first rowshatar to forsake the Ways. Good citizens would vigorously expose his corruption. He would be reported and arrested no matter where he went, his life force returned to Orvashka to preserve its remaining harmonized light.

Part of him clung to the hope that he could explain the situation and the sentence would be lifted. He could return home. Everything had just been a misunderstanding. He wasn't a traitor. He wasn't. Was he?

"I know the western communication minaret well enough to rift blind," he offered. "We just have to wait for the stars."

Jaleya's keen features remained rigid. She looked ready to plunge into the heart of an army and slay anything that moved. Or plunge her scimitar into his heart. He still half-expected her to change her mind about killing him.

"Have you ever rifted blind?" she asked.

Teza utilized the wisdom of silence.

Jaleya removed something from the kit she had taken from the skimmer and tossed it at Teza, who flinched. A water flask landed at his feet. Jaleya turned on her heel and marched away. Teza considered asking if he should expect her tonight, but her volatile demeanor trapped the words in his throat. It didn't matter. He was going to find his sister with or without Jaleya, even if all he managed to do afterward was tell her how sorry he was.

As Jaleya continued down the road, Teza finally dared to avert his gaze. He bent and retrieved the water flask, and noticed the item Jaleya had dropped in passing: a metal ring containing a single engraved key. Hope kindled in his chest. He could already feel the stars' kaza.

CHAPTER 28

Teza trailed Jaleya as she trailed the road back to Abylay. Teza kept her just within sight. She hadn't forbidden him from accompanying her, but she hadn't said he could either. Since she hadn't ditched him, he maintained his healthy distance as the hills slowly, *slowly* diminished. Walking back to Abylay was excruciating. He would have gladly accepted a beastly horse if it meant relieving his feet; he didn't think they would survive the trek. It was very unfortunate guardians weren't permitted to fly skimmers.

When Abylay finally rose above the landscape, Jaleya seamlessly merged with a bustling caravan heading toward the capital and disappeared. The stream of people was comprised mostly of merchants with guarded wagons and visiting officials and dignitaries with their retinues. Clusters of rural citizens followed in their wake. Everyone was welcome at the Festival of Shattered Swords, but attending the offering ceremony was encouraged.

Teza joined the stragglers in the back and proceeded to the thickest concentration of commoners. Dressed in tunics he had stolen from the soldiers—Teza shuddered at the memory; nothing had been spared a bloodstain—and with his hair chopped beyond recognition, he looked just like them. Just another commoner coming to witness the offering. No one paid him any attention.

While he prided himself on successfully infiltrating the caravan as Jaleya had, being ignored was…bewildering.

The officials and dignitaries wore embroidered kaftans, fine vests and trousers, or fitted dresses. Gold and silver jewelry reflected the aged sunlight. Teza had been similarly arrayed before the soldiers stripped him. That seemed like a lifetime ago, not just this morning.

Teza plodded along with the caravan until it reached Abylay; he kept an eye out for Jaleya, but she didn't reappear. The city's mighty wall beckoned him into its shelter, but for the first time in his life, Teza feared he would be denied its embrace. The gate guards searched for weapons, inspected incoming goods, and prodded livestock for contraband. They didn't seem to be stopping everyone, though. This crowd wouldn't get into the city until the festival was over if they did.

Teza sidled beside a decorated wagon; jingling and clanking goods hung on the outside. The guards stopped the driver, and he handed them a scroll. The guards reviewed the document, and noted a woman in a bright fringed shawl leaning out her carriage window behind the wagon. They waved the wagon and the carriage through. Teza followed like an assistant watching for people with light fingers. He felt the guards glance his way, and it was all he could do to not stop dead in his tracks. Surely they could hear his heart slamming against his chest, smell the nervous sweat beading his brow, see the stiff hairs on his neck.

He passed through lengthy shade, and emerged into the vibrant bustle of civilization. Teza looked back. The guards did not. He was a rowshatar, and he'd been dismissed like a dead gem. He reminded himself anonymity was a good thing in his current situation, but the hope that he could rectify it wavered.

A woman with short hair bumped his shoulder and scowled. Teza opened his mouth to chastise her, but a man with a fez atop his close-cropped head elbowed his side, knocking the words from his tongue. Three more citizens jostled Teza before he realized he was standing in the middle of a crowded boulevard. He quickly joined the human tide. He had no destination in mind, but he had to find somewhere to hide until the sun set. Iza Vor's shield wouldn't be lowered until its replenishing, but the stars' kaza would return to him before that. The people would know he was a rowshatar-estra then.

The crowd turned down a lane leading to the festival's activities. Teza paused at the intersection, and received a scoff from the man behind him. Teza pressed his back against the nearest building, seeking stationary ground. Where could he go?

In the distance, the Ora's tower esteemed its peaceful citizens from its exalted height. Harmonies adorned temple domes, and a circle of Ways flags fluttered in the mild breeze. A circle of flags? The theater? The Officials Ward was in that area. Teza considered the landmarks. Could he make it? Seal Keeper Firnak had described his home only once. Teza had attempted to locate it when he had left his guardian at the bazaar, and the result had been disastrous. The route would bring him near Iza Vor, too. If a patrol or a good citizen recognized him, all would be lost.

But he had nowhere else to go.

He stayed on the main streets and kept the theater's flags in sight as much as possible, which became difficult the closer he went. The city was packed due to the festival, but most regular labor had been paused, resulting in abandoned thoroughfares usually bustling with business. A chill slithered up Teza's spine whenever he found himself suddenly alone and exposed.

As the sky began to blush, Teza arrived at a boulevard lined with modest brick homes refined by ample porches, painted pillars, and tile trim. Seal Keeper Firnak had said raised flower and spice beds bordered his façade, but Teza found them present at multiple dwellings. He used his headscarf to wipe the sweat from his brow. If he went to the wrong door…

A golden glint caught his eye. A door knocker in the shape of the Harmony. It was the only one on the street. And peeking over the home's back wall were the branches of a lemon tree.

Teza stepped onto the porch. Hesitated. What if he was wrong? The stars' iridescence hadn't emerged on his olive skin. Pale blue clung to the waning day. And yet, he could feel the night diamonds shrouded in the sun's fire. Distant, weak, but present. Their kaza would burst forth as they claimed dominance of the sky. The stars would hold sway this night. His shredded hair was probably already turning white.

Teza knocked on the door. It opened a crack. "Rowshatar Teza?" The opening widened, and Seal Keeper Firnak returned a seal to his slotted belt. "What are you doing here?"

"I need your help," Teza said.

"Yes, of course. Come inside."

"No one can know I'm here."

"The servants are at the festival. I was about to head there myself. A few moments later, and you would've arrived at an empty house."

As the door closed behind him, Teza felt relief at being indoors again; he had missed civilization. Seal Keeper Firnak led him to the parlor. He closed the shutters and lit the wall sconces. In the fresh kazalight, the seal keeper examined Teza with concern. Teza hadn't seen a mirror since last night, but if he looked as dirty and mangy as he felt, he was a dire mess.

"What happened to you?" Seal Keeper Firnak said, guiding Teza to a chair. "Where is your guardian?"

"It's a long story," Teza said. "I'm still trying to understand it. But it's bad, horrible."

Seal Keeper Firnak laid a supporting hand on his shoulder. "You can tell me."

Teza gave him an appreciative but cautious smile. "You've always treated me well, respected me, honored me properly, and we share interest in the lost arts. That means something, right?"

"Yes, I believe it does," Seal Keeper Firnak said.

"So you consider us friends?" Teza asked.

"I always enjoy your company, Rowshatar Teza. You have a sharp mind."

"Then I can trust you?"

"Of course you can trust me. What has happened, my friend?"

Teza's shoulders sagged, and he described to his friend and teacher the events since Saunez and Jaleya had snatched him from Abylay, excluding his and his guardian's (former guardian?) plan to infiltrate Iza Vor. When he reached the Ora's betrayal and him being pronounced a traitor, his throat clenched. He angrily wiped his moistening eyes. Seal Keeper Firnak went to a decanter and filled a glass. Teza took the offered wine and gulped the sweet liquid.

"I'm not a traitor," he said. "It's all a big misunderstanding."

What about his intentions for tonight, a mere few hours from now? Were those not the actions of a traitor? This situation was making him lightheaded. He sipped the remaining wine.

"I'm glad you came to me," Firnak said. "Everything is going to be all right."

Teza's friend stood outside of arm's reach, watching him intently. He clutched a cylinder seal in his fist, but he had yet to draw upon its kaza. Why did Firnak need a seal?

Teza's eyelids drooped, and he fought to keep them open. The room began to spin; or was he spinning? The glass slipped from his limp fingers; wine droplets spotted the embroidered rug. Teza slumped forward and toppled out of the chair. He tried to prop himself up, but his muscles seemed to have liquefied. His mouth felt like it was filled with wool. The stars—the stars were slipping away! He could feel their kaza, but accessing it was like trying to catch water with his bare hands.

He'd been drugged. Firnak…Firnak had drugged him.

"W-why?" Teza said hoarsely. Firnak had said they were friends, that Teza could trust him. He had trusted him.

"It grieved me to learn of your plot to supplant the Ora," Firnak said, "but I took comfort in knowing your egregious crime was due to the Schism denying your rightful reign. Then I heard the deceit spouting from your lips. You disgust me. If I could return you to Orvashka myself, I would."

Firnak deposited the seal into his slotted belt. He hadn't used it to subdue Teza because Teza would have felt him veering kaza and could have potentially retaliated. Firnak had slipped a concoction into the wine instead, rendering him helpless with a feigned act of kindness.

Firnak retrieved a cuff from an adjacent room, and even in his bleary state, Teza felt the hollow void of obsidian.

"I'm not lying," he whimpered. "I'm not..." He clawed at the elegant rug, but his lifeless limbs didn't respond. He grasped for the dimming stars—please, please!—but their kaza evaded him.

Firnak crouched beside him and grabbed his wrist. Teza struggled—tried to—but Firnak held fast.

Teza begged in a desperate whisper, "Please. Please don't."

"I am sorry it came to this," Firnak said, "but harmony must be preserved. Forward Orvashka's Ways to Paradise eternal."

Something deep inside Teza snapped, and burst forth as white-hot rage. Kaza flooded his veins. Blood sprayed in a whoosh of mountain air, and the cuff dropped to the floor.

Teza's eyelids drooped; he could fight it no longer. The last thing he saw was his friend's shocked expression, his severed torso, and blood—so much blood!—gushing onto the rug. Reaching for Teza, to drown him as the traitor he was.

CHAPTER 29

Ameara woke to Syra buzzing in her mind. The sun had warmed the Dazmir's hull, but a chill clung to the air. Before she could assess what her ship was telling her, sandals slapping wood announced Obakwe's arrival on the lower deck.

"Patrol ship, Captain."

Ameara jumped to her feet. "Watch him." The shavinash hadn't moved since he lost consciousness last night, but until she personally confirmed he no longer drew breath, she wasn't taking any chances.

Hurrying topside, she joined Nahzida in the quarterdeck and accepted the offered spyglass.

"They're ordering us to stop," Nahzida said.

The corvette maintained its signal pennant as it maneuvered to come along Syra's port side. The crew wore Setsean uniforms, and a deep-blue flag emblazoned with a white Harmony billowed atop the mast. The cannons were aimed at Syra's stern. Syra would snap the corvette in half like kindling.

"Comply," Ameara ordered.

"What about—?"

"I'll take care of it."

At the helm, Ara disengaged the thrust, but Ameara had already asked Syra to slow and stop. There was nothing to worry about. It was just a routine inspection.

Ara and Nahzida briskly descended belowdecks to hide what Setsea considered contraband. Within moments, Kyzum met Ameara at the helm and assumed the wheel. Ameara rushed back to the brig, and found herself pausing.

The shavinash was slumped against the bars, head bowed, jaw slack. The bloodshaping had snaked over his high cheekbones and nibbled the corners of his eyes. He still hadn't moved.

"Captain?" Obakwe said.

Ameara shook herself. Their few precious minutes were ticking by at an alarming rate. Kyzum could stall the sun from rising, but they couldn't afford to be suspicious in the slightest. She had to be on deck to greet the soldiers. The shavinash's corpse was no different than any other.

Ameara cut his bonds and tossed them into a chest. She took his shoulders, Obakwe took his legs, and together they lifted his body and carried it to the middle deck. Ameara directed Obakwe to Syra's heart, where the older woman set down her burden. Obakwe opened one of the hidden floor hatches used to house cargo of a questionable nature, and then grabbed the shavinash's legs once more, ready to deposit him into the empty gap.

"Wait," Ameara said. She thought she felt…It couldn't be.

Ameara lowered her ear to the shavinash's mouth. A puff of warm air brushed her cheek.

"He's alive."

Obakwe's hands glowed with sun kaza, and she recoiled as if having been bitten. "He can already see his ancestors. We don't have time, Captain."

They were out of time. They dragged the shavinash to the compartment and jammed him inside. Ameara closed the hatch and prayed to any listening gods and ancestors that the shavinash wouldn't miraculously wake up.

She and Obakwe hurried to the main deck and lined up with the rest of the crew. Nahzida stood at rest with her staff; her bow slung on her back was strung. Kyzum wore his knives openly, and

Ara her sword. Obakwe bore her knobkerries even though veins of kaza fire undulated upon her skin. Ameara's pistol and sword hung comfortably from her belt. Vekrym were expected to be armed. It gave Setsean officials a justification to publicly sneer at them while they surreptitiously hired them. But one didn't want to give them too many justifications, hence the absence of Ara's seal bracelet and Nahzida's rifle. Ameara hadn't stashed her gun because she was the captain. She was supposed to be pretentious.

As soldiers in Setsean livery climbed aboard, Ameara identified the captain by his officer's jerkin and the insignia accompanying the Harmony on his sash.

"These waters belong to Setsea," he said. "Your vessel will be searched to ensure the safety of its citizens. Resist, and you will be arrested."

"You're welcome aboard, as soon as you show documentation that you do, in fact, represent Setsea," Ameara said.

The captain frowned, so she added, "Imposters waylaying and robbing innocent travelers sets a bad precedent, especially during the spring festival. You understand."

His frown burrowed deeper, but he nodded to his second, who produced a scroll. Ameara unrolled it and read its contents, twice, just because. It was a standard document Ameara had seen countless times before, but Kyzum read it over her shoulder on the off chance that it was forged.

"You're far from Abylay, Captain," Ameara said, handing back the scroll. "Inspections are usually closer to the city."

"The Festival of Shattered Swords is ongoing," he said, "and stars' sway is tonight. You understand."

"Of course," Ameara said pleasantly.

"Assemble your crew so they won't be underfoot."

"They are assembled."

The captain eyed the motley troop and considered Syra's lack of masts. Sailing and maintaining a Dazmir with such a skeleton crew was possible, but a mundane complication could easily degrade to a crisis without a few extra hands. Only the foolish or the very competent assumed the endeavor. Ameara knew they did not look foolish, but the patrol captain's disdain for Vekrym overruled his internal warning bells.

"Search the ship," he ordered. To her he said, "Remain here." He brushed past her, his soldiers dispersing belowdecks.

"Be careful in the heart," Ameara warned. There was always one who couldn't restrain his or her curiosity.

Ameara focused inward, her mind touching Syra's. The Dazmir-vahl-kesh's answering impressions indicated where the soldiers were poking around. She flared anxiety when one of them entered her heart, then another, and another! Her hull creaked as someone gave in to his curiosity. Syra maintained the impassive pulse of her lifeless cousins throughout. *Well done,* Ameara sent.

Shortly after that, the captain and his soldiers emerged from below. One of them cradled a burned limb.

"I did tell them to be careful," Ameara said, forestalling accusations of negligence.

The patrol captain gestured to a cask of Masatitoran beer two of his men carried. "Do you have import papers for this?"

"It's not being imported," Ameara replied. "It's part of our stores, and therefore won't leave this ship."

The captain grunted. He glared at her pistol and the various defenses her crew had unapologetically equipped.

"It's unlawful to leave weapons unattended." He signaled to another soldier, and he presented a knife the crew used for cooking.

"It's a galley knife," Ameara said.

"It's a weapon and is required to be in locked storage when not in use."

"Thank you for clarifying the distinction," Ameara said. "I'll find a safe place for it."

"No need. It's being confiscated. One less weapon to harm citizens. The beer is being confiscated, too."

Kyzum sighed a lament.

"I believe you're trying to deny the people of Setsea their due coin, but since the cask is small, I will consider its repossession just compensation and forgo the smuggling fine.

"The next matter is your lack of Vessel insignia. All Vessels are required to display their affiliation so their generous exemptions are not mistakenly denied."

"The Vekrym flag serves as affiliation for all crew aboard the vessel sailing under it, which this ship is," Ameara said, her voice heating. She hated bureaucratic games. Setsean patrols always flexed their "enlightened" laws, but this was becoming excessive. The knife should have satisfied. No one on that deck truly believed she was smuggling Kyzum's tiny half-empty beer cask into Abylay. She needed to hasten this verbal sparing to its inevitable conclusion. She had a dead—soon to be dead?—shavinash in her ship's heart. And said ship had been suspiciously distant since the soldiers returned to the main deck.

Syra? She didn't respond, nor did she let Ameara in. The vahl-kesh…pursued something? Yearned to…purge, eradicate? The disjointed flashes were reminiscent of when Ameara had stumbled upon Syra in the Dazmir graveyard and accidentally awakened her. Her consciousness had been fragmented and scattered, unable to form coherent impressions. And violent. Violent and terrifying.

"This rowshatar is a Vessel?" the persistent captain said.

Ameara took the scroll Kyzum handed her and relayed it to him. "Yes, under my command. They all are."

Syra?

The captain couldn't legally detain Obakwe, but like others before him, that didn't stop him from searching for a loophole. He scrutinized Ameara's captain certificate declaring her present crew were Vekrym, therefore exempting Obakwe from her rowshatar duty, and also like others before him, he did a double take when he read which captain they currently served.

A rayed astrolabe nestling in a cerulean sea, the Vekrym flag, rippled in Syra's stern. A Vekrym always had a heading, so the saying went. Ameara narrowed her brow, warning the captain Eclipse would make a heading right through him if he continued his attempts to entrap her. She had cooperated, and her patience was depleted. He did not want her to flex her generous exemptions.

The captain handed back the scroll. "It seems to be in order. You're free to go."

Ameara forced herself to stand her ground while the patrol boarded its corvette. Fixated on her single incoherent craving, Syra was heedlessly diving deeper and deeper into the depths of her consciousness that Ameara couldn't reach. Purge, purge, purge purge purge get rid of it get rid of it get rid of it!

Syra!

The corvette's sails brought its stern about, and Ameara bolted. She caught a glimpse of her crew's alarmed expressions, and put them out of her mind; Kyzum would handle it.

Her boots pounded the thick planks as she sprinted to the heart. She threw the door open and skidded to a stop. The alexandrite that was Syra hummed and sparked in a turbulent cadence, its light pulsing erratically. Ameara yanked up the hatch concealing the shavinash. He hadn't regained consciousness, but his limbs convulsed even in the tight compartment, his eyelids flickering. Ameara felt a sensation akin to a thunderstorm enveloping his chest and funneling into the damaged etch.

Syra! What are you doing? Syra!

Her oldest companion didn't hear her, or chose not to.

Ameara scooped her arms around the shavinash's shoulders. A jolt shot through her, but it originated from the invisible storm, not from kaza. "Syra! Syra, stop!"

The Dazmir-vahl-kesh's light stuttered, and then recoiled. The cabin plunged into darkness.

Obakwe and Nahzida jogged into the heart, and they quickly helped Ameara haul the shavinash out of the hidden compartment. Syra's light cautiously filled the alexandrite.

"What happened?" Nahzida asked.

Ameara brushed the Dazmir-vahl-kesh's consciousness, calling gently. Syra conveyed confusion at Ameara's caution, as if she wasn't aware of what she had just done. Her anxiety had returned to the elevated level it had persisted at since the shavinash disturbed her mechanism. The craving to eradicate the etch was gone.

"Captain," Obakwe said from where she crouched by the shavinash.

Ameara followed Obakwe's gaze. She blinked, and blinked again. The bloodshaping's tendrils had receded to the shavinash's shoulders. His chest rose and fell in a labored but steady rhythm.

"What did your crazy ship do?" Nahzida said.

Syra seemed just as puzzled as they were, and when Ameara inquired, a dark cloud began descending upon Syra's consciousness, and she fled from the deep memories. Ameara relented.

"Get Ara down here," she ordered.

Nahzida hastened to obey, but it was debatable whom she wanted to distance herself from more: the shavinash or Syra.

Ameara said, "Let's get him back—"

The shavinash struck out with his fist, slamming it into Obakwe's jaw and knocking her sideways. He seemed to skip the intervening movement and walloped Ameara with one of Obakwe's knobkerries. The impact rung her head, and she felt wooden planks beneath her as her mind scrambled to catch up. Kaza veins burning a fierce red, Obakwe barreled into the shavinash, her body low. She toppled the assassin, but then he was on top of her, again having skipped the full range of motion, as if it was only a suggestion. Obakwe screamed as the shavinash snapped her captured arm with a vicious twist and tore out of the heart.

Ameara staggered over to Obakwe, who lay on the deck and cradled her shattered limb. The protruding bone and surrounding tissue rippled as she shapeshifted and healed her ruptured flesh. Brow knotted in pain and deep concentration, Obakwe managed a jaw-clenched nod.

Ameara drew her pistol and raced after the shavinash. Emerging into daylight, she fired at his back, the kazashots joining Nahzida's loosed arrows. Ameara knew she wouldn't catch the shavinash—not with the lead he had, not with his suddenly functioning etch—but she pursued him anyway. She had to.

The assorted projectiles missed their target, and the shavinash's leap cleared the gunwale. Ameara leaned over the side and saw a splash disturb the gentle waves, but the shavinash didn't surface in the frothy undulations. Swimming underwater with the coastal current? It was what she would do. She quickly conferred with Syra, who confirmed her assumption.

Kyzum, Nahzida, and Ara braced for the inevitable orders.

"Ara, is your rift seal replenished?" Ameara asked.

"Yes."

"Go to shore and head him off. Only engage from a distance. Take Nahzida with you."

Ara fetched her seal bracelet from below, Nahzida her rifle, and a whirling vortex whisked them to the distant coast in a single step. Obakwe marched onto the main deck as Kyzum shivered from the closing flash of crisp air. She was bathed in perspiration, but her posture was resolute. Her arm bore no trace of injury.

"Permission to pursue?"

"Find him," Ameara told the rowshatar-korza.

Shimmering, Obakwe sprinted into a bound, and an eagle soared into the sky.

Ameara instructed Syra to follow the shavinash's bloodshaping. She and Kyzum posted themselves port and starboard and combed the sea for their quarry. Ara and Nahzida scouted the sandy shore, and eagle-Obakwe circled above. When they failed to locate the shavinash within the time he required to reach dry ground, Ameara consulted Syra, but the Dazmir-vahl-kesh shied away in shame. The shavinash had eluded her.

Ameara expanded their search, taking Syra up the coast while Ara and Nahzida rifted down. Obakwe spanned their positions from the air, a winged sentinel. An hour elapsed. All they found were shoals, patches of prickly grass, and whispering dunes.

Syra's anxiety vanished. And so had the shavinash.

CHAPTER 30

Creepers and thorns clung to the decrepit cannons that once guarded Abylay's harbor, their silent towers home to nothing but dust and spiders. Ways flags swelled in the sea breeze. The spiral tiers of Harmony Tower welcomed its pristine guests, and with its polished domes, obscured the dilapidated bricks across the dividing river. Ameara spotted dissipating smoke northeast of the city. She and Kyzum shared a significant eye.

Abylay's abundant harbor was bursting with ships varying in size and design from grand galleons to single-mast sloops. There was even another Dazmir; the Vekrym flag rippled in the sterncastle of the larger and heftier skyship.

The harbormaster directed Syra to a dock near the edge of the waterfront, which suited Ameara's preference for close proximity to open water. It made escape easier if it became necessary. The Vekrym's rayed astrolabe discouraged curiosity, but fools abounded no matter the location. No one could mistake a Dazmir. If a curious fool discovered Syra was a vahl-kesh, their problems would compound exponentially, especially in Abylay. Syra played her lifeless cousins while in port, but she would defend herself if she felt her life was threatened. Ameara would not deny her that freedom.

After paying the egregious docking fees, Ameara claimed Vekrym immunity from an inspection, as all Vekrym did. The harbor official sniffed and stalked away, scribbling furiously on her clipboard. Ameara went to her quarters and retrieved the satchel containing the resealed resistance intelligence. She situated the Vekrym band on her bicep, making sure the emblem was clearly visible.

A knock sounded on the door, followed by Kyzum.

"If I'm not back in three hours, employ the contingency plan," Ameara said.

"Being Vekrym won't shield us from vengeful shavinashi," Kyzum said.

"That's why you all know how to disappear."

Ameara double-checked her two concealed knives and her Ryvekian sword. If she was ordered to fasten it to its scabbard so it couldn't be drawn, she would comply, and then cut the binding so it only appeared she was complying. She refused to rely on others to protect her when she was fully capable of doing so and making the distinction of when it was necessary. By the time help came, it might be too late. Or help wouldn't come at all. Her pistol, its star and sun seals replenished thanks to Syra and Obakwe, would remain on the ship. It would better protect her crew if they had to flee.

"We should've disappeared at sea," Kyzum said.

"Failing to arrive in Abylay after encountering the patrol would've been suspicious," Ameara said. "According to Ara, the shavinash drew so heavily on his etch to escape it's likely he was consumed before he reached the city. He might have never made it to shore."

"She also said he'd be dead this morning," Kyzum countered. "He was a very lively corpse, and we never confirmed what his mission was."

"Hence the contingency plan, which you will carry out to the letter," Ameara said firmly. If she didn't return, they were to leave her behind. No scouting to ascertain her status. No rescue attempt.

"Yes, Captain," Kyzum mumbled.

"I mean it, Kyzum."

If their places were reversed, it wouldn't sit well with her either. She would go after him. She would go after any of her crew. Which is what worried her.

The *Skyheart's* first mate reluctantly nodded.

"What are you going to tell Whisper?" he asked.

Ameara had debated that through the strait, on the open sea, when they reached the harbor, even as they docked. She only had one rational option.

"As little as possible. Considering the lengths the rebels went to to retrieve this information, I presume there are significant circumstances and other interested parties he failed to disclose, but now that we've fulfilled the contract, we won't encounter any more trouble on my ship, unless it's expected trouble."

"Sufficient detail to avert suspicion laced with just enough believable outrage," Kyzum mused. "I taught you well."

"I learn well." She slung the satchel over her shoulder. Paused. "Keep them safe."

Ameara descended the gangplank, her gaze fixed forward. Syra pressed against her mind, sensing her apprehension. Ameara distanced herself from the vahl-kesh. Even though they weren't javati, Syra would be the first to know if something went wrong. She would not do well losing another captain while their soul's communed.

The most direct route to the shavinashi's compound took Ameara past Iza Vor's southern gate. Tiles of lapis lazuli and gold ringed the tiered dais elevating the bloodshaping altar that crowned the honeycombed archway. Flowers and fruit cascaded from the altar's base, but no amount of trimmings or polishing could hide the ingrained bloodstains. Counselor initiates, ministers, and citizens wearing Harmonies hemmed the archway and preached Orvashka's Ways to passersby, beseeching them to gift their lives so the Ora's would continue; harmony would fail without the Ora's guidance; Paradise would be lost. Offering themselves as a sacrifice didn't seem to occur to the preachers.

Two acolytes flanked the shavinashi's honeycombed gate. Dressed in muted browns, the young man and woman bore shaved pates beneath their headscarves. The northern winter of their eyes was on the brink of coalescing into the Wild Ice. They couldn't have been more than thirteen years old.

"I have business with Whisper," Ameara said as she strode past. They didn't stop her. They were there as a warning, not to vet people. If one entered the shavinashi's domain, anything that happened was on one's own head.

Ameara's footsteps echoed in the malevolent silence of the seemingly empty courtyard. Stone carvings of the Ways marched across the paving stones to a Harmony-topped dome with a honeycombed façade. Cylinder seals glinted within their minarets. Ameara felt eyes on her, a knife teasing her throat, but she couldn't locate the owners.

Sustaining her steady pace, Ameara headed toward the cluster of Harmony-draped towers connected by narrow bridges. Raked dirt swelled against silent pools bordering a branching arcade. Gardens did not exist. Restless malice seeped from the pristine architecture. Ameara reminded herself to breathe.

A woman in gray shavinash garb suddenly appeared in Ameara's path. Shorter than Ameara, as most women were, her chiseled features were impassive death. Raging against the fear a shavinash's presence always evoked, Ameara walked past the assassin without acknowledging her. The shavinash followed Ameara into a nearby tower.

As Ameara navigated the familiar corridors, shavinashi assessed and dismissed her in a single cold heartbeat. She had never been ordered to relinquish her weapons, not even during her initial contact. Her boldness amused them. A Ryvekian child believing she equaled the adult warriors. Hubris it certainly was, but hubris not without warrant.

Her shavinash tail claimed the lead at a winding staircase. The bridged towers were allocated for living quarters, education, and weapons training, but invisible webs abounded in the shadows, machinations of a cadre or a single mind, experiments to bring about life's only certainty with pain and cruelty. Glancing behind the grand façade, even accidentally, would land a knife in her gut. If they discovered she had witnessed their fallibility—had exposed it—she would earn far worse.

Her silent escort entered Whisper's quarters without announcement and proceeded to his personal sparring chamber. A large sack hung from the ceiling. The rough fabric intermittently bulged. The poor soul trapped within was waking up.

Whisper gazed out the latticed window. His undulating muscles and poised posture belied his average stature and the wrinkles bordering his dark eyes. His only distinguishing garb was the shashvin sash around his trim waist.

"Eclipse," he said. His voice was a smooth river, and as treacherous as its undertow. He dismissed his shavinash with a brush of his calloused hand.

"Whisper," Ameara replied evenly. She couldn't acknowledge his helpless victim or hesitate to deliver the satchel. She couldn't be afraid. Couldn't show weakness of any kind. She was a confident, indifferent captain who just wanted to get paid. Her sword was a reassuring weight. "I've brought your cargo, per our contract."

"Always straight to business," Whisper said. "We welcomed three new shavinashi this morning." He remained at the window. Ameara felt she was going to be sick.

"My conciseness is why you like me," she said, crossing the polished wood to the shashvin's side. Towers encircled the moderate training yard below; silhouettes filled several latticed frames. Two men and one woman stood back to back in a sand-filled ring. Six other shavinashi surrounded them. All had weapons in hand. At a signal Ameara couldn't see, the shavinashi closed on the three in the center, moving faster than the eye could comprehend. They were drawing on their etchs. Blurs of motion later, the trio was crumpled on the ground, limbs bent at odd angles, crimson pooling beneath them. The infant bloodshapings surged through their broken bodies, reviving them for another swift defeat.

"I do appreciate your brevity," Whisper said, "but it doesn't allow time to acknowledge your other aspects."

The woman and one of the men stumbled upright; the other remained on the coagulating sand. Ameara watched the pair be cut down for a third time.

"If I let Kyzum rub off on me, brevity will become your favorite aspect."

"You wound me," Whisper said, his sidelong glance hungry.

The woman refrained from rising, leaving the seasoned killers one target. He lasted a breath before he was bleeding and broken once more. The mended shavinashi did not get up. Their brethren deserted them. Thus shavinash and etch were baptized.

Whisper held out his hand. Ameara slipped the satchel over her head and hung it on his open palm. The shashvin led her to a study with maps hanging on the walls and a Ways shrine in the oriel window. He placed the satchel inside a cabinet and offered her a pouch clinking with coins.

"I will grieve the day we part ways," he said.

A warning? Had the dying shavinash reached Abylay? Did Whisper know everything?!

No. She would already be dead or worse. A reminder of her tenuous position? A test? Possibly. Most things were one or the other with Whisper. Watching the display outside certainly had been.

"You're not going to check?" Ameara said, nodding at the cabinet.

"Do I need to?" Whisper said.

"You tell me. A shavinash attempted to repossess your cargo. That suggests one of two things: there's maneuvering in your ranks that you're unaware of, which I find hard to believe, or the shavinash was following your orders. If you no longer think I'm capable, tell me, and I'll rectify it. Don't send your lackeys to undermine my contact."

Whisper didn't react. At all. He didn't even blink. It was terrifying.

Ameara felt she should prostrate herself and beg for mercy. She had just admitted to thwarting a shavinash and had accused her patron of sending him. That wasn't what she had planned to say! It was all she could do to stand her ground and project a confident front.

Whisper finally spoke. "A shavinash, you say." He began to circle her, a shark smelling blood in the water. "Where did you encounter this alleged shavinash?"

"On my ship, when we were waylaid on the strait," Ameara said. "The destroyed cannon was my handiwork." She had no doubt that he had heard reports of the skirmish.

"A night attack. Not the best circumstances to determine a person's affiliation," Whisper said. Ameara couldn't determine if he was calculating in her favor or not. She had no choice but to continue. She was already committed.

"I took a shot. I missed. He moved like you do."

"You must have been close to distinguish this shavinash's sex."

"It could've been a very tall muscular woman," Ameara allowed. "Perhaps my long-lost twin."

Her patron's brow creased, reminding her why Kyzum wasn't welcome.

The shashvin's prowling lapsed. He scrutinized her with eyes of Wild Ice, but Ameara refused to yield to the bitter cold. She would defy it to the end.

Whisper's lips twisted. "You believe I lost faith in your abilities and ordered a shavinash to secure my cargo, and yet you still returned, having fired upon one of us, no less."

Was that esteem in his smooth voice, or incredulity at her stupidity?

"Our arrangement is mutually beneficial," Ameara said. "If you wanted to terminate it, you would give me the professional courtesy of informing me before plunging the knife in. Where could I go where you couldn't find me?"

The piercing cold persisted, mercilessly creeping, creeping…

Whisper chuckled. Mirthless, but a candle in foggy waters. The sudden relief was an ache Ameara dare not soothe.

"I like you, Eclipse. Where could you go indeed. It's a shame you weren't chosen as a child. You would've been a fine addition to the shavinashi." Whisper proffered the coin pouch once more.

Ameara accepted the payment. "The contract is complete and now belongs to the sea."

"Yes, yes," Whisper said dismissively.

"I'll have no more unexpected visitors."

"If you do, they won't belong to me. My messengers will provide a courteous explanation."

Ameara withdrew a coin from the pouch. "For questioning your integrity."

The shashvin ignored the Harmony-stamped gold. "It's not my integrity in question."

Ameara returned the coin to the collection. Whisper seized her wrist, quick as a viper, and wrenched it behind her back. His arm hooked her torso, his coarse hand a hairsbreadth from her sword. He pressed his mouth against her ear, savoring her alarmed gasp.

"Be careful not to fly too high. The view is breathtaking, but the fall is that much worse."

He inhaled her long dark waves, his crude lips teasing her neck's throbbing pulse. Shadows crept from the recesses of Ameara's mind and began to infect her subdued reflexes. Whisper sighed with craving. The shadows thickened.

Whisper released her. "Give my regards to Kyzum, and your other three crewmembers."

Heart racing, fingers itching for her sword, Ameara calmly took her leave, posture assured, stride balanced. The thump of fists resounded from the sparring chamber and followed her into the corridor. Her shavinash escort was waiting.

Ameara employed the same route as earlier to return to Syra, but the crowded streets now seemed to bend and twist into eternity. When the harbor's salty air finally washed over Ameara, her starved lungs basked in the rejuvenating swells. Syra's main deck felt like a fortress. Ameara restrained her deceptive relief. She was being watched.

Kyzum followed Ameara into the captain's quarters and asked, "Are we dead?"

"Not yet," she said. "Whisper still likes me." She suppressed a chill.

Kyzum kissed his folded hands and pressed them against his forehead in gratitude to his gods. "We should use the festival as cover and celebrate."

"Shore leave will require additional caution. I have a tail. They may be watching the rest of you as well." Ameara went to the secluded strongbox and used her back to shield her trembling hands as she fumbled with the key.

"'They,' as in shavinashi?" Kyzum said.

Ameara jammed the key into the lock and turned it sharply. "I improvised and implicated the cadres in the attempted theft of our cargo. Whisper's inherent distrust will in turn rouse the other shashvini's."

Kyzum's agile wit darkened. "And your convenient brilliance avoided entangling us in the implication. Is what you would say if you could."

Her friend's justified reaction heightened her gnawing shame. She had substituted a solid plan with a probable trap—a trap proposed by a shavinash. Bereft of wind, waves, and Syra, Ameara suddenly, inexplicably *knowing* which heading flowed to calm waters was a hollow excuse, not a mariner's instinct. Her split-second decision was indefensible. She had carelessly endangered her crew. Ameara almost dropped the coin pouch while depositing it in the strongbox.

Kyzum noticed. His anger faltered. "Are there other improvisations I should be aware of?"

Whisper's rough hand imprisoning her arm. His rigid body thrust against hers. Inhaling her scent and prodding her flesh like she was a piece of savory meat. His dead eyes reminding her she was nothing more than prey.

And she had trusted his equivalent. Against all reason. She had trusted a shavinash.

She clutched the rim of the strongbox, steeling herself against her mutinous faculties.

"Gather the crew in the galley," she said. "We need to establish an account of recent events and coordinate shore leave."

"Ameara…"

"That's an order, Kyzum," she snapped, slamming the strongbox closed.

"Yes, Captain." Her friend left her quarters with an indignant stride.

Ameara reached out her hand and found Syra's hull. She sagged against the aged wood as sobs racked her body. Syra caressed her anguished mind, and Ameara let the Dazmir's steadfast presence envelop her own. She'd been afraid—terrified, but she had persevered and was still alive. She had made it through the storm, just like she had before. Just like she would again.

Ameara's breathing calmed. She locked the strongbox with a steady hand.

She was Eclipse. She did not fear others. Others feared her.

She survived. She always survived. And the day she didn't, she would meet her end on her own terms. She would never be a victim again. Never again.

CHAPTER 31

Ameara was updating Syra's ledger when Ara entered her quarters. Nahzida's enthusiastic voice gusted through the momentary gap. The young galahi was contrarily subdued.

"Did you get everything we need?" Ameara asked.

"Yes, but barely," Ara said, presenting the delivery orders. "We didn't have enough to replace Kyzum's beer."

"I expected as much, especially during the festival," Ameara said, skimming the purchases. "The bulgur and bread will sustain us until the next port. Any sign of our friends?"

"No, but that doesn't mean they're not there."

Kyzum and Obakwe had reported the same. Perhaps the shavinashi were only watching Ameara. It would be a relief, but assuming that could get them killed.

"Tread carefully, act normal, and Abylay will be at our stern tomorrow morning." Ameara slid a small pouch across the desk. "Your share."

After setting aside the dues owed the Vekrym, the fee Abylay would collect upon their departure, and the final funds to replenish the star wild gems (they had to keep up appearances), it left a paltry sum to split five ways. Six ways, actually, as a portion was also reserved for supplies and Syra's maintenance. It wasn't the first time

Ameara had refrained from filling a pouch for herself, and it wouldn't be the last. They needed to barter wild gems on the black market as soon as possible.

Ara accepted the light purse as Ameara returned to the ledger, which balanced precariously between justifiable inflation and plausible incompetence. Kyzum might be able to stretch the numbers a little further.

Ara remained by the desk.

"Is there something else?" Ameara asked.

A cloud of timidity cloaked the young galahi. "Why was Kyzum studying the cargo?"

Ameara straightened, honing her sharp features. "Who claimed he was?"

"…I saw it, in his cabin, when we were preparing for the inspection. It mentioned Dazmiri."

"You recognized the language?" *Not to mention the code it was written in,* Ameara thought but didn't say.

The barest of nods. "Old Setsean."

Ameara rested the stylus on her thumb. When the Yevyrans, empaths, and other Ora resistors had fled Parvasahalis and Tesinoc, they had taken ample knowledge of the lost arts with them. What remained had been destroyed or sequestered in the Ora's purge. The people of Ulydra, Ara's homeland, were descendants of those Ora resistors, so Ameara wasn't surprised a remnant of Old Setsean survived on the northern island. What gave her pause was one of Ara's age exhibiting fluency in the eradicated dialect. A skill reserved for galahi? Or were the Ulydrans protecting more than their way of life beyond the Talons?

Ara waited patiently in the perceptible silence, prompting neither acceptance nor rejection of her dangerous offer. Ameara wanted to know what her crew had almost died for—might still die for. She deserved to know. Kyzum had been able to decipher the cargo's topic before their timetable expired but not its purpose. Was it a threat to Syra? But meddling in the affairs of shavinashi and rebels

—especially if the rebels were Yevyrans or their warrior sect—would inexorably culminate in a prolonged, agonizing death. They were sailing choppy waters as it was. The lost arts were a prize anyone would vie for, regardless of its deficient utility.

"Old Setsean is all but extinct. Perhaps you didn't see what you thought you saw," Ameara said.

Ara nodded. "Of course. I'm probably just homesick." She shuffled her weight and needlessly adjusted her seal bracelet.

"Is there more?" Ameara asked.

"No…No. That was it." Ara inclined her head in respectful leave-taking and turned toward the door. Three vacillating steps. A resolved exhale. She whipped around, her lips a determined line.

"I don't think he was here to kill us," she blurted. "I think he was trying to free himself from the etch."

A reprimand for recalling the dead shavinash formed on Ameara's tongue. The waning daylight cascading through the window highlighted Ara's jaw, healed from the assassin's debilitating but not fatal blow.

Ameara had left Whisper's chambers alive.

"Why do you think that?" she said.

"Very few things are powerful enough to negate an etch," Ara said, "but the blast from Syra's heart did just that, and we didn't drop from the sky. He knew exactly what he was doing. I don't know how he would separate himself from the etch short of cutting it out, a procedure he probably wouldn't survive without sun kaza, but he must've had a way."

"Did you find something among his possessions indicative of that?" Ameara asked.

"No, but Syra's strange behavior could be."

Knowing she shouldn't sail into the storm could not stop Ameara from doing so. "The incident in the heart?"

Ara nodded. "Star kaza can't overcome the bond between a shavinash and an etch, but Syra veers more than star kaza. Empath power birthed her; it birthed all vahl-keshi. It's how she communicates, the means of forming javash. Bloodshaping is its substitute, and a corrupted one. An empath could very likely sever the bloodshaping's bond."

Was that what Syra had been trying to communicate with the impressions of the brig? Had Syra's anxiety stemmed not from the shavinash but from the suppressed deep memories his presence stirred? Ameara hadn't sensed helpful inclinations in any of Syra's sendings, only her desire to rid herself of the bloodshaping. The further it burrowed, the more insistent that desire became. Whatever Syra had been doing to the shavinash in the hidden compartment hadn't looked like assistance. It looked, and felt, like she was trying to kill him.

And yet, he had miraculously recovered enough to overwhelm her and Obakwe and escape, when the night before she thought he wouldn't live to see the dawn. Had the bloodshaping ceased its feast to prevent Syra from severing its connection to the shavinash? Had it been, in its own twisted way, healing the damage Syra was causing?

"Syra is not an empath," Ameara said.

"But she is an echo of empath power," Ara said. "All vahl-keshi are."

"Would an empath *echo* be able to do what you've theorized?"

Logic and hope battled across Ara's face. "I don't know. Syra seemed to think she could."

"And if she was wrong?"

"If she was wrong...If she wasn't strong enough, the effort might have killed her."

"It's good we interrupted, then," Ameara said. But she found herself wondering what would have happened if Syra had succeeded. Ameara threw the reflection overboard. A shavinash was not worth Syra's life. Syra, her consciousness prominently focused on the conversation, beamed at Ameara's affection.

"Have you shared your speculations with anyone else?" Ameara asked Ara.

"No."

"See it stays that way."

Ara frowned in confusion. "But it's the only explanation that makes sense."

Ameara's voice was a poised whip. "No, it's an irrelevant explanation you *want* to make sense. Our contract is complete, and we are alive. That's all that matters. Excluding my brief encounter during the rebel attack, the events involving our guest, including the incident in Syra's heart, never happened, and you will assume that narrative as you agreed. Is there anything else?"

Faith flashed in Ara's eyes. "He could have killed me. He could have killed Obakwe, you. All of us. He didn't."

Ameara raised her brow in warning. "Is. There. Anything. Else?"

Ara lowered her gaze. "No, Captain."

Ameara watched the abashed young woman cross her quarters. To bear an etch was to be a shavinash. The Ways' enforcers would never sever a piece of their life forces. And yet, the possibility had occurred to Ameara before Ara proposed it. The irrational, implausible, improbable possibility that the stowaway shavinash had forsaken his etch, that Dorian had survived. That she had seen recognition in his deep blue eyes.

"Ara," Ameara said.

Ara looked over her shoulder, and Ameara immediately regretted her momentary weakness. She concealed it with the legitimate unease arising from their previous cargo.

"How much did you recognize in Kyzum's cabin?"

"I had a decent glance." Ara paused, and only continued when Ameara indicated she do so. "It was information about Dazmiri: schematics, flight instructions, seal configurations. Basic, foundational materials, but enough to get you into the sky."

Ara must have had a *very* decent glance. Ameara didn't call her out on it.

"Next time, don't wait before coming to me. I value the opinion, and the theories, of all my crew, even if I don't, or can't, respond."

Ara considered Ameara's words, and then departed the captain's quarters with unburdened steps, her fair cheeks tinted red.

Ameara leaned back in her chair. Dorian had shown no interest in the rebels' information; he had completed his research before boarding Syra. Did the shavinashi's interest extend beyond seizure and suppression? Did the Ora's?

What had she given them?

Ameara shoved that thought overboard, too. They'd done a job; they'd been paid; they were alive. That was all that mattered.

Drowning thoughts regarding the stowaway shavinash was far more difficult, especially when she considered the conclusion Ara had failed to see.

What if he hadn't been trying to separate himself from the etch? He hadn't possessed any means of physically removing it, and he hadn't known Syra was an empath echo potentially capable of severing the bloodshaping's bond. What if he'd been trying to negate its power only long enough for a lethal barrage of kaza or one quick hack of steel?

The sun dipped toward the horizon, painting the sky orange and red. The ink in Ameara's stylus dried. It had been hours since the shavinash drew on the festering bloodshaping and escaped into the sea. His intentions were inconsequential. The shavinash was dead, along with his incriminating report. *That* was why she had left Whisper's chambers, why her crew lived. The shavinash was dead. Dorian was dead.

CHAPTER 32

Teza huddled in a shadowed archway as he waited for Iza Vor's shield to deactivate. Any second now…Were they late? Was he early? Had the schedule changed? He hadn't considered that possibility. Saunez would have. She always thought of everything. It must be exhausting. The infinite particulars that could shatter his fragile plan, which was in all likelihood a suicide mission, were making him want to be sick.

Laughter, music, and kaza displays permeated stars' sway, but the festival's revelry was dwindling as citizens made their way to the offering courtyard. If the heralding drums sounded, it would be too late to save Saunez.

Teza hunched deeper as a giggling couple reeking of wine staggered past. They didn't notice him. At least, he thought they didn't notice him. They hadn't looked at him. He had borrowed trousers, a tunic, a vest, and a cloak from Firnak's wardrobe, but there was nothing he could do about his skin's iridescence. The stars ruled the sky.

Someone tapped his shoulder, and he yelped out of the archway. Heart hammering, he spun to confront the assailant, veering lightning to his hands. Jaleya stood outside a pool of kazalight illuminating the paved avenue. Her perpetual frown remained intact. The merry couple was nowhere to be seen. Teza released the stars' power.

"If you want to blend in, don't steal clothing from the rich," Jaleya said. She looked into his cowl. "And dye your hair and skin."

Teza glanced at his attire. He would never ordinarily wear this uncomfortable, bizarre combination; it was favored by Northerners and dishonest merchants. Oh. He hadn't considered dye. Jaleya must be exhausted, too. Maybe that was why she was always in a foul mood. Plotting, anticipating moves and countermoves, seeing conspiracies and ulterior motives where they didn't exist. Except for when they did...

"I didn't think you'd come," he said.

"I wasn't going to," Jaleya said, "but you are my best chance of getting into Iza Vor undetected."

Teza was torn about her participation. He would need help subduing the guards if he couldn't rift past them, but Jaleya was an insolent traitor who had almost murdered him. He was mortified he had felt relief at her appearance. He was the rowshatar. He was capable of saving Saunez. Jaleya couldn't even get into Iza Vor without him.

"What are you waiting for?" Jaleya said.

"The shield is still up," Teza said.

Jaleya glanced at the black sky twinkling with the night diamonds.

"Are you sure? Or are you guessing?"

Teza hesitated. "I'm...fairly sure."

Jaleya scoffed.

"Distinguishing kaza sources when they're jumbled together is difficult," Teza said defensively. "I've lived under Iza Vor's shield most of my life. I'll know when its kaza is gone." He would. Surely, he would. Right? He really didn't want to be disintegrated, or repelled into a building, or redirected to who knew where; Jaleya would be his only company.

Teza stared at the seemingly empty space encompassing Iza Vor, as if he could will the subtly oscillating dome to collapse. Jaleya tilted her head toward the heart of the festival, listening with her tainted hearing. "We don't have a lot of time."

"I know. They'll lower it soon," Teza said. "Any minute now."

They watched for the telling glimmer. A minute passed. Then another.

"They must have changed the protocol because of the resistance," Jaleya said. "We're not rifting in. I'm trying another way."

Teza sputtered, caught between convincing her to stay and accompanying her elsewhere. He glanced at the western minaret. He had climbed that domed tower countless times. He knew it like the back of his hand. That was the way in. It was the only way in. Rifting had to work.

The minaret's heart pulsed once, twice, and the dome ignited with light, the brightest star on the dark canvas. It should have been Teza replenishing that star.

A flicker against the skyline. Teza blinked. His need playing tricks, or the shield deactivating? He raced his eyes across the kaza-draped citadel. There! The receding glimmer. Teza sought the shield's elusive undulation, and found no trace.

"Jaleya! Jaleya, it's down!" he called.

She paused, skepticism gushing from her life force's every thread. But she did return. "You're sure this time?"

"Yes," Teza said. He gazed at the shining minaret, and the distance between it and them burst his newfound confidence. This would be the furthest he had ever rifted. His first time rifting blind.

"Are we going to end up inside a wall?" Jaleya said, as if reading his mind.

"No," Teza said, but he failed to rally that conviction.

Jaleya's frown deepened. She held out her hand anyway. To say he was surprised would be…well, honest.

He took her hand, closed his eyes, and visualized the minaret's interior: the massive communication orb hanging from the ceiling; the winding stairwell with tiles tracing its curves like a vine; the mosaic on the landing; the reinforced wooden door protecting the dome's precious content; the row of pomegranate trees beyond the threshold.

Teza veered the stars' kaza, and the air warped apart.

A flash of frost, and their feet landed on solid, smooth stone. A closed wooden door stood before them. Teza recognized that door. He recognized the pomegranate trees. He lifted his head. The replenishing minaret blazed directly above them. He...He had done it. He had rifted blind. And he wasn't inside a wall.

The door's bolt slid back.

"Rift, now," Jaleya whispered tersely.

"What? To where?"

"Anywhere but here."

A guard's profile, equipped with a spear, emerged from the minaret. Teza veered a rift to the first place that panicked into his mind. Jaleya recovered from the whiff of ice first, which was unfair; he was the rowshatar. She yanked him into the shadow of the library's Harmony statue.

"Stop rifting us into the open," she hissed. She scanned the serene landscaping. "We're clear, for now. We have to keep moving."

His back against the statue's base, Teza lifted a pausing hand. "I need a minute." *That* had been his furthest rift, and his furthest blind rift. His stomach was a deep pit grumbling for sustenance. If he continued veering to such extremes, gnawing emptiness would come next, followed by emaciation.

Jaleya pursed her petulant lips, but, surprisingly, she didn't rebuke the delay. She scrutinized the library's grounds once more, and then scooted Teza and herself into the deeper shadows. Her countenance drifted into the distance, and a clumsy silence filled the Harmony's shelter. She was trying to communicate with Isesh. Were those tears rimming her eyes? That was twice in one day. He hadn't thought her capable of such emotions.

Jaleya blinked as she reclaimed her life force. Angered determination honed her keen features.

"This way," she said.

Flitting from shadow to shadow, peering around corners at

intersections, and avoiding the heavily traversed corridors, Jaleya advanced toward the Ora's tower. She never checked if Teza was following, but follow he did. He trailed Jaleya with his heart in his throat, his pulse racing, certain every step would be his last. Had there always been this many guards patrolling the citadel? It didn't feel real, sneaking around his home, hiding from his comrades and protectors—his friends. But it was real. He was a traitor.

Why did he feel the only one he had betrayed was his sister? The hole in his gut wasn't entirely due to veering.

They reached the Ways temple at the base of Harmony Tower. Jaleya crept along the perimeter, peering into the tall windows. The domed atrium appeared to be empty, which wasn't unusual given the imminent ceremony. Jaleya maneuvered Teza until he could see behind a pillar rising past the second-story gallery.

"Will this do?" Jaleya whispered.

"We don't need to rift inside," Teza said. No one guarded the honeycombed archway. Everyone was welcome in Iza Vor's temples. He and Jaleya could pretend their intention was to meditate or offer devotions.

"We can't risk being seen, especially you," Jaleya said, and she emphatically pointed at the gallery.

Teza's view of the indicated destination was hindered by the window's lattice, silk draperies, and the gallery's railing, but if he tilted his head and bent his spine…There!

Teza veered a rift to the limited cover. Jaleya yanked him through and tugged him low as soon as the cold snap passed. The temple was indeed empty. Jaleya had wasted one of Teza's rifts.

The unapologetic guardian descended to the meditation hall. Teza straightened his manhandled disguise, averting his gaze from the mirrors arching across the ceiling, the filigreed moldings, the sculpted capitals, and the larger than life mosaics. When he had… reported Saunez, the breathtaking beauty of Harmony Tower had endorsed his moral course. Endorsed everything he believed, everything he knew. He was the heart of Orvashka's Ways. Now, the magnificence scorned him. "You don't belong here," it seemed to say. "This isn't for you."

"Teza," Jaleya called quietly. So she was minding his whereabouts. He joined her as she went behind the altar and entered the curtained hallway accommodating the private meditation suites and the ministers' offices. Jaleya dismissed door after door after door, until one with a filigreed Harmony abruptly halted her baffling, relentless quest. She drew her scimitar, quietly lifted the latch, and charged inside.

The office's resident was absent. Teza sagged with relief.

Harmony banners framed a tenet tapestry that spanned the back wall. Kaza lanterns haloed the Ora figurines displayed on a cabinet. The polished wooden desk gleamed in the lifeless light.

"What are we doing in here?" Teza whispered.

Jaleya doused the kaza lanterns, plunging the spacious study into darkness. Teza's iridescent skin glimmered like a reflection in his favorite wine.

"Do you sense any other kaza in here?" Jaleya asked.

"No. What does that—?"

"Neither do I," she said. She reignited the lanterns and proceeded to tip the Ora figurines this way and that, rummage behind the chaise and cabinet, and press the tiles bordering the stone walls.

"What are you doing? We need to go up," Teza said. "The preparation chamber is in the tower's higher levels. That's where the offerings are housed. Jaleya!"

Grinding stone answered as the portion of wall upon which one of the banners hung rotated inward. A roughly hewn stairwell descended into a dim tunnel.

Jaleya removed her hand from the now-depressed tile that had revealed the hidden passageway. "Isesh is this way."

"Saunez isn't," Teza said.

"Yes, she is. Isesh confirmed it."

Teza's mouth dropped open. "You found Saunez? You should've told me."

"We still have to do the actual finding. Hence the tunnel."

"Iza Vor doesn't have tunnels," Teza said.

Jaleya pointedly eyed the gaping hole beside her.

"Saunez wouldn't be d-down there," Teza said. "Offerings are housed in the p-preparation chamber. Isesh is wrong."

"Then go up; I won't stop you. But if Isesh said he saw Saunez, then he saw Saunez. He was right about the ministers having their own entrance to Iza Vor's tunnels, and he'll be right about where they lead."

Jaleya turned on her heel and disappeared into the musty cavity.

Teza remained rooted to the stone. There were no tunnels in Iza Vor. Offerings were housed in the preparation chamber. There were no tunnels in Iza Vor. The Ora concealed nothing, and they would never flee from danger while that option was denied their citizens.

The foreboding maw refuted his denials like the chaff they were.

"Wait!" Teza hissed, and trotted after his guardian.

The stark passageways below Harmony Tower were cold and dark. Teza could touch the coarse ceiling with a raised hand and reach both crude walls with outstretched arms. The compacted earthen floor was as tough and bumpy as raw stone. The torches' flames burned ineffectively against a smothering gloom. Teza couldn't believe this foul pit and the beautiful temple were of the same tower. The expanding mound of his disbeliefs may yet bury him.

Jaleya eventually halted at an intersection that looked identical to the other half dozen they had traversed. "We need to get through the door around the corner," she whispered. "There are two guards outside, one inside. How accurate is your lightning?"

It took Teza a moment to understand what she was asking. "You want me to…?"

Jaleya sighed. "How fast can you rift?"

"I'm the fastest in Abylay."

Jaleya didn't seem impressed, as she should have been. "Rift close to the door so I can take out the guards."

Teza swallowed.

"This was *your* plan," Jaleya said. "If you truly want to save Saunez, you're going to have to get your hands dirty. You didn't mind when you betrayed her."

"That was different," Teza said.

"Sure, because a place like this is where people are taken to be helped." The sarcasm cloaking her simmering vengeance was anything but reassuring. She hadn't killed him outside the estate, but what about when he was no longer useful to her? He liked to think he would just rift away, but would he even see the blow coming?

"Ready?" Jaleya said.

Teza nodded. What choice did he have? He had to save Saunez.

He peered around the corner and focused on the reinforced door bounded by claustrophobic walls and an earthen floor. The guards noticed his trespassing, but Jaleya charged through Teza's rift before the vortex's establishing burst of ice had dissipated and attacked them from behind. Teza turned away, but every violent sound made him flinch.

Something dense thumped to the ground, followed by telling silence. Teza ventured into the short hallway. Jaleya apathetically availed herself of the keys on a guard's belt, and an exclamation and a brief clash of steel sounded in the room beyond.

Teza stared at the dead men, their life's blood pouring from their butchered flesh, their expressions frozen forever in pained shock.

"I'm sorry," he said.

Teza entered the secured room, and gagged at the stench of soiled bodies and human excrement. He pulled his tunic over his nose, but it did little to ease his sinuses. Jaleya knelt by a cell—a cell secreted beneath Harmony Tower. Isesh was imprisoned within. Jaleya tore through a ring of keys in search of the match, the thick metal gate the last barrier to their reunion. Where was Saunez?

Teza searched the aisle of parallel cells. The...dungeon. The detained men and women were bruised, cut, and scarred, their clothes less than rags. They cowered in the furthest corner of their cramped alcoves, whimpering, stifling their sobs, staring at the ground as if it would save them from his attention. They were afraid. Of him, a rowshatar. He let them be. He couldn't begin to explain the situation. If he tried, if he openly acknowledged where he was and what he was doing, the last thread of his sanity might snap.

Teza retreated to Jaleya, who had reunited with Isesh and removed the heavy shackles from his neck and limbs. The simurgh's fur was scorched, his flanks striped with welts. Feathers had been wrenched from his neck, exposing patches of raw skin. His avian eyes roiled as Jaleya popped a grotesquely bent wing back into place. The fashari trembling pitifully, Jaleya cradled his considerable head and soothed his chirping whimpers. Her eyes blazed like a wild ruby. Teza was surprised he shared her anger. He was surprised he could feel anything besides the aching void within him.

"She's not here," he said.

Jaleya grabbed the hilt of her scimitar, her rage obtaining a target, and Teza backpedaled. Isesh jerked in Jaleya's arms. A silent exchange passed between them. Jaleya released her scimitar.

"She was here. Guards took her and some others a few minutes ago."

"A few minutes ago? You should've told me!" Teza said.

"We couldn't have gotten here any faster," Jaleya said, her rage receding as Isesh recovered from the shock of adjusting his wing.

"But we can still catch them," Teza said desperately. "We have to save her."

Jaleya and Isesh shared a private conversation. Teza clung to every word he wished he could hear.

Isesh staggered to his paws. "He thinks he can find her," Jaleya said. Reluctantly?

Hope welled in Teza regardless. Everything might not be lost.

Isesh's ears peaked, listening. Jaleya tilted her head and frowned, but it wasn't her usual one.

"What is it?" Teza said.

"The offering ceremony has begun," Jaleya replied.

Her words struck Teza like a physical blow. After every deplorable thing he had done to save Saunez, he was still too late. He had failed. He had condemned his sister to death.

Then the prison shuddered as an explosion shattered the ominous silence.

CHAPTER 33

Ameara sipped her mead as two men, a Ryvekian and a Setsean, circled each other in one of the combat rings. Their weapons tapped with measuring caution. Bets and coin changed hands. The rowdy, questionably sober crowd cheered their favorite. Soldiers stationed around the rings and the combatants pavilion aspired to pounce on any citizen who thought to emulate the champions. Tournaments were a sanctioned festival activity, but only mercenaries, Vekrym, and those who wielded weapons in an official capacity could participate. Ameara's pistol and sword riled the Setseans more than her Vekrym armband.

The fighters exchanged their first serious blows, illuminated by the abundant kaza lanterns. The Ryvekian bent beneath his opponent's overhand strike, and the audience gasped and oohed. He disengaged and rolled away. The Setsean advanced with a confident stride. He was going to lose.

Ameara set her half-finished drink aside. Authentic Ryvekian mead was usually a refreshing indulgence, but it wasn't satisfying.

She spotted Obakwe navigating through the crowd. The stars' arrival had dispersed the sun's fiery veins and scarlet glaze gracing her dark skin. Her shaved head drew stares from across the tournament field even after the gawkers noticed the Vekrym emblem around her arm. Obakwe ignored them. Strangers' opinions meant nothing to Wanbasbans.

"Captain," Obakwe greeted. She lithely hopped into the wagon from which Ameara observed the bout. The mead casks in the bed and the booths on either side provided cover, and the vantage skimmed across the heads of the throng. The Ryvekian trader who owned the wagon, its contents, and one of the adjacent booths raised a mug at Obakwe. She politely declined.

"Something to add to Kyzum's report?" Ameara said quietly.

"No," Obakwe replied in a clipped tone. "The official announcement of a failed rebel plot seems to be true, if inaccurate. The patriots will be executed for refusing to bow to the Ora's godless morality." She snatched Ameara's abandoned mead and gulped the honeyed alcohol. She returned the mug empty. "It angers me."

Ameara gently squeezed Obakwe's shoulder. The older woman's recruitment and her daughter's estrangement were results of the Ora's harmony infiltrating Wanbasba. The majority of the tribes had wisely recognized it as a threat and halted its progression into their land, but they were unable to dislodge its foothold. The stalemate had lasted for years and showed no indication of ending. Ameara feigned ignorance of Obakwe's secret communications with her people, and Obakwe didn't involve Ameara or Syra's crew in the ongoing conflict.

Was a conflict sparking in Setsea? It was a big coincidence if the captured rebels and Syra's previous cargo were *not* connected. Ameara shouldn't dwell on it. Her contract was done.

In the ring, the Ryvekian anticipated the Setsean's feint and stole the offensive, driving him toward the ropes of the enclosure. The spectators cheered or booed according to their wagered coin.

"Are both your 'friends' still around?" Obakwe said.

Ameara nodded. She couldn't see the two shavinashi at the moment, but she knew they were there. She felt their barren eyes.

"Whisper wouldn't have sent a second when one sufficed," Obakwe said.

"He only sent one," Ameara confirmed. She had no definitive proof, but she'd been analyzing the shavinashi's movements through stolen glances. They maintained a wary distance of reluctant association and watched each other as much as they watched her. The spies were not of the same cadre.

"You've definitely caused a stir, or someone else has," Obakwe said.

The Ryvekian twisted the Setsean's sword from his grasp and knocked his feet from under him. He pressed his battle-ax against his opponent's throat. The Setsean yielded reluctantly. Applause and groans erupted as the Ryvekian was declared the winner. Alarmed gamblers began slinking into the crowd. They wouldn't get far.

"The unknown should never be underestimated," Obakwe said.

The Ryvekian raised his battle-ax and roared in victory, beating his chest with his fist.

"Overestimating can be just as treacherous," Ameara said. The Ryvekian's arrogance would lose him his next fight. If his gods attended him, it wouldn't be to the death.

"A precarious ridge to walk," Obakwe said.

"You learn fast or you die."

Obakwe beamed. "The Schism arena taught you much, Eclipse, but you didn't heed all its lessons. We wouldn't be in our current situation if you had. And my life and the life of my husband would have ended before our time. The decision you made cannot be undone. Stop brooding over it."

"You left the bathhouse just to tell me this?" Ameara asked.

"No, but it needed to be said. I'm detouring to Nahzida's recommended kebab vendor in the hope I can convince you to join us. The bathhouse was wonderful."

A distant drum began a commanding beat that others promptly echoed, their deep cadence heralding the offering ceremony. Setseans, and a few foreigners, broke off from the crowd, answering the summons.

"I appreciate the invitation," Ameara said, "but I'm going to watch the last bout."

"You're going to brood," Obakwe said disapprovingly. "How can you be so adept at interpreting the winds and currents yet oblivious to the ancestors' guiding hand?"

"It wasn't your ancestors," Ameara said gently. "Your captain was lucky her fool's gold diverted her patron."

"You must have felt real gold existed among the false, otherwise you wouldn't have presented it."

"Or I'm proof it's an apt name."

"Perhaps; the information you divulged to your patron concerns me and has endangered us all. However, our lives have not yet ended. The ancestors often guide with wordless whispers and seldom explain the path ahead, but their direction always has a purpose. Even if that purpose is unknown."

"That requires a lot of trust," Ameara said.

"Yes. As does sheltering strangers aboard the *Skyheart*."

Cheers ushered the next pair of combatants into the ring: two men of short stature with shaved lines across their bronze scalps. Their tunics were stark and fresh.

Obakwe hopped off the wagon. "If you change your mind, the kebab vendor is in the festival's food bazaar."

Ameara gave Obakwe a grateful nod. Her inexplicable impulses regarding her crew had served her well. But nothing was infallible, and Ameara was waiting for that fallibility to rear its ugly head.

The distant drums ceased. The Masatitoran fighters assumed their sword stances, anticipating the judge's bell.

An explosion shook the ground. Ameara's hand dropped to her pistol; the kaza displays had concluded a half hour ago. Festivalgoers gasped and began pointing toward the Nidren. Toward the dust billowing from a structure's collapse. Tendrils of smoke coiled into the heavens. Fearful whispers swallowed the tournament field. Syra pressed against Ameara's mind, the stars' replenishing kaza insufficient reassurance.

A smaller explosion rumbled near the Guild Ward, followed by violent kaza flashes. A trumpet pealed an alarm. The crowd scattered.

"Get the others and rendezvous on the *Skyheart*," Ameara ordered Obakwe. The older woman calmly plunged into the panicking populace.

Ameara utilized the side streets and alleys as she hurried to the harbor, assuring Syra she was returning. Even with the sudden turn of events, her two shadows maintained their vigilance. The curious opened windows and doors only to hastily retreat as screams pierced the starry night. Bursting kaza, clanging steel, and shouts of battle sounded behind Ameara, and gradually overtook her. The attack that had started at the collapsed structure and in the Guild Ward was spreading, and Syra feared its advance.

Ameara finally spotted the harbor; she'd been inhaling the sea's salt for blocks. As she approached the end of the lane, a shiver slithered down her spine. Instincts the Schism arena had beaten into her warned of danger. Her back against a building's brick wall, Ameara drew her pistol and cautiously peered around the corner. Ship silhouettes swayed placidly with the lapping surf, but the waterfront was strewn with the bodies of civilians and soldiers, the former far outnumbering the latter. Cries and scuffling erupted nearby, and were quickly silenced. Had the attack devolved into a rout?

Someone alighted from the rooftops behind her. Surprised, she spun, raising her pistol; she had misjudged the spies' distance. The shavinash rose from his landing crouch, the hood of his cloak concealing his features. Why was he announcing his presence? Where was his comrade? Was this Whisper's courteous messenger? She didn't bother trying to discern his cadre; how shavinashi distinguished their factions was a secret known only to them. Ameara wasn't going to strike first and be accused of assaulting a shavinash, but if her impaired judgment had come seeking retribution, she would dull every seal in her pistol.

The shavinash didn't speak, didn't taunt, didn't attack. He was a statue. Something wasn't right. He wore a cloak instead of a shavinash headscarf, and there wasn't a cloud in the sky; the night was relatively warm. His broad shoulders were slightly hunched, as if standing upright was an effort.

Ameara slowly unlatched and lifted the hood of her pistol. The expanding rays of kazalight illuminated the shavinash's pale, chiseled face and his deep blue eyes.

Ameara's mouth opened in shock, and the stowaway shavinash lashed out, slapping her pistol aside and swapping their positions with a vicious pirouette. His kick caught her in the stomach, and she staggered backward, but she managed to block his next attack, and the one after that, even as she was driven from the waterfront. She had no opportunity to steal the offensive, much less draw her sword or dive for her lost pistol. His relentless blows hit like breakers.

A dark figure dropped into the lane, and starlight reflected off steel rushing toward Ameara's assailant. A sword appearing in his hand, he parried and redirected the strike, seamlessly disengaging Ameara and targeting the newcomer. A second dark figure leapt from the rooftops and thrust his blade into the savage exchange. The two shavinash spies attacked their blue-eyed brethren simultaneously, but they remained as wary of each other as the one they sought to overpower. One spy was ruthlessly aggressive, aiming for vital organs, arteries, and the neck. The other slashed at limbs and major muscles, intending debilitating but nonlethal injuries. Definitely two cadres. The homicidal shavinash wanted the stowaway dead, but Whisper's wanted him alive. All three seemed to have forgotten Ameara.

Ameara knew she should flee to Syra; the chances of her survival —of her crew's survival—dwindled with every breath she took in that narrow, shadowed street. The shavinashi's brutal contest enthralled her. It was as terrible and beautiful as a tidal wave, their counters neither forking nor breaking the colossal billow, flowing indistinguishably with the great current. The blue-eyed shavinash guided the surge, anticipating and thwarting the spies' coordinated barrage. But intervening movement began to blur, and then escaped the eye altogether as the shavinashi drew heavily upon their etchs. Considering the state of his own, the stowaway could not prevail against the turning tide. One unbalanced step, one parry a hairsbreadth too slow, and it would cost him his life.

The spy from the unknown cadre thrust his sword at the blue-eyed shavinash's gut, the attack a mere whoosh of motion, and Ameara knew he was dead. But the blue-eyed shavinash was suddenly behind his opponent, and he stabbed a knife into the base of the spy's neck. He twisted and jerked the blade, muscle and sinew tearing, bone cracking, blood spurting and spraying. He spun aside as Whisper's shavinash lashed out, but his butchery was complete.

The defeated shavinash, his head lolling at an impossible angle, crumpled to the ground, awakening Ameara from her stupor. She ordered her frozen limbs to run, and she rounded the nearest corner as one of the shavinashi groaned in pain. A brief scuffle. More cracking bone and splitting flesh. A body thumped against the paved bricks.

The victor would now come for Ameara.

Ameara pressed her back against the long wall, eyes darting, ears straining. She should have fled when she had the chance. But fleeing would have only delayed the inevitable. The speed of the shavinashi's movements…the precision of their strikes…the seamlessness of their steps…She was insane to bargain with them, to think she could gain the upper hand. She was no match for them. She was helpless, powerless. A doomed victim.

Ameara steeled herself. No. The shavinash would take her life, but she would leave this world on her feet.

She drew her sword with trembling fingers and returned to the battleground to meet the end she had wrought.

CHAPTER 34

It seems the resistance proceeded with their plan, Isesh sent. *We may be able to reach Saunez.*

The entire city has been alerted, Jaleya sent. *We won't be able to escape if we delay.*

You weren't guaranteed escape when you entered, yet you did.

Jaleya regarded Teza, who twiddled his thumbs and shuffled his feet, glancing back and forth between her and Isesh. Jaleya sighed. Her javati was right. She had agreed to help Teza, and he had upheld his part of the bargain. She couldn't break her word. The galahi of old would have been appalled she even considered it.

"We'll try to intercept them," Jaleya told Teza.

His sharp features lifted like Isesh's ears peaking at an interesting sound.

"But if they reach the altar, we retreat. We will not engage the Ora. There's no living through that."

Teza nodded, readily accepting her terms without comprehending their bitterness.

"We will encounter guards," Jaleya continued. "I might not be able to deal with them all myself, and Isesh is injured. You'll have to help. Can you do that?"

Teza stared at the ground as if the answer would sprout from the barren dirt. Isesh began sniffing the cell that had imprisoned Saunez.

"It's their lives, or your sister's," Jaleya said. "Teza?"

A sickly pallor muddied the rowshatar's iridescence. "I think so."

That wasn't good enough, but they had already lingered too long.

Jaleya opened one of the cells and tossed its prisoners the key ring. "Free everyone and get out."

Taking point, Isesh ventured into the warren, navigating its confines with his nose. At a junction with an ascending stairwell, he circled and tested the musty air before proceeding into the left hallway.

"Shouldn't we be going up?" Teza said.

"Saunez is this way," Jaleya replied, quoting Isesh. She was as puzzled as the rowshatar; she did not like the similarity.

"Is he sure?" Teza said.

Isesh huffed. "Yes," Jaleya said, just in case Teza struggled to interpret the common expression.

Beyond an arch, the passages widened, and the ceiling expanded. Isesh turned down a branching corridor that ended in a cul-de-sac lined with thick wooden doors and corresponding numbered plaques. The scent of death seeped from every one. According to Jaleya's javash-enhanced senses, the walls should have been oozing blood. Isesh licked his nose as if he could wash away the stench. Saunez being spared the offering ceremony had averted the potential encounter with the Ora and availed them an opportunity to forestall her terrible sentence, but their altered course seemed to have led to a domain of the zar'sheni. Jaleya and Isesh needed to avoid an untimely clash with the blood-veering shavinashi. Zar'sheni lacked the embedded etch of their brethren due to its interference with other bloodshapings, but by pricking their finger on a bloodstone seal, they could incapacitate or end their enemies from a distance just as efficiently, and they were no less deadly at close quarters. Their infamous signets were an etch by another name. Lenruz's murderer was not a zar'shen.

Isesh stopped in front of a chamber designated number eight.

Pleading screams crashed futilely against the muffling planks. *In there,* Isesh sent. *She's not alone.*

With Isesh's confirmation that no one guarded the other side, Jaleya cracked the door. A narrow archway framed a section of the opposite brick wall but otherwise obstructed the inner room. She chanced a step further, and found a winding staircase on her right. Perhaps it led to a better vantage. She cautiously ascended to the landing, and thanked the Creator the upper level was empty. Spanning a single wall and hedged by stone blocks, it seemed to be a protected observation platform. Jaleya ushered Isesh and Teza aloft, and they carefully looked through the blocks' horizontal slits.

A stained altar smeared with fresh blood rose above a filled trench encircling its base. Wild gems the size of Jaleya's fist, vials of various concoctions, and implements of torture lay on a blue and white cloth draping a long table. The diamonds, rubies, and sapphires, the most powerful gemstones for their respective kaza, overflowed with inner light. An oversized cage trapped a dozen ragged men and women.

Whips in hand, soldiers selected a middle-aged man from the condemned. He kicked, thrashed, and pleaded to no avail as he was dragged to the altar and forced onto the slick stone. The soldiers bound his wrists and ankles with the attached manacles and cut off his clothes. Two zar'sheni stepped forward, their tunics steeped in scarlet. Indifferent to the poor soul's terror, the male zar'shen raised an ornate dagger, invoked Orvashka's Ways, and sliced the man's throat. Blood gushed from the gaping slash, cascading down the altar's channels and feeding the dark pool at its feet. The helpless victim twitched, his lips quivering a final appeal. The zar'sheni watched with enraptured zealotry, justice radiating from their righteous postures.

Transfixed, Teza stared in disbelieving horror. "This isn't part of the offering ceremony," he whispered hoarsely.

Jaleya shushed him, even though many, many words burned her tongue.

The crimson flow slowed to a trickle, and then an intermittent drip. The female zar'shen chopped the victim's neck with a Harmony-engraved ax and kicked the severed head aside. The zar'sheni stepped back as one.

"Bring the next sacrifice."

The soldiers collected the man's body and head and dropped them onto a heap of like corpses. A subdued woman was removed from the weeping prisoners, and she walked to the altar in a daze, as if she would wake from her nightmare any minute now, any second…

Teza tore his gaze away.

Isesh sent, *Teza may be close to the truth. This reeks of Illuminated experimentation.*

That's why the zar'sheni have wild gems, Jaleya realized. She dreaded to speculate why they were amassing the abundance of blood. This "laboratory" was number eight. How many more human slaughterhouses did the Ora possess? She swallowed the bile bubbling in her throat.

"Jaleya!" Teza blurted. Jaleya yanked him away from the slits and flattened them both against the platform; Isesh crouched low. They waited for a cry of alarm or investigative footsteps, Isesh's ears swiveling, but none came. Jaleya scanned the torture chamber. No one had detected their presence. She glared at Teza. Only momentarily abashed, he tugged her arm and pointed urgently at the prisoners. Isesh found her a heartbeat before Jaleya.

Custodian Saunez.

Hair disheveled, her dress filthy and tattered, she hunched in defeat in the back of the cramped cage.

"She's alive," Teza breathed. The hope in his voice was painful.

With a measured scurry, he began scouring the limited and limiting slits for the clearest view. Jaleya grabbed his vest, her eyebrows raised.

"I'm going to get her," Teza whispered. "I'll rift down, grab her, and rift back."

"She's surrounded by people," Jaleya said. "Your rift will kill someone, or you'll be trampled when they all charge the rift to escape, and either way, the zar'sheni will sense you veering and discover us."

"So what do we do?" Teza asked.

Jaleya surveyed the grisly scene below. Two zar'sheni: formidable at a distance and in close proximity, but their signets were less efficient when engaged from the latter. Four soldiers: an alarm summoning reinforcements, or a snare restraining them for the zar'sheni's invisible darts. The prisoners: collateral damage in the future's threads.

"We have to strike first, take the zar'sheni by surprise," Jaleya whispered. "You'll need to rift us close."

"But you said they would sense my veering," Teza protested.

"They will. We'll have to be fast. *Very* fast. You weren't lying about being able to create time bubbles, were you?"

"No," Teza said, affronted. "I'm the only rowshatar-estra who can," he preened.

"Good. You'll use time bubbles to distract the female zar'shen while I deal with the other one."

"Wha—" Jaleya clamped her hand over Teza's mouth. She lowered it slowly. "What?!" Teza sputtered. "I've never veered one around a person—a person who isn't *me*. It's completely different. I'll have to...catch her, and then she'll fight the bubble...The shavinashi are Orvashka's lamenting sword—she'll break out."

"You don't have to trap her," Jaleya said. "All you have to do is keep her occupied. Lightning would work, too."

"Lightning?" Teza wheezed.

"Do you want to save Saunez or not?" Jaleya said.

Teza clenched his eyes, and nodded.

Jaleya continued. "Isesh, protect Saunez and prevent the soldiers from sounding an alarm. Once the zar'sheni are dead, I'll back you up. Then we get Saunez and get out."

"What about the others?" Teza asked.

"We'll do what we can for them, but they're not the reason we're here."

Teza's expression scrunched in disapproval, but his fear for his sister stopped his priority from diverging, and rightly so. Isesh grieved their unenviable position.

Below, the woman had been bled and decapitated, and two soldiers were removing her body from the altar. The zar'sheni were anticipating the next victim. This was their chance.

Jaleya scooted alongside Teza, and Isesh crouched on his haunches, ready to pounce.

Watch your back, her javati sent. He wouldn't be able to.

You, too, Jaleya sent. "Rift on three," she told Teza. "One. Two. Th—"

The laboratory door swung open, and a woman tinged with the absent moon's hue glided into the gory chamber. A tiara bedecked with baubles and a fringed scarlet shawl crowned her head of streaming hair. Precious stones trimmed her dress's collar and cuffs. Her filigreed necklace was set with a brilliant sapphire. The zar'sheni and the soldiers prostrated themselves. The prisoners cowered. Jaleya's flickering hope of escape reached the end of its wick and died.

Ora Ezray had come.

CHAPTER 35

The vanquished shavinashi lay at their conqueror's feet. Blood dripped from their severed heads and seeped into the paved bricks. Their executioner's broad chest heaved with every gulping breath. His cowl had fallen. It was Dorian.

Dorian had tried to kill her. How had she misjudged so badly?

Their eyes met. Ameara dropped into a defensive stance, daring him to attack her again. Just let him try. She would run him through.

She hoped he didn't notice her sword's tremble. She couldn't hold it steady. When he charged, she would be dead in a heartbeat.

The shavinash discarded his crude scimitar; Ameara dismissed the obvious feint. The shavinash plodded toward the harbor, every wavering stride a struggle to remain upright. He placed a steadying hand on the side of a building and managed a few more arduous steps. He faltered, barely caught himself. He leaned heavily against the wall, scraped another step. A lightheaded shudder buckled his legs, and he crumpled to the ground.

Ameara waited for the trap to spring. It didn't. In the rays of kazalight escaping the unlatched hood of her defeated pistol, Ameara scanned the shavinash for wounds and found none. But the etch's festering tendrils had re-coiled around his neck and were mercilessly advancing over his cheekbones. He lay as lifeless as his headless comrades.

Glad Kyzum wasn't witnessing her foolishness, Ameara cautiously approached the fallen shavinash.

The shavinash grabbed her wrist. "They can't find me," he gasped. "Get rid of me."

All his strength was channeled to his clutching fist. She could break free with an effortless tug. The shavinash couldn't lift his head. Ameara lowered her sword.

"I have to…disappear," he panted. "Get rid of me."

His eyes rolled back; his hand dropped. Ameara prodded him in the shoulder, but he was as limp as a windless sail. The etch had regained the ground lost to Syra.

Her crew was free and clear! It was obvious the shavinashi had killed each other. Ameara would claim she had fled the confrontation. Retreat was an acceptable option when one was out of one's depth.

Except…one of the dead shavinashi was Whisper's. Whisper, and the other spy's shashvin, would learn of the damaged etch. Very few things were powerful enough to do that, and a kazashot in the dark was not one of them.

What had the dying shavinash said? "They can't find me." His brethren couldn't find him because they would discover his damaged etch, and the trail of his demise led to Ameara.

He had to disappear. If he was believed to be alive—he had provided ample evidence—his brethren would seek to dispose of him in rippleless darkness. Shavinashi did not forsake Orvashka's Ways.

Ameara looked toward the harbor, the direction he'd been heading before he collapsed.

Get rid of me.

Weigh down his body, send it to the ocean's depths. No one would ever find him.

Syra was docked on the edge of the waterfront, but Ameara could make it. If Whisper inquired, she could tell him she had fled after one of her shavinash tails engaged her unknown assailant. The designs of the shashvini were not her concern, but she was tiring of being entangled in them outside a contract. She would probably have to thank him for the shavinash's "assistance," but she could do that in a backhanded way; her report had to seem legitimate.

It would work. She and her crew would live.

Ameara sheathed her sword and retrieved her pistol. The assorted kazalight leaking through the unlatched hood melded like Syra's undulating hues. Ameara rested the barrel on her hand. The stars' power brightened her palm, as if she had captured its source. Just like the heart of a flawed, worthless crystal.

The stars. Star kaza… *Replenishing* star kaza…

Ameara looked heavenward, to the dominant night diamonds shining through the thinning smoke, and then at Dorian, who should have died yesterday.

What was she thinking? He had just tried to kill her. Or…had it been a ruse to draw out the shavinash spies? She'd been bruised —*very* bruised—but she knew how hard he could really hit. He had spent his last breath telling her how to survive the shavinashi. If his intent had been retribution, why speak?

Why, why had he harbored the worthless crystal? Why had he been on her ship?

Why couldn't she see the truth of his shavinash's garb?

Because her crew had been spared. Whisper's quarters hadn't been her pyre.

Because she sensed spring's warmth beneath the relentless ice.

As long as she glimpsed the former, she couldn't accept the latter's sway.

Ameara snapped the hood closed and holstered her pistol. She strode to the lane's end and scanned the waterfront. It was as silent and still as a Wanbasban graveyard. The fires' sear had faded from the sky, and the kaza flashes had ceased. A suspenseful hush blanketed the surrounds. The tide lapped at the docks.

Ameara returned to Dorian and began dragging him toward Syra. She wouldn't have to haul him far; she just needed a sightline to Syra's heart. Dorian wasn't bleeding and hadn't collapsed near his victims, denying his brethren (former brethren?) a blood trail—any trail. The grisly scene was a defiant taunt.

A main avenue brightened with lantern light oscillating to the cadence of a muffled march. Ameara pulled her burden faster, but a second halo spilled onto the waterfront from a side street between her and Syra. Ameara couldn't see Syra's heart, and she wouldn't be able to before the torchbearers emerged. She was cut off, a dying shavinash in her arms, two decapitated ones nearby, and her veil of shadows about to be obliterated by Setsean soldiers. The city's dark warrens beckoned her, but towing Dorian through the meandering bolt-hole would transform it into the jaws of a trap.

Ameara dragged Dorian between a galley and a sloop, the sleeping ships obscuring them from view for the moment. Challenges arose from the two companies as they reached the waterfront, but then they hailed each other with recognition. The oscillating fields of lantern light began closing the gap. Soldiers in front, ships to the sides, and the harbor behind, Ameara and Dorian were caught like a netted fish not yet reeled in. Ameara's mind raced the approaching footsteps heralding their doom. She didn't need Syra's gangplank to board her—she just needed a sightline to her heart. It might prove to be her and Dorian's final resting place, but the harbor was their only chance.

Ameara secured her wavy hair with her headband and used Dorian's cloak to fashion a crude harness around his shoulders. She eased herself and Dorian into the frigid water as the soldiers' lanterns breached the ships' concealment. Cold shocked her body and stole her breath, but, as Kyzum was fond of saying, the sea was in her blood. The depths of the waters and the heights of the skies were hers.

Towing the unconscious Dorian, Ameara swam beneath the docks toward Syra, using the pilings for momentum and to preserve her strength; Dorian was dense muscle, and his limp frame conspired to drag her under, despite the harbor's buoyancy. She paused whenever a soldier passed overhead, lest he hear her disturbing the natural current. The frigid waters exploited the delays and leeched the life from Ameara's limbs. Resuming was harder each time.

Reaching a pier that seemed to be of sufficient length, Ameara followed the slick boards deeper into the harbor, and spotted Syra's familiar stern. Her heart soared; they were going to make it. She quickly but calmly sent instructions to the Dazmir-vahl-kesh, and then pushed free of the pier. Maneuvering behind the nearest ship, she screened herself and her weighty cargo from the waterfront and the moored vessels. She signaled Syra. Ameara felt the rift form, the surrounding water spiraling—she hit solid wood, a small pool plummeting like unfurled canvas over her head.

Wiping her sodden hair away from her face, Ameara climbed to her feet. She was amidships on Syra's middle deck. *Well done,* she sent.

"Don't move," a familiar voice commanded. Ameara turned slowly, and Kyzum lowered the crossbow he had aimed at her chest. "Ameara! Thank the gods. What's happening out there? Who—?" Recognition halted his question, and his finger leapt to the crossbow's trigger. "Please tell me he is finally, actually dead and you brought his corpse aboard to dispose of it."

"Sorry to disappoint," Ameara said. "I have a hunch the commotion is, or was, rebels; it seems to be winding down. Where's Ara?"

"Ara went to the festival with Nahzida and Obakwe," Kyzum said. "They're not back yet."

"Empty sky," Ameara cursed. It was Ara's watch. Kyzum's presence had led Ameara to believe her crew had returned safe to Syra, but he had merely taken Ara's rotation. While she was worried about her crew, she knew they could take care of themselves and were wise enough to avoid the conflict. They were probably lying low until the storm blew over; please just be lying low. However, without Ara, Ameara would be sailing blind. And she couldn't afford to wait. The only sign Dorian still lived was an occasional twitch of his fingers.

Ameara would have to relinquish the wheel to Syra, and trust the Dazmir-vahl-kesh wouldn't lose herself in the buried depths of her consciousness.

"Why do you need Ara?" Kyzum said, warily scrutinizing the bloodshaping writhing beneath Dorian's pale skin.

Ameara hesitated, knowing how crazy she was going to sound. It sounded crazy even in her mind. "I think Syra can save him."

"Save him?" Kyzum said incredulously.

"I don't think a shashvin ordered him here. I think he was trying to free himself from his etch."

"Well, I obviously have some catching up to do. This morning, his every breath was a liability. What's changed since this morning?"

Ameara didn't answer—couldn't answer without confirming what they both knew: the situation hadn't changed.

"You trust me, Kyzum," she said.

"I'm questioning that trust right now. He is not the boy you grew up with. He is a shavinash, and we are all better off with him dead."

"If this doesn't work, he will be." Ameara bent to lift Dorian's shoulders. Kyzum grabbed her arm, but she twisted free. "You don't have to help," she said, "but don't get in my way."

Kyzum steadied his crossbow. He could permanently remove the liability with a single arrow. Ameara knew he wanted to. At this range, he couldn't miss.

"Kyzum, please."

Her friend grumbled a sigh, and relaxed the crossbow. "This is not a good idea."

Ameara and Kyzum carried Dorian into the heart. Basking in the stars' kaza, Syra pulsed to a content hum; the stars held sway, Ameara had returned, and the fighting had subsided. And the stars held sway. Green and purple hues pranced about the alexandrite's facets. Ameara and Kyzum laid Dorian near the jubilant heart seal. The bloodshaping's festering tendrils had reached his eyes. He seemed to cry tears of writhing ash. Ameara carefully exposed the etch, and resisted the reflex to recoil. Within the chipped obsidian was something beyond darkness. A nothingness. From that void sprung dozens and dozens of black veins that branched into dozens more, the creeping shoots wriggling hungrily even as they feasted.

"Are you sure he's not dead?" Kyzum said. He sounded a bit too hopeful for the contrary.

"He's alive," Ameara said, and added to herself, *Barely.*

"What now?" Kyzum asked.

Ameara straightened and approached the pulsing alexandrite —approached Syra. Her oldest companion. This was Ara's theory, Ameara's inexplicable impulse. The young galahi could be wrong. Ameara could be wrong. About so many things.

She rested her palm on Syra's smooth facets. Power tickled her skin, lightning crackling about her hand, yet the gem was cool. Ameara felt the potent kaza within—Syra's life force bolstered by the stars' replenishing. Syra reluctantly withdrew from the celestial bliss. Her light stuttered at the bloodshaping's proximity, but Ameara's physical touch—such a rare contact—tempered the vahl-kesh's anxiety.

Ameara opened herself to Syra and focused on Dorian's inexplicable recovery and Ara's subsequent theory, trying to convey with impressions what words failed to translate.

Can you help him? Ameara asked.

Syra shied away from the sendings. They circled where she dare not sail. A soft tremor flickered the alexandrite. The bulkhead creaked. Kyzum eyed the heart with unease.

Ameara let her mind wander to the worthless crystal found among the shavinash's possessions. Syra's consciousness stilled.

If you can, and you're willing, please try, Ameara sent. *But don't exchange your life for his. We would all be lost without you.*

Syra brightened momentarily before receding inward. Ameara stepped back. A minute passed uneventfully, then another. Syra's awareness was as distant as it had been when Dorian lay hidden in the hatch, but perhaps Ameara was mistaking the reason. Perhaps

Syra wanted no part in this, or she was dismayed she couldn't fulfill Ameara's request. She didn't answer Ameara's sendings.

Dorian inhaled sharply. He didn't wake, but his limbs jerked.

The heart seal pulsed faster. Dorian's eyelids fluttered; his groan ended in a pained gasp. The alexandrite flickered, dimming with each erratic beat.

"This will end well," Kyzum said sarcastically.

Syra blazed with light; Ameara and Kyzum shielded their eyes against the brilliance. Syra's light *heaved*. Dorian's back arched, and he screamed in raw agony. Ameara leapt on top of him, pinning his arms with her legs and clamping her hands over his mouth; Kyzum subdued his legs. Ameara sensed a clash of storms around the etch, crimson clouds churning against a cleansing deluge.

The alexandrite flared. The bloodshaping's tendrils receded from Dorian's face, loosed their suffocating grip on his neck. Retreated to the etch that bore them.

The crimson clouds flashed. Syra's seal thrummed, her light struggling to emanate beyond the gem's contours. Dorian's eyes rolled upward. Silent, he was beyond crying out, his taut muscles strained to their limits. The hull groaned.

"Ameara?" Kyzum said in alarm.

Syra flailed, desperately bursting radiance to counter a devouring oblivion. The deck shuddered, and wood splintered above their heads.

Syra! Ameara sent. *Syra, stop! Syra!*

The Dazmir-vahl-kesh pursued the battle that was killing her.

"Stop, Syra!" Ameara called. "Syraylen!"

The alexandrite that was Syra rallied its meager light and billowed in defiance. The heart and Dorian convulsed, and Ameara felt the crimson cloud burst. The etch ignited with a vengeful fire. Kyzum yanked Ameara away as the bloodstone seal and its obsidian shield exploded. Syra's light fled.

Ameara and Kyzum breathed unsteadily in the dark silence.

A moment passed. Syra's light did not return.

Another moment…

Ameara hesitantly sought the Dazmir, terrified of finding a void instead of her consciousness.

A frail glow stirred within the alexandrite, a feeble hum emerging from the paralyzing silence. Where the etch had been, a fist-sized hole bored into Dorian's chest; Ameara could see bone within the gaping wound. His blood lay splattered on the heart seal's contours.

Panicked, Ameara called to Syra. She felt something weak and faint, reaching, and then the Dazmir-vahl-kesh's familiar presence brushed against Ameara's mind. Her light pulsed wearily, but it was steady. One of them had survived.

Dorian gurgled an agonized inhale. Ameara's hand flew to her mouth; Kyzum averted his gaze. How was Dorian still alive? Kyzum had been right. She should have let him die. She had only caused him more pain.

The blood pooling in Dorian's mangled chest rippled. Fractured bone mended, and muscles began knitting together, skin expanding over the cavity. The bloodshaping…Syra hadn't destroyed all its power.

The healing slowed as the wound's edges met, and the last of the bloodshaping expended itself, leaving behind a jagged scar. Dorian's eyes sprang open, and he gulped air into his lungs like one awakening after drowning. Disoriented, he struggled to comprehend his location and unresponsive limbs.

Ameara spoke his name and approached slowly. The sound that might be foreign to his ears descended upon him with familiarity, or perhaps he merely recognized her voice. Ameara crouched beside him and gathered his unfocused gaze with her own.

"Dorian. It's Ameara. You're aboard the *Skyheart*. Dorian?"

He blinked repeatedly, but he couldn't dispel the bleariness. His entire body seemed to be in spasm, shocked by the sudden loss of the etch.

"Ameara," he stuttered. "What—? What have you done?"

He groaned and went limp, and Ameara feared he had succumbed to the aftereffects of eradicating the bloodshaping, which she had failed to even consider. But Dorian's scarred chest began to rise and fall as steadily as Syra's replenishing pulse. The shroud of pain receded. Ameara and Kyzum exchanged dumbfounded looks.

"I have no words," Kyzum admitted.

"That's a first," Ameara said.

"More like second or third. What are you going to do with him?"

"If he recovers, we'll make a deal. If he doesn't, I'll give him to the sea. You can throw him overboard."

The prospect mollified Kyzum, but only a little. "I'll hold you to that."

Ameara rested her hand on the alexandrite heart, impressing pride in Syra's bravery and gratitude for her and Dorian's lives. *Thank you.*

She broke contact before the vahl-kesh caught wind of her returning doubts. What had she done indeed.

CHAPTER 36

Ora Ezray glided past the zar'sheni and soldiers and studied the prisoners huddled in the cage. She pointed. "That one."

Soldiers waded into the prisoners. And pulled Saunez from among them. Ora Ezray inspected the custodian, the wild sapphire set in her necklace glowing with tapped kaza. She nodded, and the soldiers led an unresisting Saunez to the altar.

Panic-stricken, Teza seized the stars' kaza, but the rift that would save his sister broke upon Jaleya's resigned expression.

"She's an Ora," Jaleya said.

"But…" He glanced below. The soldiers were removing Saunez's clothing, exposing bruises and fresh wounds. She had been questioned.

"Please," Teza begged.

Jaleya couldn't bring herself to say no in the face of his wretchedness, but she couldn't say yes either.

Ora Ezray may stay her hand to avoid altering the future, Isesh sent.

She specifically chose Saunez, Jaleya replied.

But she didn't kill her outright. A ripple instead of a wave.

She's still an Ora, Jaleya sent with finality.

Teza furrowed his brow at their silent exchange. "Fine. I'll save her myself."

"You'll die." Not a rebuke. A warning.

Fear paled his kaza-touched features, but Saunez being shackled to the altar steeled his spine. "Then I'll prove a better rowshatar than you are a guardian."

Jaleya threw up her hands. Teza took a deep breath, then another. He looked through a slit, and a whisper of kaza tingled Jaleya's skin. He was actually going to rift!

Jaleya grabbed Teza's tunic, an almost involuntary action. He was a spoiled, deluded child who blindly followed the Ora and their Ways. He had betrayed his own sister. If not for him, she and Isesh would be soaring above a free Abylay, not crawling through the malevolent heart of the Illuminated's subjective morality.

And he was willing to stand against an Ora to save the one he had betrayed.

Jaleya couldn't abandon him to death, not when there was a chance, however minuscule, that life could prevail. Openly defying an Ora would be a victorious way to die. She lamented failing her vow to give Lenruz the justice she deserved.

"Stick to the plan," Jaleya said. "We'll deal with Ora Ezray after we finish the zar'sheni; we still have surprise on our side. Isesh, you'll have to handle the soldiers on your own." She looked gravely at Teza. "We can't protect you down there. You'll have to take care of yourself."

Sweat beading his brow, Teza nodded. At least he understood the enormity of the situation. Or seemed to.

The zar'sheni approached the altar.

"Wait," Jaleya told Teza. He gaped incredulously, but, remarkably, he did wait.

The zar'shen brandished his bloody dagger.

"Wait," Jaleya repeated. Isesh lowered his haunches, ready to spring.

A ripple, not a wave, Jaleya sent to Isesh.

That is the hope, the fashari replied.

The zar'shen invoked Orvashka's Ways and raised the dagger.

"Now!"

Jaleya launched herself through the rift and severed the male zar'shen's knife hand with her scimitar. He backpedaled, reaching for his signet to heal the spurting amputation. Jaleya pursued, scimitar leading, but the zar'shen blocked her blade with his signet. He pressed a finger against one of the piercing bloodstone seals inset on the stone cylinder, and a force like a solid wave struck Jaleya's mind. She faltered, and the zar'shen kicked her onto her back. Jaleya rolled aside, avoiding the full might of a second invisible breaker. She jumped upright and zigzagged across the stone, bursts of mental bloodshaping grazing the fringes of her mind. Closing the distance, she slashed wildly with her scimitar, keeping the one-handed zar'shen on his toes and forcing him to use his bloodshaping weapon as a short sword. She scored a lucky hit on his partially healed stump, and the zar'shen flinched. Jaleya darted inside his guard and thrust her scimitar into his belly. She sent his signet flying to guarantee the wound would remain fatal.

*   *   *

It took a moment for Teza to orient himself after rifting, and by then Jaleya had already engaged the male zar'shen, as if she rifted here and there every day. The female zar'shen reached for the signet hanging from her sash belt, and Teza frantically veered a time bubble. The spherical shimmer caught the zar'shen mid-motion, seeming to completely immobilize her, but Teza felt her resisting the stars' kaza, forcing her fingers closer and closer to the bloodstone seals in her hallowed weapon. Her movement was painstakingly slow —nearly imperceptible, but it was all too fast to him. He hadn't lied to Jaleya; he *was* the only rowshatar-estra who could veer time bubbles. But beyond their creation, he was as ignorant as a farmer in civilization. He had hoped brute force would compensate for his lack of finesse, but his abundant rifting had negated that possibility. His borrowed vest had become an absurd cloak. He couldn't stop her.

Out of the corner of his eye, Teza saw Ora Ezray retrieve the ornate dagger and turn to Saunez, who lay helplessly shackled to the altar. Isesh growled challenging peals, occupying the soldiers with his teeth and claws; Jaleya struggled with the other zar'shen. Saunez! Indecision captured Teza like his arresting kaza sphere. He couldn't release the female zar'shen, whose fingers were a hairsbreadth from a bloodstone seal, but he couldn't let his sister die either.

Ora Ezray raised the dagger, and her hand slowed as Teza's time bubble enveloped her. The zar'shen, now free, veered a bloodshaping, and the mental blow dropped Teza to his knees. The bubble around Ora Ezray collapsed. She—and the dagger—resumed normal motion.

Teza veered in desperation, and Ora Ezray twisted away to save her arm from the rift whirling into existence above the altar, the razor-sharp border slicing the fringe of her shawl. Ora Ezray scoffed incredulously and rounded on Teza, her eyes blazing.

"You dare raise your hand against Orvashka's Harmonized?"

The wild sapphire in her necklace brightened, and Saunez gasped, her neck muscles straining as she fought for air. Teza began to veer, but the zar'shen intensified her mental attack, dispersing the stars' kaza. Teza cried out and toppled sideways, clutching his head, the vicious bloodshaping threatening to rupture his mind.

The crushing weight suddenly ceased, and Teza recognized Jaleya as she assailed the female zar'shen, driving her away from the altar. Teza reached for the stars, but a force of moon kaza hurled him across the chamber, and he crashed into the laden table. Wood snapped; his head hit stone; and vials, torturous implements, and wild gemstones spilled onto the floor. Dazed, Teza crawled out of the debris. Ora Ezray was waiting. Her sapphire flaring, she slowly, explicitly clenched her hand into a fist. Saunez's struggles redoubled, her limbs flailing their final effort to continue living.

A suppressed storm within Teza burst loose. The lies, the deception, the betrayal. All birthed from the woman murdering his sister.

"I dare," he said.

The rift had barely formed before Teza launched himself through it. He barreled into the Ora, drove her through another rift, and smashed her into the table's wreckage. A move to make Jaleya envious. Saunez coughed and gulped the life-giving air.

Ora Ezray's sapphire brightened, and Teza was knocked aside. Moon kaza seized his body and lifted him off the ground. His limbs were yanked to their limits, stretched for sundering with the slightest pressure. An invisible vice clamped around his neck, stealing his breath. He tried to break free of the veering, but it was as if he had been encased in stone. Only his eyes obeyed his commands.

Ora Ezray placed her fallen tiara atop her head and straightened her disheveled dress. She sniffed at Teza hovering helplessly before her.

"You shine with Orvashka's harmony. You've witnessed the Ways' goodness. And you deny them like a selfish peasant. You are not a rowshatar. You're not even human. You and your kind are a disease, a parasite exploiting the benevolence of your betters. If I could deny you Paradise, I would, but since you will be perfected there, I will have to be satisfied with exterminating your earthly taint."

Teza shot a feeble bolt of lightning at the Ora, and she deflected it with a flick of her finger. Her sapphire flared, and Teza knew it heralded his death. He was going to die. Ora Ezray would rend his limbs and toss his mangled torso to the ground like refuse. When his life's blood expended itself, Ora Ezray would quench his last breath with her own hand. And she would endorse every moment. Teza saw it in her eyes, even as his own darkened.

Isesh and Jaleya sprang upon Ora Ezray, scimitar and claws slashing. A gust of moon kaza threw them off balance, but the javati twirled into their next attack. Ora Ezray mentally tugged at Isesh's injured wing, diverting the simurgh, but Jaleya's blade sliced her arm. Teza's invisible chains vanished as Ora Ezray consolidated her focus, and he dropped to the stone floor.

"Get Saunez," Jaleya ordered, her attention fixed on the Ora and her wild sapphire.

Teza's limbs were numb, and his head was spinning, but he wasn't going to point that out to Jaleya and her resolute stance. He crawled away from the guardian, the simurgh, and the Ora as they circled each other, the air pregnant with inevitable violence.

Isesh pealed a bark, Jaleya charged, and the Ora's sapphire flared with the moon's light.

*   *   *

Jaleya never stopped moving. She weaved around the Ora, lashed out with quick strikes, and pirouetted back into her swift irregular orbit. Motion hindered rowshatari-mara's ability to affect or catch their target, but the Ora had had centuries of practice. Intermittent pushes and pulls on Jaleya's limbs, clothing, and scimitar redirected her attacks, and only her guardian training saved her from being thrown across the room or captured like Teza had been. Jaleya thanked the Creator she and Isesh had intervened in time. If anyone was going to kill the gullible rowshatar-estra, it would be her.

Complementing Jaleya's randomized rhythm, Isesh pounced at Ora Ezray from behind and from the side, aiming for her filigreed necklace. They needed to separate her from the wild sapphire; then the Ora would be helpless. With a flash of the blue gemstone, Ora Ezray swatted Isesh's wounded wing, thwarting his trajectory. The fashari's natural kaza resistance was no shield against physical pain, and the veering that would normally be a minor crosswind hit like an arrow. Isesh's whimpered chirp tore at Jaleya's heart, but her javati refused to exchange positions. Even injured, he was faster than Jaleya, and therefore had a better chance of stealing the necklace.

Ora Ezray studied Jaleya as she continued circling. The sapphire began to pulse slowly, but Ora Ezray didn't attempt to seize Jaleya. Her eyes focused on an unseen horizon.

Jaleya abruptly swerved and swung her scimitar at Ora Ezray, but Ora Ezray mentally jerked the blade beyond her person. Jaleya plunged into the redirected course and twirled into a follow-up attack;

Isesh leapt at Ora Ezray's exposed back. Her eyes widening in alarm, she backpedaled and hastily veered an arresting gust at both javati. Jaleya was deflected, but Isesh's claws grazed Ora Ezray's neckline, missing the key to her power by a hairsbreadth.

Ora Ezray traced the ugly laceration, blood clinging to her fingertips. Indignation tinged with malignant curiosity suffused her kaza-touched features. "What are you?"

Being the subject of Ora Ezray's scrutiny should have frightened Jaleya, but all the Ora's might was chaff before her vindication. At long last, she stood openly defiant against the tyrannical rowshatari and their self-ordained rule. Against the Illuminated mob. Against their malevolent Ways.

"My name is Jaleya, and I'm going to prove the Ora and their Ways are false gods."

The Ora sneered. "Such frail threads are as vapor. And just as easily extinguished."

*   *   *

Teza staggered to the soldiers' corpses and focused on finding the keys to the altar's shackles and not on the gashes and crushed throats Isesh had left in his wake. Spotting the key ring on the third soldier's belt, he retrieved it with fumbling fingers and then lurched to his bound sister. The female zar'shen lay dead nearby, a deep cavity hacked into her thigh.

"What are you doing? Get out of here while you still can," Saunez ordered.

"No, I'm saving you," Teza mumbled, his scrambled brain struggling to keep pace with the chaos. He inserted the first key into the manacle binding Saunez's ankle. It didn't turn! Sweat beading his brow, Teza tried the second key. Click. The manacle popped open. To a background of Isesh's hybrid peals, Jaleya's swishing sword, and bursts of moon kaza, Teza began rounding the altar and unlocking its shackles. Click. Both ankles free. Saunez's urgings exacerbated his fingers' trembling, but he couldn't stop. If he did, he wouldn't be able to resume. Click. One wrist free. Saunez sat up and slid her legs over the side of the grisly stone. Only one more.

Jaleya cried out and was hurled toward the altar; Isesh dove after her. Saunez and Teza saw the living projectiles, but they were too slow to avoid them. The collision knocked Teza over the altar; Jaleya and Isesh hit the floor and rolled in a tangle of feathers and braids; and Saunez was jerked off her feet but yanked to a stop by the last manacle.

*   *   *

Jaleya halted her tumble with a smacking sprawl; she had lost Isesh a few rotations back. She shouldn't have taunted the Ora. As if Jaleya's words were a greater injury than physical assault, Ora Ezray had discarded the future's constraints, and by the time Jaleya recognized the concurrent veering, she had already been airborne.

Isesh climbed to his paws and prodded a groaning Teza upright. The tinkling of jewels resounded as Ora Ezray mentally gathered the scattered gemstones, their facets vibrating and sparking. Realizing the Ora's intent, time seemed to slow, Jaleya's single inhale stretching into infinite. Teza veering a rift and reaching for Isesh, who was poised to spring to Jaleya's defense even though they both knew he wouldn't be fast enough. Saunez, chained to the altar by one wrist, seeking cover where none existed. The dead female zar'shen, a mere arm's length away.

Jaleya exhaled.

The gemstones shattered, wild kaza bursting forth in a spectral explosion that Ora Ezray redirected toward Jaleya and her companions. Teza grabbed Isesh's neck feathers, halting his futile leap, and they rifted out of the barrage. Jaleya scrambled beneath the dead zar'shen and used her body as a human shield, but shards as sharp as a new spear grazed Jaleya's limbs, and the crackling blast seared her exposed skin. She heard a solid object impact flesh and a thump against stone.

The eruption of kaza subsided with a rustling rumble. Jaleya pushed the zar'shen aside; large shards protruded from her torso, blood flaked on her withered clothing, and raw blisters marred her flesh. Isesh was still a bright presence in Jaleya's mind.

Teza's wail shook the chamber. He ran to his sister. Saunez was splayed out on the altar. Shards pierced her like they pierced the zar'shen, and polished slivers had embedded themselves in her scorched skin. Teza called her name and shook her shoulder, but Saunez didn't respond to her brother's touch or pleas, her eyes half-closed. Teza crumpled over his sister's body, his forehead pressed against hers.

Ora Ezray nodded in satisfaction. Jaleya scrambled for the nearest weapon; she had lost her scimitar during her unsolicited flight. Ora Ezray stepped forward confidently, her sapphire blazing with light. And froze. Her slippered foot hovered above the floor, and did not land.

Cradling his sister, tears lining his cheeks, Teza swarmed Ora Ezray with the full force of his grief, anger, and unfettered kaza, and rendered her powerless. The Ora's eyes bulged in horror and disbelief.

Jaleya grabbed a soldier's scimitar, spun, and thrust it toward Ora Ezray. The time bubble immobilizing the rowshatar-mara popped a heartbeat before the blade pierced her back and burst out of her chest. Jaleya drove the Ora forward until steel hit stone. Ora Ezray slumped against the altar, the skewering scimitar supporting her weight. Her blood dripped down the blade and into the trench bloated with the Ways' justice.

Jaleya snatched Ora Ezray's filigreed necklace. The wild sapphire glowed with undisturbed kaza. Jaleya felt Teza's gaze, and her eyes met his. For the first time, they agreed.

The altar's dark pool rippled, the floor vibrating. The bloodshaping depictions etched upon the stained block brightened with angry light.

Jaleya yanked Teza away from the altar as a tempest of power engulfed it. The gale tugged at their clothes, and kaza flashed and whirled like lightning. Saunez and Ora Ezray shuddered. Isesh whimpered-chirped and sheltered beneath his uninjured wing.

A flare of crimson, and the depictions dimmed. The squall vanished, leaving a cautious silence in its wake. Teza rushed to his sister and called her name, desperate hope clenching his throat. Saunez didn't answer; she lay limp upon the altar. Jaleya cautiously approached Ora Ezray, but the skewered rowshatar-mara showed no signs of life. The surviving prisoners stirred from their protective postures.

Jaleya turned to Teza. He rocked his sister back and forth, tears pouring from his eyes.

"I'm sorry," Jaleya said, even though she knew how empty those words were at this moment.

Isesh's sending was gentle. *We must go.*

Jaleya sent her acknowledgment, pained though it was. At least Teza could say goodbye. Jaleya hadn't been able to.

Teza stiffened, then leaned back. Saunez's eyes fluttered open. She blinked. "Teza?"

"Saunez? Saunez!" He embraced her anew, eliciting a grunt. Saunez's reciprocation was sluggish and awkward, her confusion equal to Jaleya's wariness.

Saunez had been hit with gemstone shards and the kaza released from their shattering, but she bore no sign of the trauma. Her olive skin was as smooth as a baby's. The jutting fragments had been expelled from her body, an ability deemed impossible for kaza healing. The altar's channels and its trench were bone dry.

Teza freed his sister and offered her his tunic and vest, both siblings blushing at Saunez's nakedness. Jaleya noted the crease of ribs on Teza's torso, and based on Saunez's disapproving but resigned glance, she did, too.

Determining Saunez posed no immediate danger, Jaleya went to the cage and released the prisoners. Only three survived: two men and one woman. Jaleya told them to flee the tower—flee Abylay, but as she stipulated they could follow her and her companions only if they didn't hinder them, a scream sounded behind her. She whipped around, raising the scimitar she had removed from a dead soldier, but no threat presented itself.

Saunez clutched her head and screamed again. "What is that? What is it?"

"What is what?" Teza said, perplexed.

"I can feel them. They're everywhere! I can't stop it. It won't stop!" Saunez cried.

Teza tried to calm her, but Saunez shrugged him off, shielding her head. Her distress and ravings increased in volume. Isesh stepped forward, but Jaleya hefted her scimitar and struck Saunez with the hilt. Saunez collapsed, Teza's cushioning arms falling short. Teza gaped at Jaleya.

"She'll give away our position," Jaleya replied tersely.

Jaleya slung the unconscious Saunez over Isesh's back; Teza winced as she was jostled. Aided by Isesh's superior senses, Jaleya took the lead out of the grisly chamber, the liberated prisoners following. Footsteps and voices stirred the hushed corridors, but Jaleya remained on the direct path to the temple. They would never escape if they got lost. They had to beat their opponents to the surface.

At a T-intersection, Jaleya halted abruptly, her companions skidding to a stop. A zar'shen and a shavinash were rounding the corner ahead. A glance to her left revealed a squad of soldiers advancing toward the junction; one wore the spiked helmet of the remshiri. Spotting their quarry, both units charged, steel flying free of sheathes, stimulated kaza tingling Jaleya's skin.

Jaleya's company could stand and fight, and be killed or captured, or they could retreat and hope they found an alternate exit before the shavinash overtook them. They would never make it. Jaleya gripped her scimitar. If she killed the shavinash but perished in the process, if everyone perished, would his death be worth the cost? If it was *him*, yes. But she couldn't ascertain his identity across the distance in the dim torchlight. Her previous battle with a shavinash surfaced in her mind. Was she even able to fulfill her vow to Lenruz?

Jaleya called to Teza. "Rift. Now."

Leaning against the wall, Teza shook his head. "I can't."

Jaleya rounded on him. "You can, and you will, or we all die, right here, right now, and everything we just did will have been for nothing."

The sudden responsibility bowed Teza's shoulders, but he breathed deep and focused on a sight only he could see. A rift whirled into the corridor. Isesh, bearing Saunez, trotted through, and Jaleya ushered the others after him. She glanced over her shoulder, but found no confirmation either way.

A gust of mountain air, and Jaleya emerged onto a tree-lined walkway terminating at a familiar minaret. Teza leaned on his trembling knees. His cheeks had sunk, causing his already prominent ears to be even more pronounced. The freed prisoners encircled him and showered him with gratitude, but when they began extending their fervor to Jaleya, she allayed it with raised hands.

"Is the shield activated?" she asked Teza. He nodded. No rifting out, then. The gates would be heavily guarded, as would the wall, and when Ora Ezray's body was discovered, the citadel's entire garrison would be ordered to kill on sight.

"Iza Vor has been locked down," she told the former prisoners. "There's no way out. Our best chance is to conceal ourselves in different locations and remain there until the alert is over. Are any of you familiar with Iza Vor?"

"I am," one of the men said.

"Take these two and hide until the lockdown is lifted. Then get out of Setsea." The trio hesitated, confused. "Go, or you'll be next on the altar."

Mention of their captivity spurred them into Iza Vor's halls. They might survive. Probably not.

A gate or the wall? Jaleya sent to Isesh.

There is another option, Isesh replied, impressing his idea.

You're wounded, and there are three of us, Jaleya reminded him.

Flight is not required. Just a steep, tilted descent.

That's a very tenuous distinction.

Jaleya, we are spent. We cannot fight our way out, nor do we have the time to scour the wall for an unguarded section, if such a thing even currently exists.

Jaleya hesitated, and then reluctantly sighed her acquiescence. "This way," she told Teza.

They marched into the minaret and began ascending the winding staircase.

"We're hiding in the minaret?" Teza said.

"No, we're getting out of Iza Vor," Jaleya said.

"But you told those people—"

"We couldn't protect them. Hiding, they have a chance."

Teza's silence was a testament to his exhaustion, for which Jaleya was grateful. Why had she freed those people? All she had given them was false hope.

At the landing, Jaleya rushed through the wooden door and killed the single guard within. The communications clerk surrendered, Isesh's sending staying Jaleya's hand. The terrified clerk scurried down the stairs. They were fully committed now.

The dome hosted four lavish windows. The massive communication orb hung from the center of the ceiling. The metal casing equipped with abundant missive seals would require four people with spread arms to encompass. The freshly replenished diamond in the enclosed heart seal sent Jaleya's head spinning if she looked directly at it, hence the guard's and the clerk's tinted spectacles.

Jaleya began slicing the guard's tunic into strips and knotting them together.

"What are you doing?" Teza asked.

"You'll need to rift us one last time."

"I can't rift out of the shield. Even if it was possible, I can't veer anymore."

Isesh trotted to Jaleya, and she fastened the makeshift harness around his chest. A loop trailed down both of his shoulders.

"That's what you said in the tunnels, and yet, here we are," Jaleya said. "The shield ends just beyond Iza Vor's wall. Isesh will glide us clear, and then you'll rift us to the ground."

Teza glanced between Jaleya, the open window, and the injured simurgh. "Your plan is to jump out of this minaret and *hope* we clear the defenses so we don't fall to our deaths?"

"The fall probably won't kill us; Isesh will slow our descent. We're more likely to bleed to death from our broken bones puncturing our organs."

Teza squeaked what was probably an objection. Jaleya used the vest Saunez wore to secure her to Isesh's harness.

Isesh's ears peaked, and Jaleya strained her own until she heard the rapid footsteps echoing up the stairwell. That was faster than anticipated. Jaleya should have killed that Illuminated clerk. She went to the door and jammed Ora Ezray's necklace into the latch. Eyes bulging, Teza scrambled to snatch the wild gem from the hazardous pressure, but Jaleya caught his arm and towed him to the communication orb. "Time to go."

Jaleya pulled a lever, and the padded rests stabilizing the sphere retracted. Someone pounded on the door and ordered it be opened in preservation of harmony. Pointedly ignoring him, Jaleya and Isesh climbed onto the communication orb. Jaleya slid the loop of fabric over her shoulders and gripped Isesh's harness. She looked at Teza expectantly. Miserable, Teza clambered to Isesh's opposite side and secured himself as Jaleya had.

The door shuddered from an impact, the latch clanking against the wild sapphire. The squad attempting to break in either didn't contain a remshir, or the remshir couldn't sense the sapphire's kaza amid the diamond's. It was a prickling blur to Jaleya.

The javati and Teza rocked the sphere back and forth, back and forth, until it swung from window to window. The door lurched in its frame, the rattling hinges sprinkling dust. The moon kaza in the wild sapphire writhed angrily.

The orb rumbled backward. Isesh bent his haunches. Teza squeezed his sister's hand. Jaleya asked the Creator for a miracle.

The orb swung forward, and they flung themselves through the window into the twinkling sky; the door burst inward, clobbering the battered sapphire, and the dome collapsed in a blue and white explosion. Isesh pealed-whimpered in pain as he assumed the weight of his companions. Banking sharply to spare his injured wing, Isesh carried them over Iza Vor's battlements at an oblique angle. Abylay rushed to intercept them.

"Teza!" Jaleya called, but the rowshatar didn't answer. Buildings grew like kaza-nourished crops; spires and domes whizzed by, blood and brain matter about to splatter their honeycombed porticos. "Teza!"

A whiff of crisp air, and they tumbled out of a rift onto the street, adding to their bruises and scrapes. Jaleya slowly lifted her head, hardly believing she was alive. Isesh's ears were laid flat, his wings and limbs quivering; his consciousness was shrouded in shadows. Teza crawled to Saunez, who had fallen off Isesh, the vest torn at the seam.

Chaos had descended upon Abylay. A fiery glow haloed the Guild Ward. Smoke billowed into the sky near the river. Steel clashed to the accompaniment of piercing screams. Kaza rumbled and flashed like a storm.

Iza Vor was untouched. The Dazmiri hovered contently on their tethers anchoring them to the waning skydock. The resistance… The resistance had failed.

Isesh's sending was a weak whisper. *Now we hide.*

Jaleya voiced her reluctant agreement; they would never escape the barred city in their current condition. "Now we hide. Maybe a vacant building near the West Ward, close to the river…"

Teza hunched over Saunez as if he could meld them both into the street. Jaleya eyed him suspiciously. "Teza? You know a place?"

"I...I'm not sure."

"You're obviously thinking of somewhere. Spit it out."

Teza hesitated. "I know where Seal Keeper Firnak lives."

"We can't trust him."

"He w-won't turn us in."

"Yes, he will."

Teza held his sister tighter. He wouldn't look at Jaleya. "He won't. He c-can't. He's..." Teza swallowed. "He's d-dead."

Isesh's healthy wing wilted. Jaleya took a mental step back, reassessing the hours she and Teza had been separated in Abylay. In hindsight, she knew it had been unwise to leave Teza to fend for himself, but if she had stayed in his proximity any longer, she might have dealt the lethal blow she had withheld at the estate. Rendezvousing at Iza Vor, she had assumed Teza had stolen the fancy clothing and hunkered down until the stars began to shine. That is what she would have done. And that is where she had erred. Teza was not her. Teza could barely dress himself. He would have sought aid. Someone he thought he could trust.

It had been one betrayal too many.

"Does anyone else know he's dead?" Jaleya asked. She tried to be gentle, but this was not the time or the place to lament. Teza would have to process later.

Cringing at her words, Teza said, "I don't think so. The servants were gone, and I—. I'm not sure."

Anyone seeking the Seal Keeper will most likely assume he was summoned to fight, Isesh sent.

'Most likely' will have to do, Jaleya sent. She pulled Teza to his feet. "Show us. Carefully."

Rallying his remaining strength, Isesh volunteered to bear Saunez once more, and the weary companions ventured into the chaos. Teza's route would have utilized the main boulevards, but Jaleya kept them on the backstreets. They stumbled upon clusters of dead soldiers and resistance at intersections but encountered no active skirmishes. When they reached the affluent avenue Teza had described, Jaleya led them to the back of Firnak's house, where Isesh helped them scale the wall. A door adjacent to the private garden opened into the kitchen. The kaza lanterns were dark. Jaleya and Teza laid Saunez near the pantry, and then Jaleya ordered the others to remain there while she searched the house. It turned out Teza had been right: they were the only ones there. The metallic scent of blood saturated the upper level's parlor.

They settled in the dim kitchen away from the window and doors. Teza's iridescent skin gleamed like moonlit water. He huddled by Saunez as if she was the one thin thread sustaining his sanity. Jaleya removed the makeshift harness from Isesh, who flopped to the floor and was instantly asleep; his familiar rumblings were a comfort in the chilling night. Jaleya cut one of the harness loops into smaller strips and then approached the siblings. Teza stirred from his stupor.

"What are you doing?"

"We can't risk her screaming and revealing our position," Jaleya whispered.

Teza drooped in concession. Jaleya moved to bind and gag Saunez, but Saunez bolted upright, arms flailing defensively.

"Saunez," Teza said. "Saunez, it's all right. It's me, Teza. You're all right."

Recognizing her brother, the former custodian stilled. "Teza, where are we?"

"We're safe, for now," Jaleya said from a cautious distance.

"What—? What happened?" Saunez rubbed her temples, squinting. Jaleya placed her hand on her scimitar hilt.

"Saunez, what's wrong?" Teza said.

"It's coming back. You don't feel it?" She moaned and clutched her head as she had done in the Ora's laboratory. "It's everywhere!"

"*What is it*?" Teza said.

Saunez groaned, doubling over. Teza took his sister's arms and told her to look at him, to focus on him. His efforts failed to calm her agitation, and she babbled and flinched like a javati with a severed javash. When she involuntarily cried out, Jaleya knew she was going to have to knock the woman out again.

Isesh rose from his slumber and planted himself in front of Saunez. He caught her brown eyes with his avian ones, and held her there. Staring at the fashari as if her life depended on it, Saunez hushed. Her hands slowly, precariously, lowered.

Isesh? Jaleya sent, but her javati didn't respond. His consciousness was distant, akin to when he spoke with other fashari. Teza called his sister's name in a fearful whisper. Saunez recoiled and swatted the air, whatever torments Isesh had repelled exploiting Teza's interruption. Isesh recovered Saunez's attention, and she re-submerged herself in the simurgh's ethereal gaze.

Jaleya prodded Teza away from the absorbed pair. He relinquished a few feet but refused to budge beyond an easy bound. Jaleya crouched by the door leading to the rest of the house. In the morning, she would scout the city and find a way out. Tonight, she had to ensure their presence remained unnoticed.

And so stars' sway passed in tense silence sporadically broken by echoes of violence and crackling kaza, the scent of smoke a seeping pall. Saunez was a twitching silhouette within the kitchen's shadows, a cracked wild gem held at bay by a celestial messenger. She should be dead. Jaleya kept her hand near her scimitar. What had she and Teza wrought?

CHAPTER 37

The sea gleamed beneath the morning sun, the billows singing to the fluffy clouds lounging in the azure sky. The coast curved outside the window of the captain's quarters. Ameara gazed at the ever-distant meeting of sky and sea. Where anything could be waiting. Where anything was possible.

They had departed Abylay with the dawn. Ameara had abused her status as a Vekrym captain to do so, but she wasn't the only one eager to leave after the failed rebel attack. She had received no summons from Whisper, so she had either missed it, or he had refrained from sending one to conceal the significance of the two dead shavinashi. A matter for their next bout.

A brief knock preceded Kyzum's entrance. His blunt demeanor revealed his purpose before his words did.

"He's awake."

A part of Ameara had hoped he wouldn't, that her legitimate effort to save him had failed. The thought repulsed the rest of her, even in the face of her own misgivings she could never admit out loud.

"Bring him here," Ameara ordered.

"I still think throwing him over the side is our better option," Kyzum said.

"Noted, but it's not your decision."

"Noted, Captain."

Hard at work juggling their personal and professional relationships, Kyzum left to do as instructed. Ameara's gaze lingered on the distant horizon. The expanse that would forever remain unknown. Perhaps within lay a land that wasn't so…harsh, demanding. Complicated.

Kyzum returned a few minutes later with Ara and Obakwe, who flanked the bound shavinash. He had regained most of his color, but he moved lethargically, as if recovering from a fever. They halted in the center of the Setsean rug, and Obakwe forced the shavinash to his knees. Nahzida positioned herself in the doorway and aimed her rifle at his head.

"Thank you, Nahzida, Ara. That will be all," Ameara said.

The markswoman and the galahi obeyed, but they didn't close the door behind them. Ameara let it be. Her crew needed reassurance of her resolve, but apart from Kyzum's expected presence and Obakwe's deterring kaza, congregating in her quarters with brandished weapons projected an aura of fear. Ameara could not fear the shavinash.

"I'll make this simple." She turned from the window, crossed the short distance between them, and lowered the shavinash's tunic, revealing the jagged scar confirming the etch's absence he had no doubt felt upon awakening. He concealed his shock well, but not as well as a shavinash should.

Ameara straightened and continued. "You can't go back to the shavinashi because they'll kill you for being a rogue. You said you needed to disappear, and you have. You defended the lives of my crew, so I'm giving you yours. I never want to see you again. The scales are even. Our encounter will never be spoken of. If you breathe a word to anyone—if I hear so much as a whisper—I will hunt you down and kill you."

"Understood and agreed," the shavinash said.

Ameara went to a cabinet and retrieved his belongings. She nodded to Obakwe and Kyzum, and they escorted the shavinash out of the captain's quarters. Nahzida and Ara trailed them to the gunwale, rifle and seals discouraging ideas of violence. Obakwe untied the shavinash, flexed the sun's kaza in warning, and joined the crew's defensive crescent. Suppressing her screaming better judgment, Ameara handed the killer his bundled weapons. He accepted them slowly lest a lethal projectile accidentally pierce his suddenly vulnerable body. Ameara stepped back and nodded at the gentle billows. "Off you go."

The shavinash stood motionless. The harsh lines of his face might as well have been stone. Ameara braced for treachery.

The shavinash withdrew the flawed crystal from the scabbard's hidden compartment and offered it to her. "This belongs to you."

Ameara raised her brow. "How do you figure?"

His small, yielding exhale softened the stone ridges, a ray of sunlight warming the frozen horizon. "It was a gift. The day the shavinash took me, you put it in my hand and told me to bring it back to you." He placed the crystal on the gunwale. "Do with it as you will."

Ameara gaped. He could have killed her then, and she wouldn't have realized it until she woke in the afterlife. She had suspected —believed?—thought she recognized something in his features, his character, his eyes. Yet doubt remained. How could it not? But for him to know such an intimate detail…

"Dorian?"

"Goodbye, Ameara."

He hopped over the side to her unfinished, "Wait."

Numb, she watched him swim to shore.

"Captain?" Kyzum said from beside her.

Ameara shook herself. "Ara, get us underway."

The young woman started; the whole crew had probably heard Ameara and Dorian's brief exchange. "What heading?"

Ameara spoke the first direction that came to mind. "North. For now," she added.

Ara scurried to the helm. The others lingered in an overly thoughtful manner.

"I'm sure the rest of you have things to see to as well," Ameara said. Obakwe and Nahzida scattered. Kyzum remained. Ameara walked away before his cautionary but stern expression found words. She looked over her shoulder once. The shore was empty except for the surf and sand. The shavinash—Dorian...Dorian was gone.

CHAPTER 38

The screams had stopped. The kaza storm had passed. Shops had opened late, normal activity resuming sluggishly. A cautious air clung like the dissipated smoke. It was a fittingly surreal background to the lemon tree and the freshly turned earth beneath it. Teza tore his gaze away.

He heard a door open, and Jaleya emerged from Seal Keeper Firnak's home. She had scouted with the rising sun and reported soldiers on the streets in force. The Ora had released an official report regarding the events of last night, proclaiming misguided rebels had attacked Abylay, the shining beacon of harmony, on one of its most sacred occasions. Ora Ezray's sadness and dismay were so great, she had refrained from the offering. It was with deep regret that the apprehended rebels would be returned to Orvashka, but the citizens of Abylay—of all Setsea—could find encouragement and hope in the unfortunate deaths. The insurrection was further proof that antiquated ideas produce nothing but suffering, and with the depravity of such hateful beliefs laid bare, the Illuminated would usher the misguided to Orvashka's Ways, strengthening harmony for the good of all.

Abylay's gates had opened shortly after the executions. Festival-goers who had come for a celebration and experienced horror instead couldn't leave fast enough. That had been hours ago. The sun had passed its zenith.

"How's Saunez?" Teza asked. Even though there was space on the bench he occupied—space enough to keep distance between them—Jaleya remained standing, alert; was she even capable of relaxing? They weren't out of danger yet, but they could at least take a breather between servants arriving and Jaleya subduing and binding them in a storage closet. Orvashka knew Teza needed a breather. Part of him was still expecting to wake from this nightmare. His gaze was drawn to the lemon tree again, but he diverted it to the blooming tulips.

"She's managing to keep her mind clear when she's calm," Jaleya said. Isesh had been assisting Saunez all morning, Jaleya lending a hand in her spare time. Teza had been expelled like an incompetent servant.

"What did you do?" he said, trying to hide his resentment. He should be the one helping his sister, not Jaleya, not the creature who hadn't been able to decide between canine and bird.

"We taught her how to prevent a mind from entering hers and how to admit only those who are welcome. It's the first thing javati learn."

"She's not a javati."

Jaleya didn't immediately retort, probably because she didn't want to admit Teza was right.

"She's more than she was," Jaleya said.

"In other words, you have no idea what's happening to her."

"I don't hear you offering any suggestions."

"You kicked me out!"

"*Saunez* kicked you out."

Teza huffed and turned away. He grabbed the remaining flatbread off the plate beside him and wiped it along the bowl, collecting the last of the yogurt. He had already eaten more than a fair share of fruit, nuts, bread, sweets, cheese—anything he found that didn't require preparation. His stomach still grumbled. At least it wasn't gnawing at him anymore. The awful trousers he wore fit comfortably now, whereas that morning they had fallen off his waist.

Teza stuffed the flatbread into his mouth, but in his effort to rebuff Jaleya, he found himself face to face with the lemon tree. He spun on the bench, showing it his back.

"It's a heavy burden, but it does get easier to bear," Jaleya said.

Teza scowled. What in Orvashka was she talking about?

Jaleya captured his irate gaze, and led it to the lemon tree. The recently turned earth beneath its boughs. Teza couldn't turn away this time, trapped between the tree's condemnation and his guardian's acknowledgement. His anguish stirred into anger. The same anger he had felt before he killed Firnak, before he attacked Ora Ezray. It terrified him, and yet spurred him to action, which in turn terrified him even more.

"It gets easier?" He jumped to his feet. "That's all you have to say? I—" He couldn't even form the words. "You're a hateful person. You are. You don't care about anyone except your pet, and that's only because his death would drive you insane. You're a self-righteous brat who epitomizes everything Orvashka's Ways lift us out of. The Ora may be liars, but they're right about people like you."

"At least I have a reason for my hate," Jaleya retorted. "You Illuminated destroyed everything I love, and you ravish anything and anyone who questions your deified decrees. The zar'sheni's experiment that maimed your sister's mind is your sacred offering ceremony when it's not hiding behind jewels and drugged victims. It's the heart of your Ways, and you've witnessed it, but you're still defending it. Thinking for yourself, making your own choices, that's just too much responsibility. You'd rather remain enslaved to your Ways than admit they might be wrong."

Teza pursed his lips, folded and unfolded his arms. "It shouldn't get easier," he mumbled. "It shouldn't." He brushed past her, fleeing. But if he was fleeing from her or from her words, he didn't know.

*   *   *

Jaleya sighed and appealed to the heavens as Teza stormed off. She hadn't intended to blurt words she had wanted to slap him with for weeks. She'd been trying to offer comfort, to let him know she understood what he was going through. Ending a life was not easy. Tensions were high all around, though, and a boiling river of unspoken words stretched for miles between them.

Jaleya plopped onto the bench the rowshatar had vacated. She absentmindedly picked at the crumbs of flatbread. She should have been pleased—elated—with what they had accomplished. An Ora was dead; Jaleya had struck the lethal blow herself. She was one step closer to destroying them, their rule, and the shavinashi. The victory should have been a taste of the sweet revenge that would one day be hers. She just felt exhausted. The burned patches of her skin were tight and flaky, and her cuts and scrapes itched. No one would question the report claiming Ora Ezray refrained from the offering because of a broken heart. The people gobbled up the Ora's lies faster than the bread at the distribution centers. The Ora and their rule would live on.

Jaleya, Isesh sent, coming up beside her. *The time is ripe to leave.* His wing was splinted and heavily bandaged to keep it immobile, but he assured her he would fly again. Jaleya wondered if *they* would fly again. She kept that thought far from his consciousness.

Do you have a destination in mind? she sent.

The Wanbasbans let few cross their border, but they may make an exception for a javati. An isolated isle of Ryvek—

I can't leave Setsea, Jaleya interrupted.

The Ora will pursue us, Isesh sent. *We will be executed if we're recognized. I think your sister would prefer you live rather than pursue an imprudent vow.*

She'd prefer to not be dead.

Very well. In which random direction will you begin searching for her killer?

Isesh twitched his head sideways as only a bird could. His sass was all human. Nevertheless, it was a legitimate question. Jaleya had dreamed of choosing her own path for so long, but now that she had the opportunity, she was stranded at a crossroads.

How are you able to communicate with Saunez? Jaleya sent. The phenomenon had been burning in her mind since Isesh calmed the former custodian in the kitchen, but other pressing concerns had prevented her from inquiring. And asking now delayed having to choose a random city to begin searching for a murderer who was more ghost than human.

I sensed I could reach out to her, Isesh answered. *I was as surprised as you when I made contact. Her mind was a meadow compared to yours.*

I was young, and you're exaggerating.

You were young, and I'm not.

His affection felt through javash momentarily warmed Jaleya's heart. *So…Saunez is some kind of javati?*

Isesh's ears flicked back and forth. *Javash makes a javati, and javati always come in pairs.*

All right, then what? Jaleya prompted.

Isesh hesitated, his spectral tail slinking between his legs. Saunez had him more spooked than Jaleya thought.

It is said that empaths and fashari were able to communicate without javash, as I do with other fashari. Saunez is not my javati, and yet I am able to touch her mind.

You think Saunez was turned into an empath? Jaleya sent. *The empaths are extinct.*

Perhaps not, Isesh sent thoughtfully.

Is that what the zar'sheni were trying to do? Why? The empaths were the Ora's enemies. Would that even be possible?

With bloodshaping alone, I don't see how, Isesh sent. *Instead of a portion like the rowshatari, empaths accessed all of the Boundless Sea. To that effect, an empath cannot be born from a power that contains no kaza. However, bloodshaping was not the only power in that chamber.*

Wild gems, stars' sway, battling rowshatari, and our javash ever present. Whether or not they all contributed, I tremble to think what such a combination could create, but perhaps we have an answer.

Jaleya fiddled with one of her braids as she pondered Isesh's theory. Her knowledge of empaths stemmed from post-Schism texts and histories, so she listened with heavy skepticism to the claim that the empaths had been tyrants who used their ethereal powers to control people and imprison their souls. That the empaths had been able to read emotions and form javash, Jaleya believed, as she had found scraps of corroborating information here and there from sources that didn't worship Orvashka's Ways. The return of a people able to violate others in such a way was a fearful prospect, but Jaleya feared that less than what the Ora planned to do with such power, if their goal was in fact to create an empath and Saunez wasn't a horrible mishap.

Should we tell Saunez? Jaleya sent.

She's suffered a trauma. The knowledge will burden her further, Isesh replied. *However, since we're parting ways, she should be informed, even though all we have to offer is speculation.*

"Jaleya! Jaleya!" Teza sprinted across the garden. "Saunez is gone."

"What do you mean by 'gone'?" Jaleya said. Saunez was probably on the upper level obtaining some much-needed solitude, and not being where Teza had last seen her had panicked him.

"She left." Teza presented a piece of paper that contained three blunt sentences.

> *Teza,*
> *Thank you for your assistance in Harmony Tower, however ill advised the venture. I need to find my allies and figure out what happened to me. Don't follow.*
> *Saunez*

"We have to go after her," Teza said.

We? Jaleya thought, but spoke, "She said not to follow her."

"She doesn't know what they did to her, what's happening to her. None of us do. And she's trying to re-establish contact with rebels. She's in danger."

"She can take care of herself."

Teza sighed in frustration. "Fine. Will you at least tell me where the rebels are?"

"I don't know," Jaleya huffed. She paused. "But Saunez's most likely destinations are Isedbi for its port and Tesinoc for its potential allies. So east or north. That way," she pointed when Teza looked perplexed.

"Isedbi, Tesinoc. Yes, of course," Teza said.

"They're opposite directions," Jaleya said, just in case he had missed that very important detail. "You're going to get yourself killed."

"Then your perpetual frown will turn upside down, and Paradise will descend out of astonishment." He spun on his heel and returned to the house.

Stifling his amusement, Isesh sent, *He doesn't know the way to either city.*

He's not our problem anymore, Jaleya replied.

We wouldn't be alive right now without him.

And he wouldn't be alive without us.

Then we agree you work well together.

That's not what I said or what I meant.

That doesn't make it less true.

You want to help him search an entire country for his sister? Jaleya sent incredulously. *The sister who specifically told him* not *to come after her? Who might have inadvertently been the subject of an Ora bloodshaping experiment, and who you believe is now an empath?*

Isesh swished his feathered tail. *He's ignorant and naïve, but he is also brave and sincere. When he recognized his betrayal, he did everything in his power to correct his mistake. He forsook everything he has ever known to save Saunez.*

He only did it because the Ora betrayed him, Jaleya argued.

Perhaps. Perhaps not, Isesh replied calmly. *The foundations of his life are collapsing beneath him. He has lost his home and everyone he considers a friend. His sister fled. Right now, we are all he has.*

Jaleya folded her arms and scuffed the dirt path. None of this would have happened if Teza had rejected the Ways' lies and seen their "harmony" for the hypocrisy it was. He wouldn't have betrayed them, Saunez wouldn't have been captured and…altered, and she wouldn't have absconded.

But Teza wasn't the only one who had made a mistake. If not for Jaleya, Batebi and Imlay would be alive, the skyships would belong to the resistance, and freedom would be consolidating its long-awaited victory.

Saunez was Jaleya's only connection to the resistance. Isedbi and Tesinoc were sure to have shavinashi lurking in the shadows…

Jaleya dragged her feet as she followed Teza into the kitchen. He was tying closed one of the packs Jaleya had filled with provisions (she'd been surprised anything remained after Teza's feast). The bulges indicated he had added extra rations. Jaleya doubted he had taken the additional weight into consideration.

"What will you do when your supplies run out?" she said.

"I'll find more."

"How?"

"I'll figure it out," he said tersely. He slung the pack over his shoulders, stumbled beneath its bulk, and turned toward the front door.

Jaleya blocked his path. "Teza, wait."

"No," he snapped. "I don't care what she said in that sorry excuse for a letter. She's my sister, she's in danger, and I'm going to find her."

He attempted to bypass Jaleya, but she caught his arm, twisted, and knocked him off balance. He hit the floor with a heavy thud. Isesh sighed into Jaleya's mind.

"Will you stop and think about what you're doing just this once?" Jaleya said. "You have no independent experience, no idea where she's heading, and you'll have to evade Counselors, soldiers, and remshiri. You may be able to veer time bubbles, but a blade can kill you as easily as it kills everybody else, and while the sun and moon shine, you *are* just like everybody else."

"I don't need to think about it," Teza said. "What happened to Saunez is my fault. I have to make it right."

The harsh realization of the disillusioned clashed with denial upon his sharp, olive features. Resolve sparked in eyes that had lost the stars' light.

Jaleya offered her hand. Teza accepted it suspiciously, and she helped him to his feet.

"We're coming with you."

Teza barked a laugh, but when no punch line was forthcoming, he looked to Isesh. The simurgh inclined his head.

"You're…serious," Teza said.

Jaleya forced her gaze to remain steady. She didn't want to admit her fatal error to the rowshatar, but since it was the honorable course, like a galahi of old, she would look him in the eye while doing so.

"You're not the only one who has something to make up for. And even though swearing my oath as a guardian was done under duress, I would be a poor example if I shed myself of it when you obviously need me."

"I don't need you," Teza said. He paused. "But company would be agreeable, even if it is yours."

"You don't get to order me around," Jaleya warned, "and I'm not going to take care of you. We will share responsibilities."

"Unless those responsibilities are replenishing seals, I won't be much help," Teza said.

"I'll teach you," Jaleya replied.

Resigned to something he wasn't going to like, Teza's predictable pout was smaller than expected. Jaleya didn't need javash with Teza to know they were thinking the same thought: this was going to be a long journey.

CHAPTER 39

Ameara rested her hand on Syra's wheel as they crossed the rolling hills far below. She didn't have a destination in mind, but she wanted to put some distance between her crew and the shavinashi. Not so much distance that it appeared they were fleeing, but enough to provide a head start if necessary. Ameara still half-expected a cannon blast to ram Syra's shield. She had heeded a feeling over experience and reason, challenged Whisper, and trusted the counsel of a shavinash.

What had she been thinking?

The most terrifying part: she would do nothing different if given the chance to repeat the last few days.

Kyzum joined her on the quarterdeck and presented two wooden cups and a bottle of wine.

Ameara eyed the expensive vintage. "Do I want to know where you acquired that?"

"Courtesy of Nahzida's secret stash," Kyzum said. "Don't worry. She was compensated."

He placed the cups on the helm and filled one, but Ameara opted for the bottle instead of the wooden vessel's lesser portion. As they sipped the smooth red liquid, Kyzum said, "You know the reason you don't like beer is because the stuff Setseans brew can barely be called that. Next time we're in Masatitora, I'll find us a dark beer, and you'll finally see I'm right."

"Your beer is competing with Ryvekian mead, too," Ameara said.

"The Ryvekians converted you far too easily. The sea you all have in your blood is an abused advantage."

Shrugging, Ameara took another swig from the bottle. Kyzum tasted his conservatively. The sky darkened in the west, the first stars piercing the deep-blue heights.

"How are the crew holding up?" Ameara asked.

"They're thanking their gods to be alive. I'm questioning my sanity for staying with you all these years, but we did just pull off another seemingly impossible plan. Promise me that when we run out of those and fall from the sky and die in a massive, fiery shipwreck, we'll take as many shavinashi with us as possible."

"I'll drink to that," Ameara said, and they clicked bottle and cup together.

"How are *you* holding up?" Kyzum asked.

Ameara gazed at the gradating sky. The lengthening shadows enveloping the land below broke upon islands of light, natural and kaza. "I'm debating between Isedbi and Gurza."

"That's not what I asked."

"I know."

Kyzum spoke gently. "Ameara, I'm sorry he turned out to be your friend; I truly am. But whatever debt you think you owe him, it's more than paid."

"Our agreement is mutually beneficial," Ameara said.

"You two have to play nice lest you entrap yourselves. His brethren never agreed to sit idly by while you do so. What if *they* find *him*?"

Then they would have to hope the shavinashi's desire to quietly eliminate the defector trumped their aversion to loose ends, that he was tortured and killed for being a traitor and not for information. They had to hope he wouldn't snitch for the miniscule chance of a quick death. Ameara had considered all of that. She had still released him. She would release him again.

"You still think I should've killed him," Ameara said.

"I think you should have let him die. Holding on to the past just hurts." Kyzum paused. "You should get rid of it. Say goodbye, walk away. Move on."

He knocked back his remaining wine, coughing as it went down. "That is awful. Beer. That's what we should be drinking." He gathered the cups but didn't ask for the bottle. "Don't excuse all of us from our watch. Get some sleep, or at least pretend to, for me."

"Yes, sir," Ameara said.

Kyzum paused at the stairs. "Ameara…if you need anything…"

"You'll be scrounging the galley for good beer," she said, offering him a smile.

"I won't find any," he grumbled as he left the quarterdeck. "Your Setsean friends commandeered all of it."

Ameara lingered at the helm for a moment, then crossed the deck to the rail. The Nidren River was a glistening eel swimming in a dark sea. Clouds heavy with rain gathered above the distant, silhouetted mountains. To the east, stars twinkled in a clear sky. Syra paid the night diamonds no mind, their kaza already beginning to wane.

Ameara retrieved the worthless crystal from her tunic pocket. The crude edges had worn smooth over the many years. The evening's meager light refracted deep within, as if the stone had captured a star. Kyzum was right. She should let it go. Throw it overboard. She had confronted her past betrayal, acknowledged it, looked it in the eye. Perhaps repaired some of the damage. There was nothing else to be done.

Ameara closed her fist to dispose of the worthless crystal.

She couldn't raise her arm.

Ameara shut her eyes and sighed. *Did you know who he was?* she asked Syra. Syra had been anxious after Dorian snuck aboard, but she hadn't been alarmed or frightened until he began tampering with her mechanism, leading Ameara to believe Syra had attempted to rift at the jetty to evade the etch, not its bearer. Had Syra's empathic abilities somehow imparted recognition or revealed his connection to Ameara? Was that why Syra hadn't alerted Ameara to his presence? Had she sensed the potential for this very moment?

The Dazmir-vahl-kesh hummed contently in Ameara's mind. It was all the answer she was going to get.

Ameara looked to the distant horizon, where sky appeared to meet land. She uncurled her fingers. The crystal's star was faint, but it remained steadfast, unyielding. Dorian had returned it to her as requested. He remembered. A part of him had survived. She hoped it was the best part.

Ameara slipped the cord over her head and tucked the crystal inside her tunic. She returned to the helm and steered Syra east, toward the boundless, endless sea of glimmering stars.

Jessica Hope grew up in Illinois and studied film and writing at Columbia College Chicago, but she fell in love with the Rocky Mountains and had to move west. She discovered fantasy novels in seventh grade and since then has always been in the middle of at least one book. She became a Christian when she was thirteen, and it was the best decision she ever made. She lives in Montana.